Abrupt Mutations

Enrique Luis Revol

ABRUPT MUTATIONS

Translated from the Spanish by Priscilla Hunter

DALKEY ARCHIVE PRESS

Originally published as *Mutaciones Bruscas* by Editorial Sudamericana in 1971.

Copyright © 1971 by Enrique Luis Revol
Translation copyright © 2018 by Priscilla Hunter
First Dalkey Archive edition, 2018.

Library of Congress Cataloging-in-Publication Data
Names: Revol, Enrique L. (Enrique Luis), author. | Hunter, Priscilla, translator.
Title: Abrupt mutations / by Enrique Luis Revol ; translated from the Spanish by Priscilla Hunter.
Other titles: Mutaciones bruscas. English
Description: First Dalkey Archive edition. | Victoria, TX : Dalkey Archive Press, 2018.
Identifiers: LCCN 2017057601 | ISBN 9781628972313 (papaerback : acid-free paper)
Classification: LCC PQ7798.28.E83 M813 2018 | DDC 863/.64--dc23
LC record available at https://lccn.loc.gov/2017057601

www.dalkeyarchive.com
Victoria, TX / McLean, IL / Dublin

Dalkey Archive Press publications are, in part, made possible through the support of the University of Houston-Victoria and its programs in creative writing, publishing, and translation.

Printed on permanent/durable acid-free paper

CONTENTS

DISJECTA MEMBRA POETAE

"Tomorrow let him love, who has never loved; he who has loved,
let him love tomorrow." (*The Vigil of Venus*)

> "In the world I have a rose
> And one day I will cut it." (*Adelita*)

"Yes," she answered, "I will open my heart to you—read in it
what I do, my most minute sentiments, my thoughts, everything
will be known to you."

"Ah! Zulica," he cried, throwing himself on his knees and
kissing her hand with ardor, "with what affection I would repay
you for everything you do for me! With what pleasure I would
submit to you all my thoughts! Sovereign lady of my heart,
your orders only will regulate my conduct." (Crébillon fils, *The
Divan*)

"On the whole, I think that in the rough usage of passion the
woman is the more active. I have seen far larger scratches and
marks on men than on women . . ." (Bronislaw Malinowski, *The
Sexual Life of Savages in North-Western Melanesia*)

> "Beloved, we are always in the wrong,
> Handling so clumsily our stupid lives,
> Suffering too little or too long,
> Too careful even in our selfish loves" (W. H.
> Auden, "In Sickness and in Health")

"But if McLuhan is right, what he outlines is indeed a disturbing analogy. A curved universe, the whirl of images, sounds, and erratic spaces—doesn't it bring to mind the world hallucinogen addicts discover when they 'trip out'?" (Umberto Eco)

> "A heart which the tooth of no crime can pierce,
> I flee, pale, exhausted, haunted by my shroud,
> Fearing death while I lie alone." (Mallarmé,
> "Anguish")

"Today, whether despite or because of the technical advancements and failures of the Modern Spirit, the happening seems to be the only expressive medium capable of representing the crisis of the real and the crisis of the human." (Jean-Jacques Lebel, *Le Happening*)

> "Slowly the poison the whole blood stream fills.
> The waste remains, the waste remains and kills"
> (William Empson, "Missing Dates")

". . . regressing to the savages that they may give me lessons." (Lautréaumont, *Maldoror*)

> "Crises of expression and erotic seizures:
> this is the man of today,
> his inwardness a vacuum;
> the continuity of personality
> is preserved in suits
> that keep for ten years if the material is good."
> (Gottfried Benn, "Fragments")

"To treat of this, would ask a long discourse. All goes topsie-turuy; all Kim, Kam; all, is tricks and deuices; all Riddles and vnknowne Mysteries; you shall not finde man, with man;

we all liue in ambush, lying in wait one for another, as the Cat, for the Mouse, or the Spider for the Fly; who roming carelessely vp and downe, suffers her selfe to be taken by a slender thread, whilest that venemous vermine, seazing on her head, holds her fast, neuer leauing her, till shee hath kill'd her with her poison." (Mateo Alemán, *Vida del pícaro Guzmán de Alfarache*)

"Formerly the monsters came after *us*, or met us at the threshold of their realm, and we did our best with magic weapons and magic words. Latterly, armored in bathyscaphes and the formulas of depth psychology, we go down after them." (John Barth, "An Afterword to *Roderick Random*")

". . . the popularity of hallucinogenic substances is a symptom of a shift in modern sensibilities. Does this shift represent a change of goals or an absence of goals? Both things. The traditional symbols have lost their meaning. They are empty signs. In a world ruled by the communications media no one has anything to say or anything to hear." (Octavio Paz, "The Symposium and the Hermit")

". . . it's a Republic of Cocaigne that we need." (Danton)

ONE
THE VIGIL OF VENUS

"I'm not afraid," Laura tells herself. "If I want to, I will."

Right away she says to the man sharing her taxi:

"I'm quite sure. I'm ready to sacrifice everything for him, as long as he loves me. I just have to know one thing. Does he really love me?"

It's a gloriously sunny morning and fall is in full swing. Meteorological conditions more suitable to this kind of tearful confidences will soon set in. Kiki wants to ask the taxi driver to let him out at the park. What difference could it possibly make if he's a little late for his class again? He is stopped by the thought that *this thing*, this viscous, tearful Laura could get out of the cab with him. It's better to miss a delightful walk than to run the risk of being stuck with someone much worse than rain on a parade and without question as bad as big hail on a farmer's crop. ("Just look! She took this taxi to tell me she's ready to sacrifice everything for the guy. And did I ask? She's so unaware it doesn't even occur to her to comment on the wonderful weather.")

On the other hand, the sunny morning and the park are a temptation too great for the driver, who has finally made his way out of a tight bottleneck on the world's most opulent avenue and suddenly has to floor it. Just when Kiki feels maximally irritated at the tastelessly sentimental crybaby, she's thrown right up against him.

Even her physical features cannot arouse Kiki's sympathy, much less his desire. Laura's jaw is too prominent, has a touch

of the Indian brave in it. ("Laura, Big Chief Beaten Barn Owl!")
There's also dullness, stupidity even in her large round milky
green eyes. ("And that nose: it's like a raptor's beak; but a sad
raptor, one that's been brought down to size!")

In all honesty, his friend Horacio hasn't shown very good
taste this time. No one could say that Laura is a pretty girl. But
that isn't exactly the thing that leaves Kiki cold and actually
feeling a certain revulsion. Kiki's known a lot of girls even uglier
than Laura, but, for one reason or another, they've seemed
more attractive to him than this indisputable daughter of
puritans; granddaughter of puritans and temperance leaguers;
great-granddaughter of puritans and suffragettes; great-great-
granddaughter of puritans and, it's obvious, redskins. ("My
poor little Pocahontas, what has happened to you!")

More than anything, it may be her prudishness, her strange,
old-fashioned ways that put him off. She lives under a kind of
insecurity blanket, you might say. For example, right now, once
she has re-established her comfortable position and composure
at the other end of the seat, she begins speaking again in the
exact same tone she's used for the entire trip:

"Because, surely you know, my mother is without question
a pillar of society. So when I brought him to our house last
Christmas . . ."

Laura gives the impression that the world has not yet
discovered sexual trauma and the inferiority complex. She
exudes the suffocating shyness of the Victorian age, the kind of
behavior that can only evoke antimacassars. *And the cloying reek
of a half-rotten cadaver that has just been dug up!*

He already knows her story by heart, every single detail of it.
He's heard it at least a hundred times: Mama treats the visitor
with arrogance the whole time and he resents it:

". . . yes, of course he was resentful. You Latins are like that.
And since that day he hasn't been the same."

Exactly. At least a hundred times, and Kiki still hasn't gotten a chance to interrupt her story with Horacio's comments on the episode, who swore he didn't care in the least if Kiki repeated his withering criticism of her crazy old lady and the ruined turkey and nauseating stuffing and the dumb decorations, as boring as only the stupidest rich people can make them. On the other hand, Laura seems to be enjoying her story more every time she tells it. As for Kiki, isn't he also at least a little pleased to hear the differences in the two versions of the story? Naturally he already knows what he'll be called on to hear now: the next step up her ladder of solitude and frustration—just as he would have written it for *Love Confessions*. He likes matching the next part with that horrifying moment he'd write of, when Laura's mama insists on having Horacio served more stuffed turkey: "It was prepared using a traditional recipe of our country," Mama would declare. "But *I* wasn't prepared using your recipe!" Horacio would quip ("making a stab at humor").

"My family is what you'd call very wealthy and we belong to one of the oldest families in the country, but I will . . ."

Word-for-word, Kiki could have finished the sentence before she does, saying everything he now hears: Laura is ready to risk disinheritance, willing to go to that extreme, just to be . . .

". . . near Horacio. I have plenty of money in my savings account. I can buy a ticket and fly to him without delay. As long as . . . he says he's ready to make me his wife."

In spite of all the courses that Kiki has taught on elite culture in mass society and the extremely gruesome episodes he's written for *Love Confessions* (sentiment-soaked gruesomeness is in fact his specialty) he realizes that Laura is completely captivated by her banal story. She is now embellishing it with trash mythology. Of course she herself would never see that. But the image of a perfectly chaste Laura seduced by a perfidious Horacio—*wait, why not brutally raped?*—is clearly seducing her! She imagines herself treated like a slave by a dark villain, and she, *she,* a modest, proper, filthy rich young woman trembles as she obeys his every vile command.

It would do no good for Kiki to point out to Laura that in today's world nobody can leave this or any other supposedly civilized country (I'm just saying!), without a carry-on crammed with documents, the accumulation of which, of course, can happen only after all the forms that allow anyone even to breathe in another country are completed—all of which, if you're lucky, takes weeks of paperwork. In fact, things have gotten very bad for Laura and our generation, if we want the thrill of a romantic escape. "There's no place in the world now"—Kiki almost says out loud—"a Shelley can run to with a naive, trembling beloved, mere steps ahead of gesticulating parents' threatening scowls." No, now runaways are stopped at the border. And where would anyone find a naive, trembling beloved in today's world anyway? But waxing cynical about all this, Kiki believes, is too easy. ("Besides, Celia is truly, truly naive and trembling.") (*Was.*)

As usual, the image of Celia interrupts his thoughts. Better concentrate on the woes of this puritanical, red-skinned Beaten Barn Owl. ("It's Laura. Her name is Laura. Every time I think of her I should call her Laura." ("Yes, have a little empathy!") "It's evident the girl wants to vent her feelings to someone. And, since she knows that among the millions of people here, I'm Horacio's best friend, she assumes that I'm the perfect sounding board for her troubles." *Moreover, consider this: you're also an expert on the subject. And out there are* True Confessions *and* Love Confessions *to back up the claim. So be good and pay her a little attention. You might even earn a few bucks with a new storyline.*)

But Kiki, an expert on mass communication, already knows very well that a public hooked on the "trues" likes them exactly the way they are: always the same. A Madame Bovary doesn't want to read *Les Liaisons dangereuses,* much less *Adolphe.* She wants to read what a Madame Bovary ought to read, wants nothing but the cheap, fixed menu and wants nobody who asks for Lobster Thermidor (much less *langouste à la Thermidor*).

More to the point, Laura's soppy misadventures are no exquisite dish. ("And she's so ugly.") But make her a little prettier, chip off that puritanical crust—*careful: don't take too much!*—and you have another appealing young heroine.

Meanwhile, Laura's strident little voice continues to rise as she piles up the sad, sad details and draws ever closer to her predictably pathetic—and even more pathetic for being predictable—grand finale of desolation and ruin. Laura loves her unhappiness and has become her own most faithful public.

A couple of times already, the cabby's face has surprised Kiki, peering back at them from the front seat. A typical Italian, a man of the people, how could he not love a melodrama like Laura's? ("But he's still an idiot! And if he keeps turning to watch this nutty girl, he's going to crash right into something!") Kiki has a mortal fear of dying in an accident. Just think, before Celia, he could even have been called intrepid. Then he started to take care of himself, he was afraid she would be left all alone. He knew she was very lonely and good and naïve; and Celia had been very good and very naive. *Celia again!*

This time a truly disagreeable thought jolts Kiki from his obsession: "Oh! The driver surely links me directly to what he's been hearing from this idiotic girl. Later at home he'll repeat what he's heard on this fare and his entire family will agree that it's such a shame to welcome into the country all those suspicious foreigners, whose sole objective for immigrating is to ruin pretty girls."

The driver will describe him to his family in some ghastly way. Kiki will wind up being turned into a true cad in the eyes of the people and Kiki's faithful audience will soon imagine the expert on mass culture as some kind of sordid drug trafficker who devotes his free time to ruining the lives of chaste, rosy-cheeked schoolgirls—("all of them blond-haired and freckle-faced, of course!") It's no longer merely in the pages of *Love Confessions* that he is about to be given a place in Megalopolis's lurid mythology. *That* he can't allow! Until now, it has been only

to make a living—not what you would call a very juicy one—
that he has agreed to collaborate in the city's general brutishness.

The driver, taking advantage of another stoplight, now
turns to stare at Kiki with an obvious look of reproach. Kiki
interrupts Laura.

"Silly girl, you must pay attention to what I'm going to
say to you. I'm much older than you, and yet not too old to
remember that ten years ago I used to believe what you, it seems
to me, now believe: that feelings are the most important thing
in the world. That's why, when my only uncle, to whom I owed
so much, tried to persuade me not to marry the girl I was about
to marry, the only thing I said to him—in tones that ranged
from pleas for understanding to insults (imagine! I accused him
of trying to swindle me!)—was . . . that I was in love. And you
already know what happened to me later. My poor uncle, who
died without speaking to me again after one of those arguments,
had been *completely* right all along and I hurt him for absolutely
no good reason. Draw your own conclusions."

The driver's back seems to stiffen. He will undoubtedly not
turn to look at Kiki again with that air of reproach in his eyes
that has varied from ironic to contemptuous.

Laura, on the other hand, cedes no ground.

"This is very different."

"It always seems very different when it refers to ourselves."

"I know that you felt sorry for that girl."

Horacio has obviously told her about it.

"So tell me, don't you perhaps feel a little sorry for Horacio?
Because, you know, after all he is just a foreigner? Maybe you
feel a little sorry for *me,* for the same reason."

Laura is quiet. Kiki has started to feel very comfortable in
the role of serious man that he has assumed to cow the driver.
He anticipates Laura's objection and continues the lecture:

"And that is exactly why I fear that in the long run your
case could turn out to be very similar to mine. So I pose this
question and ask you to think about it. What purpose does it

serve to make your mother unhappy just because you want to kid yourself with a little word, a word that most of the time means only that you feel sexually attracted to someone and would like to go to bed with the someone you favor at the moment."

Kiki perfects his role substantially with those words. He is no longer merely the serious man. ("Well, yes, fundamentally he's still the serious man, but one now full of life experience.") A kind of older brother. *Better yet, a very young uncle who is also noticeably worldly.* A man of experience who is never caught by surprise, never scandalized by anything, and, moreover, has the ability to address a college girl with tact and understanding. *A bon vivant, an incipient, magnificent bachelor.* He nonchalantly lets the ash of his premier Upmann cigar fall onto his beautiful brocade vest as he looks up with a sigh from behind the cover of a rare edition, his expression firm but ever gentle, and speaks to a naughty young lady who, most certainly, awakens his memories of a teenage love.

"Of course I'd like to go to bed with Horacio," Laura thinks, "but what bad manners to just say it out loud to me like that!"

Out in the city, golden light as thick as honey makes it difficult to imagine the existence of any place in the world beyond the park and its luxuriant contours. Squirrels hurriedly rush apart, band together, scurry up trees. Their fleetness and agility seem contagious: oh, to be five, six, seven years old and heading out for the big pond off there to the left with the little toy yacht in your hands.

Reluctantly, Kiki comes back to the melodrama still unfolding in the taxi.

"Of course you would like to go to bed with Horacio!" Kiki can again see the objection forming, the reference to pure, platonic love. He decides to ignore the squirrels' games and reprise his role of all-understanding *bon vivant.* He adds certain perfections of philosophy à la Will Durant.

"Because one thing is certain. All of us tend to use pompous words to hide our most elementary physical actions and responses, our needs . . . our whims. Talking about love, in your case, Laura, means coating with respectability what in any other mode of expression would seem vulgar to you, too coarse for your taste. It's always the same with people like you, especially the ones your age. You tend to bring up vulgarity when some realistically-minded soul mentions our physical nature in any way."

("Beaten Barn Owl is listening to me intently because I am uttering the most inane banalities imaginable.") The driver seems to have lost all interest in what happens or is said on the back seat. He gives the impression that a noisy rape could be in progress back there and not even then would he turn his head. *Kiki, you've successfully turned yourself into a noble, Indian puritano.*

The cab has finally left the park behind and fallen in line with traffic going toward gloomy gray buildings in the lower section of the city. A restaurant's familiar sign alerts Kiki that he is about to reach his destination.

At that moment he would like to add something like "one always has to take into account that a beautiful girl, however angelic she may appear to be, underneath it all is just an anthropoid wearing makeup." He feels sure that a line like that, with its easy-going but mildly cynical tone, would have its maximum effect on Laura's thinking, above all now, when she's about to be alone with her thoughts. The "anthropoid" bit is especially good: it would remind little Beaten Barn Owl that he considers her his intellectual equal. With "anthropoid," he reasons, his statement would in fact be especially effective as praise. *And besides, "monkey" has no sizzle!* For, if Laura is aware of the great unattractiveness that Kiki sees in her, his implied simile, in the honest, slightly nonchalant, and skeptical manner of *Sieur* Michel de Montaigne, would suggest that *Kiki-honnête-*

homme-blasé sees in all women exactly that: apes in makeup. She would be forced to think about herself by the allusion to unattractive women—because, even if Laura harbors pretentions of being attractive, they could only be demi-pretentions—and, basically, she cannot help but know she's ugly. But, with that image of herself in mind, she would also clearly see that, in the matter of ugliness, her entire sex is in it with her!

He doesn't say this to Laura. He's sure such a statement would impose on him at least another ten or fifteen minutes of conversation with Beaten Barn Owl, something he cannot allow to happen at the moment because his students will already be waiting for him at the door of his classroom. It's better to stick with what he's already said.

"Now, Laura, to sum up: your situation for me is this. You have a lot of reflecting to do. Don't rush into anything. Don't be in a hurry to do what could make you unhappy and bring misfortune to others. Be a nice girl. I'm sure that tonight, when I see you at O Jango's (because you are going, right?), you will see things in a different way. Above all, I hope, more prudently."

With these words, he plants a light kiss on her forehead and opens the door of the taxi, which has just stopped in front of the lifeless neoclassical façade of the Free School. "What a narrow forehead!" he says to himself, "I almost kissed her *hair.*" He feels a wave of disgust.

"Yes, you're probably right, Kiki. I promise to reflect. Oh, I'll see you tonight then, Kiki, and, Kiki, I promise to be feeling better. And thank you again, Kiki, for everything. See you later!"

("She's making a face at me! A capricious, sweet-girl smirk, the little pícara! She looks horrible.") Kiki steps to the curb, looks up, and sees the familiar words carved over the Free School's entrance: *Pedes in terra, ad sidera visus,* and silently translates: "feet on the ground, eyes on the stars." The motto of the Free School is as deceptive as everything taught in it. Worried that Laura will give in to a new outburst of emotion, Kiki leans over—he should be looking at heaven but, frankly, all he sees is hell—and hurriedly closes the door of the taxi.

He almost runs to the building. ("Why did she use my nickname so many times as we said goodbye?") Only after a moment does he realize that he forgot to give her money for the taxi. ("But she has *a lot* of money, and, after all, she could never find a psychoanalyst who charges as little as taxi fare!") He also takes into account that, with just a little ingenuity, he *could* still get something out of the specific melodrama he has so patiently just had to listen to. With one or two embellishments—mostly making the heroine's physical aspects prettier—he might turn this into another celebrated tale in *Love Confessions,* or even in *True Confessions,* the real sources of his income. (*And, by the way, it's almost time to give Celia the rent money.*)

On reflection, the taxi ride wasn't bad. Above all, the worst thing, a collision, didn't occur. How long has Kiki had fears like this, really? ("No, it's not at all the case that as a boy the idea of dying didn't bother him. He was bold, that's all.") The worm of fear has always gnawed at him, the way it does at this very minute as he climbs the stairs to the Free School, repeating to himself the titles of pornographic Victorian novels he'd like to mesmerize his female students with. He would very much like to have in his hand an edition of *The Lustful Turk.* Today is the ideal occasion to read them that delicious episode—*how far pornography has fallen since the Second Industrial Revolution!*— in which the protagonist dissuades Emily from her prejudices against anal penetration. "Of course that episode is an imitation of Sade's *Justine.* But it would have been just what I need for what I want to say this afternoon about the erotic fantasies of Victoria Regina and her contemporary, Jack the Ripper."

A squirrel, one of those Kiki saw a short while ago as the taxi passed the park, has with surgical precision just ripped open the finger of a little boy who was offering it a nut. This happens at the exact instant Kiki enters his classroom. Of course, this news would not come out in the newspaper either.

When finally, after more than an hour's wait, they hand her the bound volumes, Lena Lustquist again notices (and what a repugnant feeling it is) that her sticky clothes are clinging to her body and she's perspiring uncontrollably in the oppressive heat of Buenos Aires. From the first day, she has felt cheated by the enormous, deflated city. When she was a student of Romance Languages at the University of Gothenburg, she couldn't help imagining the "*ciudad junto al río inmóvil*" as a city beside a still sea of river. It should be enormously more beautiful than this conglomeration of bricks and mortar and bovine-like beings rendered featureless by their uniform obesity and undefined blind aggression. This heap of buildings, as ragged and pretentious as a worn stamp collection, confused by its own geometric rigidity and low, undifferentiated skyline—this is the cityscape her eyes will be forced to submit to for months and months until she has served the full sentence of her grant period.

She has clearly read Mallea and Martínez Estrada. It was they who verified for her a personality between taciturn and boastful that she was delighted to be going to meet. She was convinced that, scratching, scratching, scratching, she would finally uncover the enchantingly luminous Mediterranean clarity in the primitive Hispanic mind. She had consciously even hoped to have a love affair. Precisely catalogued under her memory's bright light, an intense, dark face or a caress knowingly prolonged would energize those long, scholarly winters back in her home country. Or—*why not?*—even a little son who would combine her own muscular, pensive temperament and the proud frugality and impetuous rhythms of a man made for riding horses, a natural-born *caballero*. Instead, what she gets here are modestly lascivious glances from overfed creatures who are beginning to appeal to her as under-boiled meat that might still have a little ice at its center despite the relentless, devastating heat. It is a heat the natives don't seem to notice, though it's easy to see the asphalt melting in the streets they bolt across, weaving in and out of traffic with a skill that could have a kind of grace about it if it didn't inevitably remind her of a large troop of bullfighting clowns.

And to think of all she'd had to fight her way through to get this grant. The most-erudite and knowledgeable Dr. Soderblon, director of Spanish American studies, despite having spent no more than ten days in Latin America fifteen years ago when he went to Puerto Rico to interview some great Spanish poet there; the elderly Dr. Soderblon, always so astonishingly up-to-date on the twists and turns of bibliography—that very Dr. Soderblon had been the one who brought to her attention the fact that, in the past five years, the Puerto Rican university he had visited once had already received thirty-two monographs on Borges; and, according to the latest news, Princeton had in the works seven volumes on Julio Cortázar, while, at the Sorbonne, there were nineteen. Gothenburg itself already had a thick thesis on the author of *Hopscotch*—some four hundred pages longer than the novel itself—written by the flamboyant doctors Anita Knudsen and Rebeca Epstein. In the long run, armed with such impressive numbers, he finally persuaded her not to repeat the same mistake everyone else was making by writing a thesis on one or the other of the two great authors. Still—she had reminded him in a less than reticent tone of reproach—he, the illustrious Hispanist, was reserving for *himself*, in order to crown his career as a prolific and conscientious researcher, a comparative study of Borges's and Cortázar's views of the world, a topic she had planned for a long time to make the subject of her own final work.

So she sits in a dusty room that reeks of mold, her eyes scanning the faces of the few summer readers there. She's searching for anyone with a more or less palatable resemblance to Mallea's suffering sawmill worker—after all, the public library is too unlikely a place to run into Drieu's *l'homme à cheval.* Before her on the table lies an open volume of the literary journal she has requested. As she tries to survive the heat and her clammy clothes, she decides that her first impression of the city—"just consumers: no one here makes anything"—was accurate. She believes she is clearly not going to find in the library or even out on the street a single example of the *criollo* male she used to dream of in Gothenburg. She is more remorseful than ever that she accepted her teacher's suggestion—"where there are great authors, there must be minor writers who are not completely bereft of interest." But here she sits, in her very Nordic sense of duty, beginning work on the thesis that would be drawn from her on-the-spot assessment of three little known *porteño* fiction writers. Of course, on top of everything else, even after her hard work of verifying all the details through the cultural attaché, it turns out that one of the writers has just now definitively renounced his status as a *porteño* and gone to live in Italy, where he would no doubt lose weight; another is somewhere in the remote region of La Mesopotamia overseeing a round-up on his big hacienda. The third writer, whose story lies open in front of her, seems for his part to have permanently installed himself in the other America, a place overrun with hippies and race-rioters and bristling with skyscrapers: he's in faraway Megalopolis. And that's where her cousin Eriksson also is, the very intermediary through whom she hopes now to make contact with this third hardly great, *porteño* fiction writer. He's the one who figures in the card catalog with a large number of works on popular culture that in time she would need to consult to round out that part of her investigation *in situ.*

In the figure of the third writer, our amiable reader may have already divined the person of Kiki.

Lena is now aware that a little arroyo of sweat is sliding down her slender, Modigliani neck and shivers involuntarily. Disgusted, she bows her head. A drop of sweat falls from her burning forehead directly onto the letters forming the title of Kiki's story. This reminds her that she can't let her alma mater down. She's expected to begin reading immediately whatever comes after the scarcely promising title "Missing Reality." "While here *I* sit literally soaked with too much reality," Lena says to herself, and fails to begin reading the following text:

Missing Reality

As soon as he got to the station in the county seat of the province to complete his trip to the capital, he started the search for his favorite brand of cigarettes. Carlos, a die-hard smoker, had had to grit his teeth and tolerate the harsh, and in the end tasteless green tobacco that—except for those really strong black cigarettes that nothing in the world would ever induce him to try again—had been the only brand he had been able to get in the down-and-out town where, for strictly family reasons, he just spent more than a week. Luckily he succeeds in finding a pack of his excellent imported brand and, stocking up on newspapers and magazines, he sits down in one of the less than cozy metallic chairs lining the walls of the waiting room of the small bus station. Good tobacco and interesting reading would anesthetize his anxiety to get back to the big city, and he's already feeling more at ease after the strain he has just undergone during his stay with his country relatives. They are too good-natured (or seem so to him). He feels especially relaxed after inhaling once again the delicious fragrance of his tobacco, in which he thinks he detects delicate notes of honey, whiskey, and the green expanses of Virginia.

An extremely sensual person, a little dissolute even, he no doubt also desires *other* satisfactions. More than a week's deprivation of female flesh in that awful town where the brakes slam on good-naturedness at the bedroom door, turned out to be a torture for him. Carlos would have liked, for his remaining

nearly three hours of travel, to have the luxury of looking
forward to finding some attractive girl in the seat next to the
one he has just been assigned at the ticket window. Preferably
she'd be one of those little blonds of about twenty (so abundant
among the local *piamonteses*). Naturally, he would not hesitate
to engage her in conversation by offering a magazine for her
entertainment during the long bus ride. Perhaps, step by step,
word by word . . . But, no: Carlos is no longer twenty and has
given up such illusions. Great erotic affairs begun during travels
happen only in the movies! His experience as a traveler, to be
truthful, is not insignificant and he has come by it as often on
land as on water or in the air. Carlos already knows that the
beautiful women travel with unimpressive boyfriends or stupid
husbands or with other women equally as beautiful (a waste
of pleasure!). Or their beauty is diametrically contradicted by
female companions who are insignificant and ugly. The fact is,
whether he travels by bus, plane, or train, every time a woman
sits down beside him, she turns out to be irredeemably ugly.
There had been one exception, it's true. How could he forget
her! She was a proud redhead—and Carlos's preference, without
question, is for redheads. She had green eyes and was about
twenty-five, but—curse of Tantalus!—she carried in her arms
a baby. "A boy," the beautiful woman did not hesitate to tell
him. Of course he now no longer dreams of the good fortune
of starting up erotic relationships on public transportation.
Undoubtedly they would seat him next to a smelly, elderly man;
or some obese spinster schoolteacher from the sticks, the kind
of woman who separates the world into warring factions of
"educators" and "people needing to be educated."

A graceful, slender, twenty-something-year-old with dark
hair and delicate features—finely set nose, green eyes slightly
slanted—Julia silently enters the waiting room. Carlos is
immediately jarred out of his meditation and puts down the
newspaper that had shielded his face. This beauty would most

certainly *not* travel in the seat next to him, whatever the reason. Who knows, she probably won't even be on the same bus and is going in the opposite direction. Or she could just be here waiting for someone. The beautiful young woman with lustrous black hair ceases to interest him and he discreetly fixes his eyes on his newspaper again. He's determined to read it this time without letting himself start daydreaming. A story he finds in the literary supplement, surprisingly, manages to distract him completely and that's how he spends the hour until his bus is ready to leave. With not so much as a glance in the girl's direction—for a while she occupied a seat one chair away from him in the almost empty waiting room—he goes out to the enormous conveyance that sits awaiting new passengers.

But why is this bus already so crowded? The clerk at the ticket window sold him a seat on what is supposed to be an "express." He should have known that this behemoth had come from some remote point of departure and now would simply be completing the final leg of its route to the end of the line.

According to his ticket, Carlos has the right to sit in seat 26, midway down the coach. However, now seated in seat 26, looking notably hostile, he finds the corpulent anatomy of a *campesino* who in no way seems disposed to hand the seat over to him. Time is of the essence now. The bus is behind schedule for departure and once it starts moving (Carlos knows this from many bus rides), a status quo will be established, according to which, either by right or by physical fact, each seat belongs to its occupant. The almost asphyxiating heat inside the carriage has already started to bring on Carlos's habitual nervousness. He feels compelled to act with the aggressive energy appropriate to someone who is very annoyed. His nerves are definitely not soothed by the possibility that, in this case—"even on a bus!" he adds in his head—a status quo will set in. Disturbed, he turns abruptly to avoid an argument with the voluminous intruder who is sitting in his seat. He intends to find the bus's security agent, fill him in on the outrageous mistake, and demand that he make immediate reparation of it. He just then collides with the seductive little brunette, ticket in hand, who is looking for her seat. She is indeed a stupendous young woman. However, now is not the moment to make small talk with her, and Carlos limits himself, somewhat grumpily, to begging her pardon, then continues toward the front of the bus. He spots the driver, who is already starting the motor. The driver stops the motor and screams for the guard to end this monstrous injustice. Carlos already knows that he will get his seat back and reverses his route to claim what is by right his. Standing quietly beside his row of seats, he finds the delectable *houri* from the waiting room, who is listening resignedly to a large teenager now sitting in the seat next to the one that corresponds to Carlos's seat number. This young fellow, he soon discovers, turns out to be as much an intruder as his corpulent neighbor, and much more fearless, for with unflinching self-confidence he's telling the tender beauty:

"As for this seat, I got no plans to move an inch 'less they give *me* one."

"Don't upset yourself, miss," Carlos intervenes, "the security guard is coming to resolve *this*." And, offering his "this" with so much emphasis that it seems like a storm warning, he runs his eyes, full of disdain, over the two intruders, who, however, do not appear to notice his allusion to them.

The arrival of the guard produces an instantaneous effect. The intruders vacate the seats without batting an eye. Carlos, who still can't believe his luck at winding up with the beautiful young brunette as his traveling companion, lets her enter their row first, sacrificing his right to control the window, for which so many other times he has fought unflinchingly. It's a right that becomes precious if you think about it. On long trips, even in fairly low temperatures, the interior of a bus eventually feels like an oven. The great majority of passengers keep their windows hermetically sealed, due, apparently, to what could be classified as a mythological fear of currents of air.

Carlos is quiet. He's amused by the pretty young woman's fluster. She's even prettier now as her blushes cover a certain professorial demeanor. Is it conceivable that a girl like this could have just felt the thrill of a *coup de foudre?* Carlos has for quite a while now seen himself as a middle-aged man, his body invaded by fat, in whom nothing remains of the attractiveness that long ago frequently made him an irresistible seducer. On second thought, he realizes that he might still be of interest to a pretty young woman. First of all, in today's world women appreciate the intellectual type, such as an already graying male with nicotine-and-ink-stained fingers, the universal marks of an older man of letters. Such appreciation was inconceivable when he was fifteen years younger and had to overcome his staunchly intellectual propensities to ensure amorous conquests.

For Carlos it would have been enough now to sit quietly for a moment and let this precious young female recover a little from her confusion. But, as if what had already happened weren't enough to get things going, she opens her handbag. Carlos's quick perusal of its jumbled contents detects right away, among all the tissues and multiple keys, a pack of the very same horrible cigarettes that, for his part, he had relegated to the bottom of a jacket pocket the moment he acquired his aromatic Virginias and the existence of which (are there one or two packs in there? but no matter) he has already forgotten. During her patient search, she first picks up anise mints and lipstick and then finally brings to light a copy of *For Whom the Bell Tolls* in paperback.

"How are things going between Maria and Jordan?"

She looks over at him, at first very surprised, and then laughs heartily. She's soon mentioning a healthy list of authors, novels, and films. For a country girl, she's surprisingly up on a great many things. Except for an unimportant mistake here and there—for example, her attribution to Kafka of a travel book, when, of course, such a book doesn't figure among his works—her errors are due to who-knows-what excusable mislaying of information inside her delectable, excitable head. Or to some childlike vanity that is perfectly natural in someone who is still almost a child. So, except for a few trivial details, Carlos feels as completely at ease with her as he would with any of his intellectual friends. She may turn out to be a tough nut to crack, but it's also possible that so much reading has, as they say, liberated her . . .

"Would you like a cigarette, miss?"

She accepts without hesitation. This reinforces the second hypothesis in Carlos's mind. Furthermore, she smokes like an experienced smoker, solidly corroborating his hypothesis. She engages spontaneously in a conversation that has already left the field of fiction behind. If this girl has shoals, she keeps them well hidden. As it turns out, she is a physics teacher in a prep school in the interior, but, surprisingly, she seems on top of all the important advances in her field. What may explain it is that she regularly attends university classes in the capital. She lives there and doggedly travels out each week to teach her classes.

"Do you not believe that today physics is becoming a purely imaginative exercise?"

"Of course. But I'd frame it in the following terms: today's physics is closer than ever to poetry. And I really like good poetry a great deal . . ."

Hearing her say that, to him of all people, a poet, a *well-known* poet—a poet *di mestiere!*—makes him think this is decidedly going to go somewhere and all will be his for the asking. Some benevolent genie has decided to grant him portentous protection from bad luck. Is this the moment to disclose his identity to her? No, it would be better to wait a little longer. The way things are going, this could last all the way to the end of the bus ride. He's sure to have enough time. Yes, wait a little longer and maybe he will even be able to recite one of his poems for her, or that Ronsard, "*Mignonne, allons voir si la rose,*" which, since he has gotten older, has never failed to facilitate his conquests.

". . . can notice this, for example, in the most recent definition of probability: 'probability is the median value of the relative frequency of a distribution of factors within an irregular series.'"

Carlos tries to visualize the notion by relating it to the wonder of their encounter on the bus, but abandons the attempt when he realizes that she's now waiting expectantly. He quickly breaks the silence, praising, of course, her marvelous memory and the excellence of her information. The truth is that this highly knowledgeable, beautiful girl beside him has her own peculiarly erotic herbs and spices.

" . . . physics and poetry, as you say, but I prefer to talk about physics and fantasy literature."

"Yes, you're absolutely right, at least in part. And by the way, did you know that at Princeton, just as at many other North American universities, certain works of science fiction are *required reading* for courses in physics, chemistry, and even biology?"

"Well, it seems to me that, in that sense, they are proving me right. And, as if this were not in itself sufficient evidence, allow me to remind you that physics, this science, to say it another way, of 'solidities' until the beginning of the century, is now entering—and wholeheartedly, especially from the perspective of the layperson—into the arena of the fantastic. When it postulates the possibility that a material, a single substance, can be in two places simultaneously, is this not *story* pure and simple, and even more than science fiction, a bona fide fairy tale?"

She listens to him quietly, her enormous green eyes opened wide. ("What does she see when she looks at me? Does she see me as old and bloated, as I see myself in the mirror in the morning while I shave? Is she considering my gray hair and making a calculation to ascertain that I'm about twenty years older than she? But, if in so many other things she is so up-to-date, she must also know that the mature man is in vogue. Perhaps I simply am attractive to her. At least, she has a way of listening to me . . . But I should let her talk a little more now.") And a brilliant thought occurs to him for wrapping up his short lecture.

"That is the way of it, my wise young miss, modern physics is, in reality . . . missing reality."

She smiles at him sweetly, seems to meditate a moment, then, turning in her seat a little, begins to take off her jacket.

"May I?"

Don't think for a moment that he wants to take liberties. No, he's very careful not to let his fingers brush against that marvelous, fragrant skin on the delectably round shoulders revealed by her sleeveless blouse. He simply helps her remove her scratchy tweed jacket. How it must have irritated her skin.

"It's really hot in here, isn't it?"

"If it's not too much bother, may I ask you to open the window, just a little? Some air would not be bad at all, I think." The fresh air makes her yawn. Carlos glances discreetly at his watch and notices that they have more than an hour left on the bus.

"Is it much further?" She has the heightened senses of a cat.

"A little more than an hour."

"Oh . . . I should take a short nap."

Isn't it wonderful to be made the guardian of her sleep? The enchanting young woman again makes all the usual feminine movements involving her purse. Carlos even perceives a tender flirtatiousness in the jumble under which she buries the Hemingway paperback. She definitely won't finish reading it in the course of this bus ride. Carlos is dazzled. He observes the youthful faces she makes as she digs around in her bag. And, although it seems to him that something, maybe a pack of cigarettes, falls out of it, she doesn't notice, preoccupied at the moment by pushing her novel down to the bottom of her purse. He doesn't say anything to her about it because, in truth, the obstinacy she shows in her arduous task has bewitched him.

Carlos tries to read the book on the origins of Greek art that had so interested him during the days he spent among his already-forgotten relatives. It's no use: the words dance before his eyes and not a single idea on the page succeeds in opening a path to his intelligence. The enticing image of the sleeping woman imposes itself constantly between the text and his rational mind. He soon abandons his reading to think of her calmly. He surreptitiously admires her bare legs, snatches comfort from the sight of her smooth, round shoulders, and finally contemplates, entranced, the touching exquisiteness of her nose, so fine, so thin, slightly upturned: flawless. She, he has no doubt, is all woman with a capital "W." His admiring contemplation makes the time pass quickly. Only once during the remaining journey does he have contact with any reality other than her, when he notices that a group of big, crude kids beside him who have to ride stand-up murmur to each other, then seem to cast mocking glances his way.

"Miss, miss. I need to wake you. We arrive in about twenty-five minutes."

She looks at him, startled, as if she were looking at a perfect stranger. But she remembers immediately. Mathematics and imagination, physics and science fiction, science and fantasy literature. She smiles at him, although it doesn't seem to him that she's fully awake.

"Here, have a cigarette. It will be just the thing after your short siesta."

"Yes, thank you, but I prefer mine: they're smoother."

Carlos interrupts her beautiful movement to forage in her bag.

"Look. I have yours too. Have one of these."

Carlos has now taken out the cigarettes he had earlier rejected and dropped into the left pocket of his sports coat, which now seems more crowded than ever. This, naturally, is only the effect of nerves as he strives to accomplish each movement quickly and to perfection, a form of praise that he's rendering to this little goddess. Truthfully, the girl already seems to be feeling his praise for her in the fact that—just as in any ad on TV—

he already has her preferred brand. Perhaps, as she smokes the cigarette he has offered her, she's asking herself how he could have so brilliantly known which brand it was (without realizing that, when she opened her bag earlier, she revealed to his tender curiosity more than a few of her secrets).

He's on the verge of telling her to keep the whole pack. But this beautiful woman might interpret it as demeaning, if he, who knows a lot about smoking, keeps the good cigarettes for himself and lets her keep the bitter national ones, the only brand she's used to.

As he puts the pack back in his pocket, it occurs to him to make an innocent joke:

"They are really your cigarettes, I took them while you were sleeping!"

The lovely thing shows not the slightest alarm. Her gaze does not shift to the handbag. Instead, she gives him a big smile and their conversation resumes more or less where it left off. But now his brilliant verbal efforts converge on a single objective: he must establish a solid basis for immediate, direct contact with this ravishing (he says "*ravissante*") traveling companion. He still knows only a few, very vague facts about her, too general to be of any use for easily meeting her again.

It may be old and tired, but the stratagem of lending someone a book still gives good results. It has yielded Carlos, on more than one occasion, great satisfactions, and it works effectively in this case as well. He speaks to her of Hadamard and offers to let her keep, for as long as she likes, the Frenchman's passionate *Psychology of Invention*, a book that in all honesty Carlos has barely looked at, opened only a couple of times at that. He bought it years ago, when he was proposing an essay on Valéry, which he didn't finish. But he now talks to the adorable creature as if the book were utterly fascinating; it's an involuntary response to his strong desire to secure a concrete way of connecting with her. When the bus enters the terminal, Carlos already knows her name and address. First thing tomorrow, he will bring the excellent book to Julia Sierra, for that is her name, and he will see her as many times as he wants. This is working magnificently.

"Today has been the most enjoyable travel of my life, please believe me," he tells Julia when they say goodbye and go their separate ways home. (And he's not lying and maybe she feels more or less the same.)

Captivated by Julia Sierra, missing her already—*what, that soon?*—he barely hears the housekeeper's greeting chatter of a thousand matters. And, going against a powerful habit, he casts only a distant glance at the usually inviting pile of correspondence that has accumulated on the little table in the vestibule during his absence.

In his bedroom, he begins to undress, drunk on Julia Sierra. But before taking his shower, his rapture is not so acute that he fails to comply with a timeless ritual always performed after travel: he deposits on the chest of drawers everything that makes his bulging jacket pockets look deformed. Meanwhile Julia Sierra has already stepped out of her bath. The warm water has depressed her even more. Why was her traveling companion so standoffish with her? It's true that she wound up falling asleep, but at first she only pretended to sleep to be able to move closer to him, as if unconsciously, so there could be some contact between their bodies. But when she moved her half-bare thigh toward his leg, he pulled further back in his seat. Julia Sierra looks in the mirror and is satisfied that her charms still haven't lost their effect. Her breasts are firm and buoyant. Her thighs are slender. "Have I completely misinterpreted things? Can he really be one of *those*? Still, at first he seemed so interested in forming a relationship with me." Wrapped in a big towel, she throws herself on the bed. A cigarette would help her see this mystery more clearly. Beside her, in the middle of the accustomed clutter, is her purse. She digs around in it and finally decides to dump everything out. Lipstick, aspirin, Hemingway, mints, keys, photos, rumpled tissues with red stains. Now everything is on the bed. The cigarettes stand out in their absence. "They're your cigarettes; I took them while you slept." The words explode into her memory. And to think that at the time she thought it was a joke! Appearances are so deceptive. "How *cultured* he seemed. But, no! He's a common thief, at the very least a jerk. How could he have played such a mean trick on a lady he just met?" How atrociously vulgar! He must be one of *those* after all! Carlos is still extracting things from his pockets. He reproaches himself for having momentarily stopped contemplating Julia's already sacred image as he counts the coins that had weighed his right pocket down. There are one hundred and seventy-one pesos. He can breathe easy. One plus seven plus one make nine, one of his lucky numbers. When he starts to empty the left pocket, the image of his new love dominates his mind with greater force than at any moment since he left her. Here, under the pack of his imported cigarettes, is the pack she touched when she took one—he will smoke them too from now on, permanently. They are the brand he made her smile with when he told his innocent joke. Almost solemnly, you could say, he places this pack in the drawer of his bedside table; he knows he will keep it there as an authentic relic. He goes on taking things from his pocket. The antiquated lighter that never fails: with it he lit two cigarettes. An empty box of matches, from which at some point he has stripped the label, following a deeply rooted habit that is almost maniacal. A pack of cigarettes, those ordinary ones. "Another one? What? Where did *they* come from?" Carlos is stupefied, but the pack is in his hand. He opens the drawer of the nightstand and, of course, the other one, the sacred pack of cigarettes, is there. "So where have these come from? *Where!* They are your cigarettes, which I took while you were sleeping.'" He feels his face redden; his fingers tremble. She will undoubtedly think he's a jerk, if not a vulgar thief! Why, oh why did he think of making that stupid joke, how could he think of doing such a foolish thing? "But, *was* it simply a joke?" Or was it an involuntary confession of an embarrassing and equally involuntary act? Clearly, he had seen the contents of her handbag. When she was asleep, could he have started nosing around in it and picked up her cigarettes? "But, why?" In a state of unconscious ecstasy of some kind, maybe? No, why would he do that? "What unsuspected malice is harbored beneath my consciousness? And those rude, muttering louts! Of course! Why, they witnessed the theft . . . !" And to think, he had planned everything so thoroughly in order to lead this love affair to a happy ending! Oh! What should he do now . . . ? Will a vulgar thief, a jerk who brazenly goes through the bag of a sleeping girl, have it in him to show up and chance facing a huffy, forever disdainful Julia Sierra?

The story is full of warmth, heft, and frustration, and ends up depressing Frøken Lustquist even more. Still, her Nordic equanimity obliges her to recognize that the narrative possesses certain basic virtues, above all an inner truth imparted in a somewhat flaccid but hard-charging style—in the way of a seminal bull kept in the corral too long. She has seen this as the outstanding temperament of the *porteño* ever since her arrival in the city beside the unmoving river. "Could the story be autobiographical?" It's hard for Frøken Lustquist to imagine how a writer could be so timorous, timid even; or better, so constrained. Although it may be shocking to her to even be thinking it, it is her duty now, as a conscientious Nordic scholarship recipient, to dig deeper into the sexual mores of the Buenos Aires literati.

It's time to hand back the borrowed volumes. She will go to her hotel for a prolonged icy shower. She is sure that, after a refreshing bath, she won't be vulnerable to a disappointment like Julia's and resolves to go to the folk poetry recital for the Literary Union tonight. It's the ideal spot in the city beside that motionless river from which she will begin her new investigation. The attaché had been right after all to get her an invitation and insist she attend this event, when she, that very morning, depleted by the terrible heat and trying to wriggle out of the obligation, had told him, in an unambiguously disdainful tone, that her field of study is contemporary fiction, *not* poetry of the folk.

That night Frøken Lustquist stoically holds her own in the ravages of lascivious *porteño* literature. Seven months later she will give birth to a boy but continue to endure the gestation of her other descendant. Her little son with the decidedly mulatto features she will inscribe in the civil registry under the name Martín Fierro Lustquist before handing him over to the foundling girl. As for her second child, that is to say, her doctoral thesis, which, as such, must have an unimpeachably Scandinavian complexion, she plans to postpone the birth until after she obtains another travel grant and fulfills her new objective of interviewing Kiki in Megalopolis. But, as a result of circumstances beyond anyone's control—the disappearance of this author, who moreover suddenly becomes an ethnographic explorer, the same way another of the writers she had her eye on suddenly became Italian, the study of either of whom now belongs in another department of her university back in Gothenburg—her work will remain unfinished forever.

At first glance they could be the legs of a very slender, teenaged girl. The young poet, a kid in the class who is always talking about women, once called them "fireworks encased in silk," and without a doubt believed he'd created a beautiful image. However that may be, it is a very telling image, for the sensation that Celia causes is primordial; she impresses as something impelled by an internal force, abruptly rising into a high, graceful curve. Is she about to burst into sparkling bits of fiery light? The truth is, there is no hint so far of anything like that happening. At this exact moment, one could almost guarantee that it will not: she sits with her legs tightly crossed and is clearly absorbed in taking notes on the eminent Professor Camillo Orvieto's lecture, which is becoming increasingly slow and repetitious. To his eyes' delight, he's taking inventory of the hidden charms she offers. Kiki, of course, comes in late and the lecture hall is already crowded. And after searching patiently for several minutes, *his* eyes are finally rewarded with a brief, fragmentary glimpse of Celia's charms, the ones on view at the back of her head; that is to say, her innocent, meticulously *naif* hairdo and the backside of her very delicate neck.

Professor Orvieto's grounding in historical materialism is noticeable. It is furthermore something perfectly foreseeable in an Italian *gelehrte* of his generation who was once so devoted to *Babbo* Benedetto before being kicked into exile. The explication of the poem that Orvieto is presenting owes its conceptual core—obviously—to the ideas of Prince Mirsky.

"I wonder what has become of Mirsky? Where do he and his bones now lie?" muses the compassionate, erudite observer, so full of ill-spent tenderness (*who is always and of necessity Kiki*). The poem itself has already suffered more or less the same fate as *The Cabinet of Dr. Caligari* and *Battleship Potemkin*. (All three are masterpieces, to be sure, full of energy and drama. But over-exposure—abuse, more like it—has depleted them.)

"'I sat upon the shore, fishing, with the arid plain behind me. Shall I at least set my lands in order?'" The poet's question immediately transports Kiki to a large patio pleasantly scented by flowering jasmine. At the patio's edge a stiff-haired Airedale stands guard as Kiki sits reading Eliot's poem for the first or second time in his life. He wonders if that wasn't the question he should have been asking himself some time before the botched or malicious administration of Don Olegario, an uncle by marriage who lost the family's small fortune in arable fields, the only thing Kiki's father had left him.

Professor Orvieto, meanwhile, is speaking English with
surprising fluency. "Above all if you consider that he has lived
here only three years." His first major stop in exile was Argentina,
from where, once again, he was of course forced to flee by a
revolution that he insists on characterizing as fascist. "Yes, he
speaks it well, no question." But he doesn't manage to give the
right intonation to the fragment of a children's song he has just
read aloud. This causes a smiling murmur to run through his
audience. They are mostly very, very rich old maids and divorcées
and have known the song since earliest childhood. It's always a
curious relief to catch a professor in a mistake, especially when he
is as celebrated as this one and as gifted at quoting so aptly from
little-known bibliographical sources in no less than six languages.
Clearly, in their averted smiles and quiet, mildly ironic coughs,
there should be seen nothing more than the indulgence of a public
who is very conscious of being in the presence of one of those
rare eminences—such as Croce, Fermi, Salvemini, or Borgese—
who were moved by raw courage and talent and confronted the
bellowing Duce and his *bravi*.

Predictably, the moment in the poem now arrives when, with
all the naturalness of an Italian academic befitting our *gelehrte*,
Dr. Orvieto will show off his fine erudition as a Dante scholar:
"'*Tan m'abellis vostre cortes deman, qu'ien no me pueso ni voill a vos
cobrire. Ieu sui Arnaut, que plor e vau cantan.*' That is to say, 'Your
courteous request so pleases me, I cannot nor will I hide me from
you, I am Arnaut who weep and singing go.'"

"'*Ieu sui Arnaut . . .*'"—and he may be on the verge of
repeating the line aloud, when the hem of Celia's skirt rises a little
more; more than it should, it could be said. The eminent *dottore*
Orvieto, a disciple of Croce, the courageous *lottatore antifascista*,
is irresistibly attracted and focuses all his attention now on an
appetizing pink thigh. A defensive line of fine lace visible at the
hem of her slip disturbs him even more. Celia, unperturbed, of
course, and engrossed to all appearances in her notebook, steadily
writes in phonetic symbols the foreign verses just quoted by the

professor. She thinks maybe she will later type out the lines she has just heard—for she knows a good number of things, but not Provençal. She plans to copy the words directly from the Italian source, which the professor has so precisely referenced: *Purgatorio* 26, 140-147.

Oh! How Kiki would love for Celia to notice this disturbing hesitation by Orvieto, whom—or so Kiki thinks—she idolizes.

But in Viareggio now, a tall, stately North American newspaper reporter nicknamed Bonté (undoubtedly thanks to the French governess her parents furnished her with from the age of two) is about to say something to Orvieto. The columnar beauty's uncluttered elegance has a sovereignty that brings to mind the grand mansions of Virginia. He has just met her and doesn't suspect that very soon he will be her husband. She now makes an observation that has become one of the most meaningful and enigmatic truisms of our time: "It's curious. The male human animal feels irresistibly attracted to a feminine thigh when it is glimpsed only fleetingly due to a skirt's indiscretion, while, on a beach, that same thigh, in full view, won't awaken in him the slightest ripple of eroticism."

Celia is still writing, but other heads are turning to comment on the exceedingly long pause the professor is engaging in. "Most unusual in the loquacious scholar," old maids and divorcées comment quietly among themselves. Generally speaking, they have taken no notes; they attend the class the way people go to a bullfight or a game of real football: in order to judge performance. Kiki, meanwhile, smugly compares Orvieto's exposition to the one *he* has just presented to his last class of the day in his course, "The Avant-Garde and Kitsch." *Oh what a surprise. Kiki knows everything there is to know about kitsch.* Orvieto's exposition, on the other hand, has now completely unraveled; it seems beyond repair.

"But it's always the same," Kiki thinks. "No matter what you do, you always wind up in second place because you're from 'south of the border.' Well, the flag covers the merchandise; it's the law of the sea. But *merit* is reserved for these Europeans, so pure, so antiquated. Here, all you have to do is to be French, German, or Italian and act as if you've always lived in a millennial homeland supersaturated with a culture that has achieved its purest and most concentrated form."

While Kiki thinks this, Professor Orvieto is still in Italy and it's November 12, 1938. He's in an office at police headquarters, where he has come with his flamboyant wife, yes: Bonté, to get a passport that will let him leave the country. Anti-Semitic legislation is on the verge of becoming the law of the land and Orvieto has already lost his position at the University of Turin. *Il Duce's* demand to have immediate ethnic purity everywhere on the peninsula all at once would be comical, hilarious even!—if it weren't barbaric. All Orvieto's years of fierce devotion to Fascism, since grammar school, when he was an enthusiastic *balilla*, have given him nothing in the wake of the implacable laws the Duce has finally imposed on his people under pressure from his Austrian friend—"that nobody-of-a-painter."

Celia has stopped writing but does not give the impression that she's surprised by the cool silence that has suddenly pervaded the classroom. Orvieto's class is taking on the look and feel of a morgue and it emanates from the headman. "As usual, she's blinded by her petulance," Kiki thinks. "She can't see that her favorite professor has suffered a very serious mishap here. She thinks this silence is a concession that Orvieto is making just to let her review her notes." He knows Celia pretty well.

Celia reads what she has just written and chews on her red pencil. A violent erotic image takes hold of Kiki. During the little recess in the lesson—nearly everyone in the lecture hall is muttering now, a few brazenly offer each other cigarettes—Kiki has seen his advantage and crept along the side aisle to the front row and can now see her perfectly in profile.

Meanwhile, Professor Orvieto hears the voice of a police official who is casting clearly lascivious glances at Bonté, ever efficient

Bonté. Since childhood she has been a cliché of goodness: hence her nickname. Beneath that fresh blond elegance of hers, no one, at first glance, would suspect the existence of an incorruptible correspondent of the *Herald Tribune*. The policeman is now proposing to hand the passport over with all the required authorizations, which he has prepared, in exchange for . . . ?

Years later, Professor Orvieto would run out of a movie theater, tears streaming, after seeing a scene reminiscent of this same what-she-had-to-live-through moment in a film whose title is imprinted in indelible letters in his brain. None of this can be helped. His affinity for melodrama sometimes imposes itself on a moment and his great classical learning beats a messy retreat from life's so-called realities. The worst part of it is that, fantasizing a physical resemblance that is in no way supported by the facts, the professor would believe he had rediscovered his deceased wife in Ingrid Bergman, the actress in the film.

Yet, Bonté Andrómeda's tremendous sacrifice, *was* it, after all, so tremendous? *And where was her Theseus ex machina?* So, yes. Bonté Andrómeda: Casablanca and dromedaries, Diomedes and androgynes, myths and poets, Provençal poets and Arnaut Daniel . . .

"Forgive me, shall we continue? I didn't feel well for a moment," he says. His face looks greener than ever. The expectant silence of divorcées, old maids, and the others urges him to pick up the threads of his lecture: "Now I should say at least a thing or two about the significance of Arnaut Daniel's appearance in Dante's poetry. The life of this Provençal, or, more precisely, this *Périgord* troubadour, spans nearly fifty years exactly, from about 1150 to about 1200."

In Kiki's mind, one captivating image overruns another: European love is born; he's the first romantic; his beloved, disdainful Celia of the flowing chestnut hair, interposes a snowy whiteness of skin and soul between reality and desire; he's the rejected lover; he strums a lute, mournfully.

". . . than the Limoges poet, Girault de Borneaul. Now it's time for us to go on to the next verse: '*Quando fiam uti chelidon*—O swallow swallow . . .' The Latin: 'when will I be like the swallow . . . ' (Tonight at the party, I shall try to stay close to Señorita Celia.)" With perfidious modesty, Celia now rearranges her skirt; it devises a way almost miraculously to cover even her knees.

"(The Italian's discussion of this text is too clumsy! If Celia could only have heard the explanation *I* gave in class just half an hour ago when I compared romantic Victorian painting with the spirit of the *Pall Mall Gazette*.)"

"(Could the big-nosed wop be going to the party? O Jango is capable of anything. And I'm capable of not going if I find out he has been invited.)"

"'*Pervigilium veneris*.' You spell it like that." Orvieto has stood up to write the poem's title on the blackboard; his figure looks even more ridiculous now. His suit is uncontestably cheap, obviously from a big department-store liquidation sale. It does nothing for him in every way possible.

Kiki tries to call up a visual image of how his students see *him* when he stands up to write on the board, for example, in his understated, custom-made, dark charcoal, three-piece suit. Kiki suddenly thinks of the story inspired by Hermann Hesse ("those were the days . . . !")—his never edited, never published, and now definitively lost story. "But I can easily reconstruct it if I try. It was"—how clearly he remembers the place—"in that magnificent living room with the broad windows"—and recalls the time—"a bright, soft autumn sun flooding in . . . And Celia was there, so young in her green weskit and Scottish skirt, with her long chestnut hair." It was the first thing he wrote after their very quick wedding.

". . . yet the poet here seems to have made use of a Latin text that is far from the preferred one. In the text, as established by Monsieur Robert Schillig, ex professor of the École Française in

Rome, we find instead: '*Quando faciam uti chelidon*,' which we can translate: 'When will I *do* as the swallow?'"

Kiki realizes that Celia has finally noticed his presence in the class. What happened is that he didn't notice for a while that Celia had noticed him, and now she wants to make sure, using an extremely disdainful look, that he notices her noticing him. Completely preoccupied, he had been thinking about his novella, which is forever lost. He'd had ambitions years ago of seeing it published in a great European magazine, such as the *Nouvelle Revue Française*. His "*Gnotos eauton*"—but the title: too explicit? Well, think of a young philosopher, someone like an eighteen-year-old Empedocles who wants to see himself as others are able to see him. Pallas Athena grants him that gift, but, in the alter ego that materializes before his eyes, he sees only an impostor. Is this the emerging myth of the modern ego? Or is it all too explicit to prove a myth? Some stevedore with the Cunard Line seems to have thought so when he made the trunk with Kiki's story and some other old junk in it disappear.

". . . might understand better why Mr. Eliot incorporates that line at the end of his poem, if, on one hand, you consider the context, a kind of kaleidoscope; and if, on the other, you remember the end of our *Vigil of Venus*, that, not without merit, has been called 'a document of religious synthesis in Imperial Rome.' The anonymous author or authors of the poem end it this way: '*Illa cantat, nos tacemus. Quando uer uenit meum? Quando faciam uti chelidon, ut tacere desinam? Perdidi Musam tacendo nec me Phoebus respicit. Sic Amyclas, cum tacerent, perdidit silentum*.' Which has been translated in the following way: 'How long in coming is my lovely Spring? And when shall I, and when the Swallow sing? . . .'"

Through Celia's adorable little head—ever ingenious at ridiculing and disdaining—crosses a vision of Orvieto and his big nose perched in a tree like a swallow, doing his best on the limb he has lit on, but finally failing to sing. An ironic smile forms fleetingly on her lips. Orvieto sees it and goes on translating the verse, urgently repressing a desire to flee the classroom:

"'Sweet Philomela cease—Or here I sit, And silent lose my rapt'rous Hour of Wit: 'Tis gone, the Fit retires, the Flames decay, My tuneful Phoebus flies averse away. His own Amycle thus, as Stories run, But once was silent, and that once undone.'"

When the bell finally rings, Kiki, who in the last few minutes has kept his head bowed, suddenly looks up. Celia is closing her big leather book bag, very student-like. How young she feels carrying it! "And, besides, she's such an intelligent, dedicated student. She'll succeed, major in something, get a degree."

". . . and, of course, the chorus, with which you're undoubtedly familiar from my 'Masterworks of Ancient Lyric' course. But I prefer to give the translation of it once more for you: 'Let those who love now, who never lov'd before, Let those who always lov'd, now love the more.'"

Class is over, it's time to go, and Celia, as always, is among the first to leave the classroom. Will she go to the party O Jango is giving tonight before he returns to Brazil?

As usual, one of the freaky old biddies who go to class just to pass the time has delayed Celia too long and she barely has time now to run by her office at *La Fe* Publishing. "There won't be a problem with the boss, I can make it up by asking him to invite me to dinner. But I need to grab a few things." They are precious things, her little jars of cosmetics. "Makeup is a science today, a branch of biology. That new Arden cream has literally restored my youth. I don't think I look any older than Agnes." At times (right now, for example) Celia laments being miserly. "I ought to keep another jar of it at home. But what's the use of that, I can always just pick one up anywhere." (*Yes, always better to finish the one you've started before opening another.*)

How long can that irritating woman of indeterminate age,

with a face as bland as a raisin muffin and a smile as annoying as a dripping faucet, keep on harassing her? "She would be smiling even if she was telling me she had cancer of the uterus." But Celia wouldn't be Celia if she did not know how to wriggle out of situations like this one. All she needs now is one of those luminous but simple ideas she gets that could put an end to this long delay at the school's main door; one of those things she always thinks up that let her come out looking good at the moment and afterward never materialize—unless, of course, they're about important people—shall we say, young persons who are important to her for more or less unknown reasons?

"Yes, of course, and no worries. This Monday without fail I'll give you a copy of my notes, corrected and typed."

"You're so sweet! We have to chat more often."

"Definitely. I'm always looking for good friends like you, people who are really sincere and studious. We'll make it happen. But now, if you'll excuse me. Must go. You know how men are when they're kept waiting."

So Celia manages to disentangle from her middle-aged classmate. The latter, maybe having something of a vampire's talent for smelling maiden blood, is thrilled at the prospect of spending time with this very young woman who has the looks of a teenager: an eighteen-year-old's trim legs, a fifteen-year-old's perky breasts, and the naughty little face of a girl of twenty-two.

Celia, of course, is perfectly aware of each of her physical attributes. Wasn't it not very long ago that she heard "qu'elle est mignonne!" said of her by that superior expert in today's cherished feminine charms, the Emperor of the Golden Age himself? For so she has baptized him, and her flattery is blindly accepted by the addressee, that monster from hell, her ex-husband Kiki. In spite of everything, it should be recognized that he doesn't come up short when he hears a flattering phrase.

Celia quickly makes her getaway from the shabby halls of academia. She detests them, but they are useful for keeping a certain balance in her prestige quotient. That precise, sharp *click-click* of her exiting heels might be the best clue of all to her malicious, charming, and evasive, but, at its core, somewhat timid character. Celia knows that she's just one of the crowd but, at the same time, sees herself as perfectly unique. No one could have beaten her to the punch with the news that, at this very moment, she leaves behind three admirers feeling equally pensive: an exiled scholar and widower; an ex-husband, who calls himself a specialist in the culture of masses; and a young poet, very young, so young that he hates the ex-husband for being the ex-husband and is attending this course on modern poetry—he, *he*, who has true vision into the disappearance of classical norms in art—just to be able, regularly, three times a week, to see Celia. Whom he has not yet had the courage to engage in conversation.

Would he ever have the audacity to speak to her? Would he even be capable of sustaining a real conversation with her, or would he merely limit himself to asking her some stupid question, the answer to which he probably already knows like the back of his hand? It is for one reason alone that our timid young poet endures the torture of hearing loud praises of Montale, Eliot, and even Pound. He needs to be near her eyes, to look into them—but he can't help himself, he says, "her mischievous little eyes"—or from time to time to hear her voice, it sounds so sweet to him; or, on some afternoons, to get a whiff of her perfume, which, without a doubt, is more than mere Arpège, immensely more than that, nothing less than the aroma of the flower that is Celia. This, certainly, is worth the sacrifice he makes by having to think about lowly literary adventurers as if they were Great Classical Masters!

The timid young poet cannot conceive of the possibility that at any moment he might actually inhale from Celia's body or from *any* orifice of her adorable fragility, an aroma other than Arpège, the fragrance the young man is more or less thinking about when Kiki, now master of the school's deserted stairs, notices him clearly following his ex-wife, furtively, about ten yards behind her.

"What if she turns around and thinks I'm following her on purpose? Oh! If she'd only drop something, God, let her drop something, so I can hurry and pick it up for her. But *goddess goddess goddess* she would be as naturally swift as she is slim. I need to get closer, in case something happens to fall. But why aren't there more people on this damned street at this hour? I'm nervous as hell. I'm all but panting. I have to slow down even if *goddess goddess O goddess* she gets a little further ahead of me. It doesn't matter anyway. I won't have the courage to walk up to her."

Even so, what *would* be a good way to start a conversation with her? "I could, for example, say: 'Interesting—isn't it?— what the professor said about the importance of Gérard de Nerval's verse in the poem. And, by the way, I've heard that you were once married to one of my professors.' No, not that: it's too forced to just go from the poet to the ex like that. Besides, when the moment comes, I shouldn't even allude to him. Still and all, what I'd like to say to her more than anything is how could an angel like you *goddess* I mean I know him he's a miserable teacher and says nothing that isn't in any introductory textbook and how could you stand living with him the *cretin* always over the line with the girls how you must have suffered *my goddess* after I heard him talk three times I lost heart *goddess* and couldn't go back such a cretin I bet he had a traumatic childhood OK, that won't work either: a goddess, a true goddess has compassion for all. It's more than likely she just started to have pity on the miserable-worst-son-of-a-bitch-in-the-whole-world."

No, no, no. Nothing, none of any of that would ever work. To start a conversation with her, you need something simple.

"'Señorita, allow me to say how much I like you.'"

"'Well, just look at the saucy kid.'" (*After all, he's not ugly, he's blond, tall, healthy, okay, not all that healthy, there's the little pimple at the tip of his nose.*) "'Why, he's practically a teenager, tell me, what's your name, little boy?'"

("'Three years of the crude life in the Merchant Marines.' How stupendous. 'Yes, and I can recite entire scenes from Shakespeare' . . . Right! And that's exactly the kind of thing women aren't the least interested in.

"'If I only had the persuasive banter of those assholes who hang out at The White Horse! Look, see that guy with his grubby shirt collar?—and those raggedy guys, whose clothes are also not too clean, now we're talking about it; and those who never bathe or wash their clothes, especially the ones there in back—well, the ones up front too!

"'And on top of everything, now I have to get the sole of this left shoe fixed. My Chelsea boots seemed so elegant and sturdy when I bought them in Liverpool last year, but here, everybody keeps staring at my feet and sneering . . .'")

Kiki, still on the stairs, is on the verge of exclaiming "*Merde!*" But, as it happens almost without exception in libertines, he's quite modest and for that reason prefers to limit himself to a hardly shocking *Ça alors!*—which comes out a little forced, because that exclamation always makes him feel like the South American who has come through Paris. He takes off his glasses. He prefers not to wear them on the street anyway, though his optometrist insists on it. He wants women to be able to admire his subtly slanted green eyes. They give him something of the air of a sacred cat, as a girl from Alexandria said to him one time, almost certainly as a joke. Still, as always when his physical vanity is involved, he took it very seriously.

He has taken his glasses off in order to better observe what that boy is doing following Celia. It could be he's a sex maniac capable of "bothering" her—to use a euphemism— even in broad daylight! *It's nightfall.* Or. Right here on this peaceful residential street. In which case Kiki would be obliged to chase the obsessed assailant away in order to keep Celia, so delicate, so fragile, and, after all, so fragrant, from experiencing the horror of a shock like that. St. George liberates the damsel from the dragon, the damsel feels appreciative, takes him to her bachelorette apartment (*more accurately, her divorcée apartment*), and they spend the entire afternoon and evening looking at the engravings of Giulio Romano that he always carries in a large blue satchel. Afterward—isn't it Casanova who relates a similar episode?—they decide to practice the difficult exercises proposed with a pulse of steel by the great master.

Yes, in Kiki's opinion, an episode of that kind is just what he needs, to regain his moral authority with the timid-but-stubborn Celia. She is an infinitely sensitive organism. "No skin, not even that very smooth skin of hers, can protect her pure, intense soul. I, Kiki, have gravely offended her so many times, without even realizing it at the time."

He remembers a night well over a year ago, when they found themselves in Manhattan with the Lewinsohns. They were all walking near Rockefeller Center and decided to dine at Chez Larré's, the restaurant where the great Breton so often shed tears over his troubles like a weeping Magdalene—Breton, *l'Empereur de l'Age d'O* no less. ("Take note, any of you young men who believe you need a rough exterior to show a strong spirit!") Then suddenly the red-haired Marjorie Lewinsohn proposed they switch partners. He imagined for a moment that she was going to offer herself to him but, she being a redhead, he wasn't at all interested in that, had no doubt that at certain decisive moments she would become rank, emit intolerable odors, as always happens with redheads—there may be no generalization more allowable on the subject of women.

But, fortunately, redheaded Marjorie only wanted to be alone with him for a moment to lodge a complaint and call him *ordure*, in French. (*It wasn't for nothing that one-hundred-percent-pure-Irish Marjorie had studied at Sacré-Coeur.*) The despicable

"Lewinsohn" had come to her by way of her husband, the encyclopedic pygmy whom Celia and he, maybe Celia more than he, had baptized *Le Petit Larousse Illustré*.

"How could you do such a thing to poor sweet Celia! *Ordure*," the woman had said. And now more than a year later, Kiki still hasn't clearly identified exactly what that thing was, because the great scene with Celia happened only a few months afterward and, in the meantime, while they were still living together, he forgot (shrewd work of his Id?) to ask Celia herself what she had told Marjorie that he had done. But, honestly, Celia, *si mignonne, si naïve*, could never have said anything bad about him. It had to have been purely an invention by the redhead to stay close to him a while. Perhaps, by concocting a scene to disturb him, she could feel, if only for a moment, more powerful than he, the famous satyr, who, nevertheless, had always chastely resisted her and her redhead charms (all of them certainly fetid at critical moments in women of her color).

But now, from a street crowded with people, who also were going to the theaters and entering nightclubs last year—*Wait. Just suppose that, by way of general announcements, let's say in newspapers, you could call for those same strangers who were going to theaters and clubs that night to be here and walk on the same sidewalk today. How many of them would remember the exact time they were to show up, if even Kiki, for whom the earlier occasion is still a very vivid memory, cannot even be sure when? And, should they remember with absolute clarity exactly when such an unrealizable event was to occur, how many would actually be able to comply? Life lived is illusion*—. . . Or. Now from a street crowded with people, including some from more or less a year ago, we can see coming into focus the figure of a girl. She approaches the besotted young poet to speak to him. *Don't tell me that fool of a boy is going to make a conquest!* He at least will finally leave Celia alone, and the girl is not at all unattractive, though, by comparison, she's not much to look at. But, in all honesty, what woman is worth anything when compared with Celia, the Quintessential Eternal Feminine? *Bettina Brentano, maybe? But—unfortunately, or maybe luckily—the woman whose legs were not like fireworks but whose imagination was, died more than a hundred years ago.*

The girl's disheveled hair is a light chestnut color; her complexion, typical for her age (nineteen), her class (lower-middle), her place of origin (British Columbia), and her racial background (an intricate concoction of noble Anglo-Saxon genes and less select others: Gallic, Ancient Greek, Portuguese). It goes without saying that her rather large hands, though not devoid of a certain archaic elegance, come from formidable Anglo-Saxon ancestors, while her decidedly large and not in any way elegant feet are a fully Lusitanian inheritance but, it must be recognized, this may be illusory because they are inside those worn-out, high-top tennis shoes. Her height (5'7") is adequate for a female of her generation living north of the Río Grande and gives satisfactory evidence of powerful vital energies and successful ethnic mixtures. Her name, Barbara Dowd, witnesses in a tiredly convincing way that the age indicated on her identity card is the right one. Exactly twenty years ago, Barbara Stanwyck ruled the silver screen as the prototype of aggressive femininity whose masculine equivalent seemed, at the time, to be George Raft.

Barbara Dowd steps forward rather hesitantly. But with the splendid, unselfconscious confidence of a country girl, she goes up to the timid poet and asks if he can point out exactly where Nick lives, since he's well-known in the neighborhood.

She has interrupted the timid young poet at the precise instant in his amorous meditations at which an idea has finally occurred to him and seems to reveal a brilliant, infallible way to begin a conversation with his goddess without her feeling offended or frightened. It consists of asking her to lend him her lecture notes for a few days. If this bright idea had enlightened his mind an instant earlier, the sighing romantic—who, of course, is really neoclassical, mind you, in his embryonic *aesthetic* configuration—would have been free to continue his purposeful pursuit. The person whom Babs has approached is someone who, *how lucky*, does not in the least seem to be in a hurry. But, truthfully, in order to avoid the possibility of some blush-inducing proposition, she would have preferred to approach that enchanting, exquisite, obviously older woman whose path she crossed first. Nevertheless she speaks with no noticeable concern to the very nice young man, who is loaded down with books and wears British booties, his shoes and tomes surely two unmistakable signs of respectability.

Celia's troubadour mentally curses the girl. Now he would lose sight of his goddess for sure, just when he had come up with a strategy and had within his reach a perfect pretext for approaching her. For the moment he doesn't catch on to the fact that this recourse will still be there for him to use on some other occasion.

("Is this a joke? What would a common little pipsqueak like her want with a guy named Nick? And how am I supposed to know who this Nick is? Is this girl just a little barrio slut? Yeah, she could be a decoy sent in by the goddess's odious ex-husband. Why, that dirty dog! So that's what this is about. He corrupts them then takes advantage of them to send them out as spies, because what would *I* know about some Nick guy anyway!")

He's ready to respond to her in just those terms but observes that Barbara Dowd's lips are starting to quiver. He does not observe, because he still hasn't been able to bring himself to look into a woman's eyes, that the eyes of the woman who will turn out to be our supreme heroine are, at the moment, filling with tears. On the girl's trembling lips he sees the outline of a mocking guffaw. ("Oh, now I've *gotta* teach this girl a lesson. Yeah, if they think they can play mean tricks on me, she's gonna learn *real fast* not to trust that jerk, her corrupter.")

"Yes, miss, of course. First, you go straight until you get to the corner, then go along the avenue three blocks without turning, and, when you get to the square, look for the dry pond bed. If you don't find your friend Nick around there, and you can't miss him really, he never fails to show up there this time of day, but anyone will be able to tell you where to find him."

Celia is now out of sight.

Kiki goes down the stairs and heads off in the opposite direction.

Barbara Dowd, in search of her Nick, has memorized the details of her informant's perfidious directions.

As for the timid young poet now bereft of his guiding goddess, he goes on his way, desolate, but already half-sorry for the wicked joke he has just played on the pipsqueak. He walks slowly, his remorse growing stronger with each passing moment. He would now do well to turn around and look for the girl, confess to her that he doesn't know the Nick she was talking about, in fact knows no Nick at all. But he now reaches the pharmacy and remembers that today is Friday. The *Sunday Times* will have arrived by air from London. He never fails to read the literary section immediately; he likes to get the latest news about a wee group of brave British lads who are keeping up the noble neoclassical ideal. Literary taste takes precedence over his scruples of conscience. ("Art for art's sake: yes, but the slogan was once wasted on a bunch of pederasts, and could anyone ask for anything more befitting a *neoclassical* concept of life?") An impish smirk, at once delicate and cruel, outlines itself on the face of our very young and rascally emulator of the Abbé Delille. It would be hard at this moment for anyone to deny his capacity for irony and his cruel adhesion to the caprice of the moment, so Ancien Régime. Once inside the pharmacy, the young poet is captivated by the neon lights and the hum of the air conditioner. *How lucky*, they've reserved his copy of the *Sunday Times*, as usual.

She is surrounded on all sides by the unkempt, their disorderly costumes are their uniform; individuals of all ages and the most varied sexes: one sex, another sex, any sex, missing sex, excess sex. Somebody is reading the adventures of Batman out loud, someone else is singing flamenco, someone over there is reciting Shakespeare, somebody nearby is telling dirty stories, somewhere a person is crying, a different person somewhere else is immersed in his delivery of a neo-Marxist critique of the "paleo-Hegelian" concept of alignment, and there is a man tirelessly saying to his neighbor: yousonofabitchyousonofabitchyousonofabitch. In other words, it's a perfect slice-of-life and cross-section of the most advanced society in the most advanced era of human existence.

But Nick is nowhere to be seen.

His journal is one of Kiki's secret vices. But it should be understood that all Kiki's vices are secret. He turns to his entries with the pleasure of a self-gratifier who is re-reading for the umpteenth time a particularly dirty paragraph in a treasured little pornographic novel.

Of course, not everything he has thought, however habitually he may have thought it in third-person with the reflective tone of a journal, is then written down in it. Kiki, after many disappointments in annotations of his that at first seemed so incisive or profound, has grown used to applying maximum severity as he judges these crystallizations of his intelligence and sensitivity. After scrupulously considering each one, he throws the vast majority of them out. This way, he believes, he's saving himself from the danger and absurdity of turning into "the man with a diary." In reality, by trying to evade that sad condition, he has sunk more deeply into its trap: more and more often he thinks about everything with a certain meditative solemnity. He has become a third person, an increasingly distanced witness of himself.

Perhaps Celia didn't know he had stopped on the school's stairs, watching her and feeling melancholy and ironic as she walked away. Nor would the timid young poet have known that Kiki had observed him following her. Much less would either of them have suspected that he stood there playing with their futures, having them approach each other, separate, move farther apart, come closer together (within certain limits), as he applied doses of proximity in different measures of mutual influence that are possible between these two beings.

"Isn't this, but in a more deliberate way, what we always do with everyone else: make their destinies? What are destinies? We invent others' destinies and others invent ours. But for years I kept repeating the same big mistake, the most fatal error you can make. I, a sinner, do confess and repent having believed myself the master of my destiny. That same mistake is poisoning all of modern society and spoiling even its best minds! Each of us sits in a solitary cell, fantasizing fantasy after fantasy about our individual selves. Therefore the only thing that really exists between us and everyone else is missing communication, because, at most, we can only get to know the lives we live. Others must imagine our destinies."

Would he write this meditation in his notebook? It seems quite brilliant to him. ("Watch out. Great haste gains nothing. Let it sit in time's sieve awhile.") (*But he isn't always so cautious; that is easy to see.*) His latest entry, written a few days before in the increasingly solemn mood of his notebook, originated in an incident he observed not quite a year earlier. And it was precisely because he saw himself as his own author, when he was nothing more than an actor. One's true author is the public. Where did he read that? But did he actually read it, or merely think it and then forget? *That "merely" is perfectly symptomatic of Kiki's personality.* Before, a more or less banal episode was enough to make him believe he had found the resounding significance of his life, that is, his meaning, his destiny. Just as when he wrote the story *Missing Reality*, which is now probably forgotten and lost in the pages of an ephemeral literary journal.

"I assure you"—he actually says *"Certes"*—"the original episode, lightly distorted in my published piece, gave me a lot to think about at the time." His destiny had always been to be contiguous, soldered to others, enthusiastically exchanging signs that seemed to be from a shared language. But they were always discrete, always falling on something other.

When his story was published, his ex-companions, who remained loyal to the Party, said as much to him, in a tone of condemnation. "And they were right, from their point of view, which favored lowering one's expectations and compromising with whatever came, doing anything to stay 'in': 'Communism restores the individual's fertility.'" And he had believed it too, with the same sincere, almost religious faith as the author of that slogan. He thought he had found authentic comrades because he came to them devastated, like a sterile, ferocious little animal who kept spinning around and around, always chasing his tail in the same tight circle, locked in the prison of his mind. It was as if Celia had castrated his soul when she left him. That is why he believed that his new companions, their members iron-hard, their hearts sweet, offered him restored vigor with the zeal of religious defenders of the world's oppressed. That's why, later, when he saw how they really were, knew who these comrades in fact are, he preferred to be a man of "missing reality," a kind of flesh-and-blood phantom. But in no way a puppet.

The guerrilla fighters, all poor, fanatical kids, had taken a brutal beating in the jungle, and the intellectuals were meeting that day to discuss it in that vast living room reminiscent of the interiors of Wright's "prairie houses." Between whiskies, sitting in the delicious coolness of air-conditioning after hotly commenting on the meaning of Buñuel's films—"a reactionary, yes; but, all in all, useful"—they had finally proceeded to an analysis of the causes of the rout. They spoke of the disastrous infiltration of Trotskyites. They countered with truly disastrous infiltrations by Neo-Stalinists. They affirmed the need for duly dialectic, ideological behavior. They agreed that the person most responsible for the disaster was that quasi bourgeois, Khrushchev. One very short guy with a mop of reddish hair, wearing thick spectacles and checkered Bermuda shorts, was very *nouvelle vague*—he read a chapter of *Critique de la raison dialectique* every day (with no noticeable improvement of his intelligence). He had put on an apron and was drying the lunch plates. His wife followed the very interesting debate on partisan strategy as if it were a sports final in which she were the referee. He declared that they needed to agitate more.

But the business of the kid who wrote verses out there in the jungle, infatuated with Aragon and Neruda, the boy who, later feverish, sobbing, asked to go home; that kid (only nineteen), whose comrades, believing they were only being forceful, when they were clearly being brutal, had shot and killed him for "attempted desertion"—well, *that topic*, all *that* had no importance. It came down to "teaching a lesson."

"Discipline, above all. Iron-willed discipline," the gravelly voice of an exophthalmic Marxologist had forcefully stated. Until the topic of the fierce execution was opened for discussion, he had remained silent. (He was elaborating his plan for the seduction of his new secretary, one of those little brunettes that were his specialty, for without a doubt, it would have to be done on the sly, behind the back of his domineering, quick-tempered, multimillionaire wife.)

"Yes. Without discipline, we'll get nowhere," agreed a bearded guy who said he was a revolutionary writer. And he glanced at his magnificent gold chronometer.

So yes, missing reality. That has to be better than this kind of trafficking in the lives of innocents.

The bug-eyed Marxologist swallowed another *foie gras* canapé, joking that it was un-comradely to put such temptation within his reach since they knew the deplorable state of his liver.

"I thought it would be a good homeopathic medicine," replied the woman who owned the house, unabashed, gaily flirting with him, as she did with all her husband's friends.

The feet of another boy, one of those who had wanted to fight in the jungle like the lawyer Fidel Castro, had been rubbed raw and, worse, were riddled with worms. The boy, who had talked to his military judge like he was talking to a psychoanalyst, wanted to confess, everything, every single thing, leaving out nothing. He even shared the impression made on him when he saw his mother naked one time. It was fortunate the boy knew almost nothing, for, though he knew the little red-haired man's name, he knew nothing else. "The correct distance between the great intellectual and the rank and file preserved," the short little man told himself to ease his nerves; he couldn't rid himself of the vocabulary he had acquired at the London School of Economics. The important thing was that the vile, repugnant little traitor didn't know who he was and never would, so he could stop worrying. Someday, that boy would come out of the jungle; he was the once brilliant student of biology who had been contemplating a secure future as an agricultural geneticist. But what harm would he actually be able to do then?

The bearded guy who said he was a revolutionary writer seemed impatient and glanced again at his enormous watch. He already had airline tickets and his internationally recognized passport for his flight to Costaguana the following day. Lost in thought, his head full of sensual images of ardent mulatto women, he helped himself to another whiskey, unfortunately not "the Monks'," especially since it was his last one of the day. He had to continue editing his novel, the action of which unfolded precisely in Costaguana, a model victim of the vicious United Fruit Company. Writing the novel was, for his part, a great and noble effort in the liberation of oppressed peoples, but until tomorrow he had not yet been to that country. Paris was his favorite place of residence. Paris: La Tour d'Argent, easy liaisons, *cinéma cochon*—other industries that traffic in the lives of innocents.

That is why Kiki had preferred to situate himself inside the missing reality. "*As flies to wanton boys*," but no, even this posture had proved erroneous; no one could blame the gods, *there weren't any*. Perhaps he didn't yet know it, but his destiny was not within *his* reach either. No destiny can be within the reach of its respective life; that is perhaps a clearer way to say it. True. Even though he possessed one of the most abundant proportions of reality-to-delusion to be found anywhere among his contemporaries, or at least among his kind, the intellectuals.

Kiki glances in the mirror, washes his face again with cold water, and decides that he's presentable enough for . . . whatever O Jango's party is going to be! Oh, yes, before he leaves, he'd better write down his provisional entry. Any piece of paper will do; he will just put it in a drawer of his desk with some letters and clippings. Someday, when he's looking for something in there, he'll find it, re-think it, and decide if it's worthy of putting in his notebook. That is what he does. Nevertheless, just as that annotation will never be entered into his notebook, soon, very soon, he will return to being less selective about the things he includes in it, and, in point of fact, not just about that.

Laura Van Boren lives in the uninhibited wilds of the second half of the twentieth century in a society whose most sacred principle is Squander. "Go forth and waste!" ought to be the slogan of any wise prime minister today. Especially if he intends to emulate his French Colleague in Immortality who, more than a century ago, shouted at his compatriots: "So go get rich!" But, at twenty-two, Laura Van Boren maintains her family traditions. First, she's as obtuse as her great-grandfather, Marcus Van Boren, who hangs in the gallery of the nation's uniformly colorless vice-Presidents and distinguishes himself by being the dullest and least colorful of them all. Moreover, despite her era's colossal temptations in the worlds of clothing, transportation, and ways to waste time, Laura has inherited a pristine tendency to avarice, frequently disguised as modesty and reluctance to engage in ostentation, which in an earlier time made a significant contribution to her ancestors' fortune (*which, FYI, is now greatly diminished*), and is the kind of conduct that tends to be the normal habit of wealthy people of good stock everywhere, people *de bonne souche,* as they like to put it. For it is within their number—yes, and very enthusiastically so—that Laura sees herself as one of the people who keep up an oh-so-very-exact if capricious equivalence between good manners and miserliness. All of which is to say that she is feeling irritated that Kiki forgot to pay for the taxi, and she doesn't limit herself to attributing his attitude to mere forgetfulness.

"How clever of him! He has ingeniously found a way for me to take him to his school lecture for free."

As for her taxi ride, she had the driver stop after two blocks and has continued on foot, first paying the fare and handing over a humiliatingly small tip. But, apart from economizing on the taxi, other reasons have possibly induced Laura to walk. Ever since Horacio left the city, she has wandered aimlessly about in it, taking advantage of her long walks to ruminate on new perfections of her melodrama. She wants, as always, to have time to think about things that are happening to her. In other words, by dividing and subdividing her unhappiness, she remains faithful to the clichés that seem to rule her whole life. With an inner complacency that she would never confess to feeling, she now hopes to come finally to a clear decision. This is, of course, a bud that doesn't open. Looking at things more carefully, she perhaps faces at least two choices, and, at this very moment, two dilemmas are flowering in her conscience. Given the antecedents already in the attentive reader's possession, the first one is easy for her to summarize: "Do I decide to go find

Horacio?" The second one is this: "Do I go to O Jango's party tonight? Because why didn't I listen to Mama, always so wise and good, in the first place and give up all those dangerous liaisons when I was still in high school?"

The dangerous liaisons Laura is thinking about—unconsciously plagiarizing the title of a novel by a great strategist of the erotic, a work she of course hasn't read—are with South Americans. This almost goes without saying. "Who but a South American woman, all insinuation and attention, could have had such an adverse effect on that nice girl Agnes? During high school, she was more virtuous and spontaneous than anyone." The same thing could happen to her too, couldn't it? "So be careful, little Laura!" *Yes, watch your step.* Those violent, dark, sometimes ingeniously intuitive South Americans are seductive! "Even when they're notoriously ugly or look like Negros or their hair is frizzy." *What is this, racial prejudices popping up in you now?* "Be wise, dear girl." "South Americans *are* unpredictable and full of lust. But people from here are usually like that too!" Laura now must painfully reconnoiter on behalf of her derailed compatriots. "But those extravagant South Americans, yes, above all, they are *extravagant.* Take Horacio, for example. Is he just showing off when he says he raises polo ponies on his land or does he really have them? But even if he has some, *why* does he have them if he's not really *rich?*"

Meanwhile, thousands of miles away, with expert precision, Horacio's mallet effortlessly strikes the ball, which goes exactly to the foreseen spot. Applause and shouts of joy are heard. Horacio is playing better than ever. He feels magnificent, calm, with the tranquility that comes from a settled conscience.

"But what should I do about someone who needs me so much?" This is one of Laura's secondary questions, which, though secondary, has her on tenterhooks.

Horacio, before leaving for the polo field, had just finished the letter he will mail to her tomorrow. "Without fail."

"I should be strong and break up with him. And now that I've decided not to go to tonight's party, it's my first definitive step toward the destiny that it's my duty to pursue. Yes, there's no point in it; it's not in my best interests to be around those people who only know how to spend money and talk about sex. Horacio would only ruin my life. But, if I'm not by Horacio's side, am I not ordering his destruction?"

Just thinking this, Laura shivers with a certain voluptuousness that she would never recognize the existence of, but which nonetheless is clearly evident there in her head.

"No! I cannot leave Horacio!"

In the letter that sits waiting to be sent to her, Horacio has written the following:

"Out of pity I've hidden many things, but now I am far enough away and I find it better to tell you all of the truth. I am sick of you, Laurita. Your pimply skin makes me sick. I must have been half *crasy* when I was going after you. It was because of that sadistic Kiki. He just wanted to torture me so he insisted I continued to go out with you.

"It's because Kiki is a failure at everything. That's why he is so jealous of me, and look how he took his revenge. Just for damages I've never done anything to him to deserve. No, he did it all by himself. And then making himself, without me ever asking, into my second moral conscience . . . and even you can recognize that that has got to be a ghoulish kind of conscience.

"He isn't capable of confessing that in his heart he feels no genuine interest for my personal feelings about things, but only envies me. Envy, to be sure, can be his only 'legitimate' reason to insert himself into my most private affairs. He's jealous of how rich I am, yes, much richer than you can ever believe, you pimply, ugly little monkey-face. And because I am so good-looking. Because I am really good-looking, isn't that true, my horrible-looking Laurita? And because I of course have much more success than him with women, but not because I am rich,

like he likes to believe and make people believe, but because I
am nicer and straightforward so I spontaneously win women—
as you can vouch for and know the way I do it . . . But, all this
that I tell you now is not on topic, so let's get back to what is
important now.

"Yes, as terrible as the truth must be for you, it would be
even worse for me, now, at this stage of the game, to hide it
from you. So I repeat. You make me sick, you make me sick.
Can you understand? The smells that come from your body,
after a tennis match, for example! And to think I had always to
accompany you immediately, to talk about all manner of stupid
things, like you being the future of the *arquitectura funcional*
(and by the way, Laurita: you will never be a good *arquitecta*:
the best you're able to do is dedicate yourself to copying other
people's blueprints although I know already, I already know that
you don't need it but that way you would be able to save even
more money, which—see how well I know you?—will only fill
you with satisfaction). Just talking about stupid things with you
at times when the only thing I could have wanted to have at
hand was a gas mask. And don't think you are going to solve
things by changing soaps and applying more deodorant. That
is not it at all.

"Try to get used to the idea that you're sickening to me,
Laurita. Tell it to yourself again and again, a thousand times, a
million times if necessary, until that notion takes root in your
no way lucid head, in your mediocre head that does honor to all
your ancestors, famous only for being mediocre.

"And tell me, Laurita: did you inherit the pimply skin from
them? Or do you have so much acne on your face because you
masturbate all the time? Because here, in my backward country,
we still believe—because there is plenty of cause!—that acne
comes from masturbation. So that you can understand this, I
repeat it with words your doubtlessly seriously scowling mama
would use: the shameful abuse of one's self provokes certain

superficial cutaneous disturbances. Good, at least your strong vocation for the solitary pleasure, Laura *onanista*, has saved me from the torture of going to bed with you. What would that have been like! I shudder just imagining it."

This is but a sampling of the long letter addressed to Miss Laura Van Boren that is intended to leave for Megalopolis the following day.

Laura, for her part, is still walking and is now nearly downtown. As usual she has no fixed plan. Her meditations are crossed more and more frequently by the dilemma of her invitation to the party. Going would mean in some way being closer to Horacio, the intermediary through whom she met O Jango. And of course she wants to be closer to Horacio. She isn't going to put the final period on her relations with him—"as Mama wants"—even if their relationship is maintained only in epistolary form.

But is all this indecision just self-deception after all? In addition, O Jango is a suspicious character. Don't they say that his fortune—"and keep this firmly in mind, Laura"—proceeds in large part from the razorblade industry? And don't they call him "the king of beards" in his native country not exactly because he manufactures those little blades, but precisely because his hired gunmen, who he keeps on salary everywhere in the world, assassinated the inventor of a magnificent little razorblade sharpener that kept used blades like new for months and even years? "Well, undeniably, they do say that." But on the other hand, what would have come out of the success of such a flourishing small business? How would it have turned out for the hundreds and even thousands of barbers? "You have to think"— and it is a terrifying thought, chaste Laura—"that their wives and daughters may have had to become prostitutes. Looking at things that way, O Jango looks like a veritable benefactor of humanity," Laura tells herself. The temptation to let herself get a little closer to Horacio—but only as close as going to O Jango's party—begins to win the day.

Horacio rinses the soap from his forehead and smiles, completely satisfied. He has just given his team a decisive victory and the letter he wrote just before coming to the polo field has put an end to another idiotic incident, one of those his good heart saddles him with from time to time because of his innate addiction to getting along with everyone.

"Besides, if I go to the party, I'll be able to spend the whole time with Agnes and her friend. Of course, I still think *she's* mean, she has changed Agnes for the worse. But it's obvious that she's distinguished. She's such a big fan of good books that she seems just like people from here. So the three of us could have our own party of genteel spirits amid the hustle and bustle of the other guests. And Agnes and her friend can help me make my final decision. I'm sure *she* knows exactly what to pay attention to with people from her own country. Besides, isn't it to my advantage to corroborate with her what Professor Bellomel, our first architonic critic, told us in his latest lecture? About how no one could doubt the lack of privacy in Latin American homes? And how this influences character development and dashes almost all of the spiritual life of those poor people? What we have here may possibly be the key to understanding Horacio's psychology, so out-going and so untrustworthy. But still, a man like him can help me escape from my loneliness. And what would I do if he wrote me threatening to commit suicide or something like that?"

For an instant a shadow crosses Horacio's face just as Laura asks herself this question.

"He'll surely write me to say he can't live without me and all that. But what if Agnes and her Latin American friend don't go? Mommy took it so hard when she heard only a greatly expurgated version of what happened to my cousin Hermione at one of those intellectual and artist parties. Of course that one was unusual. It was in Cambridge (Mass.), at the end of a symposium on the relationship between poetry and pacifism, and one of the conference-goers self-identified as a member of the Neolongbeards and jumped onto the stage and invited the entire hall to a party that night. 'A logically perfect ending to this meeting that has so enlightened us spiritually,' he said. And he explained that the party was being given by his sect, in part so they could share their wise precepts. So about a hundred people, of both sexes, accepted the invitation, cousin Hermione among them. How could the poor thing know that those so-called followers of Neolongbeardism would subject her to such unmentionable humiliations?"

"That imbecile Laura is certainly going to write me gushing with love as always. I'll just tear her letter up without opening it." Horacio smiles with satisfaction at the thought of Laura's desolation because of frustrated love. Ignoring her is even better and much simpler than what had occurred to him to do earlier, which was to answer with an announcement of his death written on the office stationery he managed to steal from the same airline he left Megalopolis on. There had been no question in his mind but that Laura, with the methodical nature of a gatherer insect, would finally discover the ruse. "She would never be able to resist the temptation to know everything, to stay maximally informed. She would ask for the airline to send her reports of all the airline's accidents over the last ten years. *Sí, sí*, and that is just for starters! Say, that is *her* to perfection: a data-gathering bug: what a good definition of the scarecrow!"

"That night, the host of the Neolongbeards' party stated that they were nature mystics and, in order to commune with the Great Mother, he was inviting all the guests to remove, preferably in the bathrooms, all their clothes and cover their heads with the hoods they'd find prepared for them in there. So Hermione had no choice. She had to do what everyone else did. Poor little thing, what she had to put up with from those naked, hooded men, and her barely a woman yet, with those puny little breasts and her little legs, skinny as pipe cleaners. But in reality all artists are bad people, almost as bad as Latin people. And O

Jango, who is a Latin, says he's also an artist, although no one can see what he has done to be able to use that title."

Laura believes she has reached the uttermost depths of human thought when, in her mind, there begins to glimmer a verification that artists, so perfidious and lascivious, are usually capable of creating works of *art* and some of them are *not* made to be merely a sensual experience, but also in order to elevate, even purify the human spirit. She promises herself that, second semester, she will take another course of Art Appreciation, which will surely shed light on this enigma. "Oh, if only all problems could be solved this easily!" Now she feels very tempted by O Jango's party, which no longer consists of just a couple of small glasses of sherry accompanied by Agnes's and her Latin American friend's brilliant conversation, but also includes the true art treasures that the Brazilian has accumulated in his apartment. On the verge of getting lost in the abyss of art for art's sake, she wonders what she would give to see that fabulous Polonaise bed again. "However often O Jango celebrates his lewd rituals in it!" Then, to ease her moral conscience, she adds, "But I have nothing to do with all that, however."

What should she do? Mommy, with whom, in moments of acute crisis, she has so often communed through extrasensory channels using telepathy, as it is called, does not respond from her house in the country. "But of course! Why, at this hour, she must be at the country club playing canasta. That always takes her full attention." Seeking divine inspiration, Laura raises her heavy head—her face is, in fact, at least as pimply as Horacio described it in a letter that she will never get to read—and her eyes meet the thin face of a boy whose own very large eyes fix on her for an instant.

"I've seen him somewhere, but . . . who is he?"

Although O Jango cannot help but realize that his very existence has been made possible due to the union of his progenitors—precisely *his* progenitors—he has cherished, from the moment he discovered the story in his now quite remote childhood, an intense resentment of the grandfather who impeded the marriage of his mother, at the time an available eighteen-year-old, to the great German aristocrat who was asking for her hand. His grandfather's detectives in Berlin had easily confirmed, without needing to make prudent or clever inquiries, what was *vox populi* there and even, in a very veiled way, commented on in the *Simplizissimus!* The proud warrior stood so straight up into his a-little-over-six-foot height, so beautifully monocled and stiffly mustachioed, so cliché. So Prussian Aristocracy. Inexplicably—that is to say, explicably, but only in the inexplicable way things happen to Germans— on leaves from his regiment, the Uhlans of Death, he was also a member of the more than merely equivocal group around Kronprinz Wilhelm.

And then his mother was married to the coffee mogul.

If only—and no matter how often, in order to relieve his grief a little, he tells himself, that then he never would have really turned out to be *he*—if only he could have carried those enchanting, noble, High German names with so many *von* and *zu*. How different his life would have been then. A different rooster would have crowed.

Instead, given the father he got, how was he going to wind up as anything *but* the laughingstock of Harrow, so often seen as the issue of a noticeably Negroid, minor, tribal king by condescending parents visiting the school? No, he could not pardon his grandfather's cruel trick. So, on the occasion of a wedding celebration given by another São Paulo magnate, he composed his poem "Love Song." The title alone, when they all heard it that day, moved the emotions of the elderly, and his reading, done with the voice of a perfect courtier, astonished most of the guests gathered in celebration of this very splendid event. Present, in fact, among other illustrious personalities, were the Governor of the State and the Archbishop of the Pope's

Council of Advisors. O Jango's poem not only provoked the biggest upset of his grandmother's social life (she had frequently attended this kind of noteworthy distraction, not without some significant public successes), but it also brought on a minor apoplexy in the old man, who never spoke to him again and, unquestionably, would have disinherited him immediately if the laws of the country had permitted it. Instead, the old man found a way to take out his revenge on his daughter, O Jango's adored Mama, and on her perfumed, fiercely desired, often caressed body—except, of course, the caresser had turned out to be his father, the coffee hoarder, who long ago had found his own way to take revenge on the poem's author, by giving him an inauspicious surname along with flesh tending to obesity, and suspicious, just a tad excessively curly hair.

O Jango has never forgotten "Love Song." He still revises it from time to time, according to his state of mind. This he has done today, when, after happily finishing the guest list for his potlatch, he feels very satisfied. In fact, the poem's new version is one of the least coprophilous, but perhaps also—let the kind reader judge—the most insidious and discreetly offensive. It reads:

> They have crossed, redone, undone,
> separated and joined, added and subtracted,
> lost and found themselves.
> But there was once a young lady of Genoa,
> practically a whore sent by force to America.
> Passage cost far less than a convent
> and once aboard, she only need consent
> to leave the ship's captain satisfied.
> And do his cooking.
> They have broken, assaulted, lost and gained
> themselves on the sweat of their brows.
> But he left home, yes, let us call it a home,

after some mischief similar to hers
(in fact what was never found out was
what this similar mischief to hers was),
and he carted his whole patrimony, that is, an onion,
in a satchel (and telling his people goodbye, he could
only say,
his voice breaking: Damn! I am finally going
to get out of this place. And, as far as here goes,
it is where I'll never come back to).
They have longed for, beaten, and scratched themselves,
in effect risen
and now here you are, so proud
to be the best woman of them all:
"In my blood," you declare, "two great peoples are
present,
creators of culture, custodians of beauty"
(and in your own beauty, indeed, we can never stop
believing).
They have divided and multiplied, lost and found,
crossed, unmade, and remade themselves
and now you are here, resplendent creature,
who confided to the last of the Saxe-Hohenlohe line:
"Mama and Papa will perhaps not oppose our marriage."

   "She was still splendid. Even at that moment, when she was
already sixty-something-years-old, still very attractive—and
only partially thanks to a wonderful cosmetologist. And on
that day my dear little mama stepped forth from among the
stupefied guests." *The Governor of the State was counting the little
angels on the ceiling to repress a loud guffaw and the Archbishop's
face turned exactly the same color as his ceremonial frock.* "Yes,
mamita, mi mamita came forward and kissed her teenaged son
on the forehead. I can still feel your kiss." O Jango articulates
each syllable as clearly as if he were reciting a lesson, then, to

keep from sinking deeper into melancholy, he decides it would be good to give his guest list a final look.

At first he doesn't give it his full attention, despite how important the night's performance is to him. Something keeps running through his mind, preventing him from concentrating with the lucidity required by the list's perfectly deliberated stream of names, vices and occupations, and tenuous images of guests dance before his eyes. He decides to look up from the brand-new volume. Little by little, his mind eases and he regains a bit of the verve with which, some nights earlier, after many cocktails, he summarized for a few of his favorite friends the life of his recently deceased mother as well as his own. He would have put it all down in writing at this very minute, if he could avoid getting lost again in the twists and turns of memory. "Nothing is easier for men to adapt to than changes of fortune, if they find them favorable—and they adapt to nothing that doesn't favor them. And the same is true of ovules." That last sentence is of his own making, but he wouldn't be O Jango if, when looking into the eyes of an unsuspecting audience, he didn't let it pass for an original epigram of the Duke of La Rochefoucauld's. When his old friends confuse his talent with that of the celebrated aristocrat of the *Maxims,* his vanity is stroked.

Nick Ensor is finally almost ready to settle down to work and feels the uneasiness appropriate to the few minutes that precede his execution of the task at hand. Roslyn won't get home now until after seven, just in time to shower and dress for the party, so Nick still has four whole hours at his disposal. There is no doubt that, having that much time ahead of him, he will easily knock out something more or less palatable. Whenever he feels this uneasiness and spontaneously refers to the intellectual work in front of him as the "task," he, who is far from militarily minded, can be sure that things aren't going to go against him.

Six months earlier, his receipt of a certain sum of money, that, of course, Roslyn had pulled out of her meager savings account, had secured an invitation to him from *Minos*—"the most independent of the independent journals," to quote its guiding slogan. They wanted his "Notes on Poetry after Poetry." At the moment, what had most interested him was the opportunity to make himself a little money: Nick Ensor would have ceased to be Nick Ensor if he had not been able to contrive a way to get Roslyn to give him double the printing costs of his article. Then, as fate would have it, a copy of the relevant issue of *Minos* had fallen into the hands of the eminent Professor Dinessen. A tediously long trip by train had inspired him to read Nick's article. An undeniably involuntary reading, but what could the professor do. It was better than nothing. Especially considering that in every kiosk at the railway station he would certainly have run across *Histoire d'O,* a novel which, in a moment of his flagging attention, someone had filched from him. It was the seventh theft of that masterful book perpetrated against the professor on campus in the span of two months' time! Wretched thief! And just after he had spoken on "New Christianity's Need for a Literature." Tedium was forcing him to read Nick's "Notes," and perhaps also the hope that they would work like a good sleeping pill. But he quickly found himself very wide-awake and unsettled.

"They cite me less and less. I'm on the way to becoming as outdated as the Neo-humanists and their useless ilk. I must get in touch with the new generation of critics." So, between slugs of good bourbon from his exquisite silver flask, he wrote Nick a letter that, line after line became more complimentary, in direct correlation with the optimism the alcohol was producing in him. The next morning, he would have torn up the letter upon re-reading it—after all, he himself still retained enough prestige to go on covering himself undeservedly with excessive praise. But surpassing every other consideration was the fact that he was quoted less and less and therefore it was absolutely necessary for him to make allies among emerging critics. Still in transit, at a station along the way, needled by his need for publicity and goaded by the alcohol, he mailed the letter.

"'The tact with which you sort through the easy seductions of the –*isms* that have done so much damage to a few of the most talented critics of my generation, has interested me greatly.'" This is followed by one of those concise sentences that commentators on epistolary bibliography love to quote: "'Criticism must be eclectic or cease to exist.'" Then comes an allusion to Sainte-Beuve in an indispensable touch of very subtle, veiled flattery: "'Today our literature claims for itself a vast, elastic kind of talent.'" *Nick of course finds himself ready and able to meet that demand.* "'One word of advice: follow your road with complete autonomy.'" This was in there because everyone knows how picky those Beatniks are who write for minor journals like *Minos*. "'And accept a suggestion that is at the same time a request: I would enthusiastically welcome from you, for the next issue of *Comparative Criticism Review*, which I edit, an article that explores certain aspects only fleetingly touched on in the one I've just read. Your work, if it turns out that you wish to honor us with your collaboration'"—"*the plural is appropriate here,*" the professor thought, "*indeed, the plural will give him a sense of the academic solidity of* our *academic solidity*"—"'could be, for example, a type of general introduction to the study of the importance of myth in poetry and mass culture.'"

Nick already knows the important paragraphs of the letter by heart, if with an involuntary embellishment or two that his vanity may have added here and there. This is principally as a consequence of having read them so often to Roslyn, who already envisions him incorporated into a university as the teaching assistant of perceptive, encyclopedic, and majestic Professor Dinessen. She will gladly abandon her blue jeans: she sees her next project as making herself a turquoise silk dress to wear to faculty receptions; she has no doubt that her mom's pearl necklace will be the perfect accessory for it. When they get married, she'll ask her to give it to her as a wedding present. Because, there can be no question, they will have to regularize their situation.

But how will Nick take the idea of getting married? From his brief bout of Marxist measles, what Nick seems to have most assiduously conserved are his anti-matrimonial prejudices. And the truth is, she herself has contributed in no small measure to their establishment in his views, due to her insistence on ridiculing the attitudes, clothes, thoughts, feelings, all, *every little thing, as they say*, and anything whatsoever to do with married women. "Fools like Dinessen and Van Wyck Brooks haven't the foggiest idea of what it is to do literary criticism." Hasn't she heard Nick, more than once, if not a thousand times just two weeks ago, express some such pejorative judgments about the very professor who now, suddenly, resoundingly, has become a great master, the only worthy name among all men of letters approximately sixty years old? Then it should be possible to make him change his opinion of marriage. It shouldn't take much to make him see that his university career will depend on his having a solid private life. "To not be afraid of Virginia Woolf, daddy will have to be a preacher."

Approximately thirty books are piled on the little table at which Nick is getting ready to work. Nick is and is not a beatnik. For one thing, lysergic trips don't make him nauseous. But, for another, he peppers his writing with ridiculous, weird words like "nullity" and detritus left from his frequent reading of the classics, themselves the residue of a university education that will now no longer be a waste. By the same token, he is, on one hand, accepting of his little table of badly painted wood and in principle is now ready to work at it, until you hear otherwise. A Jack Kerouac and a Lawrence Ferlinghetti may have relied on a support structure like Nick's table to write the works that have given them such well-deserved fame and this, unquestionably, can be a comforting thought. But, on the other hand, Nick can't help considering that among the beatniks of the world he must be the unique and very *rara avis* that requires the support of thirty or more books in order to squeeze out something like a dozen pages. And thirty or more books require a substantial, solid base of support, not this broken-down little table with four, toothpick-thin legs.

This thought doesn't fail to alarm him, though he is finally ready to sit down and write the abstract for the lead of his article, including a general reference to "the extremely important publications coming out of Chicago to renovate the history of religion," by which he means the works of Chicago-based Romanian scholar Mircea Eliade—*a perfectly awful novelist, but that's another story*—and his many followers, "who, fortunately, haven't taken up the art of fiction."

The little table starts to shake as soon as he starts typing on his Remington and it bothers him. On top of that, the vibration of an underground train rumbles through the building's foundation. And up from the street and through the window, which, as usual, he has forgotten to close, roars the customary din of traffic and a thousand compounding voices, above which now soars the unmistakable, half-fierce, half-lascivious voice of a singer:

Babbo non vuole, mamma nemmeno,
Come faremo a fare l'amor.

"Some Italian wearing a red-striped t-shirt." *That Italian doesn't exist: he's a cliché.* In Eliade's place, a Henry James—and this is exactly what Eliade didn't know how to do—would have made him an impeccable fellowship winner just back from Italy. Or someone like that: hadn't *Nick* started seducing that plain-looking girl, "what was her name, I believe it was Laura," with that same song? "I wonder what's become of Laura. Laura?

Yes, yes, of course, Laura. And after her was Irina, and after her . . . Right, Roslyn came along." He's been with Roslyn such a long time now! It doesn't seem possible . . .

Nick gets irritated and stands up. He's in the middle of the disorder of a small room. Roslyn of course forgot to make the bed.

"I'll start the essay in a minute." The most important thing is that he already knows how to get on Dinessen's good side, and, at the moment the key to things is to think about what he's going to do with Roslyn. He again feels the uneasiness of the few minutes that precede his execution of a task, but now with even greater intensity than before, when he was getting ready to start his article. He's almost as nervous as when he had to write and tell Lorraine, "I don't want to see you anymore, I'm sick of tenderness," indeed, even almost as anxious as that time he was crawling with his squad toward a North Korean machine gun nest. Nick, the anti-military fan of war similes, surprises himself by thinking that maybe his true vocation was exactly in weapons, a strict discipline that doesn't leave you time to think, the kind of strict discipline that only lets up to let you enjoy the most basic pleasures. "Don't confuse basic with rudimentary," Nick writes to himself in a mental footnote.

On the white-washed walls of the room, hanging among reproductions—Uccello's fantastical dragon-butterfly at the Jacquemart-André Museum, Seurat's preliminary study for "La Grande Jatte," an aerostatic eye by Redon—are tempting photographs in full color, pin-ups cut from the pages of *Playboy* or *Cavalier*. In his Korea days, there was nothing better than Varga's girls. But they were only drawings. These photos, on the other hand, show you flesh-and-blood girls you could run into at the coffee shop, if not the public library. They offer all the advantages of reality with none of the rough edges. "What a shame women aren't like that in real life, so odorless and silky." Or maybe they are until you go to bed with them, but a garter belt leaves marks on a woman's waist that sometimes look like a rash. "And however close they shave their bushy armpits, there are always little bristles that are really hard and put the frost on desire." He was getting on top of Roslyn one time, it was barely their second time and so their erotic charge was still practically intact, and he unintentionally caught a glimpse of her left armpit. What came into his mind was a plucked chicken and he remembered the disgust he felt as a boy when they would give him pieces of chicken that still had little bits of quill stuck in the skin. "It's such a shame real girls can't be like the girls in *Playboy*. And they can't, even if they're the same girls!" So what if Roslyn posed for Peter Basch and claims that, when she was in Paris, she made her living for a few weeks by working for Jeanloup Sieff. He would rather have her in the flesh, but like in her photos, the ones she carefully keeps copies of in her family album. "This generation desperately needs those 'feelies' that Aldous Huxley talked about!" In feelies, there are always pin-ups, the true goddesses of any self-respecting onanist. "And inside every genuine intellectual, isn't there a vigorous masturbator, at least a potential one? Was it Gide who confessed to masturbating as a young schoolboy and well into adulthood?" Why, all these reflections could be the basis of a chapter of a book whose title Nick's known for years, though its content is only now beginning to take concrete form in his mind: "Variations of the Intellectual Experience," a chapter on the intellectual and the mass-man. "It would be fantastic to have a little help on it from Kiki—but that egotist could never collaborate with anybody! I'll do it on my own." Or a chapter on the essential onanism of the intellectual since the baroque— "The Dissociation of Sensibility as a Masturbatory Principle," could be the title. And a chapter on what he was thinking about just *before* that last part about onanism. Sometimes it's hard for Nick to remember ideas that only seconds ago were in his mind with perfect clarity. But, it was that exact thing that had moved him to think about the significance that pin-ups have for intellectuals. "Oh, I remember now: the intellectual and the temptations of military discipline. Colonel T.E. Lawrence, Ernst Jünger, Hemingway (*Hemingway?*), Malraux . . . In some way this is related to the theme of myth."

Suddenly realizing this, Nick regrets all the time that he has wasted woolgathering and decides to get back to the matter at hand. It's only 4:30. He still has a long time before Roslyn reappears, that's enough time to write at least three pages.

Wait a minute! Did I say "reappears" instead of "returns"? Why did I do that?

The poet's verses fit Barbara Dowd like a glove: she is in fact the promise of pneumatic bliss.

"Is Nick here?"

The girl's breasts are still heaving from the five flights of stairs she has just run up, for she has finally found where Nick lives! What is more, they seem lifted, well separated, and very firm (hopefully not falsies, but you'll have to take a little time, you sly dog of a picaro Nick, to find out for yourself). Her legs can be sized up without difficulty, owing to her very short, green-and-red plaid mini-skirt: they're well filled out, pillars really, two well-defined pillars covered in golden down. Will she wind up becoming overly passionate? This question somehow makes even more enticing the business at hand: that being to get those legs apart. Only one thing is left for Nick to verify right now. What will her delicate little face of the folk, seemingly open to everything, the high cheekbones strikingly prominent; what will her dear little face that is only that, a little face that could, despite its jaw, inspire in the inattentive observer a deceptive feeling of power; what will this face look like in the throes of pleasure? Those sweet, green eyes: what will they do at that moment? Though slanted a bit, they are all innocence. And, even if her ample, unclouded forehead announces a Barbara

Dowd of purity and prudence that never could have really existed, it is the one that perhaps will come into existence after the search for her Holy Grail.

"Is Nick here?" she repeats. She half-fears that she's gotten the address wrong.

"Well, yes. I'm Nick."

What? How can this be Nick? This little man with the thick glasses and solicitous manner who, when he talks, looks like he's about to lick something. The true Nick is that splendidly contemptuous, agile boy who came into her town one night and into the drugstore where she worked the soda counter, and made a date with her, and, to be classy, deflowered her that same night in an abandoned barn and left town the next morning, not on the sly, but explaining to her that they were waiting for him to get back to the city to get the role of Peer Gynt in a new—the definitive!—production of the great work. (But here it's appropriate to clarify that, until that moment, Barbara Dowd had never heard of either it or of Ibsen, because, in her pre-university courses, she had never taken History of Modern Drama.) Yes, very soon they would be putting the play on, with him, her lover, in the starring role, and he, so faithful, so modest, emphasized how much he wanted her at his side, forever, and would wait for her there in the Village, which is the artists' neighborhood, where all she'd need to do to find him was to ask for Nick, because everyone knew him in the artists' neighborhood.

"I'm Nick," Nick Ensor insists, repeating it to the confused the girl.

But was it only to reach this confusing conclusion that the little heroine had slipped out of town on tiptoes, leaving her parents only a brief note announcing that nothing could stop her, for she was going in search of her happiness, and asking them to forgive her for snatching a handful of one-dollar bills from them? Was it only to reach this bewildering ending that she had found herself forced to make certain concessions ("but not that many really!") to a pair of truck drivers and even a bearded guy on a motorcycle? Was it to get to this false finish that she had left Clover, her piggy bank, in pieces, in the end to get just a few coins?

And is it reasonable, now, to say to the man with the thick glasses: "No, you are *not* Nick"? Our valiant little girl is ignorant of the ways of the immense city and fears offending him.

"Nick! Yes, that's me." Nick Ensor assures her for the third time and feels tremendously idiotic for having to make such an obvious affirmation. But he instantly realizes with complete certainty that this luscious beauty, this absolutely gorgeous girl, this object truly worthy of *Playboy* (*just wait until Nick Ensor sees her with her back turned!*), is in search of another Nick, and that, poor little thing, she's not from here, she's terrified, she's lost. But, in his view, he owes it to himself not to lose a catch like this.

"Come in a minute, come in. Let's clear up the confusion. I know several other Nicks here in the neighborhood and it will be easier for the two of us to locate the one you're searching for, miss . . ."

"Barbara Dowd."

How many Nicks can there be in this tentacle-laden metropolis of more than twelve million souls? Moreover, is the one she wants locatable, even if one supposes that the James Dean-Bond-Casanova in question is really from here or is at least staying here somewhere, and further supposing that his name is in fact Nick?

The time is now nearly seven thirty. Roslyn is punctual and, just as she has the virtue of not making people wait, she also possesses the gift of not arriving early. So Nick lets this little goddess of the wheat fields, this foolish little deity on the verge of tears, tell her story, spontaneously and starting from the end. He has not moved too near to her on the sofa, where he has

managed to have her lie back, in part to let her rest a little—
after a journey like that, how could she not be exhausted?—and
in part so that she has a clear view of those pin-ups adorning the
wall facing her. In their presence anything can happen: who's to
say they won't even set an example for her?

Naturally, in spite of her nervousness, Barbara starts to fall
asleep and, for the moment, all Nick can do is contemplate the
way the delicious girl's agitation, even though she's half-asleep,
doesn't dissipate all together and how her quick, unconscious
movements reveal some of her most intimate charms. Nick is
pleased to note that, however provincial she may be, she is above
all one of her generation and has opted not to wear panties.
"This always makes the job easier," the young critic can't help
thinking.

But now, the succulent young thing is snoring and maybe—
she looked really tired—will go on doing so for hours. The
minutes have never seemed so precious to Nick as at the present
moment. Roslyn's return is immanent and getting to his goal
may take longer than with the neighborhood girls. He must take
into account how archaic the norms are out in the country. And
this girl is evidently provincial, perhaps even full of prejudices,
however much her skirt has casually ridden up almost to her
belly button. Which, of course, instigates our Nick's immediate
reaction. As always when he wants to see things of the spirit
more clearly, he turns down the lamp. He doesn't leave the end
of the sofa, where he chastely sits. Then he removes his glasses:
there is a significant probability that the other Nick doesn't wear
them.

"Here I am, darling, it's Nick. Hey, wake up, it's your Nick."

"Where am I?" That is the very first thing—how could it be
otherwise—that our intrepid little girl says, almost beside herself
with fear and, in the shadowy darkness of the room, unable to
discern or, of course, quite remember where she is. She's having
a hard time coming out of a dream in which she found herself

in the Village, but the Village in her dream was more faithful to that name and was full of villagers in picturesque Dutch costumes.

"It's your Nick," Nick Ensor repeats, now whispering to her, bringing his lips nearer to her face, holding himself back with great effort to keep from throwing himself on her.

Yes, the Village has disappointed Barbara, who imagined it more village-like, more rustic, and more, how can I put it, spry. But, in fact, she has wound up in an urban neighborhood more or less like any other. That is possibly why she's still trying to get back down into her dream, when she's completely awakened by another reiteration, spoken this time in a quasi-irritated tone, as if her darling already had her in his mouth and was ready to start shaking her in his jaws.

"I am Nick. Nick! Do you hear?"

Losing no time, he covers her face with kisses while his hands, quickly—you might even think they had doubled or tripled in number—proceed to strip her of her blouse and brassiere. Then, all of a sudden—her breasts, so firm to the touch, her nipples, so inviting!—our little Barbara receives him with a soft sigh that for an instant alarms Nick. Shouldn't the size of his member surprise her? But his alarm lasts only a moment, for he is soon tranquilized by the girl's increasingly enthusiastic rhythm, to which he responds with not unexpected energy, until both reach the final delirium of pleasure. Nick Ensor calculates—and a furtive glance at the luminous face of his watch corroborates—that he still has an hour and a half of free time. Ignoring the girl's gentle protests—*yes, gentle and also protesting*—he begins to kiss her belly. Almost imperceptibly, or, you could say, cunningly, he is moving down, down, and finally the young thing's legs tremble convulsively and almost strangle him, until she lets out a sigh of complete satisfaction. Perfidious and ecstatic—*but don't ever forget that perfidious!*—Nick Ensor is then able to free himself from the embrace.

Now it's time to invert their roles. It is only the authority with which he orders it, after having asked and entreated her with no results, that makes her finally kneel down. Nick softly caresses her splendid hair. Oh! If only he could turn the light on now! He finds consolation in the fact that he doesn't have a mirror quite up to the job anyway and contents himself with caressing her hair and whispering instructions to her that he intersperses with perverse insults that he knows how to utter in a tone of tenderness.

"Why did you call me 'whore'? You think I'm a *whore*?"

The young critic responds after a long silence, which to Barbara seems to hold ominous signs.

"Yes, I do. You're a whore. To be more precise, you're a *little* whore."

Just as he had foreseen when he gave her such a deliberately hostile response, our heroine now sobs convulsively.

"How can you say such a thing to me? You know you were the first one! That was *obvious*!"

"To who, me? *I* am not *Nick*! Or, I'm Nick, all right, but not yours, if there really is such a person."

The poor young woman thinks she's going crazy. *At least this is the formula that any writer of melodramas would in good conscience have adopted here to describe the state she is now in.* ("We must keep in mind that, yes, our heroine is clearly faithful to the spirit of melodrama. Its powerful vestiges remain perfectly intact in the second half of the twentieth century, thanks to authors who, like our friend Kiki, contribute to *True Confessions* and other publications of the kind. For, as we know, they are read with enthusiasm and devotion by all the Barbaras who serve mankind at drugstore counters up and down the civilized world.") Nevertheless, in spite of her great confusion, this valiant young woman has the self-control needed to be able to pull herself together after every deception that, in the mere half a day she's been here, this Megalopolis has thrown at her, revealing its diabolical face. ("At this stage of the game, for the benefit of literary comparatists and a pedant or two, it should be noted that, a long time ago, the same aversion to the Big City took hold of one Pierre Glendinning, Melville's fool of a hero. But it's also appropriate to point out that, unlike Pierre, our admirable Barbara does not give in to her desperation.") Faithful to a literary tradition loaded with names of more or less famous heroines, Barbara overcomes her disappointments and attempts to deceive herself, trying to come up with arguments that will shore up her quavering faith in reason and human nature.

Clever Nick slyly guesses that this is the mental process unfolding in young Barbara and, in order to completely convince her that he is her Nick, he denies it, leans back on the sofa, and, locating the button on the lamp, clicks it. He turns on the light in the room and—we must add—the darkness in Barbara's mind.

Well, is this Nick or not? He seems a lot less robust than before, and his face is in no way comparable, it's less virile. But now that he's not wearing glasses, she can see that, yes, it's true, he is her Nick. How silly of her not to have recognized him at once. Or even to have remembered that Nick is an actor and that actors, as everyone knows . . . But she was so tired earlier.

"I could hardly keep my eyes open, you know? Can you ever forgive me, sweetheart?"

When he finally convinces Barbara to leave, he will have promised to find her again later at an apartment at an address he gives her, where that night there will be the most sumptuous, mind-blowing party in the annals of Megalopolis.

Nick has only forty minutes until Roslyn's return.

"No, don't come by for me. Just do what you can to get ready at the office and go straight to O Jango's. I'll meet you there. I have to go out to find a book I need for tomorrow morning—early, and . . . the library closes at seven. See you later, sweetheart."

This is the second time in two minutes that he has told a

lover goodbye. But can one really call Barbara a lover? Be that as it may, it's amusing to think that, in the midst of the party's clamor, two women will be looking for their Nick, two Nicks who in reality are the same one—or neither one. Can he really *know* that his true self is not out there somewhere, in another person, perhaps in this very city, this very barrio? Who is Nick? Couldn't he be *he*, at least starting from some predetermined moment? Couldn't *he* also really be somebody *else*, even in this very neighborhood? While he rearranges his clothes, which were left in disorder by his recent amorous mishap, Nick goes over to the window. "Is that someone now in this neighborhood?" He opens the window wide. He lies to himself, saying he's doing it only to let the fresh air wash away the strong traces of the girl's cheap perfume lingering in the room. He knows that it would be of great interest to Roslyn to be able to detect that another woman has been there in her absence; but deep down he knows that opening the window is a maniacal compulsion. At the moment he really believes that out there, walking by on the sidewalk six stories below, he's theoretically incarnate in another body. "In some man, woman, or child, or maybe just a roving dog?" He ponders on some other being he has not yet seen, yet will recognize instantly.

Confused noises reach him from the street. The alleged Italian who was singing *Babbo non vuole* a little while ago is silent, but Nick can make out a voice yelling curses, then loud laughter and the monotonous spiel of the avocado seller and car horns, so many car horns. These are the sounds that are always there. They are no doubt the exact same sounds that were there two years ago, the day that, as Kiki told me in his letter, Celia opened the window and made her threat. How Kiki has hated me since then! Is it because he wrote me a letter of confession? Or does he realize I didn't take it seriously? *That's good, Nick, now you're safe. For the moment. Move further away from the window.* ("And do whatever you want to do, but stay away from it.")

Nick goes over to a disorderly pile of papers and searches through them for the letter in which, two years ago, Kiki told him in confidence the sad episode that ended his and Celia's marriage:

"Dear Nick,

"Something happened last night between my wife and me and it leaves no possibility that false excuses can exist between you and me ever again. There in our little apartment, the one you know so well, right across from the Women's Prison, I suddenly realized something I've been incapable of comprehending for the last six years: Celia—my poor, darling girl!—has always been a victim of my gross self-obsession. From the day we got married, that marvelous girl, unable to defend against it, had to find within herself the necessary fortitude to put up with the horrendous pressure of my pathological egotism.

"As my most trusted confidant since our student days, you formed an equally close relationship with Celia. So I believe it's almost my duty (and Kiki had energetically underlined those last two words) to give you a detailed account of the events that took place here yesterday afternoon. The only actors were my Celia, my poor, poor Celia—oh, no! Is it my stupid egotism that still makes me call this little goddess, this angel of purity and goodness, 'mine'? Yes!—and myself. And, however hard it is for me to confess it to you, I must place the blame for such an ignominious trampling only on the second of the two actors in that horrendous event. Me (this word was also underlined).

"Given your natural generosity and tendency to forgive others, for even their most idiotic foul-ups, I begin my narration of this disgraceful event—in which, I repeat, I bear all the blame—by acknowledging up-front that right now we're having the hottest month of August in the meteorological history of this city. Maybe you've seen in the newspapers how many cases of sunstroke—a lot of them fatal!—we've had here in the last weeks. In addition, you've always known how the heat affects my nerves. But this time you won't be able to blame the heat, this was my responsibility alone. Precisely because of the heat, being fully aware of the bad effects it has on me, I ought to have made sure I could exercise over my every action and word an extra portion of control, instead of letting myself go in a truly pathological explosion of emotion. (I do need to see a psychiatrist. Urgently! Celia's been wisely telling me that for a long time.) But instead my anger exploded, and it was for the most insignificant reason imaginable! It was just because, instead of coming out with me to a movie, Celia preferred to stay in and chat with a young girl she protects and, without charging her a cent for it, tutors in Spanish. Truly, my very good friend, you can't blame any of this on the heat. Another man, any other, nobler man, would have been less violent, even in a much worse situation."

When he gets to this point in the letter, Nick can no longer hold back the loud guffaw that, for a while now, his throat has been working with some effort to push down. Without thinking, he crumples up the pages of the letter and they fly through the window: why go on reading this? Why had he even kept these pages for the last two years? He knows by heart what comes next in them ("and not in them!"). Celia sits on the edge of the open window and threatens to throw herself out of it if Kiki doesn't leave her alone. Kiki evidently doesn't understand what it's all about and attributes everything to a sad, noble desire that has been growing inside of Celia and now tempts her to throw herself out of the window because, like a monster, he has finally stood up and told her ("so egotistically!") to pay a little less attention to her tutees and a little more to him! He doesn't want to leave, but Celia asks him to because she's trying to save him the shocking spectacle of her suicide. "Without a doubt," Kiki tells himself, "after hearing my unbelievable cruelties, Celia can only believe that she has no place in my life and wants to sacrifice herself to set me free." But instead of leaving, as his wife is so strongly urging him to do; instead of going immediately to the movies or anywhere, Kiki kneels down in front of her and begs her to believe him. He tells her he loves her so much, needs her so much, can't live one instant without her. And Celia, in even more peremptory terms, repeats her threat and showers him with insults of all kinds, which he lets run over his spirit like a divine balm that will purify his corrupt being. Kiki, now prostrate, listens with immense relief to a Celia who is suddenly the picture of calm, a Celia who says:

"If you *ever* want to see me again alive, you'll go to your damn movie this instant."

What movies were playing that night? For a moment Nick is sorry he threw the letter out. Infinitely detailed, it included the titles of the three films that on that hot August night Kiki forced himself to sit through in a shabby Village movie theater, titles that Kiki was pleased to include in his letter like three pieces of evidence that made his fierce crime worse. Nick no longer remembers the movies' titles, but he is very clear about what comes next in the letter: about midnight Kiki calls the apartment from a bookstore, for, dumbfounded with the shame of his cruel demands, he cannot now inflict his presence on his good Celia against her will. When Celia answers, there is a smile in her question:

"*It is you, my darling?*" The cutting words come when he identifies himself:

"I've decided we can't now go on living together. I've done what I could to help you, but I realize that my help only harms you. Believe me, what you need now is a psychiatrist and I'm leaving you alone so you can take care of that. Take my advice. You already know I love you, but my suitcases are packed, so be good and take my advice. And, since I'm leaving right now, you can come back to the apartment anytime you wish. You'll hear from me. No, no, don't worry about me. We'll always be friends. So just take my advice."

How hard he had laughed at Kiki's letter! The next morning, poor old Kiki, predictably, sat waiting outside the office of a prestigious Freudian psychiatrist, who immediately proceeded to fleece him, as expected, emptying his savings account without improving his attitude. Kiki's real problems have nothing to do with grave or deep disorders of the psyche; they are an acute manifestation of his galloping sentimentalism, something that life experience and the passage of time alone are able to cure.

"Blind, miserable Kiki!" How he had laughed to himself at his friend who was so ignorant of what was in plain sight at every moment, right before his eyes. That is to say, Celia's "frigidity," which Kiki had attributed to energetic blunders of his own in the sex act. Had pathetic Kiki now realized what it was all really about in Celia's case? "And why didn't I open his eyes to it? The truth is, at first I couldn't believe he was so dumb, I thought he was faking his ignorance and, through Celia, trying to hide his own proclivities." But Nick is like that, always distrustful, disgusted with people. As it always turns out, everyone is really healthier and more virtuous than he will ever be. "They're so tedious. All these girls you can seduce with a snap of the fingers; all these people, men and women, who let themselves be fooled so easily. Do they *want* to be fooled? And pathetic old Professor Dinessen, what a fossilized, strutting peacock he is! Then there's Roslyn, viciously avid, always sniffing around my incursions into other cunts. It's all shit!"

Nick realizes that the last thing he has said is not just another simple sentence. His exclamation has in fact been so audible that he fears it was heard by his neighbors in the building. But its repercussion has been even more dynamic inside him. "In point of fact, everything *is* shit." Now he sees with total clarity exactly why he has cultivated himself with such diligence as a critic. It isn't out of love for something, it is out of hate. Because everything is shit and must be denounced and he needs to denounce it. But before it has always been on the condition that people still would think that someplace—past, present, or future, somewhere, anywhere—*there are* things that aren't shit. Nonetheless, once you've been struck by a certainty that hits you all of a sudden, a devastating electrical charge and you know that every, everything, every-thing indeed *is* really, inevitably, only shit, a great, sovereign, bone-crushing, abracadabra-ing pile of shit, shit yes shit all always only shit, shit all over here, all over there, just all over.

Once that happens, even *criticism* no longer makes sense. And then what does? Only the immediate extinction of the perceiving subject, the being that's cognizant of the shit that is the world. So, ably sweet-talked by Celia and her dirty tricks, uber jerk, gullible Kiki, on that tragicomic night was on the verge of throwing *himself* out of the window to the street far below; into the void, which Nick now gazes down on and, contemplating it with rising disgust, leans far out to see.

Does Nick lose his balance? We're quite sure this question is bothering our kind reader. We will recount the facts. Nick watches the human anthill toiling away below and realizes that he's also part of the cannibal termite hive. He remembers how distracted he was by the foolishness of his good friend Kiki, who just wandered around in desolation for days and days. He thinks of all the many meals and drinks he made his foolish friend pay for, in exchange for keeping him company and listening to his nonsensical confessions. And, meanwhile, he, Nick, was promising himself to turn them into literary material, which unfortunately he never has done. Nick remembers all this and he feels disgusted and he loses his balance (we will never know, to tell the truth, whether to say deliberately).

And he starts falling. A human projectile has now been launched toward the center of the earth—which, to be sure, is no small target for the prideful. (*And it bears remembering here that our friend Nick is in an essential way only that.*) In this new situation of effectively hurtling irretrievably toward his death, his first reflection is one of vanity. He feels, finally, liberated from his disgust and sees himself in the same place as that prestigious Irish airman who, foreseeing his own imminent demise, said to himself:

In balance with this life, this death.

But Nick sees immediately that he isn't giving his life up to the great stupidity of an epic struggle and that his act will be, at most, an insignificant curiosity squeezed into the next morning's police chronicle. No, he is not in truth the poet's despairing hero, though his poem, even at a moment like this (*training shows!*), Nick can remember. The inner critic who has possessed him throughout his whole life does not fail to show up and embitter his final moments. His death, Nick recognizes, is a supreme banality—he is simply one more particulate of the great world of shit and his death is now inevitable.

The body smashes against the pavement.

* * *

His silent insults tear into the intruding girl and he almost groans when he realizes he has lost the goddess's trail. Now he will have to wait three whole days to see her again. Will he ever be able to screw up the courage he would need to follow her down the street again, practically in plain sight? He has done it today by forcing himself to keep going forward, not to mention the even more challenging test of speaking directly to her.

He was feeling so satisfied with himself. He had at last hit on a more or less reasonable ploy to strengthen his relationship with the goddess. "Timid enchantress," "unwary goddess": the two phrases come into his mind again and revive his vacillation about the first line of the new sonnet he's writing to her. Trying to choose between them had even distracted him for a fraction of a second as he adored her in class a little while ago. It might have been possible for him finally to decide which epithet to use, if it weren't for the image of the dead mouse that now suddenly crosses his mind. It was the victim of poisoning that his mother showed him this morning at the foot of the stairs in the rundown apartment where they have lived since his father died. He's an exemplary young man in the eyes of the world—which start with the eyes of his mother. She had been nearly his whole world, until he discovered the existence of his Celia. He supports his mother, modestly, yes, but quite honorably, through his work as an office boy in a public relations firm. Someday, rising through the ranks, he might even be able to become a magnificently paid author of TV jingles. He is sure that, in that land of opportunity, he will triumph, as so many others have. He is what you'd call a perfect young man. His only vice is reading; that is easy to see from the stacks of books scattered about his studio room. Books are the only luxury he allows himself.

And it has now been proven—by Mama, neat, hardworking Mama: the voracious mouse that had adopted his library as a delicacy didn't live in his room. Its hideaway was somewhere else and at night it would slip in to feast greedily on the volumes he laboriously acquires in secondhand bookstores. "Mama, always so sensitive to others! She asked my *permission* to leave a plate with little pieces of cheese on it near the bookshelves, cheddar, the kind I like so much, smeared with poison, and this morning she showed me the poor, dead little animal." (*Recognize that you felt its pain, though, of course, that is an act of romanticism, a mephitic inheritance from Rousseau.*) Its whiskers were still comical. (*So there can be comedy in something that inspires suffering?*) What seems perfectly clear is that the mouse ate its fill of poisoned cheese and was returning satisfied to its hole, but only managed to reach the foot of the stairs. Perhaps, going down the last steps, it already felt the intolerable pains in its little belly? Or it could have even started to feel sick while it was still eating. (*Might it be that mice are like elephants, those corpulent, incurable romantics* ("who are perhaps incurable because they're so corpulent") *and the little mouse decided at that exact moment to go to his hideout to die?*) "Is that romantic? No! It's a biological fact and nature's perfection is always classical." Now the young neoclassical poet is no longer bothered by the strange tenderness that the mouse's last minutes have just inspired in him. "Its reaction was atavistic; a fact of nature compelled him to return to his cave." Still, the young poet feels his eyes grow moist as he thinks of the mouse caught up short by horrendous pains, its little belly on fire, trying to reach its goal, wanting—why wouldn't it?—to die among its own.

More important, however, is the subterfuge he has finally come up with to establish more intimate contact with his Celia—a timid enchantress, an unwary goddess. He would work out what to do with those two expressions later. Because isn't his own trick also a poison that is already beginning to corrupt him? Mouse, trick, and sonnet occupy him a long time this afternoon as he wanders aimlessly around the Village. "At least I told Mama I'd possibly be a little late getting home." *Right.* (You rascal, you know you were hoping to spend all this time with Her and you didn't say anything to Mama about that!) "Right. Mama. Just last night she was saying she was my 'little woman' and me going along with it using my most innocent smile and her building castles in the air, saying one day we'd go to a beach in the tropics and stay in a fancy hotel together and all that, one of those Hiltons people say are so expensive and luxurious; just as soon as I 'move up,' as they say, and become the author of jingles fought over by the principal ad agencies. Mama can already see herself—my poor little mama!—lying beside me on the golden sand under whispering palms."

The timid young poet feels very tired and very, very thirsty. He has lost count of the blocks he has covered, but notices that he is staring into the plaza, where, with some trepidation, he can see some kind of action unfolding. His love of words finally prevails over the fear of seeing himself involved in a commotion that might lead to a fierce charge by mounted policemen. "What would become of Mama? And the goddess!" But he stops anyway and starts to read, putting his full attention on the words written on large signs that a crowd of bearded men and shameless women carry as they proclaim their support for the dogs that run loose in the city streets, as well as their opposition to new anti-canine laws passed by a sadistic city council. The marchers' slogans are in many different languages, as befits the internationalism not only of these new Vandals who want to be called *hippies*, but also of this Megalopolis that is the most polyglot city in the world. Their signs reflect their defense of canine causes and wave to save the city's Dalmatians, poodles, Dachshunds, Pekinese, Scotch terriers, Chihuahuas, great Danes, and, who could forget, although they usually make common cause with the authorities, the Alsatian police dogs. But it seems clear: these despicable people, whom he now moves away from, are hereditary victims of an erroneous concept of love. They are Romantics now in the final stages of rot.

The timid young poet has already passed the noxious White Horse Tavern for the second time, but when he passed it earlier, he was so engrossed in thoughts of Celia that he didn't notice. "That poet who was always fighting with his wife in there (and she was always as drunk as he was) had once been its most faithful and pugnacious patron. He was the poet who came here just to die. After crossing the ocean—how furiously the ocean raged that fall—he got to the Village and died exactly here, his brain literally gnawed away by alcohol." Certainly no timid young poet, the poet of the tempestuous voice was what they call "a wreck of a man who locked himself up with a case of whiskey in his wretched room in a nearby mean hotel and they found him the next morning already in a coma." (*A great poet, or merely the undeniable forefather of those surly, unkempt, smelly, swinish people the young poet sees protesting there in the streets?*) "The dead poet certainly had the gift of poetry in him, but he was destroyed by bad poetics. For 'poetics' also covers conduct: Goethe said 'I call the classical health . . .'

"And, nowadays, nobody in his right mind in the Village dares repeat what was once dogma here exactly fifty years ago: 'religion is the opium of the people.' Answering that formula, which was always false, is another one that today has proven true: "opium is the religion of the masses. Yes," the timid young poet allows, "the latter definition is the correct one, the rationale the asocial unwashed use to enact their 'political system-icide.' In the era of dead ideologies, only the drugs or the True Faith will survive, that's a fact."

But just as the timid young poet isn't really in love with Celia, though he believes he is, he also doesn't follow any true faith, though he believes he does. It's more reasonable to assume that, until now, he has really been looking for the father he lost when he was fourteen. But as soon as he turns the next corner his thirst will be assuaged. And it will be accomplished by something greater than what is offered in the glass of beer that he has not dared to go into the sadly famous Tavern of the White Horse to drink. In fact, no sooner does the timid young poet turn the next corner than he sees Nick falling.

"Is that some kind of trick he's doing?"

But the timid young poet soon realizes what is happening. When the body is only a few yards away from crushing itself against the pavement, the stunned poet sees that, in the face he has just looked into and read so clearly for a tiny fraction of a second, there is no hope of a waiting net. He feels a strong urge to vomit, but is drawn to the horrible, bleeding sack of flesh by an animal curiosity that overcomes his fear, and then something soft and warm, something that makes him feel good, envelops and presses itself into him. ("A pretty blond nape; a handsome, firm neck; an encouragingly solid back.") Something is seeking protection and begins to rub against him very softly, almost imperceptibly. ("This lovely boy! How hard it is not to see his face. He must be beautiful.") In the circle of the curious that surrounds the body splayed out on the sidewalk, the timid young poet is the first one to approach it, fascinated by his own terror; he occupies a space on its closest perimeter. Behind him ("You're so loving, who gave you your strange name?" the young poet will ask her later, as he caresses her full, generously formed breasts) is a woman who continues to enjoy the macabre spectacle before them at the same time she feels the full effect of the nearness of their bodies and slowly, attentively continues to rub her breasts and belly against him. Dorkas is her name and she gives in completely to the emotion of it all (*how dangerous her surrender*) as she stands behind him, where the buttocks are not the most erogenous zones of the timid young poet's body.

He's on the verge of ceasing to be timid.

Something, which only much later could have become understandable to him, makes him turn around and take hold of a plump arm. She can now admire the freckled young man's beautiful face. Shining blond hair that has fallen over his right eye gives him an air of mystery; the divine left eye, so blue, so very blue, seems to burn with sensuality.

"It's as if the vision of him looking at me like that is revealing to me his deepest secrets. He's so magnificently young, so full of powerful, new sexuality," the woman Dorkas says to herself. She will initiate him into the truths of pleasure. The young poet will no longer be timid. He will know what true pleasure is. She takes him to her apartment to enjoy him. It will be she who is seduced.

"Never leave me," she begs him.

The young poet's memory has partitioned off from this afternoon the two figures who have pursued him all day. ("After all, Mama can easily get work. And what have I been doing up to now but writing bad poetry? Throw out the poems, yes, throw them out, don't look for an editor, who justifiably will never materialize. I'll start over again right now. Now I know where poetry comes from. And I'm full of poetry!")

"I'm leaving you my necktie as a surety, until tomorrow."

How insistently he needs to feel his neck's nakedness. "This young man," will say anyone who is like he was until a couple of hours ago, "is heading for a fate worse than death." And there may be some value in the judgment. People often start by confusing poetry with sensuality and wind up as disheveled, hairy hippies hysterically strumming zithers. But, for the moment, one fact can't be missed: Nick's holocaust has been given added meaning: it has served to move the young poet out of his larval foolishness. Of course, skeptics will always be able to point out that, though he has changed, the boy's spiritual side hasn't been very much improved.

It is a strange thing. This is the first time the timid young poet has not felt fear when he descends into the subway system. He disdains the plodding escalator. He feels agile, even athletic, and runs down the stairs two by two. He isn't worried about where to place his feet; he is sure of hitting the right spot. From now on, he will always land in the right spot. A beautiful girl, with the right amount of everything, rewards his athletic feat with a suggestive smile.

Another strange thing: this is the first time the timid young poet isn't at all worried by the haggard faces of those riding up the escalator to his right. He has gone over the rings of the universal worm of Angst. He smiles back at the beautiful girl who rewarded his prowess with a smile and he follows her, doing his best to calculate the distance between them to avoid getting into the same train car as she. "If she likes me, let her come find me."

At this hour offices are closing, the station platform is filling up. He's brushed by many bodies; he doesn't move. They push against him. They can because there are more and more of them, and that is the only reason, for he notices that he is solid. The timid young poet feels himself turning to steel. They move with him closer and closer to the edge of the platform.

He doesn't think of the possibility—and "terror" is really the appropriate word to describe what in general used to cause him to think of this possibility—of falling onto the tracks. He is not terrorized. He's perfectly certain that no shove will be able to knock him down there.

Luckily, a lot of people get off the train. ("But where did I put the newspaper I was carrying before I met Dorkas?") The trip home is long and he wants to keep himself entertained. At this point it could have been with anything, for example, a story by Mickey Spillane. He finds his paper at last, folded neatly in the same inside pocket where he keeps his wallet.

Directly across from him sits another beauty.

He reads a few book reviews—this is the first time it has occurred to him to do that, particularly in this London paper, his favorite—and they bore him. ("Maybe I'll stop buying it.") At the bottom of a page, his attention is caught by the title of a prose poem. ("Ugh! That shattered body on the pavement.") He had forgotten.

He grimaces in disgust. That is exactly it: disgust.

Celebrating the Suicide

Sometimes it becomes necessary to yell at the top of your lungs at life itself.

And tell it: the afternoon lost in the muggy heat's furious embrace is also life's own stupid surrender: to sweat, or, two thousand miles away, to dilapidation in the heat of last night's crime.

Sometimes you have to dispute life with life itself.

With the life of the murdered man who has now drunk his last gin-and-tonic (just think of it: the last gin-and-tonic of his life!), that chubby, flaccid, sensual, slightly cruel man. With the life of Hölderlin, too, including every time he threw himself from another cliff under pseudonyms that would knock only him off track.

And what do you think life itself might answer?

All right, that it was always a trick.

Sí, como todo.

Yes, like the lazy poet who returned home just so the letter on the table that collapsed from exhaustion would be nailed into memory forever; or like that young Polish woman: her mother was a doorman in the Bronx, but the daughter liked to fall asleep with a Debrett's under the pillow.

In your own words: "*sí, como todo,* 'yes, I eat everything,' *sí, como todo,* 'yes, like everything'!"

That's why, as soon as a poet wanted to contribute a myth to his never used up but wasted land, he threw himself into the sea from a ship that was far away from his native Brooklyn. And one must give a thought or two to the strength of those nine sailors who tried to stop him. Because he threw himself into the sea not so much from a desire to drown as from a desire to become myth.

But life itself is so trifling and innocuous now. Even the myth of Genesis can do nothing for it as a tonic.

"What garbage," states the young, formerly timid poet. "It's like they want to write stories but don't know how and come out with this stuff. I *know* I won't buy this newspaper anymore." He murmurs sarcastically, "Celebrating the Suicide," rolls the newspaper into a ball, and throws it out the open window. "More crap that ought to be kept out of print."

"I would agree!" the girl answers, without knowing what he's talking about.

But the young, formerly timid poet only mutters to himself, "I have to start thinking strictly strategically now." And judging from the looks of him, we would say he still has lurking within him a fear of falling back into the hesitancy from which the panacea of orgasm has just cured him.

He leans toward the train window and pushes it all the way open. The girl's hair becomes a golden eddy. She's delighted, smiles. He looks out into the blackness of the tunnel, wanting a source of inspiration for a secure tactical direction to take. Then a speck of something stings his right eye. It feels as big as a grain of sand but is probably only a carbon particulate.

His eye hurts and starts to swell. It really burns. He tears up.

"It's better not to rub it."

"Right, and I know it's the wrong thing to do, but how can I not?"

A single movement is enough to bring the girl into the seat beside him and his face into her very soft, very sweet-smelling, very clean hands. "Let me see to it, I'll have it out in a flash." Afterward she advises him to close his eyes for a minute, "while I count to two hundred."

"No, it's better if I do. Women can't count." The young, formerly timid poet takes her two small hands into his left hand. Using the index finger of his right hand, he begins to count. His eye has stopped bothering him, but he keeps it closed all the same, submissive. The timid young poet's index finger moves more and more slowly from each of her small, graceful, pink fingers to the next. They are any couple in love. The train starts to move again.

"Oh, no, look! We've passed your stop! You were going to the 185."

And he realizes they're leaving the station where he should have gotten off the train. Suddenly he knows all is well: that's not where he should have gotten off.

"Do you know how I redeem myself when I break the rules of the game?" He has noticed an adorable playfulness in this clever girl's provocative dimples. And she smells very good.

"No, tell me then. How?"

"It's all the rage. Like this."

The black laundress now riding in the seat facing the young lovers, smiles at them. He has just kissed the surprised girl on the mouth. *Yes, a triumph of instinct. The dark gods rule.*

And he kisses her again and, her natural shyness overcome, she kisses him back.

They kiss a long time.

"What are you doing . . . or, do you do now?"

". . . What does that mean, what am I doing, or, do I do now?"

"Oh. I meant to say, are you studying somewhere? Do you work?"

"Recently I've had to give up my studies. But, when I am again able to, in the future, I'll return to school, I'm thinking of becoming a TV cameraman."

"That's wonderful. You'll make a lot of money. So you work somewhere now?"

"I do. I have to take care of my mom. She's a widow. Still young, though, and it would be good for her to get married again. Don't you think a woman barely forty-five years old is wasting her life as a widow?

"I do. I'd love to meet your mama."

Whoa, one thing at a time, my still-a-bit-timid young poet! One thing at a time. But you know that giving him this advice at the moment is a waste of time. And he has already renounced poetry, and his shyness, well, he proposes to conquer it forever. *He's young.* And he really likes this girl. She's so happy, so sincere; she's what people consider someone very good to be with. What's more, he has just resolved to immediately change his course of study and his school. For some time now, he has secretly wanted to get into the world of television, which he hears so much about at the publicity agency where he works. And, now that he's acquired some self-confidence, it looks to him like a done deal: he sees himself rising in the company. Director's Assistant, Television Section. Section Head, Television Division. Assistant Supervisor, Corporate. Second Vice President. First Vice President. *And then?* Anything is possible.

There can be no doubt about it. It is Louise J. Bird's destiny to be constantly betrayed by her lovers and her friends. It would be interesting to ascertain precisely what motivates them to abandon their neurotic patroness, such a sure source of income, if, as people usually put it, you know how to get away with things. Some of them leave her just because of their annoyance with the little old multimillionaire's physical ugliness. Others, because of the unfairness of it all: a less deserving inheritor of wealth than Louise is inconceivable; she was only able to get hers thanks to the empire of J. Bird Bank and the imbalance of powers that exists between it and this broken-down, frequently malicious old scarecrow. But most of her people abandon her out of sheer envy: they covet the magnificent specimens that this eyesore of a woman demands to have around her in exchange for the prestige temporarily bestowed on them by her palace and immense fortune. Such is now the case with Celia and a certain plump, tasty morsel endowed with an air of innocence that seems as innocent as her name—although Agnes herself is actually no fool (as in due time Louise J. Bird, after a police investigation, will have to find out in a truly spectacular and painful way).

But sometimes these motives all work together. It is then that Louise must put up with the most awful kind of betrayals: the unforeseen ones! For example, Patrick's seduction—or brutal rape, in Louise's opinion—of her blond virgin, the girl with the looks of a delicate ephebus. Louise calls her the Page. "But, and it's so obvious," Louise says to herself now, always with a catch in her throat when she thinks of her Page—she completely missed the signs of the girl's, at the time, latent hermaphroditism. But why did *Patrick* steal the Page? In order to make Louise suffer, of course, to show her—"and how vulgar he is!"—that not everything can be bought with her millions. So he decided to *souiller la petite* and then splash Louise with their barnyard filth, since he could no longer have either his rents or his paintings or make himself out to be—and to what end?—her greatest treasure. He abducted the Page, perhaps even resorted to *drugging* her first, yes, well of course, what doubt can there be, he had to first *drug* her most valuable treasure. (Of course, Mrs. J. Bird would not have used such a hokey tone to relate all this, and that may actually explain for the reader the eternal discord—melodramatic as it can be and straight out of the soap-opera handbook—which exists between her and her descendant.)

But, in another way, what happened was very simple and boils down to this: the Page and her cunning little face, lightly freckled and framed by the most childlike, naughty locks of golden hair and a decidedly medieval little bang. How could any sensible person have the courage to renounce the spectacle that that bang will present at the moment of orgasm, if only seeing it is already such a supreme delight? The Page—and please don't shake my quill and dare me to call things by their names now—had become enthusiastic about the possibility of being enjoyed sodomitically. An insinuating remark of Patrick's, perhaps out of sheer bravado, had set her imagination into frenetic motion that only stopped whirling madly when, a few months later, she got fed up and they left on the quiet—all made possible by Patrick's savings, garnered mainly from the quick sale of some of his canvases (in which, let it be said in passing, as always happens and always will, the principal beneficiary turned out to be Monsieur Feldstein, the well-known art dealer). This gave them more than enough money to install a bargain-basement household in the Etruscan village of Volterra, Italy, so they set themselves up immediately in a cottage of their own that was fit for a moderately strong-backed farm worker. Patrick's ambition was to complete his education as an artist in Italy by carrying out archeological investigations on the same soil—*vide* D.H. Lawrence—upon which, so long ago, there lived a people so pure, healthy, and sexy that their scenes of fellatio seemed to be good even for the sarcophaguses.

Patrick's art education, however, has remained forever incomplete. The shovel and hoe he initially acquired with some urgency to begin his work on the land became relics of one of his many great frustrations. As unsullied as the day they left the factory, they just stood there against a wall of their miserable shack, which he insisted on calling his atelier. It's true that the Page was the cook in the dilapidated barn they lived in on that land that the hand of God had long ago let go of (and, honestly, their meals weren't all that good either, which the Page continuously blamed on the total lack of good culinary materials, like peanut butter and maple syrup). But it's equally true that the principal weight of the domestic chores fell on Patrick's shoulders. He even had to learn to carry on his head, from a fountain that was situated more than a half mile away, the immense jug of water that the Page diabolically always consumed in diabolically record time. It was really something to see Patrick climbing up the road to the old barn, exhausted, dusty, sweaty—Patrick, once the most exquisite painter in Megalopolis—with a pack of grubby little kids at his heels, mocking him, their shrill voices singing out: "*Guarda la donna!* He is such a nice girl!" And worse. The children became more and more aggressive, even started throwing stones at him, because the Page, although she did not applaud them, egged them on. She would appear at the window whenever she heard the uproar outside and, laughing loudly at her lover's pitiful appearance, sometimes even mimicking him, she actively participated in the children's fun and games. How much desire to do archeology could he have left after that! In addition, and worst of all, however anomalous their existence together may have been, the experience of sharing his life with a woman—if that is how the Page, as such, classified herself—had the effect of freeing certain atavistic traits of masculinity that began to appear in Patrick. "We will end up like run-of-the-mill married people, one man, one woman," she had told him shortly before they abandoned the Santa Vitalina farm in Volterra. Later, his run-ins with the noisy kids almost forgotten, it seemed to Patrick that he had spent the best days of his life there, in spite of the feelings of jealousy that disturbed him more often every day. Eventually, as soon as he came in from doing chores, if he found the Page chatting with anyone, man, woman, other, young, old, child, his jealousy would flare up. Patrick had begun to believe he was on the verge of turning into an almost normal man. He started making plans for the future. But he hadn't counted on the Page's temperament, her mockery to the point of harsh cruelty (those photos she got it into her head to send to Louise!) and her capriciousness to the absolute limits of arbitrariness that would always be characteristic of the Page. So, filled with nostalgia for what he was leaving behind, already possibly sensing the worst, Patrick had no alternative but to leave for Naples with her.

There the definitive separation occurred.

"*La signorina è andata via* and she won't be coming back. But, she said, she will write to you right away. It was urgently necessary that she leave. She said for you to excuse her."

It was the concierge of the Neapolitan boardinghouse, who, with a very sad face, transmitted the Page's goodbye to Patrick. The latter, at the moment, was bringing her a book he had just bought for her. It's true, he paid a mere handful of liras for it, but she was always so interested in the literature of Spain and would doubtlessly have appreciated it for its full symbolic and commercial value, even down to the detail of his feeling that he had swindled the bookseller in the bargain. It was the first printed edition of the *Vida del pícaro Guzmán de Alfarache, criado del Rey Felipe III, Nuestro Señor, y natural vecino de Sevilla,* that is to say, Mateo Alemán's masterpiece, which she had mentioned so often. Once, in fact, less than three years before, when she was still at Mount Holyoke, she even planned to specialize in the picaresque novel and go to Spain with a scholarship to study it. All that had been before the Page fell under the corrupting influence of Louise J. Bird.

Melodramatically, the way almost all lovers do, Patrick could never accept the version of events that the Page told him, detailing with her usual self-confidence her seduction of the multimillionaire. Instead, seeing only destructive force in the old bird, he went more and more deeply into debt, always feeling called upon to try and rescue an innocent from Louise's influence. And now just think of it! Not only did his Santa Vitalina projects, all of them without exception, come to nothing, but where would the Page wind up? She would surely never return to her studies. The poor little thing must now feel completely lost, while he has in his possession the symbol, the instrument of her salvation: the picaro's hazardous life full of turmoil, bad smells, and brutalities; of energies dissipated for no reason at all. Just like the market earlier that day, where, beside a seafood vendor's stall, he had been rummaging through a box overflowing with insignificant books—devotionals and theological treatises spongy with grime, textbooks missing an average of half their pages—and suddenly there appeared the worn but, by some miracle, complete books of this novel.

And they soon turned into his constant companions, the most effective palliative of his long, unproductive wait for some sign of life from the Page. Naturally, no sooner did she board the boat that would take her to Marseilles than she forgot about the promise to write him contained in the message she had asked the concierge of the boardinghouse to deliver to him. Perhaps she had also already forgotten the existence of Patrick. He, meanwhile, lived *à bout de souffle,* his savings depleted, as he followed the adventures of Guzmán de Alfarache across the Catholic Sovereign's dominions, needing to escape his own increasingly desperate hope that his Page would deign to give him some sign of life.

That sign never arrived. Nevertheless, the books have brought him luck and, though he has now arrived at his worst moments in terms of finances, it's good that he has kept them permanently with him since Naples, holding onto them despite his full awareness that these volumes could get him more than a pretty penny in a first-rate specialized bookstore.

For many days, at first, he would sit reading them in the *trattoria* that he and the Page had discovered and which had become his regular restaurant. Then one night, after finishing his spaghetti à la marinara, he was trying to distract his thirst for another *bicchiere di rosso,* which his flat pocketbook would not authorize him to order, and he sat reading a few more pages of the *Guzmán.* He suddenly felt himself being observed and looked up. That night he would not ascertain what happened to Guzmán in Madrid after he was detained in his rooms and accused by a constable of committing "criminal conversation" with a teenaged girl. It was the first time Patrick set eyes on the refined, dark, and imposing figure of O Jango. To tell the truth, for all the grief that the Brazilian subsequently brought him, including his present destitution and dejection, their meeting was a piece of unimpeachable good luck for Patrick. O Jango brought back to life in him his upright hardness of an interested man, his hunger for worldly success, his need for luxurious things. That the business at hand that night eventually turned out badly was yet another story. But those volumes, whose covers he has never attempted to restore, have constituted his lucky charm.

Tonight, having decided to crash O Jango's party, he's ready for whatever might come his way. Whether or not it be the reconciliation he secretly longs for, or a fantastic scandal he perhaps does not long for any less, his spirit feels pacified. Yet he's perfectly aware that his nerves could still betray him at the party or even before he ever gets there.

In order to fortify himself against adversity and gather his self-assurance, he decides that a few pages of the pícaro's fabulous and truthful story would do him a great deal of good, for in the protagonist—although he hasn't yet told himself this—he's beginning to see himself. Soon he's lost in the story. This does begin to calm him down, and as the tensions he's feeling begin to lessen, his overcharged mind relaxes. Letters begin to dance before his eyes; the words he's scrutinizing create the most astonishing associations in his thoughts. And he's soon asleep.

Patrick sleeps deeply, while, in her secret hideout, Louise, having recuperated a little from her earlier crises, is now searching one drawer after another for those terrible photographs that arrived one day by airmail from Italy.

It had been the Page's idea, of course, but Louise J. Bird won't accept the possibility of such evil in her little darling. For her, the guilty one would always be Patrick. He was the insolent upstart who obviously envied her fortune and illustrious lineage. (It is illustrious, to be sure, although, as the reader will now be told, the first J. Bird, whose name sums it all up, was a bad egg, historically speaking, a *jail*bird.) Patrick seized some power over the girl—who knows what wiles he used, but undoubtedly involving drugs. But Louise does not want to even think about his dirty tricks. "He did it all just *pour souiller sa jeunesse aimable.*" (But why, it must be asked, does French, which is not her native language, always invade Louise's thinking at this point in the story?) Ah! Finally. Yes. Here are the smutty pictures. On the back of one, in clear, intentional, school-girl script, the Page had written: *"Nous faisons des cochonneries en nous souvenant de vous."* The grammar may be imperfect but Patrick's perfidious intention and the meaning are clear: "We do nasty things and remember you." There was no room for doubt, he forced her. "Maybe even had to torture her!" (As she thinks this, although she wouldn't want to confess it to herself, a rare voluptuousness takes hold of Louise.) "Yes, the Page was forced to write that dirty caption, which is filthier even than the photos of her and Patrick wallowing on each other, or of the girl flattened under the weight of her corruptor while he penetrated her, the filthy sodomite—what doubt about it could there possibly be?—through *la voie defendue.*"

Patrick had not wanted to set the camera for delayed shots and take those photos. But the Page's threats yielded results: it was always better to please her by going along with her quirky whims. The aftermath of a little girl's childishness when she has found a fun new toy, isn't, after all, as serious as facing the consequences that would result from his obstinate "no." ("First of all, the child will run away then and there, for good.") And that is why Louise J. Bird, armed with a magnifying glass, her fury barely contained, is now examining Patrick's face, turned forever, idiotically toward the lens of a camera that soon would wind up somewhere in Madrid's famous flea market. She sees in Patrick's forever idiotic face in the photograph that his bulging eyes bulge more stupidly than usual, are even more bulging, malicious, and myopic than Louise has ever seen them on the man's face of flesh and blood.

Louise now doggedly peruses another photo until her jaws crackle and hurt. In it the Page appears on her knees in front of that wretched Patrick's naked body, her petite, not quite nubile breasts plastered against his knees. She's engaged in the task that Egyptian mythology reserves, with adoration, for Isis. Oh, if only she, Louise, could have been in the Page's place at that moment! She would have joyfully clenched harder and harder until he was horribly mutilated. In the meantime, she has just damaged a molar that has a cavity (*oh my, Louise, don't forget to make yourself a dentist appointment*) by grinding her teeth too long and extremely hard. She starts singing to save herself from the new horror that she faces:

In a cavern, in a canyon,
Excavating for a mine . . .

Vaguely, beginning very far away from the sidewalk of
this squalid neighborhood where Laura stands looking up at
a three-story building that to her, without a doubt, given her
age, would be a historic relic if it weren't for the unimpressive
flatness of its aspect—that is to say: very, very vaguely, through
a recent, thick fog of time, there come to Laura the imprecise
echoes of the wittiest of phrases, as she continues to stare dully,
with unwitting impertinence, at the window that the bug-eyed
guy has just brusquely closed. She begins to make out in the
dimness—her memory fails her regularly when it's about lived
experiences and not printed words—a cautiously luxurious
ambience and a person who is speaking even more cautiously.
Nonetheless, she senses, yes, he's an acquaintance and it's her
duty to greet him.

"I wonder if he thought I was spying on him just now. Oh,
I'm always a big *dummy*," she tells herself. "Mama is so right,
she criticizes me for that. Why can't I learn? Without meaning
to, I've just come across in an incredibly bad light to someone
who could turn out to be important." In her mind, a certain
luster can't help but associate itself with the man's head, which
Laura has seen for perhaps less than a second.

Patrick O'Dont, on the other hand, recognizes her instantly.
She was the girl with the Latin aristocrat. "He was so obnoxious
but so good-looking. Yes, she was that stupid girl who talked
constantly about her important last name and kept mentioning
the grand Megalopolitan families." It seems to Patrick that she
was *trying* not to remember him just now. "Of course not, she
is Miss Van Boren." With a last name like hers, what a career
he could have had. "O Jango . . . yes, it was in O Jango's first
apartment here, that's where I met her, two years ago, before he

had completely finished moving into his penthouse. For sure, he wouldn't have dared throw me in a corner back then! Oh yes, her and her good-looking Latin—those athletic, handsome *tapettes* are the most vicious ones of all, you can see I'm right: veritable queens. Oh yes, I'm certain they'll be invited to the party tonight."

But with a name like Patrick's: just the name's commonness alone . . . ! "Oh, poor Mama. After all, in her way she used to be good. Almost a lady. And I take after her, not after that animal who never knew how to get us any money."

Patrick wants to consider himself from someone else's perspective. His favorite game, especially lately, since he has been living in poverty, consists of tearing himself down as painfully as possible, in absolutely merciless, blistering self-criticism. He in fact already has plenty of wounds from this entertainment. O'Dont, his unbelievable surname, isn't even Irish! It was probably made up as a nickname to mock the moralistic narrowness of some grandfather, great-grandfather, or great-great-grandfather of his.

"What difference does it make anyway: they all surely worked on the docks or in ship holds and none of them had enough of anything to even leave their descendants photos. Or daguerrotypes, if they lived that long ago. And what good would photos do me! They'd only show me what I'm sure were all just coarse faces, swollen up and puffy from drinking rotgut. Truthfully, what could a real last name get me at this point? But, considering everything, the hypothesis I've come up with about the origin of the surname O'Dont does not lack for cleverness."

Oh, if he only had O Jango to explain a thing or two about names to him. Still, for Patrick this isn't a mere hypothesis. It's a given, especially because his family name helps him feel mortified.

"Anyway, my last name doesn't have a real meaning and, if I could, I wouldn't have one at all. And the terrible thing is that now I think they've discovered where I give refuge to my humiliation. I'm sure that little bitch won't hesitate to spread the story of where I live now, here with the bums of Megalopolis, and then O Jango will not delay his launch of the biting commentaries I know he's capable of. How well I know him! 'Well, he's finally among his own.' I'm sure that's what he'll say.

"Still, I can explain all of it. But what good would that do you, you idiot! Why did you close the window so fast? It's precisely because you're ashamed. You're nothing but a *wimp*. But if I say it's a rakish hideaway, *un pied à terre* . . . *canaille*, to which I retreat sometimes, isn't that something a strong artistic temperament would do? When I feel, the, the, *la nostalgie de la boue*? And miss the filthy masses, the mud? I dare anyone to attack that alibi, so that bitch can just go to hell with all her money-grubbing forebears, those, those . . . *usurers*! Yes, but O Jango *knows*! I know he knows that I've been practically penniless since I left him. But did *I* leave *him*? You better sharpen up, Patrick O', don't stretch the truth so much. Say it, say *he* left *you*. OK! He threw me into the incinerator along with my art, but he still wants everyone to believe he's the big patron of the arts: Mr. Mecenas! He just loves to hear his adulation as the Protector of artists here, Defender of artists there. And he threw *me* in the incinerator! Why? Because I'm not into promiscuity. And today I was just standing there at my window, had before my eyes, not this miserable landscape, no, I was escaping the poverty of this slum. I was looking at the whole beach of Maracas in front of the Hotel Prince of Wales, where I was staying again, but liberated from O Jango's tyranny and not committing a single faux pas, I was the aristocratic millionaire artist that I should have been!"

And Patrick will submerge himself happily in that daydream again, until, suddenly thinking "false steps," he remembers the image of Laura Van Boren standing down there, spying on him, sent by O Jango and maybe spurred on by that athlete . . .

". . . who without a doubt is a *tapette*—and he and that other Latin American guy must already be lovers, oh, those nouveau riche show-offs understand each other so well."

But another major faux pas of his was even worse than this last one. It also happened in front of Laura, in fact, precisely because of her. Laura Van Boren, who was just back from Paris, didn't spare him that humiliating information, while he hadn't been to Europe in fifteen years! So, moved by vanity, he was trying to show that he was "with it," *bien à la page*. He had used the word *partouze* and realized that the idiot girl wasn't giving a single sign that she understood what he was trying to say to her. "Not one sign of comprehension! Slang changes so much in such a short time." He knew at once that he must have committed a serious faux pas, but he could do nothing except forge ahead with it. "And then O Jango wiped me from his memory."

For two weeks now, from the moment he heard by chance from someone in a bar in the Village that his ex friend was getting ready to leave the country and would be having a Mastodon of a farewell party, Patrick has deluded himself with the possibility of a last-minute reconciliation. Something along the lines of a discrete R.S.V.P. Oh, with what fervor he would have responded; but projecting a certain appearance of coolness: "I know how he is, don't I? It wouldn't be the thing, especially with O Jango, to surrender completely, in any *improv* move. O Jango specializes in inflicting his cruelty on those who show their enthusiasm.

"But I used to be such a joker. And now everyone jokes about *me*. I ask for one small grant and here come the letters, actually the same one, over and over: 'We regret to inform you that . . . The Board of Trustees does not consider it . . .' 'The Governing Board judges it inopportune now to . . .' 'As you will understand, we must follow the new economic strategy that . . .' 'We hope that next year . . .' Always, always exactly the same thing! Meanwhile dozens of those thick-haired kids who imitate male magazine accessory models prosper, in Paris, Rome, London, Madrid. Madrid! That flamenco dancer!"

Patrick's curriculum vitae has been angrily ripped apart. It lies scattered all over the grimy wood floor. But didn't someone always polish that floor before? It is, after all, somewhat comforting to think that, a hundred years ago, this was a chic barrio. "There were boys around, barely out of high school then, and think of that poor old Romanian Jew, Jules Pascin. I got to meet him. And I met Zadkine too—hey, I think he's even still alive! I used to imitate his gouaches and earn a lot of money. But I had no idea how to save any of it. Poor Mama always fussed at me about that. Back then, individual expositions to the nth degree. But for more than half a decade now I haven't been able even to get a *marchand,* the kind of agent I deserve. What, Monsieur Feldstein? No, no, don't even think about *him.* He uses the excuse that artists are squanderers and keeps everything for himself. 'Your things don't spark an interest now, maybe it's the times, but what can we do if one doesn't catch people's attention? Wait a little while.' 'I don't think that is serious art, either, of course, why, just look at it, it's Batman! But it's pleasing, people like it, it's the latest thing.' 'No, you have to wait . . . ' That's all apparently easy to say to someone, but what do I live on in the meantime? Patrick O', I dare you to look at the fact that you're getting old! Oh, that is not really true. I *feel* young. Besides I still *am* very young. Only forty-eight."

Patrick O'Dont lies to himself shamelessly. ("You took six years off your age years ago, Patrick.") *How you magnify it!* Of course Patrick has learned each line of praise by heart, underlining it in red to make things easy for grant committees. Now on the floor is also the residue of reviews torn from national and foreign publications, saved by him for decades as treasures, now in shreds, however well they are preserved in his memory.

"'A perverse knowledge of line that denotes the evidently exquisite influence of Aubrey Beardsley. In his gouaches women's flesh becomes, we could say, an ethereal principle of Evil.'"

There it is, that old puerile Manicheanism in you! You remember it, don't you, Patrick? Back then, Woman was Evil and Man represented Goodness. How much you've learned since then! In the entire universe now, there is only evil. "'Like Bérard, he is a *petit maître* of elegance. Decorative art? Certainly it is. But he does not lack, in his own way, a certain psychological depth when it concerns the portraits of celebrities and prominent social figures of the time.'" No, it wouldn't be possible for you to remember that critic's whole, long paragraph; certainly not with the same detail with which you've remembered other reviews. And it did have in it something of what you remember. But you shouldn't trust your embellishments. Yes, there is a reference to Bébé Bérard, and it's not hard to resurrect the way it swelled your pride at the moment. Just think of it: you, a poor boy from Megalopolis compared to no less than the very sensitive and French Bébé.

"But who remembers Bérard in today's world? Perhaps a few old relics committed or housed near Chaillot. And think of it. Why doesn't Megalopolis have its own sacred ground, after all, even for its social fossils?" (*But be careful, Patrick O'Dont. Talking this way, you're almost on the verge of bitterness.*) "Bitterness! Me? No way. Haven't I had my moments, my own small share of triumphs?" (*Will his inflated sense of pride again prevent his seeing himself as bitter, despite the hate oozing from his every pore?*) "Not bitter at all! No, this time I'm going to demonstrate beyond a shadow of a doubt that I have some real virtues. I'll go to O Jango's party, then, and say I've been invited and have overcome my pride. (Which has been damaged by his *ingratitude*.)"

And Patrick applauds his emerging decision with a tremendous kick to O Jango's portrait. It's the only piece of his own work that he has saved. Of course it is in fairly poor shape: it's from his "Bébé Bérard period." But the canvas, leaning against a wall, doesn't rip. Only a few muddy smears stick to it. (In the judgment of more than one critic, this possibly improves it significantly.)

Meanwhile his aggressor foot starts to hurt. He thinks, with great alarm, that it might swell up and keep him from attending the party, something he has now definitively decided to do. He begins to berate his friend, then breaks into the most blush-inducing string of insults imaginable: "You faggot *fairy* nobody!" is the least abusive thing he says.

At the time Patrick was painting his full-body portrait of O Jango, our artist gave his subject yellowish skin ("you dirty-macaque-low-yellow of a fierce Brazilian primitive!") and virile features that he flatteringly exalted ("mere enhancement of your fakery, you little princess of my dreams!"). Contemplating the portrait now, he's tempted by the possibility of carrying out a voodoo operation on the effigy. Should he castrate it? "But what for, if 'it' hasn't stood up for such a long time anyway? Better to paralyze him!" Yes, that is what he will do. He wants to see him in a wheelchair at the mercy of caretakers who swindle him, humiliate him, and mistreat him, to put it in plain language. "Yes! Let him have an accident and lose his left leg!"

Patrick looks for a sharp instrument: knife, scissors, letter opener, anything he can find with which to perform his magic operation of terrible revenge. The kick he delivered to the portrait a moment ago has given him a limp that shows up as he searches and he suddenly realizes that his tantrum has been providential and forgets about his projected, iconoclastic surgery. He still has a beautiful ebony walking stick with a gold handle, an accessory he bought in London one time, in those remote days of the high life. He has never wanted to sell it or even hock it. Why *has* he never wanted to get rid of it? (The Freudian answer is obvious.) (*Too obvious.*)

With his walking stick, his foot wrapped in a large bandage that he now puts on himself, he will show up at O Jango's party tonight limping like a Dien Bien Phu hero and, when he, a proud invalid, bursts in, that emotional macaque of a Brazilian will shed tears and good times will return. His fasts of the last few months have also given him back the youthful slenderness he had when O Jango first met him—"and this is bad of me to say, because it's out of vanity, but he *instantly* fell in love with me that night at the trattoria in Naples!" His waist is again as slim and flexible as a sylph's and his charisma, his swaying allure, will overpower the Brazilian's will power. Patrick O'Dont now casts a melancholy look at O Jango's image and sees it is ruined. But he thinks he will have more than enough time later to restore it in the tranquility of O Jango's *fazenda*, which will be staffed by lots of obsequious little black Brazilians.

Laura has just finished her walk. Still ruminating on her dilemmas with the slow pace of a genuine ruminator, she now finds herself in the part of the city with all the art galleries. Suddenly, as she stands before a Monet canvas exhibited in the outside window of Galería Gris, the light shifts, and she sees before her eyes, enacted with absolute clarity, the exact moment two hours ago, when she was still wandering in one of the city's most run-down neighborhoods, and she remembers the correct name and surname of the boy she glimpsed through the window he slammed shut.

"Yes, a sensitive painter your Monsieur Monet, but useless when it comes to the human figure," she hears someone say. And she sees Patrick again.

"Of course, it was Patrick! Patrick O'Dont, the painter. The one who made that splendid portrait of Mama when I was still a little girl. It was *his* face I saw looking out of that window for a second or two." An exquisite painter, Patrick O'Dont, whose relations with O Jango she remembers hearing very dirty, unbelievable rumors about.

"But people are so wicked!"

("Yes, O'Dont, O'Don't, the painter. *So suggestively polite!*")

And to think that such a refined artist could be so understanding with her when she saw him that time at O Jango's. "I was with Horacio and Horacio liked him so much."

Instantly Laura Van Boren makes a decision that will be definitive: she will go to the party. Surely he will be there. And how else is she going to find him? She will have herself painted—"it will be like I'm as important as Mama ('imagine *that*, dear!')"—and she will have her own portrait and, instead of a letter, she will send Horacio a great artist's image of her. "It will be for Horacio, who is so far away." But will the honorarium be too expensive? And how much will the freight turn out to cost? "It doesn't matter. I have a lot put away in savings and the money is there for just such occasions as this. Yes, the portrait, and a card with a really funny message, like maybe, 'When this you see, remember me.'"

Now, isn't this infinitely better than a long letter full of sobs?

"I used to think I was ashamed. But, more than anything, I was scared! The news in the letter I've just read has convinced me of that, and now I can see it. It's right here staring me in the face, and I believe it: I *know it* now. More than anything, I've been afraid; of what I am, and when I've yielded to it, I've been overcome by my own success.

"And now. They have finally torn the house down and they are going to open the avenue they've been threatening to complete since I was a girl. Back then, when I first heard about the project, I must have been twelve or thirteen, and my father was still alive. He told us the house would gain in value, so he was going to make every sacrifice to buy it outright. But a few months later a stupid accident ended all that. We had to keep renting and Mama opened it as a boardinghouse. I . . . I had had so many illusions. We used to go riding in Papa's beat-up car—the same one that cost him his life. It still hurts me to hear the name Ford. I always think that whoever says it does it to hurt me and I see Papa, all bloody again, and hear him talking to us with so much conviction: 'it's nothing, don't be upset, because this is nothing.' We were out for a ride in that beat-up old Ford, I must have been thirteen, yes I was thirteen, thirteen years old and ever since I've been superstitious. So now it's the thirteenth of the month and that's *two* thirteens! But that day we could smell the rich dirt of the fields beside the road and I imagined that Papa was sitting beside me on the back seat and we were coming back from a picnic riding in a shiny black car, a very fancy car with a closed-in top like the one I saw Joan Crawford in in her latest movie. Because she was the great actress of the moment. And I imagined my brother up in the front, at the steering wheel, wearing a chauffeur's uniform, beside my mother, and she had on a uniform too, she could be my and Papa's footman.

"'Idiot,' my brother would call me when I'd tell one of my family fantasies: 'there's no such thing as foot*women*.' Oh? Well, just to please one old cretin of a woman, I put on a uniform sometimes. But, if he saw me in it, in his illiterate ignorance, he'd probably think I just dressed up like that to go to a masquerade, though his life as a stupid clerk can't possibly have given him any idea of what a masquerade is. And anyway, if he knew, he'd probably just call it 'a Carnival dance.' And it *was* February, almost time for Carnival, and the patio flowerpots had filled up with pretty dahlias, but there I was, all dressed in black, all black, and me so white and pink. What a shame. They never do smell sweet, and in February Mama had to take the first boarders in but why did she take his side? 'Leave him alone, he's having fun, he's still a kid,' Mama always took his side but I wanted him to stop playing that toy trumpet because we were in mourning. 'I'm never going to understand this girl,' she would say and scold me, she was always scolding me, then Poor Auntie Bianca came, loaded down with kids and that lame midget, who always puffed himself up, claiming that back in his country, full of Indians, he belonged to an old aristocratic family, but 'what kind of aristocrats are those,' I'd ask Aunt

Bianca, and she would just smile sadly, 'don't you realize he's nothing but a pretentious half-breed?' And Mama, 'this girl is crazy, and what can you do with crazy people, nothing, just go along with them wherever they take you.'

"But I did love my little cousins, those poor, ill-mannered little things. Only when Kiki appeared did I start to feel different from them. Whenever they visited, and they were almost always visiting us, they would make a lot of racket, but pretty soon Kiki started coming in, all loaded down with books, and I'd order them to be quiet because they were always drowning Kiki's voice out, and they didn't always obey, but all that time, to let me practice English, he'd be reading me some verses by Eliot, 'nobody not even the rain has such small hands,' no, wait, that's not Eliot, no, but he was always reciting something for me, and my little cousins would get louder and louder and sing crazy songs like I will give you, I will give you, niña hermosa, una cosa . . . que yo solo sé . . . empieza con c: café! And, who knows, but I never had the courage to ask Kiki if he thought they meant anything by it, the naive little things, but you had to recognize that there really was something sneaky in the way they sang the words, how could I forget, I will give you, give you, pretty girl, I will give you something, Something, something that only I know, it begins with *o*, but they were just kids, little *pibes*.

"Oh, that's really strange, it's been such a long time since I've heard that word and now it sounds wrong. But *pibes!* Mama always used to call to us, *pibes*, and so did that guy, the one who at first seemed to be so good and one night grabbed me by the arm, '*che, pibita*, don't you like to have a little fun?' and Mama had to intervene, she told him 'move out of this house this instant;' and then me, just a poor kid out there on the huge patio with the bare walls, terrified, I had to force myself to keep from crying, and then I discovered a wonderful word because I saw a firefly on a fern, but it is sad that dahlias never smell as sweet as roses and then Mama came to the patio door, accusing me, she said 'you're laughing, you ungrateful thing!' and slapped me in the face so hard I fell to the ground, 'just look at the major client you've caused me to lose;' but I was just a scared *pibita* still in mourning for Papa, and oh if he were only still alive. But I'm going to study a lot, really hard, and become outstanding, I will be somebody despite Mama accusing me of going around stirring up the pensioners, and how could *I* help it anyway? My legs were very pretty! And they're still so pretty, aren't they, just ask Louise, and look how much Kiki used to adore them, because what won his heart was my legs more than my face.

"Which wasn't, still isn't half bad either. Some girls even say I look like Audrey Hepburn, but back then no Audrey Hepburn had ever appeared in the movies, and instead Kiki would start reading even louder and it was all: 'we are the hollow men'— *una cosa que empieza con o*—'we are the stuffed men'— ¡*olé*!— and the chorus soon was deafening and then more howls and laughter from *los pibes*, oh they were so gross, but then I was on Kiki's lap one day but without my underwear because I'd just washed them and I didn't feel ashamed that his free hand was caressing my naked, softly endearing belly but because of those little voices and the guffaws that were coming from the other side of the door, because Mama had to go out and we were alone and locked the room from the inside and all those big, dark, gloomy things in the bedroom set were the only inheritance we had left from Papa who had worked so hard and in the end it was for nothing, and though I didn't completely like what Kiki was doing to me I knew that he wasn't doing it for a bad reason but couldn't help himself and I was now thinking that the hammock chair we were in might not hold the weight with both of us in it and could fall apart and we'd fall and so I asked him to let go of me so I could go and make the kids shut up but Kiki is always the egotist and held on to me and his hand felt like a strong pair of tongs on my small white and pink belly and I had to struggle to get up, me furious and as quiet as I was furious, because I'd realized that he had a hard thing like a flesh-and-blood spear and I was afraid that he was going to injure me, but with one jerk I got away and ran off and the poor little kids started crying because I said I would hurt them and then I ran back in and this time we sat on the bed and Kiki went on with his recitation and I knew that his hand was missing my small virgin belly, and oh I knew that I had, had, had to do whatever he wanted because everything depended on me conquering him . . . because if afterward he ever left me who could ever bring him to account for the daughter of a woman with a bad reputation who barely ran a second-class boardinghouse or maybe even third-class?

"It was a dump. And anyway. Yes, a derelict she could rent out, but me I was going to be a lady sitting beside Papa in the black car with the chauffeur and Mama the footman up front who looked so funny in her uniform, and I really hated that old ruin, but now I could cry for it because they've torn it down and it feels like they've torn down my childhood. But for all of it? Even Mama and her lover, the Russian who used to look at me and look at me and never dared touch me? But sometimes Mama would tell me to go to the movies and I knew why and at night it was so disgusting to be in the same room with them as if nothing had happened.

"And even Kiki, who was so elegant and arrogant and came to find me to see if I remembered the title of a book? And of course I did, it was a dictionary and it was in the bookstore where I started working. I was so afraid the glass door on the bookcase would break, me pulling it really hard when it got stuck and wouldn't open, and he helped me, smiling, such a well-mannered person from the best part of society who pinched my naked bottom and I had to put up with it if I wanted to get out of that dump we lived in because I couldn't even take a bath in peace, no, there were all those little holes they made with a drill to watch me and my shame, because I felt such shame in that shower, like I was being looked at by everybody, but it was Kiki who took my clothes off that day and started to kiss me on the forehead and his kisses went lower and lower what a scrumptious little Greek slave oh yes that's what I told myself I was and let him do what he wanted to because I wanted to get out of that slum that now I'm crying for just as if they had demolished my whole adolescence. And yes I undressed for him, already knew I had to do it after all the eyes in the walls of the bathroom, all those lookers had made me feel as if the shower water instead of washing me clean was making me dirtier and dirtier.

"Later I bragged to all my girlfriends about what a wonderful feeling it was to be free. Then I left them behind one after the other, until I got to the short little girl who was such a good girl, and I knew that Kiki looked at her with alarm, but what could I do? All right I was disgusted by him, yes; but it's only a matter of getting used to things, that's all, and so there was nothing in the world I would have gone out with her again for either, except that she so loved going with me to the movies and on the way home. I wonder if that movie theater still exists now, but I flew from all my whining, mostly grimy, always hungry, low-life, trashy people and Mama, Mama, Mommy she wanted us to call her, me always seeing her wearing footman's clothes and my little brother stuffed into his chauffeur uniform, and yes of course I hated him, but not at the beginning. I grew to hate him, I learned to hate him. But oh, what a pleasure not having to sleep next to Mama anymore so I took off my clothes for him as often as he wanted me to, but I could never give myself completely to him. But I was afraid, so afraid that he wouldn't get up the courage to gore me with his monstrous thing and one day I started to hate him because I realized that he only saw me as a cliché, not as me, and to him I was an entire dispossessed class, a poor, pretty girl, any pretty poor girl at all and, if that wasn't enough, a while later he started to talk to me as if it was really all about some third person in his period of social romanticism, when we went to the city of all pleasure.

"Because at that moment he seemed transparent to me and I knew he was leaving me night after night to go out with girlfriends with prostitutes yes with whores, Mommy was the one I always dressed up as a footman, 'I will give you something that starts with o,' that's when I started to denigrate him behind his back to *my* girlfriends and to Nick but I was able to do whatever I wanted and there was not one of my girlfriends who didn't hate him, so I was starting to really suffer deep down inside and I felt an enormous knot forming in me and about then he learned to get on his knees at my feet and I still believe that the thing I was enjoying most about that was his humiliating position because he was so vain and I wanted to keep him on his knees eternally because I was secretly always afraid of myself and that's why I slandered him behind his back and told everyone that he was crazy because to me he seemed crazy yes and how would I be able to stand it if he ever realized that I had started to detest him and yes to me he was crazy but he was different from me that was all.

"Or not. There is something else I know, oh yes, *nobody* can fool me, oh no, I know that secretly he can't stand me either, however much he pretends it's love. I maintain and will state publically if I have to, that, without knowing it, he despises me just like he despises all women. And there is more! What I honestly believe, of course, is that he's a repressed homosexual, but how well he knows how to hide it!

"So, courage, Celia: get out there and play your part."

She looks in the mirror and is finally satisfied with her makeup. She closes the lipstick and picks up the bottle of Arpège. She is sure she'll perform her part well at O Jango's and that Agnes will admire her more than ever. But she still has to talk to the old dimwit, because she has got "to make sure she won't show up and surprise us there." This will be simply a matter of provoking one of her nervous crises. Which, as will soon be seen, does not really cost Celia much at all.

Louise J. Bird, who has been purifying for almost ten minutes in the gentle sunlight pouring through the leadlight panes of a rustic window into a small interior attributed to Vermeer, once again feels herself dragged down by dark forces that have pursued her tenaciously for as long as she can remember. She shudders with disgust and terror because, this time, not even her guardian angel, the painter from Delft, has been able to counteract the powers of the abyss. On the contrary, the middle-class girl from the seventeenth century, who is also taking in the purifying sunlight, has quite contrarily initiated in Louise's mind, which is always on the edge of an unfathomable precipice, a chain of the most atrocious, horrifying associations.

Much earlier in Louise's life, her mother was one of the idols of what, at the time, constituted the *true* international high society. Those remote, good old days belonged to her mother, for it was before expressions like "jet set" were coined, when the august ghosts of Henry James and Marcel Proust still wandered about and the use of good manners was still cared for outside the bedroom. She was witty and elegant, even when stripped of her splendid clothes (as anyone could prove who had access to the nude of the multimillionaire model, Mrs. Bird, that, in emulation of the legendary Cayetana, the thirteenth Duchess of Alba, she had had Walter Sickert paint of her). Mrs. Bird sparkled with wit even in the exclusive company of women. In fact, her mother—and who could doubt it—was the exact opposite of that plump, bourgeois Dutch girl enjoying the eternal sunshine of Vermeer and keeping Louise company.

The two images, however, now conjoin in Louise's mind and for one horrifying moment, she sees her mother where the docile figure of the milkmaid should be. That is so typical of Mrs. Bird and that singular sense of humor of hers that Louise has always hated. Mrs. Bird was a Messalina and adored disguises. So now she stands bathed in sunlight in the very clean, softly colored Dutch den, her lovely face, nothing else, replacing the chubby cheeks of the original model. The new image sets Louise's vast room even more brightly aglow and a new grace—it could even be called an erotic grace—fills the tapestries that adorn the walls and even the black and white marble mosaics, once so relentlessly polished by industrious members of the middle-class in the colonial Megalopolis of Mrs. Bird's ancestors and also, inevitably, of Louise's. For, however well Louise can cover up her doubts about who her father had been, there is no doubt in her mind that her mother was the loose, multimillionaire parent who tried to emulate last century's Spanish duchess. Louise's face is a poor imitation, a really bad copy of the delicate features of the young Mrs. Bird's; but in it are recorded her origins, even if it's only a biological source. The resemblance can be discerned at the corners of her mouth, across her clear, high forehead, on her eyelids, and here and there in every ounce of her body. Besides that, would her mother have given her even the small amount of attention she gave her as a child, if she hadn't been her daughter?

How fervently Louise for years gave in to her fantasies, until well past adolescence. She imagined herself to be Mr. Bird's illegitimate daughter, adopted only reluctantly by his wife, who, by means of that adoption, succeeded in having her own constant infidelities (the *only* constant in Mrs. Bird) forgiven. The attentive, impartial observer will unquestionably see that there is also no doubt at all that Louise is the daughter of *Mr.* Bird, Cornelius J. Bird II, to be precise. Otherwise, what is the purpose of that "J." in front of the surname of every member of the family? Louise is always mindful of the false version of the story, undoubtedly spread by some less fortunate rival who had been ruined by the deft speculations of Bird Bank—which still bankrolls the founder's opulent dynasty. In that version, Mr. Bird was a knave and a scoundrel of the worst sort in his early days. A bastard son without a family name, he was known among the bad element, which was his milieu, by his nickname of "Jailbird;" but in time, as the founder's financial bloodline kept growing and endowing cultural foundations and hospitals, "Jailbird" turned into the singular but respectable surname, "J. Bird."

Nor has Louise J. Bird, the great, great granddaughter of the lofty crook, proved the identity of her bloodline wrong. She has the slight stammer that is legendary in her family, and has been for centuries; and she's only slightly taller than her father, who was even less corpulent than his. To tell the truth, her head, because of the resemblance to her mother, gives the impression of having been stolen from another woman, projecting itself as a typical J. Bird theft committed by a typical J. Bird body.

And Louise J. Bird had, in fact, cut her mother's head off. For a while afterward, they kept her incarcerated near Zurich—"so peaceful, so snowy, so many mandalas"—and the celebrated psychiatrist who treated her took advantage of his work with his patient to produce a stubbornly Jungian interpretation of a certain novel by Thomas Mann. The members of the Eranos Institut applauded a long time after his erudite lecture that year and it was decided to grant him the outstanding honor of a prominent place in the next *Jahrbuch*. But it's doubtful that Louise was ever cured of her macabre obsession. She is now sitting on, or rather has fallen down onto the floor and is babbling incoherent words. Does Celia bear any blame? At least it can be stated with confidence that in this little love nest there are never any servants to see Louise's crises. Only a handful, really a very few, at times probably not very happy, people are even aware of the existence of Louise's *pied-à-terre*, the preferred name for her secret place. For J. Bird Palace is still her official residence, at least in winter. There attend her the men of letters who want to publish in *Jaguar*, a sumptuous magazine that she finances and nominally directs. But, in fact, until she got irritated with Kiki because of Celia, *he* was her right-hand man and handled every aspect of running the magazine.

All this is present with her, clearly on different levels of Louise's psychological reality, as she continues to moan and cry, splayed out on the bare wooden floor. (Louise J. Bird would never condescend to putting Persian carpets or other fine accessories in this hideaway, which she wants to keep ascetic, however often, as a result of her kicking, she has more than once gotten splinters in her butt from the unpolished wood floor; and, one time, because of that, more bad luck, she got a prodigious abscess.) It cannot possibly be that Celia is the one to blame. "That poor girl just wants to help me grow stronger and that is why she brings up those things that I myself told her about at the beginning. That is the only reason she called me a little while ago, because she knew I was already extremely depressed last night and she had a premonition that it was going to happen again and only wanted to warn me about it. She herself has suffered so much. And maybe she lacks tact, but that's probably just her way of doing things: avoiding her own nervous crises by *anticipating* them.

A little earlier, Celia had indeed called Louise from her office at *La Fe* Publications to tell her that she had a crisis coming on. With precise, persuasive language Celia in fact predicted Louise's very crisis, and told her to defy her obsession with its elements: her beheaded mother, her escaped Page—"my beloved little woman! My slender little boy!"—and her brother, who is still breathing, but for whom the electroshocks have turned out to be as ineffective as the insulin shocks, and his paroxysms of anger were only stopped in Lisbon when they gave him a lobotomy. Since then the straightjacket is no longer part of his usual attire, but there is the fact that he's fallen into complete idiocy. "But she is cruel, cruel, though I forgive you, my dear girl, for reminding me of all that."

"And, above all, don't let yourself get beaten down by disgust and terror, my dear Louise. Remember the nightmare that that insensitive coward Patrick told you about? You must remember that he had that nightmare, not you."

A long time ago, yes, a really long time ago, because the Page was still hers then and only hers, that wretched man had told her an abominable dream he'd had the night before, after he called his mother on the telephone (she was in an old people's home, Patrick had been very careful to tell her). He was a little tiny boy, no bigger than a telephone, since he *was* a little telephone and, slowly, tiny step by tiny step, and filled with anxiety, he was moving forward and couldn't stop his little feet, which were taking him back into his mama's nurturing uterus. She was the young mama of his earliest infancy. But she was also Papa, frightening stinky Papa! So he smiled at her and kept licking himself while the uterus sucked him in. Horrified, Patrick woke up. He was beside himself with fear and had to energetically repress his feelings to keep from howling. And, afterward, Patrick, that cynic, managed to get himself under control, and, in the same way, later learned to go on living without The Page! The cynical bastard could get used to anything! ("He was like Kiki: a man, what a pig!")

But Louise has now made the nightmare hers again. (She collects obsessions like her grandparents collected artwork of unquestionable value.) She has made Patrick's nightmare more and more her own private property, above all, since Patrick, obviously out of pure perversity, took her little woman away from her. And the stingy man corrupted her boyish girl in the most repugnant ways. (Yes, yes, the Page later told her all about it, between sobs, in a dream). And while he was corrupting not only that sweet little thing with the blond bangs, but even the fragrance of thyme in her Etruscan bodice, he *enjoyed* destroying her. And poor, poor Louise, time and time again, has watched herself, with ever increasing horror, enter the sucking uterus of her very headless mother, while off to one side, sometimes in a chair, other times on the floor, the missing head would be smiling at her sarcastically.

As she vomits, Louise now forgives Celia again: "she's so pure, and I deserve this punishment for trying to fool her. I was unfaithful to her and just look at what it's gotten me. Without knowing it, she has punished me. No, how can I go to O Jango's party in this condition!"

"She's no longer a kid, our Little Missy Agnes. That she is learning. She got so nervous when I told her we would meet at the party! She believed Louise was going to discover our affair. But I'm going to teach that rich old bitch that she is no longer going to get everything she wants just by using her millions. She's undoubtedly up there right now, beating on the floor, kicking her feet, enjoying one of her hysterical attacks, or epileptic fits, who knows what they are, but she's lying on the floor, her hair a mess, vomiting all over herself, like I've seen her do so many times before. I'm sick of having to watch that, of being part of her disgusting shit! And what about all those times she wanted to feel macho and thought she was Don Juan! What that poor miserable bitch needs is to run into fifteen or so inches, that's what they say Orvieto has in his pants. Now, *that* is a great idea! Set them up and see what happens! My dear little Celia: don't forget this idea. It would be so funny to see what happens between that idiot and Orvieto. Yes, but what happens tonight, if, after my best efforts, that other little cretin shows up and starts going on all full of piss and vinegar about being Agnes's high school friend, feeling all justified for sticking to her the whole time, as if Agnes were her private property? Just one look at that impertinent scarecrow and you worry about catching all those pimples. No, the time has come, my wise little Celia, to take charge of things and devise some infallible system to get rid of that idiot too, forever. Now you have no choice. So don't be a wimp: get on with it. *Sois sage, mon enfant.*"

* * *

"It is *more* life than any other life, and, exactly for that reason, it's more problematic."

"But being, as you say, 'more problematic,' is it not, for that very reason, synonymous with '*less* life'?"

The old woman with the enormous head, who speaks by yelling, is the first thing that Barbara Dowd distinguishes in the smoky twilight of this large, crowded room. How is she ever going to find her Nick among all these people? It's clear that screaming his name will do her no good: who would be able to hear her voice in all this turbulence? If you want to run into your lover here, little Barbara, you'll have to make your way through the throng. It's obvious that this is going to require her to call up a lot of courage. This intimidatingly dense, screaming, smoking, wolfing mass of bad-mannered people will not suddenly yield automatically to her passage. ("We have to take into account that our girl finds herself among famous and unrecognized celebrities.") Compared to personages like these who are already so skilled at survival, who is she to start elbowing her way to the achievement of her objectives? (*We will soon see who.*) Her objectives, without a doubt, they must certainly already know. *Yes, our poor little Barbara still even believes that.*

She knows she must find Nick, her Nick, her gallant of gallants of the deliciously wise and knowingly treacherous caresses.

"...genius...but only scanty, perhaps very scanty genius..."

". . . then I said to you, I didn't ever want to have anything else to do with him . . ."

"...I think he's going to keep the grand finale a big surprise..."

". . . please, explain to me now what you meant in that note on Henry James . . ."

". . . so many parties to choose from, and you had to walk into this one?"

". . . so many people to choose from, and you had to walk over to me?"

". . . cannot explain it to you right this minute, but believe me . . ."

". . . Somebody told me that a man I met remembered conceiving an irremissible hatred of his father in earliest infancy, when he heard him fart for the first time."

The last speaker is a good-looking, baby-faced blond with eyelashes so long they could be false. But if our little heroine is lingering near him and has to put up with an anecdote so truly worthy of a coprophilic Sigmund Freud, it's because, inside the maelstrom in which she's slowly turning, she has suddenly come to a complete stop, paralyzed by a pain. It's a pain veined with feelings of indignation and enormous outrage. Fingers, undoubtedly very expert at inflicting the smallest of cruelties with the measured dexterity of a Swiss watchmaker assembling a Vacheron & Constantin chronometer, have pinched her, first on the left buttock, then on the right one. The good-looking blond guy observes her for a second, as if trying to place her in his memory, then immediately discards her and goes on telling the story of his acquaintance, who has recently committed suicide. Meanwhile, buttocks lacerated, our adorable little girl renews her search, and, at first slowly, very slowly, makes her way through the labyrinth, whose twists and turns are more and more confusing to her.

". . . Picasso! Possessed by the Devil! That's what I have to say to your great Picass— . . ."

". . . the greatest . . ."

". . . People don't know how to *give* any— . . ."

". . . we know how to receive, if suddenly someone knew how to give?"

". . . waited for you all morning, and for what? Because I'm a foolish woman! A fool, oh yes, a *fool.* I should have stopped believing you a long time ago . . ."

". . . an odd guy, a little stupid . . ."

". . . Hey, everyone, up here! This is where he keeps something dirty! . . ."

". . . How would a millionaire be able . . ."

Barbara Dowd is beginning to get used to the rules of the new game. While it is certain that a whole hand has just painstakingly made its way across the entire expanse of her bottom and that she has again stopped moving forward, this time she doesn't feel indignation. After the cruel pinches, she interprets this second action as almost a caress.

". . . and you're lying to me again! You always lie to me. I'm so tired of your empty promises! You never keep them!"

"No, I swear, darling! I swear to you: this isn't just another promise."

These two girls, dressed all in black, turn their lovely, perfumed heads angrily toward Barbara Dowd, who has no idea of what to do to excuse herself for having overheard them. ("But, really, they are not so much girls, and I've seen one of them recently. But where? A place . . .")

She Barbara Dowd immediately concentrates Barbara Dowd on her bold Barbara Dowd objective Barbara Dowd. And Celia, in a low but even more intense voice, goes on rebuking her little friend, who is on the verge of tears.

". . . How can a millionaire . . ."—this stentorian voice appears to come from very far away and, when it arrives, it already seems to be nearly drowning in the general din.

". . . this is his farewell . . ."

". . . and pay a little more attention. How could a millionaire . . ." But the remote, stentorian voice is squelched again.

"And where could this little country bumpkin of a girl have come from?" Kiki asks himself, even as he states, for the second time: "*Every* novel is a police story." He's still speaking to the old woman (*and her e-normous head*).

"Would it not perhaps be more accurate to say that every *life* is a police *novel?*" yells the old woman and finally notices the proximity of the girl, who, for her part, again finds herself beside the couple she saw when she first arrived and so realizes that she has covered the crowded hall from one end to the other crossing it from side to side.

But our Barbara Dowd does not lose heart. For how could our Barbara Dowd lose heart so quickly at this point, my friends? No, so many voices crowding together make her feel giddy, the dense smoke getting into her bronchial tubes tickles her throat, the worrisome air floating in the gas-enveloped room carries every little thing, and the bizarre smatterings of things she has been hearing are intertwining with the whole collection of her most recent experiences. All of this is absolutely novel to her practically brand-new conscience. This group of people and the strange new things that come with them have again made her feel the way she did that afternoon, the idyllic afternoon at the soda fountain counter. In short: the newness of it all has once again seduced her. (*Our little imp of a girl!*) She still doesn't suspect how often, in the future; how every day more and more, she will need to renew her stock of novelties. For the moment, a moderate ration of this drug is enough to bring back her zest for life (*without her embryonic intelligence needing to let her see things clearly yet*). She intuits that, for the very first time, she's entering a game she too will now play. For the moment, the game is still to bump into Nick.

Nonetheless, she's unable to resume her search right away. On one hand, the voices are beginning to hush around her and all movement among the guests is ceasing. She has no alternative but to stand quietly beside the odd couple who, on the other hand, don't seem at all intimidated by the silence that is settling over the room. In a loud whisper, they continue their dialogue:

"God," according to the elegant young man, "is the *un*-real perpetrator of a more than real *crime*."

"On the contrary: God," according to the old woman, to whom disagreeing with her companion seems indispensable, "is the *real* name that explains an *unreal* crime."

These metaphysical-theological-eschatological contentions manage to distract Barbara for only an instant, because—poor little thing!—a conscientious hand has just lifted the back of her skirt unnoticed and is now roaming her buttocks. And, it should be said, it moves expertly and methodically: first, all across the right one and, when that one has been covered, all across the left one, with even more detailed precision—if that's possible.

"If God exists, then anything is permissible"—she manages to hear the young man whisper assertively to the large-headed crone. Barbara, immediately putting two and two together, decides that, yes, God exists, but she's going to whirl around abruptly anyway and swiftly respond by slapping the face of the owner of those learned fingers that are becoming brazenly more aggressive as they insert themselves more and more in the direction of her innermost parts.

Her brusque attempt to turn activates the movement of her left arm, which is already quite out of control, because of her feelings of shame and rage, and—why not go on and say it?—because of a shocking pleasure she suddenly experiences. That arm strikes the huge-headed old relic of a female's right hand, upsetting the martini it holds. Two of their neighbors (as well as the elderly woman, obviously) react instantly to the perceived aggression, each believing it directed at him- or herself. The two neighbors glare at the old lady with blazing anger—"what hateful eyes!" our small, horrified heroine says to herself—and the old lady is demonstrably ready to revile Barbara, while Barbara turns as red as a tomato, for how could she possibly know what to do, how to beg them to excuse her unpardonable clumsiness? Barbara decides not to turn and face her own aggressor, who is the one to blame for, no-question, everything! And, as it happens, that erudite-in-illicit-touches hand has stopped meddling with her most secret charms. In addition, just when the old woman is clearly about to launch a terrible insult at Barbara, the murmur of voices around them stops altogether (as does all action of the most wise hand) and the old lady simultaneously barely manages to stifle the bad word at the very instant it almost, almost breaks out of her mouth. Barbara, who seems to be on the verge of running away in tears, hurriedly fishes out a hanky that, although already pretty well smeared with lipstick and snot, gives her a tool that can accomplish, at least in part, an attempted reparation of the real damage she has caused, and she starts to dry off the, what you might call, already-stained-forever jacket of the old relic's suit, which is still soaking up extra-dry martini. The pugnacious old woman reacts by taking a step back, fearing the irruption of who knows what new havoc, and Barbara no longer dares to attempt any new action: she's just a little country girl looking into the face of a celebrated anthropologist who is as deaf as any sexagenarian or even octogenarian could ever hope to be, and who is in the company of a brilliant young critic of our contemporary culture of mass communication.

Unsure of what to do, our terrified heroine locks her eyes on an enormous, cheerless canvas that hangs near the doorway of the great hall. She's surprised to see the waiting room of a train station. In it are three blond, completely naked women. ("Oh, this is so embarrassing! Even those little hairs are visible.") The nudes placidly dedicate themselves to ordinary tasks: one is arranging glasses on a little coffee table, another is busy knitting, and the third is selling a newspaper to a formal gentleman of about fifty who is dressed with great decorum in a frock coat. He doesn't seem the least surprised by the absence of clothing that the three damsels exhibit. His circumspection is a noticeable contrast to the state of mind of our Barbara, who is now blushing again. She's quite disgusted: she has just observed the earnest clitoris that the artist has allocated to his knitter.

A question has already been repeated four times before the voices finally begin to hush—after all, it is appropriate to show a certain degree of courtesy for the one who is giving the party, even if the rumor is that he is about to return to his very tropical country. The fifth time, the question explodes into an audience that has itself already spoken a profusion of nonsense as well as a terrifying and/or deep thought or two. This is a group of friends, although, as so often happens in these situations, among them are a certain number of total strangers (like our little Barbara); they generally already feel an incipient alcoholic high (those martinis are really extra-dry!). Except for the three or four cases of full-blown, fall-down drunkenness, they are predisposed to letting themselves be surprised; however, they're less than startled by the question, now asked five times. (But that "five times" fact is clearly not the reason for it.)

The asker is, as it turns out, the Paulist, Paulistine arch-millionaire from Saõ Paulo, Joaõ Almeida e Souza Amaral ("O Jango," to his not few intimate friends, as well as to society-column writers among whom he has been enjoying immense popularity for a while because of his fabulous largesse). And the question he has now asked five times is only this: "How can a millionaire *not* find himself in the middle class in the age of technology, if he lacks the fertile imagination of an artist that will enable him to create a novel life for himself?" (Kiki quickly explains to the old woman: "This lacks any originality whatsoever. He's plagiarizing Marshall McLuhan.") It takes the question a while to make its slow way through those gin-soaked brains but it finally arrives in the place into which it has been directed.

Luckily for our heroine Barbara, the moccasins she is now wearing let her glide with catlike stealth and she moves silently away from the ill-matched couple, feeling badly for the future of the young man. He's so handsome and, in an unmistakable gesture, has just placed an arm around the shoulders of the nearly pygmy-sized, unequivocally know-it-all, old woman with all that slightly disheveled hair. But Barbara must continue the search for her Holy Grail; due to her feelings of intimidation, she has suspended it for a long time now. And, like a Spitfire glued to the tail of a Luftwaffe dive-bomber, the eminent critic Orvieto follows her, his little eyes very lively. He's distracted momentarily by the sight of Celia in a black velvet suit. She is immersed in a back-and-forth dispute with a girl in an almost identical suit, and he realizes with whom he would have had to compete if, in fact, he'd acted on his very lascivious plans of the morning.

Barbara, more terrified than ever by recent events, is now doubly rattled: first, by the strength of her intention to meet her darling Nick and, second, by her efforts to pay attention to what that imposing brown gentleman is saying. Casting a casual glance at Celia, she suddenly remembers who she is, or, rather, who she is for her: the very elegant and young but not all that young lady whose path she crossed this morning as she entered the Neighborhood. And she can't help it if, one, she hears a few of the words the lady is speaking to her companion, who seems very much younger than Celia and is apparently quite terrorized; and, two, she notices how stiffly Celia holds her body, how hardened by rage and willfulness her face has grown. Could this be the fury of desire?

"Yes! Here and now! Right under everybody's noses, in that golden bed sitting back there."

With the exception of the interlocutor, Barbara is almost certainly the only person, among the dozens of guests jammed into the great hall, who hears this urgent demand. The tenacious Spitfire—("All eyes and ears now, look! No hands")—doesn't take his eyes off the opulent, charming rear with which Barbara involuntarily tempts him. But his ears are tuned only to the nasalized speech into which the host has launched subsequent to his introductory question.

No, no, there is absolutely no need to worry, dear readers, I see no point in letting myself tire you out with a verbatim transcription of the words spoken on this occasion by the illustrious Gentleman "Jango" Almeida e Souza Amaral. After all, in order to keep the attention of by now at least hundreds of thousands, oh, let's grant him millions of readers, Alexandre Dumas (*père*) didn't fall into stenographic versions of the speeches of *his* heroes, and *they*, many times, were *not* merely excessively rich and South American, as is the case of this Senhor Jango (whose notably colored complexion alone is enough to arouse suspicion). Dumas *père*'s heroes were instead often *prohombres* of world history, a Cardinal Richelieu, a French Regent, Napoleon Bonaparte.

For that reason, we feel obliged to offer only excerpts of this fine piece of oratory, although such edits risk causing the reader to lose what, though evidently not its essential message, is, on the other hand, its principal attraction; to wit, its many meanders and agile reticence—in two words, its flirtatiousness. What you will have here, then, in rapid synthesis, are the most substantive pronouncements of the address given by O Jango, including, certainly, the juiciest bits. But "oh!"—someone won't be able to resist exclaiming—"you want to turn it all into dried soup!" (*That is one way to put it.*)

It seems human capacities have hit a dead-end.

(Now, to demonstrate this, the Brazilian Croesus uses no less than seven and a half minutes, an interval in which the adventurous hands of Dr. Orvieto do not refrain from taking action again and Barbara, desperately, but unsuccessfully, searches for some sharp-pointed object she may have at hand, tucked away deep in the confusion of the multitudinous effects she carries in her large shoulder bag; any object that could now serve to respond unexpectedly and effectively to the cocky and sustained attack on her *derrière*.)

2. In the second half of the twentieth century, man is an animal hounded by his conquests and finds himself at the end of his tether because of the excessive exercise of his own powers.

(When O Jango gets to this point, a few murmurs can be heard. Apparently the *cognoscenti* among the guests are incapable of avoiding a display of their brilliant "er-yu-dition," as the English say. Without a doubt, this is meant to contribute more to their own personal sheen than to any genuine desire to enlighten the less informed. But above the murmuring is *not* heard an explosive complaint or scream of pain: therefore it can only be imagined that the dexterous *dottore* Orvieto is continuing to carry forth his exploration with some success.)

3. How can the man of today liberate his most important energies, supposing he still has any?

(In much less abrupt terms than the preceding words imply, almost two minutes of the host's dilated oratory are consumed by asking this new question, after which, in a genuine gesture of oratorical feeling, he engages in a pause. During this pause, you could, as the set phrase has it, almost hear a fly fly, despite some very suspicious panting coming from the rear of the enormous room; from the great, golden bed, to be precise, toward which a few eyes do not hesitate instinctively to turn, but find nothing to be alarmed at, their vision blocked of course by the wall of people gathered there and by the smoky blue haze that fills the room. Let us finish the parenthesis by saying that Orvieto's hands have also found mana: they have located the zipper of Barbara's skirt and are proceeding to unzip it: a moment, really, of great solemnity.)

4. The orator now officially announces what, via whispers, has been known by almost everyone for quite a while. Due to a family matter—although many will probably say that it's really because of the bankruptcy of his principal business enterprise,

the manufacture of razor blades—he's now required to depart Megalopolis and "to return briefly to my lair."

(We have put in quotation marks the exact phrase just spoken by O Jango. For our inclusion of it, the most fervent fans of Dumas, *père,* must find a way to pardon us.)

5a. The orator feels enormous gratitude: Megalopolis and his Megalopolitan friends have provided him with so many refinements of the intellect, not to mention those of the senses. In return, to express the magnitude of his appreciation, he wants to cheer them with some good news. It is this: happenings, which are already annoying, even to themselves, are now at risk of allowing what is, in its essence, such an excellent diversion, to become, irreparably, one more piece of run-of-the-mill junk.

(At this point come a new pause by the orator and the complete success of doctor Orvieto's most recent efforts: the Scottish plaid skirt suddenly lies at the feet of our tender heroine, who contemplates with horror what she, however, still considers merely another mishap of no consequence to the outcome of her quest. But when she attempts to bend over to pick up her evasive article of clothing, she unexpectedly bumps up against some sector of Dr. Orvieto, which for its part, most naturally, is waiting for her.)

5b. Infusing the happening with everlasting life ought to be the mission of every person conscious of the fact that the exhaustion of man's imaginative capacity is equal to the extinction of the human species itself.

(Doctor Orvieto feels that he has established pleasurable contact, but Barbara interrupts his desperate project by immediately standing straight up, so the pleasure of the Italian *gelehrte* is very brief; this lets him pay a little more attention to the ongoing speech.)

5c. The happening can now be re-valued. It may even become the ritual act of which modern man is so in need, for it will enable him to construct the starting point of a new religiosity in the midst of the excessive spiritual indigence that exists in our time. But this can happen *only* as long as, by rising above the plane of merely anarchic protest, it (the happening) is converted into an authentic show of *luxe* by means of a genuinely iconoclastic move that derives from the categorical, emphatically explicit negation of all that which, otherwise, always ought to be the goal of one's legitimate aspirations. In other words: one has to have the courage to *deny,* for, in order to have the right to *affirm,* one must deny with savage valor that which is frenziedly ambitioned.

(You can easily imagine that, for the delivery of this tirade, the Brazilian is required to use eleven of his valuable minutes. At its end, in an unequivocal sign of boredom, the sound of a few little coughs rises in the auditorium. The speaker then logically pauses, in contrast to the tenacious peninsular *gelehrte,* who has once again taken his work in hand, and, even though the work is not literally his to work on, his hand roves, with deep satisfaction, over a couple of springy, altogether naked hemispheres, pinching them here and there each time he feels the almost irresistible temptation to pinch something. After her moment of greatest agitation, Barbara, our little Barbara, having inventoried the scant possibilities of successfully fending off this renewed attack, now comes to two tolerably wise conclusions. First, the absence of the entire bottom part of her attire need not make her feel any more upset than she would feel if she were practicing nudism, as she has so often read that girls her age do on the beaches of Germany, France, and Sweden. But, unlike those women in the big painting she contemplated a moment ago, she will concentrate on limiting the view that prying eyes have of that miniscule tangle of hair below her belly. And, second, those pinches? They haven't really turned out to be any more bothersome and are without a doubt less dangerous than bedbug bites. So, if her father, who was a raw recruit in the Great War, long before the invention of DDT, knew how to put up so courageously with the onslaught of the blockheads, as well as that of those horribly annoying insects, she owes it to everyone not to do less and will also put up with it.)

6. For more than two centuries, occidental man has tried to integrate himself into some authentic order and has cast nostalgic looks back toward the primitive world. That is what (always in synthesis) O Jango says as he renews his discourse. But (I still summarize) modern man has yet to achieve anything other than a superficial imitation of primitive man, for he seems to lack the courage necessary to really negate his most elevated accomplishments. The words that here follow are exactly the ones spoken at this point by the drab-olive nabob:

"Listen to the voice of order now: let us throw our most precious treasures right out the window! It is imperative that we return to the practice of the potlatch!"

(This idea, like an efficient palliative for the barely bearable stinging that covers the surface of one and then the other of her beautiful posterior hemispheres, triggers in Barbara a memory of everything she has learned about the potlatch, all thanks to her pre-university course on cultural anthropology. It is a welcome distraction: this essentially anti-economical ceremony of the Kwakiutl and many other primitive tribes was perfected in some instances, especially by the virtuous, ostentatious, and righteous destruction of important tribal riches. So absorbed is our little girl in this clear memory of what she knows, that she forgets where she is, forgets she is searching for Nick, even forgets the tireless hands that now roam obstinately over a very exact portion of her very attractive anatomy. Barbara is sitting in class again and two years younger. In her mind, confusing images overtake one another as paint-daubed savages dance and throw things onto a fire: scholarly books, armfuls of marble figures, a portrait of a national hero that presides over a classroom, precious fabrics embroidered with mythological creatures . . . and in this classroom she hears again the *smack* with which she responds with complete accuracy to the little freckled-face, red-haired boy sitting on the bench behind her, who has just dunked one of her pigtails into an ink bottle.

Ah, little heroine, if only you could be back in your small town! The town you abandoned to chase a chimera!

Barbara's eyes once again fill with tears and she makes an effort not to cry. Where is Nick? Is it possible that he's deliberately hiding from her among the throng of guests? She concentrates on the speech, which has just resumed.)

7. O Jango now announces that he is going to produce for his guests a spectacle that has no precedent whatsoever at any time or place in the history of Megalopolis, a city very jealous of its artistic treasures. Certainly no one can deny that! Before his guests' privileged eyes will file for the very last time in their existence the richest ornaments of his apartment, so many, many of which were created in their moment for royalty, and each and every piece of which is worthy of being in a museum. And all of them will be destroyed tonight, right here. Many will be condemned to burn—the furniture and paintings— and those not reduced to ashes—the more fragile relics such as porcelains and glassware—will be demolished with hammers or simply dashed against the parquet floor.

(As for Barbara, she has not been able to form a clear image of any art treasures that might be in her vicinity: she has barely caught a glimpse of a gigantic gold bed, and the one painting she has managed to observe with some attention didn't seem to her in any way to be a masterpiece. Rather, it made her blush. From another university-prep course she took, Art History, she knows that authentic great art is not only a joy forever but also deeply moral, as the woman in charge of the course never tired of repeating when she had to show them certain reproductions of the Great Masters. The other guests, already versed in the actual treasures that the monstrously rich Brazilian's apartment holds, begin to tremble—*is it the onset of an orgasm?*—in anticipation of the Vandalistic spectacle that is to be offered to them within minutes that are countable. Kiki, for his part, thinks of that little Capo di Monte porcelain monkey that looks so much like him: "it's so *funny!*" And they are going to reduce it to shards before his eyes, when maybe it could have been his since forever ago, if he'd only asked for it at the right time from the one-of-a-kind *paulista, paulistano* Mecenas. Our *gelehrte* Dr. Orvieto's hands have stopped moving and lie at his sides as he focuses his inventiveness on a new plan he has begun to hatch: his rescue from imminent disaster of a scrumptious designer cradle: "a delightful product of the eighteenth century, made for the House of Savoy." If he manages to save it, he doesn't stop telling himself, he will have also performed an act of patriotism. Barbara, who feels even more naked now that the hands seem to have marched off, believes she feels a draft, a completely inconceivable phenomenon in this great room chock full of people, where the temperature has risen to at least 91.4°F or higher and more than a few people are sweating oceans in spite of their highly accredited antiperspirants. Roslyn, who hasn't been able to find *her* Nick in this crowd either, thinks nostalgically of the great Johanes Enricus Senft and his superb, in-laid marquetry spinet, that absolute masterpiece on which sage blond damsels must have played extraordinarily beautiful pieces at the end of the eighteenth century and on which perhaps were made to sound in France for the first time the vibrant romantic motifs of Beethoven. *It cannot be denied, let it be said in passing, that this Roslyn possesses a decent amount of historical imagination.*

Kiki asks himself where O Jango is coming from with all this talk. The Brazilian is normally a reader only of Oscar Wilde and Aubrey Beardsley. Now he's spouting anthropological knowledge. The living answer to this enigma is standing beside Kiki. She's wildly enthusiastic about the tremendous ceremony they are going to witness—her first really important potlatch in a whole life dedicated to the sciences of man!—but Kiki doesn't catch on. He is nevertheless now filled with tenderness, which comes from an affectionate nature to which also contribute the nine extra dry martinis he has rapidly consumed without touching a bite of food since morning. This tenderness now associates itself with the childlike joy of the horrid old woman, whose worthiness to pose as a witch for any of Goya's atrocious *Caprichos* is noticeable. She claps her hands enthusiastically after the host's announcement. In this tender mood, Kiki gives a firm squeeze with the arm he has put around the shoulders of the quasi hunchback. If the firmness of his arm does not desist for a few minutes, his thoughts are nevertheless running in a different direction. How often Celia used to get irritated by just such distractions in her one-time husband! *And just think. Kiki's annoying lapses of attention had their beginnings in a homemade technique he came up with to be a better lover and prolong coitus!* Closer to home, the old relic now shows symptoms of erotic enthusiasm for her gallant—as if he would have anything in common with those Eskimos, Zulus, or Maoris with whom she has always known how to cohabit so enthusiastically as to leave literally exhausted even the most vigorous warriors of the tribe.

Kiki himself, in the crystal-clear mental style of his annotations, is thinking—or writing?—deep within his mind: "What *is* a party? It is the inefficient answer that Megalopolis man comes up with in the face of a constant lack of friendly contact in the streets, at his work place, in all public locations. But a *party*, a suffocating gathering of strangers, actually fogs the thoughts and feelings even more, and, as a consequence, offers nothing resembling friendliness. Anyway, genuine friendship is impossible in this city, in this era. Well, at least we still love people." "Well, at least we still love women," Celia tells herself at the same time. She now reposes—but "repose," of course, isn't the most appropriate word to define her actual state at this moment. Nevertheless, she is in the splendorous

Polonaise bed, that other jewel of the eighteenth century, now also condemned to immediate destruction. The golden bed's sumptuous canopy curtains do not completely conceal agitated limbs—some, pink and sunny; some, quite suntanned—that now jerk spasmodically, as if in a fight to the death. The limbs belong to Celia and her dear friend, for earlier, there is no doubt about it now, her young interlocutor decided to accept Celia's challenge. *Or, to put it better, to obey her command.*)

8. The holocaust is ready to begin . . .

O Jango explains to his guests that, in the final moments of so many beautiful objects, there will come to life again, before their very eyes, the same magic that permeated each object when it first took form before its maker's eyes. Moving its creator to create it, almost by force, something then emerged whose mere creation would make it indispensable to the ongoing equilibrium of the world. These objects will now recover the full power of seduction they first exercised, long before the patina of time enhanced their value, when they initially appeared to those who became their original owners simply by converting them into splendors whose historicity has stripped them of the freshness of the first morning of their initial enchantment. O Jango, sensing the poetry in his words, intuits that he is at last whole, a poet, he, who had so doubted his literary gifts. Every one of his guests, his deeply respectful *dramatis personae*, are moving flock-like away from the dais on which the foppish, corpulent, *paulistano e paulista* subjugator has been speaking to them. He has just asked them to clear a space for the pyre, a pyre on which those objects, whose total destruction can be fully accomplished in no other way, will burn.

(Kiki gently pulls the overly large-headed old woman along by the hand and she responds with a sweet smile that is a bit more than friendly, then with another that is unmistakably romantically inclined. He's pulling her toward the far end of the great hall where the superb giltwood *lit à la polonaise* stands.

He thinks the bed can serve his amorous peccadillos until it is its turn to be axed and/or burned. But once he gets to the bed and opens the canopy's side curtain to deposit the transported sexagenarian inside it, he's confronted first by the frightened face of a girl to whom Celia used to give free Spanish lessons, and then by a face burning with fury that belongs to Celia, who crosses her arms to hide her naked breasts from him as she blisters him with the most vicious insults in her rather formidable repertory. Kiki, embarrassed, rapidly seeks refuge back at the opposite end of the huge room and pushes his companion along at a run; she, as deaf as she is, is still proud of the quick conquest she has made and completely ignorant of the atrocities that have just been heaped on her beloved.

For Barbara, the fact that the good-looking, sad-faced boy and the huge-headed woman stop right in front of her is happily providential: her efforts to pull the tail of her blouse down far enough to cover a little of the lower part of her body have become precarious and the looks coming her way from some of the other guests are beginning to show an impertinent insistence on her tentative lack of a miniskirt. The glorious exile from Fascism desists from his projected profitable and patriotic act of saving the designer cradle for the House of Savoy. This object, at this very moment, is being moved by one of O Jango's *mignons* toward the lit pyre and the knowledgeable Dante exegete returns to his travels behind Barbara's back. Her reddening face and tearing eyes can now be attributed as much to that as to the same cause that is heating up so many faces and causing tears to flow from so many eyes: the pyre burning behind a ring of asbestos and upon which the precious cradle is about to fall.

O Jango hasn't left the dais and the heat of the growing bonfire obliges him to remove first his smoking jacket and then his shirt. He presides over his potlatch, torso naked; and some guests, thinking that it's meant for them to follow his example, also remove their jackets and shirts, laughing loudly. ("It's important to add here that there are no lack of women who proudly display their naked torsos as well, and are neither more nor less taken note of than if they were in Knossos.") And O Jango, whose dark skin is taking on reddish reflections from the flames, looks splendid on the dais. There is little doubt that he is conscious of the imposing spectacle that he himself offers. Oh, if he only had a horse to sit on! He twirls the tips of his mustache and brushes aside a curl that has inopportunely fallen over his brow. O Jango makes a regal condottiere and, however much a horse is missed, constantly at his side on the dais is his minion, the delicate, ephebic, off-white boy, who, with a penetrating voice more appropriate to an auctioneer, announces the approach of each object that is to be destroyed.

Barbara feels compassion for that young man and identifies O Jango with Mephistopheles. *But where is Margarita?*

Celia, overtaken by a violent irritation, in order to make sure no one else has the nerve to interrupt her lesbian activities, gives a hard pull on one of the canopy curtains, which comes down and completely covers her and her playmate. Kiki is still recovering from the shock of his alarming encounter with her and the stunning discovery he has just made, so not even he notices this occurrence.

The other guests are generally preoccupied with grabbing the cocktails that are now being passed around by serious serving boys in short shorts and powdered wigs, who perform prodigious feats of balance and glamor with a discretion perfectly worthy of the livery they wear (which was thought up by O Jango). They thread their way with some difficulty among the avid guests, whose mouths, very dry from the smoke, do not tire of pouring down more or less potent liquors that are then skillfully combined with the most insidious narcotics imaginable.

"A chaise longue. From the early reign of Louis Quinze," the minion at O Jango's side announces. He then adds, in order to enlighten the distinguished guests, who are already excited from their concocted drinks and threaten to transform the pleasant gathering into a resolute orgy: "it carries the stamp 'P. Bara.' Pierre Bara joined the Corporation in 1758 and was an acclaimed chair maker. He is registered in Saberte's work, *Les Ébénistes du 18ème siècle*." After a brief pause, in a much lower voice, he adds: "Paris, 1927." And, amid the clamor, an attentive ear, if it's at all feasible that there still exist attentive ears in such a Witch's Sabbath of a party, would have been able to discern the sound of an axe and the crackle of burning wood.

"An oval mirror. Venetian with Murano glass. Gold plate. Decorated with garlands of flowers in bas relief. Period: Louis Seize."

"The first time Marie Antoinette saw her majestic face reflected in it," our adorable Barbara muses, and her eyes once more fill with tears. She thinks of the misfortunes and martyrdom of that unhappy queen and her august husband. This consoles her a little for the martyrdom to which she's still being subjected by a sadistic *gelehrte* whom she literally does not know even by sight.

Meanwhile, crouching to lift his decrepit companion up a little, Kiki has succeeded in pecking the great-headed one on a cheek. Then, carried away by the diabolical brew that he has profusely imbibed, he swears his eternal love to the sexagenarian or octogenarian, who is deaf as a post, half-hunchbacked, wholly anthropological, and outrageously large-headed, and, what's more, he demands that she marry him.

A not inconsequential crash leaves a pair of Indochinese male dancers carved in marble suddenly lying in pieces. "Probably expressive of something about the entourage of Qwan Yin," the minion adds laconically. And it is in his face that Roslyn, who long ago lost hope of finding her Nick, discovers a certain fascinating power, probably expressive of something about the proverbial wisdom of the Orient that is perhaps also suggested by the dancers' catastrophe.

Enormous Head in Love entrusts to her Kiki the perfect future happiness that awaits them among the aboriginal Baikas, the only Amazonian tribe that has not yet been driven crazy by Methodist pastors or ethnographic investigators, but about whom are nevertheless told shocking things, such as the stories concerning sacred, bicephalous children. Kiki is now over the moon thinking of the new rewards his stay *chez les sauvages* will permit him to tack onto his already in no way sparse curricular history, and he enthusiastically caresses the rubbery breasts that the old lady has on display in her pectoral area. His caresses are so enthusiastic that he doesn't notice when one of his rich-in-years Beatrice's breasts, excessively pulled at by his zealous hands, is no longer in the place it should be in and now looks something like a big pimple on one side of her ribcage.

A *Susanna and the Elders* attributed to Lucas de Leyden now goes up in a great cloud of smoke, which Roslyn astutely uses as camouflage to move closer to the dais. Meanwhile, with unequivocally seductive designs, she pulls the neckline of her dress's amply filled bodice a little lower. Wisdom of the Orient, as she has now baptized the minion, is definitely attractive and she is going to try (*how unfruitful her efforts will be!*) to spark his attraction to her. "The minute O Jango leaves town, I'm going right over to accept the proposition of that old oilman from Texas: his tastes can't be as bizarre as they say and he'll be good for expenses," the pale ephebe with the romantic face has already resolved, and Roslyn's mammary abundance is not the thing that will change his plans.

Some of the serving boys have opened the wide windows that look out over the avenue, no doubt at O Jango's order, who may fear the onset of asphyxiation among his guests due to the heated, highly polluted atmosphere of the apartment. However, the smoke is actually dissipating a little now. Because, actually, in the last ten minutes, they have been destroying porcelain and crystal.

Elsewhere, after trying out a variety of drinks, our little Barbara is feeling quite overcome—*yes! our sweet girl, the prototype of natural vim and vigor!*—and she finds it hard to catch her breath. She doesn't notice the cause of this, until, making a great effort with her scrumptious little blond head, she is alarmed to realize that the very hands that have been mortifying her all evening, the hands of Invisible Pursuer—but what a romantic name *she* has now given *him*! ("This certainly has become a night for baptizing strangers!")—are the hands that now gently encircle her neck. *Well, to tell the truth, not all that gently.* She can only manage to produce a squeak of warning when her eyes hit the right spot and she sees, under disorderly, heavy bed curtains, something moving as if it were alive in the enormous gold bed that four footmen are straining to drag toward the pyre.

More smoke. New levels of raucous laughter. Added screams, and it's very true that not all the screaming seems to be for joy. A few shrieks of pain and terror. Some howls of desperation. Increasingly shrill cries. And along with all that, the crackling of a lot of burning wood.

"You'll always have me at your side," murmurs the honeyed, almost-Quasimodo.

"You'll always have me at your feet," responds Kiki trustworthily.

Now it's the Regency Period chandelier's turn and there is a loud crash of broken glass. Next, the carved Chippendale console is up, but produces very little smoke; it's appropriate to notice the great quality of the wood. Now, it's the portrait of the Count of Lautréamont, just a fantasy of Giorgio De Chirico's; it disappoints: it catches fire and crumbles to ashes in practically a second.

On the other hand, Barbara, for her part, is now aware of the very natural inconvenience caused by an unflagging finger committed to its attempt to delve into her ultimate and most remote depths. And suddenly she feels sad, profoundly sad—*a girl with a heart of gold, our little one!*—when she observes that, at a gesture from the minion who still presides on the dais, two servants start removing from the wall the large, dark canvas with the naked women and the newspaper buyer. And to think: only a few short hours earlier—maybe no more than three—an object like that could make her blush. Oh, but so much has happened since then.

The mound of ashes at the center of the great hall is now enormous and could easily be mistaken for a geological formation. Boyish footmen are finding it very hard to make their way through thousands of scattered fragments and pieces of broken bottles, mirrors, and doodads that lie everywhere.

But: Barbara! Darling, sentimental girl! Why do you feel so sad and bow reverentially as that painting passes slowly in front of you! You now unwisely offer your own well-filled-out rump to the tenacious, unseen stranger who has been pursuing you for hours and hours! (*In fact, Barbara is now going to feel a stabbing pain. She will manage to tell herself only that the cruel finger has finally accomplished its goal. She immediately recalculates, however, when she considers that there are still two hands on her small, snowy neck, and they now press it more forcefully.*)

All obstacles finally overcome, the *gelehrte* vows to quickly repeat the experience, but first he considers it only fair to declare that the eminent critic he was reading at lunch has it right:

"Yes! In fact, we *are* living in a curved universe 'and only the youngest can truly acclimate to it.' Therefore long live the universal curve! We must keep our footsteps glued to those of *i giovanissimi!*"

Patrick has again just arrived in Naples, the city of palm trees seafood and grungy idlers locally known as *lazzaroni*. Waves again sweep the astronomical golden beach on which lie fine bodies oiled bodies muscular bodies delicate bodies young the young the young the even younger their stupendous phalluses standing as straight as bayonets breasts as firm as apples or sweet-and-sour lemons. This time Patrick comes to claim what is his, what belongs to him, not to his distant cousins with their nasal Lusitanian voices, of the kind who, instead of cousins, are merely impostors. It's only to him that the glittering ducal crown of the city belongs, and the relatives who usurped his position know very well that the people are only waiting for the order from the handsome legitimate heir so they may rise up against the usurpers and after they beat and mistreat them, spit on them castrate them tar and feather them bite them castrate them, they exile them and the relatives give up their perfidious pretentions and ask only that they be allowed to live in the palace they have occupied like vile impostors and serve the indisputable lord as his servants because they will be his most faithful most humble and most servantly servants because it's not for nothing that they are the relatives, very distant relatives oh yes, of the legitimate lord of Naples the city of infinite expanses of beaches where sand is as smooth as a teenaged belly in the heat of desire, his city of the golden butterfly and the saturnine octopus, the city of fan palms and emeralds.

Patrick is carried to the *palazzo* his *palazzo* and finally a little old man who in some way resembles his father because after all his family's bearing is undeniable shows him the splendid private rooms that henceforth will be his and are even better furnished in gold and precious stones than the rest of the unending sumptuous mansion and he believes in the indistinct images of servants no he sees this is nothing but a trick of his vision he's bedazzled by such magnificence and he recognizes the old relations from the other city the infernal city and his vague relations dissolve in the blinding light as the lace at his wrists discretely quivers in a very soft breeze that curls in and *behold* there is a large bedroom and his enormous bed truly a splendor a smidge too splendid following Neapolitan taste for the slightly gaudy and its turquoise canopy undulating in the big room the grand bedroom with a urinal and he shivers what a fate-filled fantasy because this is his bedroom and now there is only the reverent/more than reverent/servilely deferential/what you'd call a natural practitioner of deference/a deferencer it is his distant relative/the stuttering impostor in here with Patrick the magnanimous prince fully confident of his power/Patrick the munificent generator of beauty and at the pinnacle of his splendor he does not renounce his humility as a great lord a Big Lesson then he probably does not renounce his undershirt of Egyptian cotton with some, but, since it is almost new, very few holes and over his holey utilitarian undershirt agrees to wear only a night shirt of finest batiste which displays across his buttocks his principle coats of arms displaying the buffalo and the palm tree embroidered in fine gold and it is already midnight and Patrick is already sleeping deeply so unusually deep is his sleep and it's so sweet and his mother is feeding him pearls of dawn in a little spoon of flying sea-blue-green alabaster in such *such* a sweet dream oh so so so very but the loud crack is an earthquake ? he manages to ask himself in the darkness for it wakes him and he feels terror and worse than that shame for his sphincter unavoidably loosening and his body now tossed in a blanket rises and falls rises and falls falls and falls falls and then someone why it's the old man his relative who now knows about it and leans his buttocks those empty wineskin buttocks stinky and horrid-looking against his face and fills him with a feeling of absolutely humiliating atrocity.

Now his face smeared dislocated Patrick sees they have set a vicious trap for him he will have to abandon the city his city where palm trees and agile bodies fly over golden sand and overcome by pain and shame as the book falls onto the floor, Patrick wakes up. He barely has enough time left to get ready (he has to shave), if he doesn't want to get to the party after O Jango is already dead drunk and so stupid from alcohol that he won't be able to see who he is. It would be even worse, though, to arrive even one second before stupefaction begins to set in, before O Jango will have given in to the cocktails' onslaught and instead is still in a hostile mood, for then he could literally have him kicked out. And O Jango never lacks for able-bodied henchmen, keeps them around *pour la besogne* at moments like this.

Laura is also running late. After innumerable vacillations, having convinced herself finally that the boy she glimpsed at that window is a loose end that fortune is calling her to tie up in a definitive way with respect to her lover, she has returned to the hotel and there literally loses all notion of time building castles in the air. She sees herself, for example, with Horacio, far away, on the exotic pampa inhabited by the indomitable Drinker of Maté who gallops endlessly on a tiny polo pony just like Horacio's. And she tries on one dress after another, until she finally realizes that, if she doesn't hurry, she'll miss the party. In a matter of seconds she decides on a vaporous dress in a color they're calling champagne and styled with a generous *décolleté*— "oh my, how audacious, if Mama could only see me now . . ." It reveals the presence of incipient breasts that are prematurely withered and have a touch of acne. Once she's at the door of O Jango's apartment, she feels intimidated again, this time by the din that reaches her through the thick cedar door. At least this time it has not occurred to O Jango to place a couple of his lackeys there to guard the entrance to the party. Still, Laura is suddenly struck by a certain timidity, or, to put it a different way, an oversized fear. What if the boy she saw, who looked at her from the window, isn't here? And what if she becomes a victim of the general profligacy that commonly reigns at this kind of gathering? "Remember the insults and humiliations your little cousin Hermione suffered!" In addition, a mist of some kind is growing thicker and thicker in the corridor and Laura starts to feel as if she's choking. "It's psychological," she says to cheer herself up.

But she really wants to call out, and, again, feels foolish. "I miss my mama so much. Don't be mad at me, Mama, because I keep forgetting all the things you've taught me! But it's because I'm a member of my generation and a fully-grown woman, not a slave, or a child; and I need to prove to myself *yesterday* at the latest who I am. I don't want to feel ashamed of myself or unworthy of Horacio, or, what would be worse, sense that I cannot live up to the famous last name I bear or am in some way unworthy of the Van Boren lineage. Really, I'm sure my reaction is psychological. Or maybe the electricity is down, failures of the electric power are the order of the day in Megalopolis. Or maybe the lights aren't really getting misty at all! It's probably my nerves making my vision blur. I feel so stupid! And all this is so boring because architects never calculate the ventilation correctly for the landings of luxury apartment buildings, no, no, *paliers* are just throwaway space to those egotists, who *never* consider the service people at all, because, and so, but this nausea, it has to be from my fears coming out but I think I'm suffocating, except, no, it's only *psychological*."

Dense smoke is curling out of the keyhole in O Jango's front door and, on the other side of it, the sound of loud crashing has increased. All this is now unbearable for Laura, who is coughing harder and harder ("can it be this hard to cough up a lung?"). At this particular moment she feels an anguishing scratch of vomit in her throat just before bile splatters onto her elegant, vaporous, champagne-colored cocktail dress, which now looks very much like a cocktail of champagne and chartreuse.

"Botticelli's *derelitta*!" Patrick can't help exclaiming as the elevator door opens and, through the congealing smoke, he is looking at her, splayed there on a bench beside the apartment's front door. The prevailing mistiness softens the natural harshness of Laura's features, who seems almost pretty to him and in whom, certainly, he doesn't yet recognize the idiot he saw spying on him earlier in the day. But suddenly, when he realizes who she is, it's already too late to go back, that is, to simply take one step back and go into O Jango's apartment. Laura, on the other hand, who has had Patrick's image in her mind almost all afternoon, has instantly recognized him and feels flattered—of course!—by the comparison of which she has been the subject. Her energy returns in the presence of one of Horacio's good friends and this calms her, for it also presents to her someone of whom her mother has already approved enough to have entrusted to him her own true image, but who is still a young, amazingly slender man undoubtedly capable of understanding and alleviating problems, specifically any conflict of a worried *jeune fille*.

O Jango's potlatch is now culminating in the burning of the magnificent bed. Bursts of horrific laughter are so loud that it could be said they are cries of terror. From out here on the landing, who could tell if, among the confusion of voices and noises, the blustery laughs, the loud creaks and crackling of wood, the whacks of hatchets—really, who could discern it—if someone were screaming for help?

Patrick is feeling stoical. He is Savonarola denouncing the arrogance of lords and their nude, but smothered-in-gold-and-precious-stone, young courtesans. "All that noisy rejoicing is just a cry for help," he declares. Moreover, he is Savonarola who is afraid to join the orgy because he realizes that it's too late for him to make a triumphal entry, or even a basically decorous one. He fears he will look ridiculous, be seen as the uninvited stone guest, if he goes in to accuse now. The alcohol-impaired, Don Juan-esque crowd inside would all run to him as soon as they saw him carting in the enormous portrait of O Jango, which (in order better to get his proposed effect) he has not bothered to wrap up in any kind of paper at all. Any dramatic impression he would have wanted to make has now been stopped short by his late arrival.

Not all is lost, however.

He barely pays any attention to Laura; nonetheless, he sits down beside her. She, for her part, feels happy and accompanied and is soon clear about the mysterious mist. Patrick has, in the end, made her see how it is smoke and is getting darker and darker as it curls more and more densely out of the keyhole of O Jango's lock; specifically, from that medieval lock's immense period keyhole.

Laura feels chatty and volunteers to call the fire department. "We'll see," Patrick responds laconically, meditating mainly on what he's going to do with the painting, which has begun to be more of a bother to him than anything else. "Of course," Laura tells herself, "he's thinking appreciatively of my humanitarian generosity, my civic concern. And besides, it is, after all, pretty heroic of me to still be here if all this is about a real fire, isn't it?"

It's more likely that Patrick is very aware of and remembering how O Jango wastes things. He's not at all confident (*yes, that's the word: confident: not at all confident*) that the fire was accidental. The door has become transparent to his fantasy and he sees O Jango and his acolytes, the Grand Inquisitor with his Familiars, the Tribunal of the Holy Office, as they realistically parody a witch burning. In his imagination, he sees a young girl and an ephebe, TV extras, who are completely naked and contort as if the flames had succeeded in reaching them on the stakes to which they are tied, ingeniously held safely away from the fire by barely visible asbestos cords.

"Will it be too much to ask you to walk me home? I'm starting to feel a little sick again." ("That's not true, she's afraid that there really is a fire," he thinks. "Or—and it's still not true that she feels sick—she wants to hook up with me.")

"Of course, right away," he says. "It is a little sickening, isn't it, here in this cheap version of hell? Just let me lean this canvas against the door. You are my witness that I now return it, carefully restored, to its owner, and that I've left it leaning on the door of his house." And won't O Jango be *sorry* when the door opens and he realizes that Patrick has been there and, with not a word of reproach, has left him the final and most valuable link that has existed between them.

"How professionally carefree of you as an artist to let go of your masterpieces."

And no sooner is Laura in the elevator than she presses as close to Patrick as the modesty of her Van Boren heritage will allow. Laura starts to talk to him about Mama's portrait. Patrick vaguely remembers the fussy old hag, but as an overly made-up cockatoo of a woman who insinuated that she was ready to follow the example of the infamous Cayetana, Thirteenth Duchess of Alba, thus adopting a naughty fashion popular among Megalopolitan matrons since Sickert painted the wealthy Mrs. Bird in the nude. ("All in all, the girl is a little less repulsive than the mother and, fortunately, seems to be somewhat dumber.") (*Wait till you talk to her about painting!*)

She is going to stop talking, at least for now, as soon as she gets him to start talking in the diner. They've taken refuge from the rain halfway to the hotel for decent, rich young ladies, where she dutifully lodges when she's in Megalopolis.

"I call it my second home. The management is very serious and, of course, a little elderly. I remember that Horacio . . ." (*Stop there. Say nothing that will lead him to that theme. Keep in mind that from now on Horacio is your rival.*) But Laura persists. Now nothing can be done about it.

"Well, *a little* friendly to him. Because he shares . . . with, and I don't know if you're old enough yet to understand exactly what this means, but he shares O Jango's vice, so, sure, I was friendly, but don't get the idea that I got to know him very well. I ran into him, maybe once or twice, you know, hanging around with O Jango, or sometimes just here and there, maybe, anywhere, you know, in bars in the Village, maybe. I remember seeing him with you that one time, and I could never forget him, since he was usually with you."

While she chews her peanut butter sandwich, Laura considers her right to have her portrait painted by the artist who painted her mother. Meanwhile, he pushes his saucer back in disgust, with its two mandatory little pickles, an indigestible complement without which it seems impossible to have a sandwich in Megalopolis.

But Patrick O'Dont can foresee the possibility of something better, something that could very well allow him to escape completely from both his poverty and the pickles. At the very least, it seems to him, as they say about reigning houses, here is a connection that will put him probably even a step up the social ladder from O Jango, the *parvenu*. (*How did the thing go?*) ("Oh, yes: 'In my veins are two great peoples / creators of culture, custodians of beauty.'")

He takes Laura's hand. A great deal of discreet passion is expressed by a single squeeze of the hand.

Meanwhile, a feminine foot presses down on the fleshy lips of O Jango exactly as Patrick has painted them. After the potlatch, amid black smoke and coughs, heaves, loud guffaws, and shrieks of terror, an uncontrollable stampede of fleeing guests now trample, dirty, stain, deform, tear, split, rip, and destroy O Jango's portrait. He himself, as soon as his guests depart, falls asleep on a table in the kitchen, the hermetically-sealed door of which prevents his suffocating from smoke inhalation.

And Laura Van Boren proposes from now on to be more modern. She must be worthy of her college sorority, her intrepid alma mater. (*What's that line after "post jucundam juventutem"?*) But—*and above all*—she must make her entire bloodline proud. Her blood, she finally seems to realize, has grown too thick. Her old heritage of discoverers, founders, colonizers, and inventors requires an influx of new blood. (Even if it comes, *I'm just saying*, in old wineskins.) And what could be better than having a great artist as the father of her children? "Besides, nobody pays much attention to age differences in a couple."

"I'll take advantage of the wedding trip," Patrick thinks, "and put up great shows in Paris and London. Tomorrow first thing, I'm going to lock myself completely away: this girl will do all my errands and even cook for me and I can shut myself in and work. I'll need at least a dozen large canvases and twenty-five of the small ones. And my little eyesore here will be my scarecrow. But I also have to get together (*oh, you'll find a way!*) a small sum of money for materials. The scarecrow will scare away my desire and heal my humiliation. The day is coming for my revenge, so start shaking, O Jango! Laura Van Boren, you're truly boring, but, from now on, you will also be the quintessence of all my past humiliations and the key to my cosmos.")

And Laura Van Boren is moved watching Patrick's face. It has suddenly taken on an almost ferocious intensity. "It is his will to create forms!" She sees the artist in him. "He is Van Gogh, and the rest of those guys! No, of course it isn't easy to be a painter's wife: everybody already knows that. Our feminine flesh is too tempting to them, but it will be OK. And I will make him work, work, work. Oh, I will make you happy, Patrick O'Dont, my husband. I, Laura Van Boren, will be your faithful guard dog, I mean, in the sense of your guardian angel, and I . . . I will b-be, but who would have predicted such a thing . . . ? Meek little mouse me, I will become your compliant courtesan.")

Meanwhile, O Jango, scary Chief Bison Butt, is in mid-escape in his canoe under a storm of whistling arrows, none of which, unfortunately, even graze him, and distant war cries, the far distant shrieks of warriors, make him realize that he's a very, very small boy and is in the garage at the *fazenda* spying on auntie Amelia ("why does Tia Amelia have that beard between her legs?" And that beard, watch out, it's jumping, get away from the big hairy spider!") who is also the half-naked chauffer he feels attracted to and who protects him from war cries, among many other dangers.

As we already know, just moments ago, Kiki got barely a glimpse of Celia's half-naked body. It was enough time, however, for him to corroborate something he has always, yes, it can be stated that it is what he has always, suspected about her, regardless of never having dared declare it to his conscious mind.

And, rather than feeling defrauded, he reins in his imagination. He routes everything "Celia" definitively away from the confusing spectacle of all those body parts he has just seen, beginning with the breasts he so often and so energetically used to kiss and kiss and wanted to go on kissing until just minutes ago. He separates all thought of her from the disturbing spectacle of familiar limbs, which, until that moment, were so full of mystery to him but have now twisted into terrible vulgarities, intertwined with another woman's body. All his tenderness instantly removes itself from the object on which until then he had been fixated, almost since adolescence.

Really, Kiki's quick change is a case of abrupt reversal no less significant than Nick's, Orvieto's, the ex-timid young poet's, or our precious heroine's. And Kiki is in absolutely no way confused. On the contrary, one could say he feels perfectly lucid, and also justified. The All-Knowing Great-Headed Woman doesn't know Celia and, unfamiliar as well with Kiki's history, seems to have noticed nothing at the party. As Kiki's interest now veers toward her, he understands (*or perhaps simply believes that he understands*) that the Wise Large-Headed Woman will henceforth be the only object of his devotion.

Her only comment on things was: "Caramba, you look really pale!"

Kiki admires the delicacy and purity of that observation. In exchange for her brief words, Kiki promises himself that he will recount for the Super-Understanding Old Crone the unfortunate story of his and Celia's love. It is a turbulent story that has a slightly foul smell to it and is no doubt sad; and it is possibly the only funeral prayer ever raised by anyone for his ex, a perfidious woman who, in life, was, undeniably, a *Belle Dame sans Merçi*.

Kiki's storytelling takes place that very night, as soon as he can manage it, after that unbearable, dense smoke suddenly obliged everyone to make a lighting-fast exodus from the party. The further he gets into his tale, in fact, the warmer he feels toward the humpbacked ethnographer. Inevitably, he ends up proposing marriage. And she doesn't hesitate to extend one of her claws to him, for she needs an assistant to accompany her on her imminent expedition in search of the latest Baikas; until now she has had no luck finding one. She has a knack for putting eroticism into play with subordinates, exacting ridiculous, voluptuous demands that she picked up in her time with the Maoris, Bantús, and Eskimos during her long residencies among *les bons sauvages*. Her ways have been *vox populi* for years, and her scientific prestige isn't incentive enough to entice young researchers to accompany her, more because they fear her and her indefatigable vagina than because they are afraid of cannibals.

At the end of the seventeenth century, Madame d'Aulnoy wrote *Relation du Voyage d'Spagne*—in which, while there were a few who *were*, not everyone was insane. In it she referred to "loving, penitent Hispanics, sometimes great lords, who," the *bas-bleu* writes, "whip themselves with miraculous patience . . . And when they find a well-shaped woman, they lash themselves in a certain way that makes their blood splash on her. It is a great compliment and the lady, thus recognized, thanks them." Later we shall see how our Monstrous Investigator thanks our Freudian Age penitent.

Meanwhile, it's time to delve a little deeper into the soul of said penitent.

For Kiki, the days following the celebration of the potlatch at O Jango's are a flurry of such vast and varied activity they seem to be an extension of that demented night. Besides, as the days progress, he faces, from a practical point of view, problems he has to solve rapidly as he makes plans for both his wedding to the Humpbacked Big-Head of Knowledge and their immediate expeditionary voyage. His nerves are also fraying under the irritating, inexplicable disappearance of Celia, who should have contacted him by now about the rent; and also because of Nick's suicide. Nick had truly been his best friend since their student days. (*But friends, well . . . you know.*)

All in all, though, Nick's death is hard for Kiki. And, despite the whirl of worries he's caught up in, he has found a free moment or two to remember the phenomenon of his friendship with Nick. This in some way has rekindled in him uneasy suspicions he has felt for a long time about the companion of so many episodes of his life. Never, in so many words, would he have revealed to Nick his unspoken doubts about the motivations his friend presented to him with such sincerity (no, it is better to say, with such insincerity) to explain the bankruptcy of Kiki's marriage. Hadn't Nick always been a little in love with Celia? Even without wanting to, wouldn't he then have taken her side in her treacherous account of events leading to the divorce? Or even this: hadn't there always existed in Nick a more or less latent but powerful homosexual impulse, and wouldn't their friendship perhaps have been just a mask for a physical passion that Nick could not even confess to himself? This possibility might contribute, incidentally, to an explanation of his unusual suicide. If Nick had acted out of spite because he believed the grossly mendacious Celia, he would also know full well that the one he would hurt the worst was the old friend who confided all his troubles to him. But, even if this reality weren't so grave, it is very clear that Nick was not truly his friend, not his good friend, and the best thing for him to do now would be to just forget all the questions that have anguished him about his relationship with Nick.

This way of seeing things comes along unexpectedly and

alleviates forever the grief Kiki has been feeling for Nick. It is undeniable—their relationship wasn't a true, deep friendship.

"However, what *is* true friendship?"

Kiki's speculative approach to things hasn't disappeared. He freely reflects on this question with some frequency in the midst of these last few days' cyclone of activity. And he believes he has approached it from every angle. He has applied philosophical, psychological, and even biological knowledge to it. ("Once, when he could still count on sufficient income to permit himself such luxuries, Kiki had an ambition to be Goethe and started studying biology.") His attack on the burning question of how friendship should be defined has inspired abundant notes and he has inscribed them in his notebook. He's looking forward to his future essays and cannot pass up any opportunity he is offered to enrich his bibliographical fortunes.

We now offer a *florilegio de sus doxa*. (*The reader alone will decide if this little "treasury" of Kiki's "flowering beliefs" has much, little, or anything to do with the theme of friendship.*)

—Certain types of human behavior can only be defined, in any strict sense, by one word: *portmanteau*. This is regarding *reptilinear* men."

—There are those who won't forgive you for their factual betrayal of you (and to think that there are people even worse than they are!)."[1]

—Why the cult of feminine virginity? Because the human male aspires to demonstrate that his woman is nothing without him."

—A legitimate morality is possible only after all the possibilities as well as all the limitations of the species are taken into account."

---

1   Who is Kiki alluding to when he says this? Is it to people who do not forgive others for not having betrayed them? Does this have anything to do with a curious hypothesis about Nick's conduct in relation to Celia? Would Celia have made Nick abridge certain expectations, as is generally supposed? (N. of A.)

—A *breakdown* is what occurs when the partially constructed ego cracks and threatens to fall, or, alternatively, when the scaffolding still needed for its construction is badly made and begins to collapse. Then the builder, an ego that wants to be whole and this being one of its destinies, realizes that at any given moment—perhaps even very near the beginning of construction—it must already have committed some error in its calculations.

—In the Devonian, all those hundreds of millions of years ago, the formidable fauna of armor-plated fish go extinct. In the Cretaceous, the dinosaurs, the proudest, most useless forms ever generated by nature, disappear. Man, a culture-plated being, is also being called on to vanish. Proving their radical uselessness, will all hyper-complex structures that have ever been thought of in vane, disappear?

—Why does man alone have history? Von Weizsäcker's answer: because he's the only animal that is provided with a conscience.

—Nature's wonder: an embryonic form is independently (but, how independently?) alive and has the whole world for its womb. Dig in and study this point (Bolk, Portmann, Ashley Montagu).

—The big city, immense, exceedingly modern, oppressor of the *ville radieuse*: in it, individuals devolve into small tribes. (At least, that may be what they would like. But they have no totemic faith.)

—'All of humanity's problems . . .' Thus Pascal's acclaimed principle begins. How comforting this sounds to the fellow riding in a train crossing the green landscapes of a strange country, while tons of unhappiness weigh on his mind because his sweet little woman has abandoned him (or some trifling thing like that). But let's take a moment to consider the possibility that another individual—and it takes all kinds to make the world—listens carefully to Pascal's counsel, heeds it to the letter of the law starting long before the moment he suffers some bad misfortune ('bad' at least in his judgment, but doubtlessly not equal to Calderón's). He stays in his room, just stays put, until he finally ceases to be human. (By the way, what we have in that second case offers a possible and quite plausible explanation of *The Metamorphosis*.)

In the annotation that follows, Kiki, who seems to have yielded a little to the force of the whirlwind of those last days before his marriage, writes:

—Is this all there is in his life? Where are the outrageous erotic fantasies that for so many years had bombarded him and traced his entire biography? What has become of his fear of dying? (In a sense, although no friend of his might suspect it, his entire life so far has been a constant *Timor mortis conturbat me.*) But has he really felt the terror of it? Perhaps it would make more sense to qualify the phenomenon as a deliberate confrontation with death that has been ongoing since he was eighteen, on that night of the sinister fire when he discovered that he was alone forever and might have wanted to call out for his mama—who was so close, only half a room away. Since then, all those men and all those women have done him so much damage, isolating him even more.

—Return to your roots. To say, like that old (North) American anthropologist A.G., that every culture, in the end, is reduced to the individual, is a false proposition. In a huge majority of cultures—as innumerable ethnographic investigations have shown us—the individual, in the way we conceive of him in our civilization, that is as a legitimate *in*-dividual, barely exists at all.

—Remembered from Barbey d'Aurevilly (if I use this quote, I should, when it's convenient, run to the public library to verify its accuracy): *'les poètes, come les tortues, portent leur maison sur leur dos et cette maison c'est le palais des premiers songes, qu'ils emportent à jamais sur leur pensée (et où qu'ils aillent!), comme une écaille brillante ou sombre.'*

—How many years have I, d'Artagnan, sought my three Musketeers to no avail! Novels are a bad preparation for life. 'Thanks for telling me!'—Cervantes might say to that, but let's not forget that 'the immortal with one hand,' as our professor of compulsory literature in high school used to call him, also wrote novels. And Don Quixote, after all, is not very much more effective as a model than d'Artagnan.

—Those very vivid memories of yours have been yet other deaths. Of epiphanic death.

—The instant that each of us dies implies every person's final judgment day. Is Nick's death my redemption? Can Nick's death redeem me?

We leave Kiki for a moment and let him contemplate these questions. They may be an obsession with him, but let's step away a few paces (shall we say ten or a dozen, even?) and observe him from that distance. It then becomes evident that this individual, to tell the truth, is so self-engrossed, although he believes himself to constantly worry about others, that *he* is the only thing that matters to him.

As far as that goes, it's worth pointing out that, in the preceding annotations, written precisely at the time he was about to contract matrimony with his Redemptive Humpback, there is no mention of her in them. Look at this very carefully: it's not that there is no favorable mention; it's that, in the whole batch— with the exception of another, final annotation, which sounds somewhat forced—there is absolutely no reference even passably recognizable as being about his fiancé. As a consequence, those of us who already know a little about her see her only as old, erudite, and oversexed: a nutjob. So why not admit it? She is another victim of Kiki's enormous ego, the trait for which Celia so often reproached him (and now it seems she was right) and that Nick also noticed, but found it worthy of only a little surreptitious rancor that he harbored toward his justly criticized friend.

Regarding Orvieto, since Celia's disappearance has decisively ended for Kiki any possible rivalry with him, his curious figure also no longer holds any interest for Kiki. Scanning the daily news—Kiki is only interested in references to his imminent expedition in search of the Baikas—he never notices it when the peninsular *gelehrte* publicly announces that he has just married a young lady named Barbara Dowd. (*We will leave it to our reader's own imagination to trace the course of that adorable little thing's life as a slightly matronly adolescent.*) It almost goes without saying, therefore, that egotistical Kiki, who always reads the police news with interest, also does not catch on—not even by simply tying up what are called loose ends, never mind how vast he thinks his powers of imagination are—when the sensationalist press widely reports details of a discovery of charred human bones (belonging to two young females, according to forensics reports), which were found by garbage collectors at the end of a run. The bones appeared unaccountably mixed in with pieces of ceramic and partially melted metallic objects in garbage picked up from the most elegant neighborhood of Megalopolis.

We should not be surprised: Kiki is a man who has never been adept at this simplest of all the imaginative arts. That's why he has for years kept among his papers an item that might have given him redemption or, at least, provided the palliative par excellence for his spirit, which is so often upset as he searches for the meaning of friendship. He has kept tucked away this open-sesame that could possibly have opened the doors to a happier life for him—and he's even able to recite it from memory using his implacable and impeccable memory—but only because it was a piece of beautiful poetry. We're talking about a poem that he wrote and dedicated to his old friend L.E. Lover. *"What has become of Lover?"* he still asks himself from time to time. It is typical of his egotism that he has never taken a step to reestablish his relationship with that brilliant boy, now so faraway, for he, in contrast to Kiki, wisely remained in his old stomping grounds. But, since Kiki has kept a copy of this poem in his notebook, we can now present it to the Reader, and offer additional enlightening information.

The Poet Accepts Oblivion's Arrival

On December 14, 1944 you mailed a letter.
It was to a girl you loved.
It is worth recognizing that on the same day
you had your hair clipped and your fingernails cut.
Where is that hair? Where are those nails?
Where is that girl? Where are you inside her?
In a prosaic enumeration of losses,
writing the story of forgetting becomes less difficult.
You had friends then
and told them everything you had inside you:
the thoughts, the feelings, the love, the pain.
Do you by chance know which corners of their minds
hold your gifts?
One may be in Chicago and there you will not show up,
Hamlet's father filled with revenge,
to remind him that you exist, that you and he talked
once, before, in the mountains, in the hotel of a Swiss.
One, maybe in Buenos Aires, once while he sleeps,
includes you among his dream interlocutors:
yours may be the face in the mirror, maybe not; maybe
you are only you
because of a sweater you no longer wear.
And she, what shall I tell you about her? She remembers
a book.
You gave it to her with a fervent dedication
written in schoolboy French.
(Oh! You were such a snob in those days!)
Maybe on her way somewhere she lost the book.

But once, if she still has it,
she could leafthrough it.
With a sigh or a tenuous smile, you think, but
what if she only shrugs her shoulders?
(What you have to fear
is—consider this—her disdain: the thrown away page.)
In reality, minds have many corridors,
dark entrails of gestures and words
as natural as the cycle of a fruit or your own body.
You are born, grow up, and die buried in them.
Maybe you want to stay there permanently, a thorn
to convert the tangle of their nerves
into fabric as lethal as Medusa's hair?
Since that is—and I agree: it is a shame—the only
alternative.

The final notation in Kiki's journal is hardly lacking in interest. (And that's not only because it gives something like closure to his life in Megalopolis. Almost certainly, since this must soon be seen with more clarity anyway, it also seems to give closure to his self).

Kiki writes:

"I now feel that, until finding myself, only a short time ago (but how long I've needed you!), with this adorable woman, whose physical deafness is amply compensated by her exceptional spiritual openness, my whole life has been too much under the influence of literature. I have never confessed this to anyone, not even poor Nick, but, when my rotten destroyer threatened me that day, feigning, though I didn't know it then, that she would throw herself out of the window, for an instant I felt the same temptation that had hounded me persistently during the last sea voyage she and I made together. On the day of her torturous threat—even though I still loved her madly! even though I was begging her not to throw herself out the window!—I believe there was only one thing that saved me from *pushing* her. And that was my suddenly remembering the conclusion I'd come to on that crossing, after no insignificant amount of deep thinking about my terror of throwing her into the ocean in a moment of irrationality. For I'd begun to see that my obsession had its origins back in my country, many years before, when I read a play by T.S. Eliot called *The Family Reunion*, in which the protagonist is the victim of a similar obsession. Literature has ruled the course of my life! That is so sad!

"And what can I say about the countless days I've spent believing I was seeing a horrendous scene, a nightmare veiled from my memory, simply because . . . somewhere: in a bar or, more believably, in a telephone booth, during one of those many times I felt an urgent need to communicate with Celia, to beg her to come back to me (I was such an imbecile!), I had lost a . . . just my old copy of Pascal's *Pensées,* on the cover of which—I can still see that cover so clearly—feeling Pascal-like one time (what *arrogance!*), I wrote my own 'thought' (how *vulgar!*): 'Each man's death implies everyone's final judgment.'"

The boy smiles in relief. He has managed to noiselessly open and close the outside door. His mother, who nearly four hours ago threw herself on her bed, tearful, hair disheveled, knows he has now finally come in. But it's already too late. She'll pretend to sleep deeply. The boy can hear her snore. He had given himself away while he slept once, when he murmured a name, some Señorita Celia or other. "How ungrateful." The boy listens to the snoring: "Poor Mama. And when she hears my news . . ." She must feign until the end, must keep pretending she's fast asleep. "I'm going to get married, Mama, you know?" She has left the kitchen light on for him. "Poor Mama, always worried about me." "Is this how he's going to show me his gratitude?" "It's life, Mama." "The light is on." "I know she has left something for me to eat. Is this how I ought to show her my gratitude? But it's the way life evolves, Mama." "I knew the moment would come when he wouldn't love me anymore, when he would rebel against my rules." "It's a natural thing to do now, Mama, human nature. I have to follow life's dictate." "It is the nature of life, the wicked law of human nature. You take such good care of them, you deprive yourself, even of indispensable things. I've only been deluding myself thinking that with him it was going to be different. No, he's exactly like his father and there's nothing you can do about it. How stupid I've been!" His bowl of noodles with tomato sauce is still there warming. But the boy feels no desire to eat, even though, for the first time in his life, he's been with a woman. "And I was so hungry after that." Remembering it, he feels ashamed. "That was strictly physical! But *then*." The mother has been on the verge of leaping up and running to him. "I could still get it all back. My darling boy, come here into your good Mama's loving arms. No, oh, no! That is only another illusion. You have lost him forever, now, so what good is anything! It's best to lose him completely." The boy's intense feelings of love, laughably, have killed his appetite altogether. "I got down the rat poison I bought to protect his books." "Poor little Mama, as soon as she wakes up, she'll undoubtedly go in to see if I've eaten my supper. But I'm not hungry." "He won't feel it, it will be almost nothing; a few seconds and he will be free of all his deception." "But what should I do? I have no appetite. I should let her see that this time I haven't taken a bite. Isn't it really better to give her a sign that things have changed? Oh, her small hands, so lovely, they felt so cool when she stopped the burning in my eye. Tomorrow as soon as I get to the office, I'll call her. She asked me to only call her at her house at night, but . . ." The mother, still lying in her bed, is imagining his movements, her hearing sharp, she feels tense. "I'll call her really early, as a surprise. I wonder if she likes to lie in bed a little while in the morning?" The boy takes off his jacket. A very recent, lucid memory takes hold of him. Even so, he feels very tired and goes up to his studio. "Ingrate! You don't even come in here to see if I'm asleep." He's ready to just throw himself on his bed. "Damn! I forgot to turn off the kitchen light. Wow, I'm really tired. She leaves the light on, as if it's nothing, as if every electric bill we get doesn't represent a serious problem for me. No. I've got to stay calm. Mama has to realize that this isn't just a passing thing. It's not kid stuff." Making an effort, the boy goes down to the kitchen to turn off the light. The table, set so carefully for him, softens his feelings. How can he disappoint poor Mama, especially over such an inconsequential little thing. "It's not her fault. She has a mother's natural egotism. I'm her only son. I have to take all these facts into account." He sits down at the table and picks up the fork. "What have I done! Oh my God!" She's running to him. *Run!* The fork has fallen to the floor.

Fetid smoke still obscures the deserted, grand living room; the floor is covered with ashes and littered with debris. It is an hour after the crowd's escape. O Jango lies neutralized, but who knows for how much longer; he's stretched out on a kitchen table, dreaming, legs relaxed.

"It's time to get moving," the minion says aloud, as if to give himself some encouragement, although he's already completely convinced of his plan's security. He, of course, has been in on everything for a long time, known every detail of the "happening," "potlatch," "party," or whatever you call it. "Holocaust" may be the precise term. He helped O Jango come up with the idea and after that it was up to the minion's genius and foresight to do the rest. And he has prepared meticulously for the occasion, hasn't omitted a single detail. Now he is alone—O Jango presents no danger, submerged as he is in one of those nightmares he likes to tell later. He always embellishes them. But, even so, one thing can't be missed: they worry him. The minion is completely at home in the vast apartment. And it now offers him, according to his calculations, a fabulous haul. "Maybe it will be enough to give me a couple of years free of Jangos. The Texas multimillionaire actually *could* be as tyrannical as they say."

No sooner had he helped O Jango up from his throne and left him in a safe place in the hermetically-sealed kitchen, than he ran for the refuge he had prepared in the spacious armoire in his room. It was something he had thought to ask for and gotten. He was now certain no one could still be in the living room, or any of the rooms. "At the most you would trip over the body of some drunk. But in that case, it would be more accurate to talk about a cadaver: after being exposed so long to the smoke, anyone would have been asphyxiated."

No, considering this possibility is not a calming thought. At this point he has to move swiftly if he wants to carry out his plan without any hitches. He pulls on the shiny black rubber gloves and quickly slips on the gas mask he bought in a war surplus store. Only then does he dare open the door of the armoire, however sure he may be that no smoke could have penetrated his room. It's the one furthest away from the bonfire. And, in fact, the very small amount of misty smoke that has appeared in his room does not impede his admiring himself in the armoire mirror for a long time in his strange outfit. He recognizes with some enthusiasm that he looks impressively macabre and a lot like a mutant. After all, the minion, among other things, is clearly also a frustrated actor; he has always wanted to play Peer Gynt. His vanity impedes his acceptance of the possibility that his current sinister appearance has nothing to do with his natural genius for playing roles, and everything to do with his choice of armor, the black rubber gloves and the gas mask.

Opening the door of his room, he easily verifies that the smoke is still very thick. He is surprised. He has no option but to retrieve the electric lantern he left in the armoire; he thought he wouldn't need it.

He gingerly makes his way to the coat closet. If any bodies litter the floor, he sees none in his path. The only noises come up from the street. The coast is clear, but it's prudent to close the windows so that none of those well-meaning squares who never fail to show up call the fire department afraid something is burning. How odd he didn't think of that till now: his whole plan could have been ruined. What if firemen are on their way up right now and find him, as usually happens, with his fingers in the cookie jar? But, no, all he needs to do is deadbolt the front door, which the crowd undoubtedly left wide-open in their rush to escape to safety. Any firemen have to ring the bell and bang on the door a good while before forcing their way in and they're all so square he can count on having more than enough time to get back to his room and lie down on his bed and pretend to be asleep, dead drunk like the host.

As he gets ready to secure the front door, he sees a tattered portrait of O Jango on the threshold. He smiles. Instantly crossing his mind is an image of Dorian Gray, who at least was a lot handsomer. What a lesson *this* is going to teach his conceited boss when he finds it tomorrow. He can't waste any time now and lets go of the idea of perfecting the lesson with a little excrement. He must get on with his own project; that is the important thing now: to collect the booty. Just as he imagined, the coat closet is overflowing with women's handbags. Real treasure chests! And not just in terms of the jewelry, gold lighters, and cash here and there in them—all of which he will take. However much all that may be worth, it's the least considerable portion of his haul. Letters. Letters: that is what he wants to get his hands on; above all, those confidences about intimate relations that tomorrow he will use to blackmail their authors. His very careful management of those assets will assure him of a small but adequate income for the rest of his days, which he, obviously, will be able to spend in Mexico in the pleasant company of other exiles of his kind. He can finally stop worrying about finishing that definitive, annotated edition of his favorite poet, Keats: "What shocks the virtuous philosopher, delights the chameleon Poet" and "a Poet is the most un-poetical thing of any in existence." In those two affirmations is the best program for his survival among squares.

Generally speaking, the haul gives him no reason to complain. In terms of cash, honestly, he doesn't find very much. But on the other hand, the number of valuable, small objects—even some stunning emerald earrings—exceeds his earlier estimates by far. And of course he has carefully preserved any page that is written on in anything like a confidential tone.

His inventory done now, all he has left to do is leave O Jango's, and the sooner the better. "See you again never, you son of a bitch!" Still, he stops a moment on his way out and, even though every minute represents a loss, spits very carefully in the eye of the ruined portrait. "Too bad I don't have time to defecate on you."

In the elevator he rips off the gas mask, which he will throw in the first garbage bin he sees. The black rubber gloves he wants to leave on, since he really likes the sinister aspect of his hands in them. "After all, we're in a free country. Everybody wears whatever they like." But, near the end of his quick taxi ride to the hotel in the Village, where, some days before, he reserved a room, he decides that it's better not to awaken the concierge's suspicions, especially considering the hour. Sighing, he proceeds to take them off. "In Mexico I'll be able to use them all the time. Unless it's too hot, which would be a real shame, because I truly love the way they feel on me."

The night clerk hands him the key to his room, where two suitcases, his only luggage, already wait, and then watches him all the way to the elevator. He's trying to imagine how any guest could have gotten so covered with the smell of smoke, especially since there isn't the least trace of soot on his face and hands. A superstitious Negro cast formed from an old-fashioned mold, he shudders at the thought that the new guest could be an escapee from hell.

In all, O Jango's minion has garnered fourteen extortive letters based on the usual abortions and adulteries, in addition to a particularly promising exchange of letters among a lesbian trio, one of which is an old drunk, that half-idiot millionaire. "A great haul!" he exclaims joyously. But, immediately, remembering the story of the milkmaid and the pitcher, he sits down to study a strange typewritten document. He remembers very well the things he found in that imitation leather purse, undoubtedly belonging to a common typist. And obviously a lady's accessory glaringly out of place at O Jango's. That purse held a photo of a really ugly guy in thick glasses and shirtsleeves surrounded by piles of books and hunched over a portable electric typewriter, and a few coins and this document, which is several pages long. That's all there was in the handbag, but the document itself is very intriguing, starting with the title:

Eternal Points of Prestige in Fiction

"The *most* mysterious art is the one that explains itself. A game, on the other hand, is always an explanation of itself and definitively suppresses any interest in it. In another way, that *is* the game, unless it becomes desirable to think otherwise in order to stop tripping over some more or less Platonic conception of the ludic.

"Therefore, self-referential fiction becomes the most fully fictitious kind, that is to say, the most mysterious kind of fiction of all.

"Then why is fiction seductive? Why does the sultan not take matters into his own hands and suspend the labyrinthine outpouring of narratives, or, more accurately stated, of a single narrative, as dense and vast as any obsession? Why does he not dare to order Scheherazade to stop talking? Undeniably, an answer that cannot satisfactorily explain the phenomenon was given ages ago by, for example, a superficial commentator in the language of an academician's apprentice: *'Le roy aime les histoires et aimera Schéhérazade . . . et sa petite soeur Dinarzade qui a grandi pendant les trois années du récit. Schéhérazade, ayant prouvé que la poésie est souvent plus puissante que l'acte d'amour, devient reine.'* An explanation of this sort—'The king loves the stories and will love Scheherazade and her little sister Dinarzade, who grows up during the three years of the recital, and Scheherazade, having proven that poetry is often more powerful than the act of making love, becomes queen'—does not suffice. For one thing, we sense—and our experiences as readers corroborate—that the king was fundamentally aware that his favorite was laying a slow, clever trap for him (it's clearly the same trap that a Chesterton or a Marcel Proust, a Simenon or a Kafka sets for us to fall into over and over again). But, for another thing, we're still ignorant of the root of the *virtus* of poetry (better, read: 'of fiction') and that ignorance can make it more potent than even the act of love.

"It turns out that fiction sets man down on the very tenuous—but not less secure because of its intangibility— point of demarcation between the order of dreams (which for our consciousness is nothing but a chaos) and the disorder of experience (which from time immemorial consciousness has proudly labored to put in order through its metaphysics and other systems of reasoning). The disorder of this "ordered" wakefulness that we call reality exists for us, first and foremost, when we're awake, including for the Freudian who, while he was awake, may have read his teacher through his intelligence. What we call reality may be similar to what has been described as a *one-and-the-sameness* that expresses itself in two modes, *'una eademque res sed duobus modus expressa.'*

"But fiction introduces the creative principle into our vigilance. Through it, reality ceases to be pure fact, something that pre-exists the individual and co-exists with him, but is

independent of him by being previous to him. With fiction in
the mix, the course of reality, the 'how things develop,' depends,
from that moment, on the strength of its creativity and can
fill up with strange formations (beings, situations, moods),
like those that appear in dreams . . . but, how can I put it,
becomes more solid and, especially, more 'graspable.' For that
very reason, whoever hears or reads a piece of fiction feels that
in some way he has succeeded, with the narrator's help, in
satisfying another timeless human longing: to control the very
order that operates in the world of dreams, a domination highly
resistant to the exercise of our will. One of the old 'aphorisms
from hell,' and something also recently told us by a novelist
brand-new on the scene, will facilitate the comprehension of
the above. William Blake assures us that 'what is now proven,
once was only imagined.' For his part, the young French writer
Michel Butor, in whom we have to recognize one of the few
bright lights of our generation, maintains that 'True realism is
not possible unless the part that imagination plays is conceded,
unless one understands that the imaginary is in the real and
that we see the real through it. A description of the world that
doesn't take into account the fact that we dream, would be
nothing but a dream.'

"Fiction is better than pure daily reality at teaching man how
one life connects to others, how external events concatenate and
exert influence on our lives (that umbrella of Karl Rossmann's!),
and how lives move events, which in turn . . .

"All in all, we're talking about something very close, if not
identical, to the lucidity with which a sleeper senses beforehand
the intentions of objects in his dream, even in situations that
at first look very innocent. In fiction, lucidity acts upon the
most familiar materials of the most inoffensive appearance that
at all times are under the influence of one's awareness, under
the imperative of utility. In this sense, it must be admitted that
fiction always constitutes a lesson in prudence: man is not as

much a master of quotidian reality as he can appear to be at first, as modern sciences usually teach us—with one or two notable exceptions.

"Thanks to the fact that practically every anthropologist worthy of our credibility has commented on this, it's known that archaic man didn't draw a clean dividing line between the realms of sleep and wake: the night's contents were, for him, no less concrete or more solid than those of the morning on which he went into the jungle to hunt the tapir or traversed the river in his pirogue, making his way through voracious families of caimans. However, similar notions of equalizing night and day have been abhorrent to the waking mind of modern man for a long time. (In this sense, our 'modernity' goes back at least as far as the emergence of the philosophical conscience in Greece.) As far as the modern conscious mind has been concerned, modern human nature aspires at every moment to be perfectly faithful to reason. Yet, under the spell of fiction, even the most rational person finds himself forced to repeat attitudes of archaic man, because, in the middle of his clearest thinking, he must also concede to the contents of the invading imagination.

"All fiction—and Joyce's *Ulysses* cannot be excluded—is always and necessarily, with exhausting care, an abbreviation of awareness. In fiction, events can rush together and push each other (as occurs constantly in our waking life). But also in fiction, all events are always pre-selected and woven together in some way and possess meaning and have their respective goals, and it's clear at every moment that they have them. However much we are ignorant of what those meanings and goals are (as happens always in dreams), that ignorance must dissipate when a piece of fiction, be it a fairy tale or a novel of Tolstoy, reaches its end—contrary to what happens in the case of dreams, whose hidden meanings, can only be clarified, very precariously, if we consult a psychoanalyst.

"For a certain kind of mindset, hostility imposes its spirit fairly spontaneously when someone makes an apology for fiction. At this point, whoever may have been following this exposition with a more or less stated hostility will be able to respond that, even accepting all that's been stated here, it always comes down to the fact that *fiction* is a synonym of *lie*.

"Then what is a lie?

"The author—let it be clearly understood henceforth by all—is not about to launch into a defense of lying. Our shared morals prohibit lying because, when a lie is efficacious, it dissolves the internal order as much as the external order, the internal *no less* than the external. Our shared knowledge is intended—although, we well know, no small number of times unsuccessfully—to be a method of eradicating the lie from the relationships we have with exterior and interior reality, as well as absolutely stripping a body of knowledge of its mendacity. Without that, what would come of our lives in our excessively technical world?

"But it happens that, in everyday life, we ought to distinguish among the slick lie, the flat lie, and the overflow of pure imagination (that is: the lie without a 'useful' purpose). An eminent German anthropologist, Richard Thurnwald, has warned that 'only "civilization" opposes the impulse to lie.' And we could go further: we could affirm, perhaps without exaggeration, that scientific-technological progress, a distinctive characteristic of our civilization, has only been possible since the lie was condemned as an immoral evil. Archaic man has lied for millennia and, look at him: condemned to remain, at his highest point, in the Neolithic.

"Regarding the same primitive peoples, the same anthropologist writes that 'things taken as true rapidly petrify in dogmatic repetitions not only of formalities but of doctrines and precepts. It is here,' he writes, 'that men have difficulty confronting their imaginations with facts and then rectifying the imagined in view of the foregoing.' (*Cf.* Thurnwald, R.: *Des*

Menschengeistes Erwachen, Wachsen und Irren, Verlag Duncker &
Humblot, Berlin.) Let us, with all our might, then, repudiate—
as Rotarians and Soviets ask us with one voice to do—attitudes
that impede the advancement of the empirical sciences and
therefore of technologies (although, truthfully speaking, at least
for our present time, we don't have good reason to build up our
hopes for any advancements in the mechanical and electronic
fields).

"But what must be said about that other kind of lie, the
one that, in its nascent state, is not harbored by the tribe as an
immutable principle safe from rectification, but only (only?)
as a fiction? Let us think, for example, of a pre-fifth-century
Athenian who shows up at the Agora to inform his fellow
citizens that he has just seen something similar to what today
we call *Sputnik* . . ."

Here the document is brusquely interrupted. (Roslyn had
not had time to get a clean version of the whole essay. At this
time of year, free minutes at the office are scarce.) No, the
thing certainly has no commercial value, especially in that
special sense of commerce as understood by the Minion. But
it cannot be denied that the document holds a certain kind of
interest, as attested to by the fact that he has reread a paragraph
or two of it. He would have wanted the unknown author to
explain—"and with less fake morality, please!"—the similarities
and differences between fiction and lie. In any case, he is still
dubious about the unknown author for just having suggested
he ponder such a burning question about human nature. "Only
human nature? Can't a god lie? And animals, don't they ever
come up with fictions? Maybe the thing about man, exclusively,
is that he uses the same power to both create a new reality and
distort facts.

"In which case," the minion recapitulates, feeling satisfied,
"man is only complete when"—as in his own case—"he's also

able to lie. Ah, but, on the other hand, the guy really shows his ignorance when he says that poetry is more powerful than the act of making love. Oh, but of course. He must be referring to the tedious relations between men and women only, just round after round interrupted by menstruation. Another typical prejudice of heterosexuals. No. Instead true poetry is simply an *attempt* to experience love—not *attempt* as in a failed try, but an uprising that one wants to be in to experience true love that is freely given, sure," the minion emphasizes to himself, as if he's afraid he's wrong and wants to stay in his error, "between individuals of the same sex. Just as, only between them, can you also have absolute hate. Either way, I'll be picked and one day I have to wind up on the path to it and follow it. But, meanwhile, I better shake a leg and kick up some dust. The jet leaves for Mexico at 5:00 and this is something too important for me to mess up."

He takes a long bath with aromatic salts to get rid of the repulsive odor of smoke he's noticed on his skin since he closed the door to his hotel room. Then, using the phone in his room, he orders an Old Fashioned from the bar, promising a generous tip to make up for the late hour. Savoring it, he decides to stretch out a while on the bed and sets his watch alarm for 3:30. He loves the little gold watch with a black face, so reliable, his best friend, it never fails him. He adores things that are black and gold, oh, if Africans only had golden hair!

At 3:30, while the minion is shaking off sleep, feeling very rested and very satisfied with himself, Roslyn, hair askew, face black with soot, tattered silk dress ("its color a little shrill, by the way"), Roslyn is now half-dead from exhaustion; she is in a very bad way. Above all, she is wracked with anguish—her heart in her mouth, to tell the truth—as she sits sprawled across the top steps that lead to Nick's apartment. She has lost her purse and with it her door key. She's tired of knocking, pounding with her fists, sighing, screaming, and sobbing.

No one answers. Did Nick see her at the party without her noticing he was there, when she was tempted, but for only a moment and nearly at the very end, by the strapping boy who was with O Jango? An attack of jealousy could explain Nick's silence. "Let him hit me, let him do anything he wants to me, anything, anything, but not this silence!"

Without realizing it, Roslyn is putting into action all the common responses that melodrama authorizes for situations like this. "This deadly silence . . ." she says to herself. "No, don't give in, Roslyn, you're a big girl now. What can I do to distract myself while I wait for daylight to bring the doorman out. Yes, because then I'll ask him to open the door for me with his master key, even if I have to subject him to a huge scandal when the door opens. And what if they use the scandal as a pretext and throw us out of the building? But remember: since we've been here, Nick has never hit me. Who cares: let them all, let the whole neighborhood hear! I'm going to go in, come what may. And I'm going to throw myself at his feet.

"He will say I'm being melodramatic. I know that already, I already know it. But I'll throw myself on the floor at his feet anyway. I'm going to caress him, so very softly, just the way he likes me to. I'll pet him—crying. Am I crying already? Come, come, old girl, be a little tougher. You just have to distract yourself. Think of something else. The office! Tomorrow I'll have to play sick at the office. And it's already the third time this month. And tomorrow, today, I mean, is only the fourteenth! The boss is going to make such a face, and the worst thing is that, afterward, as usual, he'll try to collect on what he calls his small rights of seniority and he'll leave my butt full of bruises again. But it doesn't matter, because as soon as Nick receives Professor Dinessen's invitation to join the university, I'll ask him . . . but will I still be able to ask him after what has just happened . . .

is still happening?" *Stop. No, my girl, you're going down the wrong road. Always back to Nick. Something else, anything else, I'm telling you. Think about yourself for a change.* "What you need is a dose of ego. That's why men use you like an object and then throw you away, exactly as if you *were* an object. Of course, but it's because I like them. What can anybody do about that? And as for you, you, Nick, baby, my adored Nick, I love you so, so much. Oh, enough about Nick! That's an order! You listen to me: think about yourself a little bit. Reconsider things. Imagine how worried you'd be if something similar happened to—no, don't say his name! For at least a *minute*! Right! And my purse is nothing, didn't have anything valuable in it. Well, of course there was the key. But nothing else. (*Are you sure about that, nothing but the key?*) Wait a minute. The key, the key, and . . . something much more precious than the key too, you imbecile! The pages of that essay that Nick trusted to you to type. Remember?!"

She feels cold terror and can barely breathe. She has lost the essay Nick charged to her keeping with many, many recommendations that she take every precaution with it. One part of it at least is lost. How can she face him now, without those precious pages that she typed with such care, with actual, true devotion? Yes, he will despise her and deservedly. She has it coming. "Punish me, Nick, beat me, make me suffer, but forgive me!"

She cruelly digs her nails into her crossed arms (they are pretty, perfectly proportioned), pre-administering to herself the chastisement she begs for as expiation for her mistake. The physical pain calms her a little, but makes her feel even more exhausted. All at once a light goes on in her memory. "Yes! Yes! I left the originals safe in the middle drawer of my desk! All I'll have to do is type up a clean version, and this time I'll make two, no three copies of it. And I'll be absolutely meticulous when I type, there will not be a single erasure. My dearest Nick is going to realize that at least I'm useful to him as a secretary.

"Nick, my love, I'm dying to go to sleep. Where are you? Won't you just open the door? I want to get cleaned up a little and leave immediately for the office to type your manuscript. How crazy, though, when I'm typing it I can't even follow the thread of your ideas. And that long title in German is always really, really hard for me . . ."

TWO
ENAMELS AND CAMEOS

Per nomen mirabile
atque ineffabile
Dei tetra grammaton
   ut expaveatis
   et perhorreatis;
vos exorciso, Larve, Fauni, Manes,
Nymphe, Sirene, Hamadryades,
Satyri, Incubi, Penates,
   ut cito abeatis,
   chaos in colatis,
   ne vos corrumpatis
christianitatis.
(From the manuscript at *Benediktbeuren*)

Who Is Who in Megalopolis

At this juncture of his honest tale, the author feels a need to introduce into it a character who is entirely fictitious, Police Commissioner (Chief) Peter Ploughman, who is surrounded by a veritable swarm of individuals yanked from the most convincing reality, as will immediately be seen. Against the multiplicity of reality, fiction offers concrete, specific human lives, which are always somewhat viscous and at least a little dual. This gives it a highly appreciable advantage, namely: in fiction, experience has already been evaluated, developed, and tightly tied down so that it isn't susceptible to modification by every new possibility (or temptation, if religious terminology is preferred) that the individual is offered at every turn. In other words, fiction is always infinitely more objective than anyone's biographical experience. It can constitute a fixed center, a starting point to which it's always possible to return as one life follows another in the course of things, while that life makes faces, acts like a coward, falls into vices, and rises (very rarely) into one excellence or another. No better organizational element than this Peter Ploughman, police chief, could be found in the whole of tentacular, mastodont Megalopolis to describe the inevitable criminal investigation that begins with the discovery of charred human bones in garbage that—it has now been established beyond a shadow of a doubt—came from O Jango's apartment. It might be a good idea to clarify here, in addition, that Chief Ploughman, a hybrid of many kinds of detective, as fans of police novels can easily verify, owes his existence above all to G. K. Chesterton, thus his main concern is to make an inquiry with a theological bent; and to Ed McBain, due to which fact, readers should not declare their astonishment if at any given moment they see him proceed with straightforward brutality. It's also possible that his figure has a bit of the good-natured but infallible inspector Maigret.

Our Chief Ploughman, at the moment, is in his shabby office at central police headquarters, absorbed in thought. He has scrupulously reviewed certain documents found at O Jango's and some of them seem to have a singular importance. (It should be understood that this perception is due to one of those celebrated "palpitations" of his that the final solution invariably corroborates.) He is very aware that said documents were discovered inside a volume bound in blue Moroccan leather that once held the embellished foolishness of Théophile Gautier. Written on its spine, not at all austere in ornamentation, the name of the poet and the title *Émaux et Camées* also constitute an unfailing clue to the mystery of the macabre discovery that is shaking public opinion in Megalopolis and giving full rein to the oratory of xenophobic demagogues who speak with great success about undesirable millionaires who are also foreigners, as well as cannibals.

Chief Ploughman, a kind man, is not quite obese, but, overall, is a bit languid, and is a formidable 6'6" tall. He has unquestionably penetrating gray eyes and retains a good portion of his blond hair, despite his seventy-two years. When he wrinkles his brow, his vision seems to get lost as it descends into the very center of his being.

He is faraway from the world right now, and it looks as if, between them were intervening something more than the thick, lightly misted lenses in his tortoiseshell frames that make him look like a movie critic. Good-natured, slow-moving, almost excessively overweight, Chief Peter Ploughman is absorbed in a kind of meditative coma. His brow stays furrowed. At this moment, more than ever, he is "Nobodaddy," that is, nobody's daddy. He is called "Nobodaddy," sometimes with affection and always with respect, by the criminals of Megalopolis and of the entire nation. Joyce himself would have coveted this piece of linguistic art, this apt *trouvaille*, except that everybody everywhere knows that the chief's nickname was given to him by Billy Caprino, the lascivious "chopping assassin" of retired women schoolteachers. At the time, it seems, Caprino was a devoted reader of William Blake and therein found the precise epithet he wanted to use for his revenge. But was it really revenge he exacted with it? For his enemy later gained his affection; they even say the convict sobbed and embraced the commissioner when he was fetched for his final walk to the gallows, upon which he went on to quote: "The fox condemns the trap, not himself" and "The lust of the goat is the bounty of God."

But just now "Nobodaddy" is in no mood for proverbs from Hell. He has cleared his mind of almost everything, which is to say, he has completely forgotten the glass of beer warming there that he asked to have brought to him half an hour ago. His mind is tirelessly shifting between two propositions. After his intense reading of every page of *Émaux et camées* (in O Jango's completely revised version), he can't explain why it has triggered in his mind a certain inscription he found long ago, on the front cover of an old copy of Pascal's *Pensées*. That copy—and it's not at all a bad idea to add this information—was found lying next to the cadaver of that almost mythical actress and associate of the Comédie Française, Justine Noirceuil. Some reader may possibly still remember that Justine Noirceuil's projected triumphal final world tour was cut short in Megalopolis by the hand of an assassin, when Mademoiselle was strangled. But first she was raped. (*Well, each to his own taste and don't think that this consideration is banal here.*) Mlle. Noirceuil was already in her seventies at the time her contributions to the stage forcibly ended. Nobodaddy now conjectures a link between that banged-up little old lady's corpse and the case he now finds in his hands. The single reason for this seems to be that the volume now on his desk, just like that old copy of the *Pensées*, is partially burned. It's pretty badly singed anyway.

The assassin in that old case was never found and, it may be said in passing, handed Nobodaddy one of the only two defeats in his career as a criminologist. Maybe that's why the case is so fresh in his mind, still prickling with the humiliation of defeat. The killer was a barbaric maniac, "the vampire of Megalopolis," as one impatient reporter, hoping to hit it big, said at the time. The killer must have tried to use the fire to destroy an important piece of evidence, but didn't have time to see the operation through to its end. After so much time, can this new crime by some chance be related to that same criminal? Nobodaddy knows that an assassin of that type, *once a maniac always a maniac*, cannot hide in the shadows month after month before striking again. No, if that volume of the *Pensées* has popped into his mind, it is for some other reason, something handwritten on the book's cover: a new *"pensée"* put there by someone—but who?—acting on his own without coercion. (*Really?*) By adding a "thought" to those the religio-mathematic genius of Clermont-Ferrand had put inside the *Pensées*, was the thought's author trying to compete with the Frenchman's using the fruits of his own mere spiritual harvest? (What a waste of time, we add, begging the permission of the amiable reader.)

But the added thought has remained engraved with indelible letters in the chief's spirit (which tends to oscillate between inflexibility and kindness), for it impinges directly on his profession. He has sent a great many murderers to the gallows while reciting it word-for-word from memory: "The moment of each man's death implies every man's judgment day." But did a murderer write that?

These thoughts suddenly cease to interest Nobodaddy. The pendulum swing of his memory has deposited them next to his second fascinating proposition. It's the same one that so worried Lawrence of Arabia, the commissioner's favorite hero, and, more than a proposition per se, it is better understood as a dilemma: you save the baby or the cathedral. (*It's true, this case isn't about cathedrals, exactly; but as for babies . . .*)

Nobodaddy has at his disposal a complete list of O Jango's art treasures, each one a true jewel in the universe of appearances, every one of them destroyed on the more smoky than resplendent night of the potlatch. Nododaddy has also verified the names of the guests invited to the party, having assiduously perused the individual files in the deceptive volume covered in blue Moroccan leather with labyrinthine golden arabesques on the spine. Inside the cover is commentary so personal and caustic that it incriminates O Jango as the author. But Nobodaddy, a homebody, never goes to parties and so has no inkling of the fact that they always include intruders. He innocently thinks that all he has to do is identify the guests—and he will, at the appropriate time, he isn't worried about that—who, on that fevered night, did not leave O Jango's apartment. What most concerns him now, considering them all together and each one in particular, is the sociological sample of humanity that the list of those in attendance at the party-holocaust can provide him with. And, it's quite fair to say already, this is the most refined portion of the multihued humanity of Megalopolis.

The moment of each man's death implies every man's judgment day and one must choose: the cathedral or the baby still at the breast? Nobodaddy's meditation switches back and forth between them, alternating tirelessly between these two focal points of his intelligence, and nothing can distract him. His beer has noticeably lost its frothy head. Through the half-open door, his subordinates cast commiserating glances his way.

But Nobodaddy's thoughts are now beginning to whirl. Is this about *choosing* death? Is dying a work of art? When he feels he's starting to lean toward this solution, he notices that he's on the brink of paranoia and manages to haul in the net of his spirit, snagged on something out there, and he opens the book on his desk again.

The commissioner rereads once more the descriptions (so critical) of O Jango's friends that are sketched in a stupendous calligraphy made by a pen soaked in venom, violet venom, because this is the color of the writing that covers the flexible, yet thick, soft-cream-colored paper, the likes of which, until now, Nobodaddy has never encountered in his criminological travels.

No, those first letters at the head of every character's portrait cannot be the work of O Jango. On the whole, they reveal the presence of an expert miniaturist, a wise, patient *artist*. And, in the image of O Jango that has been forming in the mind of the great detective, the multimillionaire from São Paulo has little of wisdom and a great deal less of patience about him. No, he must have contracted a specialist for those fascinating, sometimes terrifying, miniaturized symbols. And it's just wrong to throw away such subtle artistry on all that poison; yet, everybody already knows, money can do anything and . . . it's just better if everyone minds their own business.

"Back to work now," Nobodaddy tells himself again, this time armed with the English translation of Cirlot's *Diccionario de símbolos*. But that great work of erudition does not help him much: although he knows exactly what an ouroboros is, and a salamander and mandrake, he still can't seem to find a link that allows him to connect these mythological beings and the personages near whose names they appear in the volume entitled *Émaux et camées*. So Nobodaddy, quite out of character, fails to tie up the loose ends between these powerful symbols of the distant past and the present inhabitants of the same Megalopolis. They just lie perversely characterized before his eyes. He'll now have to reappraise O Jango's "gallery" once more and look for an irritatingly, elusively viscous cypher.

And once more he reads:

Lys Vallée.

Over fifty, evidently menopausal. Prone to affectation, as her name indicates. What her name doesn't indicate, on the other hand, is that she's from Tegucigalpa. (But who doesn't already know, at the very least, how much natives of Central America overdo it in the business of names?)

She was an outstanding opera singer in Europe in the roaring twenties. Really, you could say that it was she who roared out the whole decade. She retired at the right time, under the pretext of marrying a Puerto Rican magnate, Benito de Concepción, and they produced a baby daughter, Lys II, who accidentally drowned in the family pool in Chantilly in a moment of inattentiveness on the part of her nanny, who, they say, was called into her *patrón's* office for an unknown reason.

Lys I suffered a prolonged nervous crisis after that and moved to the United States in search of a more effective therapy than those offered by French psychiatrists. Then at the rest home where she was living, she met who else but the pugnacious and enterprising poet Caël, a patient there, like her, but he boarded for free: the clinic was satisfied just to have his literary fame and impresario abilities visible in their records. Caël was recovering at the time from the flight of his fourth wife, the notorious *danseuse nue* Victoria Stafford (*née* Rabinovitch). He soon completed his cure by having Lys reenact the brave escape of the woman he had been mourning. So one day the magnate, who had stayed behind in Paris scheming how to finally get accepted into the Jockey Club, received a short cablegram from some undisclosed place in Mexico that informed him of the dissolution of his marriage. Lys had already abandoned her art for the Puerto Rican's millions, and now she magnificently abandoned her magnate for the hermetic art of Caël. It just comes down to an irreproachable shift of dialectics, the prophetic meaning of which would, of course, not be lost on the poet—how could he miss a thing like that! This was soon made evident in his much-anthologized poem, "*Dans le lys il y a une vallée*," which can be translated, "In the Lily There Is a Valley."

At the death of her new husband, who was hit by a helicopter while sunbathing on the terrace of the building where they lived, Lys opted to move permanently to Megalopolis.

Motive for Invitation to the Potlatch: to set aflame, before her very eyes, a magical portrait of Lys II, that unsettling painting by Omar del Ramo in which the little girl appears at the bottom of the sea, surrounded by the vast fauna of the abyss and dressed in a diving suit without a helmet, her little-girl face prodigiously enameled. It's time to shake the old woman up again. All those airs she flaunts show that she's feeling like an empress.

Honey De Sucker.

Could be seventeen, could be thirty-seven. Two divorces, nearly two thousand pieces of fake Toltec ceramics from

Brooklyn, limpid blue eyes, a strict religious education at the Couvent des Oiseaux, where she was hastily sent by her progenitors after she was deflowered (not only with her consent, but also at her instigation) by an office boy at the reputable De Sucker Creameries.

She speaks German with a charming French accent and Castilian Spanish with the vigorous intonations of Jalisco (though she has never been there). She studied archeology under the supervision of M. Jacques Soustelle, which has presented no obstacle to her having found only fake artifacts in her excavations, demonstrating once more that what Nature does not give, Salamanca does not lend.

She claims that this was due solely to the vengeance of her first ex-husband (improbable).

She has recently returned to Megalopolis after three years in Italy and it's known that she did very well there as a *ragazza-squilla*. She was deported on grounds of a denunciation submitted by one of her clients who had gotten infected with the tenacious eczema that covers her shoulders. (N.B.: except for that persistent eczema, Honey is, without dispute, one of the great beauties of the moment, in Megalopolis or anywhere in the world.)

She claims—and the thing is, Honey is always claiming something—that her expulsion from Italy was because of a vengeful meanness in her second husband (impossible: for years her second ex has reposed in the private cemetery on my *fazenda* in Minas Geraes; but I don't plan to ever clarify this for her, for it could wind up compromising me in some way, although I had absolutely nothing to do with his accidental death while he was practicing prohibited games with a bazooka).

Motives for Inviting Her: her sincerity when she begged me to introduce her to Louise J. Bird (besides that, what a laugh it would be if she infected *her* with that obstinate eczema!). And my limitless curiosity to figure out where that Jaliscan accent comes from.

Olguita Agote Riesling.

I have before me her birth certificate and for that reason I believe that on the sixteenth of next month she will be twenty-seven years old.

They say she's extremely beautiful, and once they've said that she is extremely beautiful they invariably add: "in that Spanish way."

To me she looks exactly like Liz Taylor, a real peach! Dieunon (God no!), who once got it into his head to watch her while she was taking off her swim suit, swore that she has a little tail, like an old world Macaque (and it isn't every day that one has the privilege to count on the presence of a little simian that is so nice to look at).

Mosca (alias *Fatso*).

Restating: "the poet is the least poetic of all beings."

He could as easily be a clean-cut young Falangist as a hairy hippie; as easily a sonneteer in the floral games in Chascomús as an expressionist-abstract-concrete sculptor; as easily the most exemplary penitent in Ignatian spiritual exercises as the streetwise promoter of striptease dancers.

"Fatso" Mosca is anything and everything. And nothing.

He is as much man as woman. I have no doubt that he is the closest thing to the fabulous Tiresias of antiquity that realistically can be found today.

On the other hand, he's also capable of committing copycat suicide!

Ojal, Renato.

He, on the other hand, has reached forty-nine years of age trying hard to copy only one person.

He *is* Hemingway, without making war, without having any mortar shrapnel in his body, without fighting in Caporetto, without writing *Fiesta* or *The Old Man and the Sea*, without carrying a drunk James Joyce to his apartment while good-naturedly putting up with the screams of Irish Nora, without facing fierce bulls in the ring or bears in the mountains or rhinos in Africa. And, above all, without committing suicide. This essential difference from our friend Fatso is important: nothing in the world could bring Renato to suicide.

He also doesn't have Hemingway's great physical vigor. But he is certainly vigorous enough to *believe* he is Hemingway because, being a *petit rentier*, he has enough rental income at his disposal—but barely enough—to get drunk everyday on Valpolicella.

Except that now the dipsomaniac *ojal*, in earlier times a cross between the laughable and the repugnant, is getting his letters of nobility. In this, Renato is prototypical. And the allegorical "(button) hole" in his family name can't be denied.

Solar y Soler, Marie-Louise.

Oh the refinement of one who can feel the *nostalgie de la boue* with such intensity that she must diligently cover herself with *bosta*—as if she was in one of those mud baths they give you at certain thermal spas. Except she smells like fertilizer and cow dung, not *boue*, and leaves smears of shit on everything.

She has never been pretty, or what they call pretty, or known how to dress attractively. She is not a horrible person, and she knows how to distinguish a sketch by Toulouse-Lautrec from one by Degas, and back in the day she could write an ingenious dedication in a copy of the poems of Andrew Marvell.

But with an *ostinato* rigor she has stubbornly gone green, turned herself into a retailer of fruits and vegetables. Her head has acquired powers of prognostication that have to be considered atavistic.

Who can deny that Marie-Louise is a prototype?

Albamonte, Elodio.

He is fifty-two and always devises ways to anticipate the times, almost since his adolescence. For the last thirty years he has climbed socially—and now it's his ambition to be an ambassador and from what I hear he's on his way. He has cultivated a reputation as a man of culture, when actually he is almost illiterate. His only argument is that his ethnic composition is more than suspicious.

He's not even five feet tall and has the facial features of a hippopotamus and the manners and social graces of a recently freed Mucambo who would do anything but thank Dom Pedro II for the ill-fated idea with which he favored him.

Almost from birth he has promised to write a book, which without doubt should turn out to be pretty interesting if it's his autobiography and he narrates the facts objectively, for he's the very image of a *picaro* of the era of total literacy, a Lazarillo de Tormes of mass media.

Unhappily, perhaps due precisely to his organic structure, he never completes what he promises. But this could, after all, be added to his list of pluses.

Pip.

Age: seventeen. I know the risk I'm taking by having her come, given that she's a minor, but her presence seems indispensable to me because she is the always-indulgent feminine sex, ready to surrender herself at any time to anyone.

She is perfectly innocent. It's clear to me that she has no knowledge of malice. They say her father got it into his head to build a tri-motor plane in his basement, and, of course, it never successfully took off in such a confined space. Pip is a lot like her dad. An insatiable young woman, a man-eater who has never cannibalized anyone, she is always left feeling unsatisfied.

She can't . . . take off.

Igor Pérez-Smith.

As his double surname indicates, not only is he not Russian, it's very possible he doesn't know a single word of Russian. But when he talks about Moscow, where he once spent five days on an Intourist Excursion, his curly, extremely gray beard (which makes me think he can't be any younger than fifty-five) quivers, because his artistic temperament is, of necessity, revolutionary.

He doesn't paint, sculpt, compose, or write. But he has the temperament of a Bohemian artist!

If Igor is in a restaurant and the waiter is slow to attend the poet or painter he's attached to for the moment, then, exactly like mist clinging to the keels of ships to weather them, his temperamental-bohemian fury explodes all over the poor guy, who looks at him in embarrassment.

Igor is revolutionary: that is never in doubt.

Maybe I can persuade him to be an offering in the great holocaust.

Espinal, Silvina.

She speaks foreign languages horribly. With the years (she has to be at least forty) she has gotten very ugly. What they call frightful. Well maybe not yet, but she's on her way, almost there.

She lacks any known artistic talent, is notoriously frigid erotically, is always quiet at parties, hates sports, has absolutely no professional knowledge or artistic or intellectual skills, has inherited a mediocre last name, but is always everywhere and everybody knows her and always talks to her and the magazines keep publishing her photo among the most elegant women and most sought-after cabaret stars.

Reason for this invitation: it's impossible not to invite her.

Néstor de Talleyrand-Berrichon. (. . . et de la main gauche).

Seventy-two years old, and he's still not convinced that none of us believes the cheap prostitutes he spends time with are dear teenagers seduced by his (illusory) *criollo* male virility and then marinated with his French aristocrat's savoir-faire (also illusory).

No greater fortune than talent, no greater talent than a limitless audacity to elbow his way through the places most crowded with frantic prostitutes, he has tried his hand at all of the literary genres, including extortion. At least that's what I'm told by little Dieunon, who has reason to know (if he doesn't *know* . . .). And now our man's writing for television: "hot topics," his very words, "on the social question." He's had thirty years to find out how flattering it feels to flirt with lefties. We can only hope he doesn't live thirty more years and then finally figure out that Gide and Malraux wound up distancing themselves from the "progressive sectors."

Reason for Inviting Him: I want to hear M. Left Hand say "demi-mondaine" in his French accent. It gives me a delicious feeling of being among belle-époque trash.

Soledad Weisskopf.

Forty-two years old, ninety-nine lbs, 5'2" tall.

Dumb, what you call really dumb. Vain, the vainest. Mediocre in every other respect, even her prettiness, which is undeniable and boring.

She married a man with some intelligence and envied him for it, just as she had envied, from the day she met him, his modest title in the Dutch nobility. But, unfortunately, the marriage couldn't make her intelligent; though it transformed her into a baroness. As soon as she discovered this, she resolved to turn her home into a hell. But her husband, who at least for once knew he'd better exercise his intelligence for practical effect, ran away with a typist from the commercial delegation that employed him as chief of public relations.

Soledad keeps pretending to be a baroness. All the same, this loyalty to the noble class moves me.

Elke Trakl.

Twenty-seven years old.

She's gorgeous! Almost ravishing enough to make one feel tempted by a woman.

I can almost feel her presence. It's as if in this exact moment I had her in front of me again, in Paris, somewhere around 1959.

She's in dungarees and a plaid shirt, leather sandals, her blond hair so long I see it as a symbol of liberation. She is diminutive, her little face beautiful and intelligent almost beyond belief, and she's dancing an aboriginal samba from Latin America with an indescribable gracefulness, dancing to the sound of the reed flute she herself is playing, She has the perfect autonomy of a jungle spirit, a delectable elf, or the naughtiest little genie.

Fortunately, she's not drawn to men, and her work as a photographer for a television news department is always taking her away. I see in today's paper that they're going to give her an important prize for her work filming war actions in Vietnam.

Elke Trakl! Do you really exist?

A phantom, a delight.

Sol Whitman.

Thirty-three. Ex-Miss Megalopolis.

She's a born beauty queen and has in her all the foolish indifference the role requires. Married five times; if I was feeling melodramatic I'd say she has destroyed five lives. It was certainly premeditated, with malice aforethought, that she announced to her first husband, my late friend, the great Chilean historian Jorge Lester, that she was through with him, wanted nothing more to do with him, just like that. Jorge really worshipped her, was absolutely faithful to her. He had a considerable fortune that she could use as much of as she wanted and every year he took her to her city. From there they'd go to Europe and winter at the Georges Cinq or at the Claridge, not the hotels I prefer, but no one can deny that they are "first-class," as the tourism promoters say.

She told him, "Really it's just that I'm bored with you and that's that." Jorge shot himself in the soft pallet and she got a bunch of benefits.

Nine years and three husbands later, I happened to run into her again on the S.S. Uruguay. She was making the crossing from Rio de Janeiro to Megalopolis with her only son, a little boy about five, who she had with my friend the historian. So I'm a witness to the scene: she told the French nurse to leave the boy with her and go take a sunbath. Of course, it was not out of generosity for the nursemaid, her servant, but because she wanted to be admired for her magnificent beauty and elegance while she acted like a good mother.

And that's not just a suspicion on my part, because on that same occasion the kid was sobbing, doubtlessly because he was alone with a person cold to him, instead of finding himself under the watchful eye of his nurse. I heard her, not giving a fig about my presence there, tell him: "If you keep crying I'm going to throw you over the rail so the sharks can eat you." Then she immediately turned around to smile beguilingly at this Canadian tycoon who, at the moment, was admiring her radiant beauty. I can't imagine what traumas Jorge's son is going to suffer when he's grown; maybe Sol, without intending it, is contributing to the enrichment of the entire psychiatric profession's varied repertory.

Sol doesn't like men or women or children or animals or plants. The only thing in the whole world she likes is that face and figure that appears in front of her when she looks in a mirror. Nothing else. Sol Whitman—I'm sure of *this* too—doesn't like the flesh and blood Sol Whitman either.

Am I inviting her to exact revenge for poor Jorge's sake because he couldn't finish his book on the conquest of America?

Tilbury, Marcia.

Née Panetone. At twenty-seven she's still bothered by her real family name, being obviously of Italian extraction. She has kept her husband's name but lost her husband, who opted for running away with another woman, a chorus girl of some sort, instead of sticking around to put up with her frivolous beauty—and he wanted her that way: a frivolous beauty. *Her* only aspiration, once she was married, was to resemble, in every way and degree possible, his insipid relatives, the Van Borens.

A writer friend once helped himself to her in a flash, just by stating that a great Anglo-Saxon Protestant lady *has* to yield— "it's a great New England custom"—to the passions of an intellectual. "Neo-English ladies have always been characterized by their impartiality concerning books and authors."

He told me that, at the moment of coitus, little Marcia was still asking him, "Are you sure we're doing it the way we're supposed to?" She didn't ask that out of any scrupulous morality. What she really wanted to know was if she would be able to reach orgasm without slipping from her role of "daughter of the Revolution."

Motive for the Invitation. Of course, without realizing it, she's practically a whore. But besides that she has a certain charm also found in museum pieces. I bet that in all of this gi-normous Megalopolis she's the only young woman today still interested in keeping alive the most withered of the old vernacular traditions.

And isn't it just a little poetic to try and imagine what their grandfathers, great-grandfathers, and great-great-grandfathers used to be doing while the ladies of Boston and Concord were weeping over the fortunes of little Topsy?

Mariana Marx.

What was the name of Candide's beloved?

How I'd enjoy offering her nude and securely attached to an

easel, for a few of my guests, whose names even here it's better for me to suppress.

And how easy it would be for me to do it, given how in love she evidently is with me. It's too bad that her father, according to my very good source, controls an important part of the press here, and, worse yet, it's the most scandalous type.

Nineteen years old. Romantic: she writes poetry and recites *Toi et Moi* to me, which she knows perfectly by heart. And a good skier—not surprising since they educated her in Switzerland. Could even be a virgin, I suppose.

The characteristic beauty of the plump, naive kind. Indispensable for the potlatch, of course.

Omar del Ramo.

An ardent artist, big and healthy as a lion. Robust body, strong limbs. His beautiful hands, covered with soft, dark hair, are impetuous, energetic, generous—he has all the women at his feet. He imitates a drawing by Ingres with the same perfection he achieves when preparing a Spanish omelet with onions. Naturally elegant, relaxed, not at all insolent, but sure of himself. He paints with pleasure and brio. His words can be biting when the occasion calls for it. He's not interested in money, but he earns it by the handful and always generously helps less fortunate colleagues, none of whom, however, are jealous of him. He respects his friends' wives as if they were vestal virgins and adores his own wife, and he deceives her so ably that she never catches on to it. He traces his own life story with the same skill his hands have when he creates figures and forms on paper that embody at one and the same time a delicate, powerful, fantasy fauna, a pure humanity, a golden, airy world. He has it all, everything, as they say. I need him. I feel it, I need him. O how I'd love to drink his blood, all of it. Then I could be happy forever.

Roslyn Lupescu.

Twenty-five.

When you look at her, the first thing you say is: commonplace.

She's the woman whose high heel always breaks in the subway as she's about to board the train.

The woman who is out to be modern, but really only wants to do housework, surrounded by stinking, squealing kiddies while she tortures a dutifully bovine husband for years.

The woman who reads books she doesn't understand. And respectfully stops to look at pictures she doesn't like.

The woman who smiles but doesn't really want to, ever. Who is envious and doesn't realize that she envies anyone.

She tells people that she has earned a living posing nude for photographers and at the same time believes she needs to be forgiven for it and so says it's art. She drops names, Stieglitz, Sougez, Weston, Maspons. It'a a lie: she's never even seen them. But would it make any difference if she *didn't* sprinkle their names around?

To tell the truth, no. And she isn't a commonplace: she's the point at which two opposite commonplaces cross.

Topaze McCulloch.

Sixty-seven.

The severe factions of a clan chieftan. All of her, Scots-bony. Because of her appearance, she could be believed to be a net product of the Highlands: frugal to the point of asceticism; her moral sense, a bluish sheen of burnished steel; and her eyes, a miraculous blue, as limpid as a mountain lake. But her gaze can also be as deep and dangerous as a whirlpool.

Her ancestors fought to conquer Bonnie Prince Charlie, the Frenchified lad. Generations and generations passed. Then she was sent off to Paris to complete her education in an accredited convent; the old flame of love for Gaul hadn't extinguished completely. She suffered through the rosary every afternoon in order to escape every night to Montparnasse. She read Cocteau behind the good little nuns' backs. Her German, learned as a child, allowed her to keep up, in her own way, with Freud and psychoanalysis. She admired the Russian ballet in its heyday, applauding Stravinsky, wanting to be of age already and freely dispose of her wealth, buy herself a Picasso, a Matisse, and a Dérain. She tried cocaine and stopped using it exactly when she wanted to. But she let herself go wild with another debauchery and kept having abortions. The little nuns couldn't continue keeping her; her father warned her to come home immediately under pain of disinheritance. Nonetheless, she stayed on in Paris for as long as she wanted to. She says that she had to work as a prostitute at the Sphinx, dressed as a Scottish bagpipe player.

In the end, she did go home. Bob, the only son of her only brother, was always a very fragile little boy, very shy, to the point of being unsociable. He would have been about sixteen then. He was a virgin and it was supposed that, given his retiring character, he might be practicing "bad habits." He silently adored his aunt, she so enjoyable, so modern, smoking at the table between courses with complete self-confidence, absentmindedly facing up to the furious looks the elder McCulloch was giving her.

Topaze made the young lover confess. She gave him a pinch of cocaine and the next day she invited him to go for a ride in her new Duesenberg roadster—Topaze was then of age and disposed of the inheritance of her mother at will. She took Bob to see her *pied-à-terre* here in Megalopolis (the larger family still resided abroad, at least officially, at the immense, austere McCulloch mansion) and gave him a cocktail, his first one. She told him that he was like a juggler in a Picasso and to take off his clothes so she could admire all of his slender frailty. The boy obeyed, disturbed, trembling. She herself undressed. It may be that her intention was not evil: it may be that, educated to Freud, she understood it that way. What is unavoidably true is that the next day they found the boy in his room with a bullet in his head. He hadn't been able to digest the experience his so admired, so modern aunt had submitted him to.

It was she who told me about it. Her brother never knew. If he were to find out, it's possible he would kill her. Her conscience has never been bothered by this episode. She has never felt remorse for the simple reason that she has no conscience.

One day she learned through her proxy that her brother had been left penniless, in the street, as they say, but in reality, he is managing things well and he still has enough to live on.

She has decided to become a nurse. She will be able to go on giving free rein to her cold sadism. Who can deny that her presence is absolutely necessary at my potlatch?

At this point in the text, Nobodaddy doesn't raise his eyes from the volume, but picks up the glass of beer they always leave sitting in the same spot whenever they see him absorbed by his place on the page. He drinks deeply and makes a face. The warm beer has lost all its punch, and, to top things off, he has unwittingly dumped ash from his pipe into the glass.

He orders another beer—this time a stein—and a prosciutto sandwich and settles in his chair again. He fills his pipe, showing genuine affection for it. It's the old Breton he keeps as a souvenir of D-Day, on which he saw action as a Marine and to which he owes a slight limp in his right foot. This done, he lets out a sigh, perhaps of relief, and dives back into the latest version of *Émaux et Camées*.

Alenzar, Isabela.

Fifty-two years old.

Lawyer. Nymphomaniac. Racist. And a *rastacuera* snob.

Better known by her nickname, "Hairy Spider Woman."

But Adonis and I between us were so brave that time we confronted her when she launched a frontal assault on our

"flies." I'll always think of it as some of the most fun I've ever had
in my life. Macoco Nadal had invited us to spend a weekend on
his new yacht and really I have no idea how the nympho came
into it. Oh, yes, I believe it was through the niece of an associate
she was opportunely on good terms with for some reason.

When the others went up on deck that night, some of the
girls were going to compete in a striptease, and so she was alone
in the bar with Adonis and me because he and I wanted to talk
for a little while about the possibilities of a musical comedy
based on the life of Proust. And I saw what she intended to do
right away.

"Explain to her that I don't like to go to bed with women,"
I told Adonis in a loud voice so she could not allege ignorance
even to please the court of her own conscience.

"*You* better explain to her that what *I* like are *real* women."
That Adonis is so quick with his genius for repartee, so that's
how he answered me.

It did no good: she was on us in a flash. I had been observing
her during our whole dinner—I'm fascinated by ugliness, as long
as it's also grotesque and has at least a smidge of the macabre,
and Hairy Spider Woman met the requirements perfectly—so
I saw how she was drinking exactly the way people drink who
want to get drunk and commit some kind of uproar and then
allege they weren't in control of their faculties as an excuse.

So I more or less knew what was going to go down when she
started to cast glances at the region of our lower-intestines. It
was supposed to be insinuating but in reality it was just plain
lewd and I tried to go on with our discussion.

"Can't you just see Olivier in the role of Swann?"

"The one who'd be fantastic in the role of Odette would be
Loren, don't you think?"

We kept talking like this, calmly holding on to our scotches,
and she jumped us. I think she managed to grab Adonis for an
instant exactly where she wanted to. And, not too disturbed,

Adonis emptied his drink on her head.

Then she tried to scratch him. So I intervened, grabbing her with all my strength and pulling one of her ears: I almost ripped it off. She bit my other hand and Adonis saved me, but afterward it was infected for more than two weeks and I had to endure (sadly, I'm not at all masochistic, although there's no shortage of people who believe I am) tens of antibiotic injections. Adonis grabbed her by the hair and gave her a couple of resounding punches in the face. Hairy Spider fell to the floor, simpering, trying to act like a little girl.

The whole next day she stayed in her cabin. The day after that she comes into the bar and sees us chatting, still about the Proust musical, and, just like nothing happened, walks calmly over to us and joins right in our conversation. She tells us that *À la recherche* is her bedtime reading and, just about then, without realizing what she was doing, I think, she takes off her dark glasses and we saw that her left eye was very black and blue.

How delicious would it be if she had another one of those furi-uterine meltdowns at the potlatch and got it into her head to mix it up with Orvieto; or, better yet, with Kiki! I don't know why, but, of all the stories they used to read to me when I was a child, none impressed me like—and I'm impressed again, just remembering it—"Beauty and the Beast."

Jambon, Iris.

"B. 1898. LL.D. (Harvard), Ph.D. (Oxford), advanced studies in Paris under the direction of Dr. Paul Rivet and in London with Professor Bronislaw Malinowski. A. A. A., F. R. S. A., *Membre correspondant de l'Institut*. Research on hallucinogens in primitive societies and the sexual practices of native peoples. Fieldwork among the Zunis, the Arakuans (central Brazil), the Tamacos (Ecuador), the Kokolimbas (central Africa). Currently organizing an expedition under the auspices of B. A. D. to study the customs of the Baikas of Brazil. She has taught at the Brighton School of Sociology (1945-1947) and the Musée de l'Homme (1951-1952) and is now Director of Advanced Anthropological Studies at the Megalopolitan Museum of Natural Sciences. Honorary memberships: National Council for Interracial Understanding. Other: Advisory Member, Committee for the Rational Investigation of Prejudice for UNESCOL. Principal publications: "Unconscious Modelling of Clothing Customs" (1924, doctoral thesis), *Sex, Race, and Peace* (1942), *Anthropological Reflections After the Bomb* (1945; 27th aug. ed., 1959), *Conflict and Harmony in Cultures* (1955), *Handbook of Ethnological Toxicology* (1961; 5th ed., 1962); in preparation: "Coitus as a Communicative Style." Professional collaborations (print): *Amer. Anthr., Antropos, L'Homme, Nature, Man, Journal of the British Soc. for Social Anthr., Paideuma, Bull. der Schweizerischen Gesells. für Anthropol."*

Etc. All the above I've pasted in from *Who's Who*. I was really surprised that such a friendly publication didn't include anything about the doutora's hobby. Then I learned by chance that the High Trustee of the Organization of the United Nations for the Protection and Promotion of the Kokolimba Peoples had launched a monstrous accusation against the knowledgeable woman, which did not succeed: corruption of Kokolimba minors of both sexes. So I put two and two together and attended her brilliant lectures. It was from them—I must confess—that I got the idea of the potlatch. Therefore, I would've never been able to resist inviting her. She, in addition, will nobly represent Science at the holocaust.

Almeida, Jefferson.
Forty-three.
Nearly illiterate. Managing Editor of one of the weeklies with the biggest circulation in the entire world. Lazy. The man large international organizations, for example, run to when they need someone to take charge of a mission that requires what in

newspaper jargon is called "feverish activity." Unscrupulous in financial matters. No bank asks him for even one guarantee, they all just hand him a loan for any amount. A shameless liar, and he tells you he's lying. Invariably, no one dares contradict the lies he tells. Unexpectedly, he's not at all robust. He's pudgy, with milk-colored skin that most certainly does not come from his supposed ancestry. And his face is dignified by nothing, not even a little coarseness. In speech and act, the man is ordinariness itself. But, it cannot be ignored, in some mysterious way he is able to exercise a real, hypnotic power over people.

I myself don't know for sure if I've invited him to the potlatch to get a kick out of the disgust he inspires in me, or because he wanted me to invite him and ordered me to do it through ESP.

Minos, Kiki.

No, it can't be a coincidence that he winds up right after Jefferson Almeida. If I said to either of them that they have a connection, an invisible but indestructible link, they would take turns guffawing. First of all, they barely know each other. There is nonetheless a link between them. More than anything, it's because they can't stand each other; each represents everything the other denies. That, in my view, is precisely the tie that binds them and cannot be dissolved.

Kiki has read every book all of the way through and, as in cases like his, his body is in awful condition. He is outrageously gullible when it comes to women and just as easily taken in by men, and he even fools and extorts *himself,* constantly. He always tears down anything people offer him with generosity and spontaneity, but he's hardheaded and doggedly pursues whatever is denied to him. Usually, the worse a particular thing is for him, the more *ostinato* he becomes.

At times I think he suffers from a persecution complex. Just look, for example, how furious he got when he learned that a group of young literati had brought out the first issue of a journal dedicated to the vanguard. All because the title coincided with his last name! I tried in vain to get him to focus on the mythological suggestions in the title. Nothing. He still believes that baptizing the little journal *Minos* was just to make fun of him. Of course, I'll keep financing the publication, whose title did come to me, naturally, when I was thinking about Kiki. He designs for himself the most convoluted labyrinths, just so he can get lost in them.

Reason for Inviting Him: he's a born victim.

Ayesha Flintless.

Sixty-four years old.

A flapper. 1920s, *The Last Time I Saw Paris*, all that. But now she's sixty-four!

One of the misfortunes that tend to embitter very egotistical people is their not counting on the passage of time or the defeats that, one by one, that fierce enemy inevitably inflicts on you.

Ayesha now has two daughters about forty. One, no doubt a firsthand witness of the havoc caused in several lives by her flapper-mama, is a solid little middle-class woman whose true, ideal self I think might be a dairy cow, preferably a Holando-Argentina. The other one, who tried to follow in her mother's footsteps, is around here somewhere in a mental institution, they say she'll never get out. She didn't realize that in order to act out her mother's life and have something like the success at it that she did, it's necessary to have a stone-cold insensitivity to suffering. Ayesha calls it "a Zen doctrine." Having gone through three different Churches, twenty-seven more or less fervent Sects, and an incalculable number of Spiritual Movements, she calls herself an adept at Zen Buddhism.

Which presents no obstacle—we can all suppose, even in her most intensely meditative trances—to keeping an eye right on that husband of hers. The poor guy is almost twenty-five years her junior.

Motive for Inviting Her? To punish her! She'll come, oh yes, she'll come: the aroma of wealth and luxury is irresistible to her. And she'll come alone because—yes, it's true—her invitation doesn't include her hubby. And I wonder what that poor miserable man, who is starving for sex, will do in those hours of freedom? Well, anything can happen. But she won't miss the potlatch.

Ixion, Friedrich Wilhelm.
He was born in 1920.
Everything about him is summed up in the following sentence, which I heard him use to describe his feeling as an expert horseman: "The voluptuous pleasure, I get from whipping the noble animal's flanks with my riding crop." A sentence as stupendously bad as this one is deserving of immortality. It's the *non plus ultra*, as Ixion himself would say—of tastelessness! Its gaudy tackiness is actually perfect. If anyone tries to "perfect" it, replacing the word "animal" with "steed," for example, it only loses its power. Such a highfalutin word is too extravagant for today's ear.
"The voluptuous pleasure, I get from whipping the noble animal's flanks with my riding crop." Isn't this reason enough to require his presence at the potlatch?

Selene Freund.
She must be around thirty.
Ah, but she only clearly remembers the events of her earliest childhood—when she was a very little girl, of course, full of poetry. The rest of her life she just lumps together as incidents with absolutely no importance in her mellow world of sticky childhood. This arrangement lets her skip over the last twenty years of her life in favor of the first ten. She made this one guy leave his family for her and then would not even deign to give herself to him. She dumped him, he was one of those

inconsequential incidents. Another guy, who was desperately trying to get her, she made enlist in the Foreign Legion. He wound up bones only, the ones he left in Dien-Bien-Phu, just one more meaningless incident. She lives exclusively in an immaculate, magical world of happy, fulfilled childhood. I'm extremely curious to find out how she'll transform the potlatch into one of her sound, naïve, childhood experiences.

Enos, Rodolfo.
Born in 1879.

He knew Claude Debussy, George Bernard Shaw, Prince Kropotkin, Marcel Proust, Oscar Wilde, Count Tolstoi, Benito Pérez Galdós, Arsène Lupin, Haeckel, Thomas Hardy, Gabriele d'Annunzio, Émile Durkheim, Stephan George, Lenin, Aubrey Beardsley, La Bella Otero, Jules Verne, the Viscount of Montesquiou-Fenzac, El Caballero Audaz, Eleonora Duse, Pancho Villa, the Lumière brothers, Emperor Franz Joseph, Cléo de Mérode, Antonio Gaudí, Isadora Duncan, Otto Lilienthal, Eduardo VII, Von Tirpitz, Sherlock Holmes, Ramón y Cajal, Carlos Gardel, Tsar Nicolas II, Sarah Bernhardt, Lord Kitchener, Ambrose Bierce, Jakob Burckhardt, Jarry, Giuseppe Verdi, Woodrow Wilson, Captain Dreyfus, Rouletabille, Diághilev, Lord Rutherford, Fantomas, and the inevitable, well-known names, like Mata-Hari and Rasputin, not to mention other illustrious personalities.

In stark contrast with immense humanity's long documented history, the complete works of don Rodolfo consist, at present, of one twenty-seven-page pamphlet. Its title is "Social Relativity in the Feminist Question" and it was privately published in Helsinki, Finland, in 1902, when he was employed there as third honorary secretary of the Costaguana Legation. However, his secret memoirs are *legendary*—literally, legendary. Some people claim to have seen them. According to several of the claimants, it must be about five thousand pages long. Others, who without a doubt exaggerate more, raise the number to fifty thousand.

Don Rodolfo persistently claims that this work will be published only after his death. Whenever the topic comes up in his presence—something he always manages to make happen— he glances at those around him and his glance is heavy with suggestion and mystery. This gives him what he's looking for: those enigmatic glances are interpreted, by anyone listening to him, as symptoms of his interest in including them in "the titanic undertaking," as he usually calls it. That's how he manages to be constantly invited everywhere. In any year, there are no more than five weeks, total, that he spends in the miniscule apartment he has in the Village (a loan from Louise J. Bird, it should be said in passing). He enjoys the rest of his time aboard yachts, in castles, at *fazendas*, on safaris, in bungalows, at Swiss chalets, and on all manner of weekend outings that he often knows how to prolong for weeks and even whole months. His hosts invariably appear to be satisfied with the thought that their names will one day figure in the memoirs of don Rodolfo, maybe between those of Cléo de Mérode and the Wright brothers.

But this work only exists in the imagination of don Rodolfo (and, it's clear, in the imaginations of his credulous listeners). This was confessed to me by his wife, an abject woman (whom I could see doing much better by making her way in life as a new species of parrot in a zoo somewhere—and she actually has the body type for it). She told me this a long time ago, when she was particularly heated about don Rodolfo's having wasted what at the beginning was an appreciable inheritance and then having taken up the habit of stripping her of her few jewels. He needed them to go on paying his Bond Street tailor, with whom the grievous author's trick of veiled promises of immortality to be spent in the bosom of the Immense as part of a fictitious compilation of characters, places, and anecdotes seems to have failed.

Reason for Inviting Him: my other guests, unlike me, don't know that don Rodolfo's memoirs have not yet begun to be written, and never will be. (How could don Rodolfo have time for a job like that when he's constantly playing life's grand, dramatic writer on some yacht, foxhunt, or safari or other?) So at the potlatch, they, at least the vain among them—and it seems to me that every one of them in his own way is by definition vain—will act as if all Eternity is watching the faces they make and listening intently to their words. No, it won't be merely don Rodolfo's empty pen that will make them look ridiculous for generations to come! The vain always behave ridiculously on their own, completely naturally.

Tríada, Joaquín de.

Was he born of woman? Will he never die?

Two diametrically opposing versions of him exist. Curiously they both proceed directly from him.

In one of them, he was born in Saint-Jean-de-Luz in 1899 and he studied law but didn't finish with a degree, etc., etc. This is the version that shows up, for example, in the resume he presented in his application to the J. Bird Foundation for a renewal of his research grant to complete his comparative study of the illuminati of sixteenth-century Spain and the Neo-Lognostic Beardsmen of Boston.

The second version he expresses verbally and with rising enthusiasm, almost always reaching a state that Doutora Jambon would no doubt characterize as "shamanic." This would alarm any psychiatrist enough, surely, to persuade him to suggest the immediate use of a straitjacket. In this version, don Joaquín is the spokesman of the Holy Ghost. But, in his moments of greatest enthusiasm, he doesn't dwell on details and states that he—always pronounced in a way that corresponds to the use of a capital letter on that "he"—*is* the Holy Ghost and no two ways about it.

During don Joaquín's most virulent lapses, the whole universe revolves around his infinite knowledge. He can interpret the hermetic meaning of the cave paintings of Altamira and Lascaux as easily as assign a profound, eternal meaning to the miniskirt. The last time I saw him, his right ankle was swollen; he had twisted his foot stepping out of a taxi, purely by accident of course. This negligible event led him to construct in *seconds* a very complex theological picture of the Universe, in his version of which, his inflamed ankle occupied a place of privilege.

For don Joaquín, anything that happens to him becomes the Aleph. And I'm very curious to know which apocalyptic version of things the potlatch will inspire in him.

Incatasciatto, Moncho.

B. 1913.

That same year, the first volume of *À la recherche du temps perdu* appeared. It was inevitable then that the next year would produce the uprising in Sarajevo and afterward would come everything that then had to come.

The Belle Époque had died. Forever, for everybody except Moncho. He feels called to be Marcel Proust and plays his role with great restraint and decorum and selflessness. He was certainly not made to reconsider this by the tremendous surgical intervention he had done in order to look more like the Great Rememberer.

In order to be Marcel, however, he's sorely lacking in three details: Paris about 1900, the Prousts' fortune, and asthma. It is very likely he's now preparing to eliminate at least the third problem by the acquisition of a previous infection. He may be able to cause this by psychically inducing a trauma, or in some other way—and then, stemming from the resultant infection, a fine Proustian asthma. The poor man is desperate to pant!

How could I not invite him to the potlatch? I have absolutely no doubt that he will see in the lamentable Nestor, the Duke of Guermantes; in Pip, Mlle. Vinteuil; and in me, of course, the Baron of Charlus himself. If I didn't invite him, I would be acting as cruelly to him as to me.

Louise J. Bird.

Under this name appears a blank page. Of course, the first time Nobodaddy came across the missing entry he was surprised. He thought it could therefore hold an important clue. He ordered Archives to send him all possible information on everybody with this name in the police files.

Now he faces the empty page again. He becomes irritated at the delay in satisfying his request.

He notices his desk covered with the large *chopps* and sandwiches that, deep in thought, he has distractedly ordered and instantly forgotten. He sees with annoyance that his colorful, Scotch-plaid vest is covered with ashes and brushes at them while he presses the button and calls Records.

"And the info on Bird, Louise J. that I requested hours ago? Can I be advised what has happened to it?"

"Yes, sir, chief, of course, sir: what has happened to it is that as of this moment we've got background on 111 individuals with that name and . . ."

Nobodaddy pales. Nobodaddy—who, time and again, using nothing but his fists, has faced down the most dangerous criminals, all armed to the teeth—pales.

"This is too much!" he mutters and sinks into his big chair, leaving the telephone still connected.

The big man sighs and a sinister smile spreads on the face of his invisible interlocutor. At last they've stumped Nobodaddy. Or rather, the archives have, and now he has a case far beyond his own capacities to solve. Surely this time he won't be able to come off as the rock star, which he has always managed to do before. He'll have to ask for help.

"Then when you have all the material together, get it to

me—the sooner the better! It's urgent, you know, *urgent*, do I make myself clear?"

He knows he should not have let himself collapse like that; he clearly should not have let himself sigh that way. He realizes the opportunity that, in one short moment of weakness, he has just given those vermin in Records. They hate him and his successes, mostly for always making them do work and then correcting them in the same threatening tone with which he has just said "the sooner the better."

His mouth feels dry, but he doesn't dare taste the warm beer, already flat, in any of the many glasses that cover his desk. On the other hand, how lovely it always feels just to take a warm shower and immediately drink a gigantic stein of ice-cold lager, and stretch out in the living room of his apartment in Suburbia and relax while his wife relates to him the latest episode of Batman while the aroma of cooking cabbage wafts in from the kitchen.

He signals for an ice-cold *chopp* to be brought to him and asks for two sandwiches (he suddenly feels terribly hungry), one with Westphalian ham and mustard, the other with sardines and onion.

"No, wait, I've changed my mind. Better bring me two *chopps* with the sandwiches, a couple of those extra-large steins they have.

He goes back to lovingly filling his pipe but notices with disgust that he has hardly any tobacco in the sealskin bag. He'll have to send home to get his favorite blend, which he prepares himself from eighteen different tobaccos. This is a bad sign. Before both of his earlier investigations failed, he also had to send home for more tobacco.

"And what must my poor face look like," he asks. But he knows: ravaged and with very noticeable stubble on yellowish-green cheeks. He already sees himself that way and doesn't need to look in the bathroom mirror. With this image fresh in his mind, he returns to the latest edition of Gautier's poetic work.

Van Boren, Laura.

Ageless, sexless, brainless.

What would you expect, based on her origins? You only have to look at her for half a second to guess she has a long, illustrious family line from which emanate the anemic, who confuse the exclusive ingestion of lettuce with spiritual life, and the theologically irate, who take great pleasure in terrifying the faithful with forays into the great beyond—a great beyond where an enormous Jehovah makes the sinful soul's hair stand on end with His tales of famous fantastical castigations.

Besides, she's horribly ugly.

But what can you do, you have to give her credit: she does have style. There is a kind of radar built into some part of her being—no, not *there*. It leads her infallibly to the best looking or, at worst, the most brilliant man in the place. Will it lead her to me again tonight? Then again, what I really want to know is this: will she interpret the potlatch as a preview of her ancestors' favorite topic: the plight of sinners in the hands of their irritated God?

Ovinario, Fred.

He preaches the outdoor life, simple clothing, frugal meals, instructive reading, love for little ones, tolerance for servants, sympathy for every humble thing, going to great museums, exercising rigorous discipline at work (especially when tempered by cordiality: the spirit of camaraderie should always be present in everything).

One day, he was feeling even more expansive than usual, after downing half a bottle of Chivas Regal I had just brought him—it was his saint's day and we were in his modest but sparkling-clean apartment in Suburbia—and he confided to me that nothing would make him happier than if all his friends would decide to call him The Benefactor.

When we finished the bottle of scotch—which he practically drank all by himself—I confirmed two or three other things as well about The Benefactor. One, that he owns one of the principal holdings of stock in Standard Guns. "Why, what would certain governments, like the one in Costaguana, do without their small, but deadly efficient Tommy guns?" And that is saying nothing of the relationship between the company The Benefactor works for and the Cosa Nostra families. Two, that he is a functionary at UNESCOL so he can exercise his "wille zur" the "macht." And he *easily* knocks the mighty down at will, because he constantly engages in intrigues with diplomatic delegations. He rises through the ranks with absolutely infallible precision. At every step, he moves through higher-and-higher-ranked and increasingly delicate assignments in the ceaseless pursuit of his maximum ambition, which there is no doubt he will accomplish. He wants to be the Secretary General Attached to the Office of Education for Peace. And three, his hobby consists of collecting women's wigs in different colors, which he never takes off in the intimacy of his home, especially while he reads his favorite newspaper, *The Wall Street Journal*. In addition to that one, he has a complementary hobby that's much more costly. It consists of viewing, through an intermediary in Paris, the latest, most sumptuous originals— exclusives!—of houses like Fath, Dior, and Balenciaga. So, kindly—and I prefer to think of it as "kindly"—so, kindly, on the afternoon I visited him, he wanted to give me a demonstration of his intimate habits and he put on a beautiful evening number from Dior, which he complemented with a daring, black-and-gold-striped wig. I cannot deny that he succeeded in giving me a very adequate (that is, for The Benefactor) and highly instructive show, in terms of the contrast that can be drawn between costume and physical constitution. Meaning: The Benefactor's body tends to fat, is rather short and very muscular, and his face looks a little like Orson Welles's. He would possibly look more like him if he shaved off his enormous black beard.

Motive for Inviting Him: I also have that inclination to perform acts of generosity, and I want my potlatch to be instructive for him. Besides, on this occasion I'll run no risk of having to go flying out the door to save myself from his . . . "fraternal arms," as he called them, drooling.

Uirakocha, Joachim von.
  B. 1909.
  Profession: young poet. Since his first book, *Exterminio del Caos*, published in 1928, he has been the permanent promise of Latin American poetry. Today, his face is leathery and a really cadaverous green color, two qualities that make him look like a mummified ancestor he possibly has. He certainly makes a person wonder if that theory—today so discredited by Dr. Jambon—could be right in asking if the pre-Columbian civilizations originated in Egypt. Because poet von Uirakocha has an extraordinary resemblance, above all, to the mummy of Amenophis IV. Be that as it may, he keeps on writing these experimental poems that have no punctuation whatsoever and are terribly daring. That's what is meant, of course, by "promising."
  He's possibly the most perfect example of envy that could be celebrated in all of Megalopolis today. Von Uirakocha has spent his entire life feigning a personality that isn't his. I can just see him, as he once was, up there in his remote village that is set like a gem in the Andes. It's more or less the 1920s and he's reading by the light of an oil lamp in the little room he shares with his two older brothers who have already left for the mines where they are foremen, and he's reading . . . what is he reading? An anthology of poetry published at the beginning of the twentieth century by *The Mercury of France.* Yes, in one of those inexplicable accidents that are nevertheless so frequent in our countries south of the Rio Grande, it took an unexpected detour into his village's school library. It's true, I read in "von

Uirakocha" a pseudonym that he was clearly inspired to adopt one day when his sense of admiration split between the monarchist von Hofmannsthal and the imperial socialist of the great Incas. Or maybe it happens before, when he is just an avid little half-breed of a reader who has no sense of continuity and goes from *Treasure Island, Corazón: diario de un niño,* and some book by Emilio Salgari, to Verlaine, Richepin, and even Rimbaud and Mallarmé. It couldn't have been easy for him to translate those poems on his own, with his self-taught beginner's French (which, it may be said in passing, doesn't seem to have ever improved).

But, as I always say in cases like this, all his efforts do not authorize his ultimate petulance. It's not a very praiseworthy virtue to do little and do it badly just because one runs into difficulties that are more or less unsalvageable from the beginning. When von Uirakocha began his long-lived trajectory as a young poet, almost certainly what he wanted, more than anything, was to become famous, live well, drink absinthe, and have a blond darling who would talk to him in French . . . and that's it, that was all. So I have to wonder: wouldn't he *have* all that now, in abundance and much better than his adolescent self could have ever imagined, if, instead of going the way of Corbière, Laforgue, and Apollinaire, he had devoted himself to the enrichment of his country's folklore, writing songs that, even here in Megalopolis, would be blaring from jukeboxes and transistor radios today?

But von Uirakocha dreams of *being* blond and European, languid and slightly effeminate. And look at the result: an individual who hates himself, I mean, who *envies* himself, that is, his true self, the Andean man with enormous, long-suffering, pugnacious muscles that atavistically prefer *chicha* and coca to champagne (or whiskey) and synthetic drugs. Yes, von Uirakocha is envious of that man who exists through the composition of his body and will remain in his native

Andean village forever, while *he* must be here, among *us*, with his impertinent monocle, making himself into someone who despises and adores the thing that, in all reality, for one reason or another, he isn't capable of letting himself appear to be.

So I invited him to the potlatch in order to give him a great satisfaction. All in all, I think I have something of a weakness for the symbolist-dadaist-surrealist-abstract poet Joachim von Uirakocha (and if that's a surprise, yes, I'm complex!). I know his heart will leap for joy when fire consumes that tapestry attributed to Fragonard, or when that vase that belonged to María Teresa of Austria shatters.

How can I *not* invite him? Despite his perfume (he smells like *violets*).

Silver, Don.
   B. 1933.
   He had the good luck to witness firsthand, when he was only five, the moment when his robust and mustached mama pushed his scrawny papa, the telegrapher, out of a window, because he had had the bad luck to pay attention to anonymous letters raining down to inform him that his wife was receiving others in his absence. The letters I'm talking about are in the genre the French call *fait divers*, sensationalist accounts that provide trashy news, the most frequent, insipid, and prosaic kind. There must be dozens of instances of news being disseminated like that every week, in Megalopolis alone. But, as a genre, they make so small an impact that not even the daily tabloids publish them.

Don, nevertheless, figured out a way to get something positive out of the miserable episode he had witnessed: he became its exclusive archivist. If later he was reading Dostoevsky and Freud, it was to perfect those letters, which were constantly running through his mind. But his "reading," it seems clear, also soon motivated him to write. First it was a story, pretty succinct and fairly close to the facts that were still fresh in his memory—and he had a veritable headlamp of a memory. Then he doctored the facts with horrifying sexual experiences that he'd come across in his more or less scientific readings of suspiciously abstruse psychiatry, and they turned into a story cycle. But he realized that the real gold mine was the novel; and, so, for the umpteenth time, now with more embellishments than the whole collection of gargoyles on Notre-Dame Cathedral, he offered the initial episode again, duly larded with incest, rape, and scenes of cannibalism. It was a resounding success. Instantly the great public launched itself in pursuit of the young author, their new Erskine Caldwell. And he is scheduled to make his debut as a dramatist any minute now. The title of the play he's preparing is "The Death of the Telegraph Operator."

I want to have him at my potlatch so I can suggest to him, once the Dantesque spectacle has made a sufficient impression on him and his will-power is more inclined to yield, that he give his play a less gruesome title, such as "Death of a Father." If I'm successful, my potlatch will have lasted surreptitiously long enough, due to the thousands of foreseen representations of this new title.

Ferroni, Amleto.
    B. 1926.
    It's true, he is very good-looking, in a way that, it can even be said, never goes out of fashion. True too that he's very intelligent, although maybe not with a spectacular or sharp brilliance (but I've heard that, if he wanted, he could do great things as a neuro-chemist). And he's a good sportsman, never falls into the vulgarity of staying around too long as a master of any one sport. In that way, he's also an appreciated amateur of the arts. He's quite well-mannered to boot; truly, he has the always slightly aloof ways of an authentic gentleman. And the women! About his success with women it can only be said that he is fascinating to them, while he, so modest, so prudent, so

cleverly inquisitive, takes no notice of that swarm of beauties who adore him. He only asks, "Are they aiming for me or my money?" Because Amleto is also rich. What you'd call filthy rich. Like me. No, maybe not that rich, but sufficiently rich. And he's wise with his money.

No sooner does he ask himself that question, which is something he invariably does as soon as one of his "romances" starts to prosper, than he makes a retreat. And then the beauty of the day initiates her pursuit, becomes a curious huntress who, as soon as she spies her prey, hands herself over to him. But is it right to say that his women give themselves to him? Well, that's what they *want*. But Amleto, faithful to his prophetic Shakespearean name . . . gets disgusted; too easily, let's say.

Women have made him suffer the unspeakable, about which he's stoically silent.

At the potlatch there will be no fewer than four women who on different occasions have wanted, naturally, to be his, but, of course, without success. I for one can't resist the temptation to observe our lone victim surrounded by so many executioners. Besides—why not go ahead and say it?—I'm gripped by curiosity about exactly how Amleto arranges things so he can end up the victim so often. I'm captivated by the idea that some guest may possibly attempt to victimize him with her charms; Mariana Marx, for example, or, no: the best of all would be Elke Trakl. But Elke in heat! That wouldn't be possible to believe, even if you saw it with your own eyes!

Almirón.

Almirón Almirón Almirón Almirón Almirón Almirón Almirón Almirón Almirón Almirón Almirón Almirón Almirón Almirón Almirón Almirón—wait! Am I copying his style? Oh, yes, I'm clearly infected. That is because everyone keeps talking about Almirón Almirón Almirón here and Almirón Almirón Almirón there.

Isn't there a kind of premonition in his surname? I always think of him in terms of the very strange associations that, for certain individuals, preside over their choice of a career, meaning the way their vocation is sometimes inextricably written right in their name. I put to you the case of a great neurologist named Brain; it's something to think about.

And Almirón *is* quite the *mirón*, the spectator and Peeping Tom of contemporary literature, which has a lot of *ralentisseurs,* just one speed bump after another built right into the text. Joyce or Proust or Musil, e.g., are (only very imperfect) precursors of Almirón. For Almirón is the writer of the fixed take. He clips something from reality and names it, then names it names it names it so that the thing grows and grows until its mass pushes out the whole world, leaving no place for the world to occupy, because the same name fills all the spaces. So, for Almirón—and, I think, for certain readers of his too—the world is transformed into . . . a rose, a frog, a hand. So, for example, in his last work, Almirón—for Almirón is always glued to a keyhole—in one chapter of at least fifteen pages, writes only the word "hair." Except there's one typographical error that reads "hat." It's a defect that, as Almirón explained to me, has to be cleaned up in the next edition. You can't imagine how enormous a hair can become in Almirón's treatment of it! Almirón transforms the whole universe into a hair. We soon figure out that we're all alive by merely a hair.

I've been told that the famous novelist is now preparing his autobiography at the request of a major publishing house, which, of course, only echoes the desires of his fans. I am sure that Almirón, unlike don Rodolfo Enos, will not defraud us. And I sincerely want my in no way modest potlatch invitation to wind up registered repeatedly in his book. I would consider myself altogether satisfied if, as a consequence of his being at the potlatch, he were to write into his work-in-progress a chapter, however brief, let's say, about nine pages, that consists only

---

of the alternating words "Jango" and "potlatch." In addition, thinking about it a little more—and this proves Almirón right with respect to literary procedures—the chapter itself would be a potlatch! Nothing less than a potlatch of the destruction of language.

Ulises.

He is fifty-five years old.

And that big tranny-bi-fag better not get it into his head—which always wants what somebody else has—to try and finagle Dieunon (God no!) away from me!

Ulises, it looks to me like, has absolutely never done anything merely because it's what he really wanted to do, he just does things that are OK because they're acceptable to people. That spirit is deeply ingrained in him, and it's so unhealthy to always need to be considered "ok," to comply, stick to convention, and follow the fashion. And the proportions it has now reached in him are truly alarming. It's true that he has turned homosexual, but that was only because, in his native Montevideo back in those remote years of his youth, he was limited to the social circles he ran in, and in them homosexuality was considered a proof of refinement. And that's the only reason he turned.

But his purely mimetic tendencies by themselves don't go nearly far enough to explain him. Envy and suspicion also play a big part in his seasoning, because they are the inevitable corollaries of his fundamentally cowardly and opportunistic nature. I say cowardly and opportunistic because deep down he is *amorphous* and ready to assume any form whatsoever . . . as long as everyone considers it OK to be that.

One thing is for sure: he's definitely going to want to imitate *me* this time. He'll immediately organize that "pawnshop" of junk that he calls his collections into his own potlatch. And I'm already loving thinking how devastated the idiot is going to be afterward, pining for his destroyed trash.

Troika Soares.

Fifty-eight years old.

She believes there exists an obligation for everyone to always be happy. To that point, her friend Trinidad, in a witty remark I would never have believed her capable of uttering if I hadn't heard it with my own ears, gave the best description of Troika ever. Trinidad was complaining about her and said: "Oh, no! Just think, as soon as Troika gets here, we will all have to keep *laughing*."

Mediocre in everything, except her ugliness (which is extreme), and I've seen portrait photos of her and, even when she was a little girl, she looked just like Disraeli as an old man, but, of course, with much darker skin.

Part of the reason for the potlatch is to get her to look in the Venetian mirror that belonged to Dubarry.

Celia de Minos.

She must be about thirty, but I have to admit that she plays the impish little girl extremely well. Truthfully, she's effective at anything that smacks of imitation. (Oh, if only Ulises had that gift!) She manages to look like the victim every time she rides roughshod over somebody, and is able to always look intelligent and really energetic and active when she's only very clever and, in general, very lazy. When it's convenient for her, she can also pass for profoundly religious, even though her soul is the most naturally unbelieving in all Christendom: I've seen her, on a Holy Thursday, eat a sumptuous lunch at the Chambord, during which she certainly did not turn down the *boeuf poivré* or the mousse *au chocolat*, and then go right back to her office at that half-ecclesiastical weekly *La Fe*, where a bishop sat waiting and immediately accompanied her to her interview with the Nuncio Apostolico, to whom she presented her detailed report on the Observance of Religious Holidays in the Archdiocese of Megalopolis.

Celia does possess one undeniable virtue, however: those beautiful legs. And she knows how to manage them with the unquestionable effectiveness of a bank. I'm not at all blind to what her legs used to represent—and maybe still do—for Kiki. Or to the ecstasy they offer—but then, how much is an offer worth?—even to horny old Orvieto.

It's therefore my duty as host to make sure Celia doesn't miss the potlatch.

Hurenstein, Moshe.
   B. 1930.
He made his way to Megalopolis, according to what I've been told, from some corner of Latin America that used to be more or less his homeland. He got here weighed down with a wife, multiple kids, some basic texts, a few whole tracts, and his Marxist morals and householder virtues. He also came with a scholarship—his, after winning an arduous contest with two or three hundred other candidates. He came to study sociological realism in eighteenth-century literature (no less). Once here he discerned that his South American scholarship was turning out to be too meager to cover even basic daily needs. He noticed also that his four little boys were too noisy, as well as quite ill-mannered. At the university library where he was working on his thesis, he chanced to meet a girl who had popped in to look for certain graphic material on the first Megalopolitan nightclubs that she wanted to use for a TV script. His relationship with the girl grew more intimate and, while this was happening, Moshe could soon see other things too, like the fact that his wife had varicose veins, her clothes lacked all elegance, and realistic literature of the eighteenth century had already been over-exploited by French, English, and German academics. So he abandoned his laborious research—despite which, it won't be out of line to clarify, he didn't deprive himself of his monthly scholarship stipend. He went to work, first as a translator, then

as a producer, and, pretty soon now, he is to make his debut as a director for Megalopolitan Television. The programs shown above his name today, already figure among the network's most popular and sought-after.

His wife, rather, ex-wife, has been back for quite a while now in that underdeveloped corner of Latin America out of which came the dynamic Moshe, and he's on his way to becoming a magnate. He has also replaced—twice now, I understand—the young lady who opened his eyes in the university library.

It's essential to get along well with him if you want to count on good TV coverage in Megalopolis.

Orvieto, Camillo.
  B. 1905.
  He is an educated man. And a hero. But mostly he's a lecher.

The educated man in him, on one hand, leans for support on the famous duelist that he is (or was). As a man of arms, fervent fighter for liberty, he easily crushes ardent defenders of any cause that is dissimilar or opposite to (or even the same as) his, using his verbal skills in seven languages. He as a lecher— well, any occasion is propitious for him there. In this sense— as in many others—no one can slander him, for example, by calling him prejudiced.

He is daring, as befits both the knowledgeable and the lecherous man in him. His daring befits, in particular, his exile. That is an enterprise he has exercised with brilliance for about thirty years. It's useless trying to tell him that, in the country whose citizenship he jealously hangs onto, the abhorrent laws that brought him to these shores disappeared a long time ago. Back in his country, he would have to leave behind his lucrative work here as an exile, and without it, after so many years, he would be certain to miss it.

He's intelligent, likeable, and immensely prissy, and he's my friend.

Israel Goldstein.

This is not his real name but he has adopted it definitively because it's the one that appears on the passport he bought in Paris, right after the *deuxième Mondiale.* I suspect he is also not from the place his name on the passport makes you think of immediately. Sometimes I think all this really reveals an S.S. officer conveniently disguised in the skin of his victim.

It is evident that he has known concentration camps in abundance in Mittel Europa, from where—also evidently— he originally hails. What I'm still dubious about is if he got acquainted with those interesting inventions of the contemporary technological spirit of the times as a victim or as an executioner. His knowledge seems to me to be too exact and scientific to be a victim's. Normally, a death-row prisoner doesn't get to know how the guillotine mechanism works or the potency of the discharge in the electric chair. He really doesn't need that kind of knowledge, either: society is satisfied if he just provides the body.

On a night of confidences, the alleged Israel told me the following story. The Nazis had scarcely been vanquished when, in the Rumanian village where he was hidden, vengeance—if vengeance is the right word here—was exacted on any pretty girl who had had intimate relations with German officers. Israel met a girl, terrified, who was aware of the possibility that partisans could catch up with her and, just like they had done to so many others, would surely rape her, strip her, and maybe even tar and feather her. Israel calmed her down. He promised to hide her in the little cottage where he had been tucked away—according to his version, for more than two years—and he confessed to her that he was doing it because he wanted her, wanted her so much that, "in exchange for one night of pleasure" (*sic*), he would share with her, in addition to a safe place to stay, half the gold coins he kept hidden in his belt.

When they got to the cottage, Israel took her to the bedroom and barred the door. The girl undressed and Israel, clearly faithful to his promise, handed her a fistful of shiny pounds sterling. The girl tried to kiss him then, but Israel abruptly pushed her away. He made her spend the whole night on her knees, naked, sucking and licking the bedroom doorknob. Then, of course, the next morning he took back his pounds sterling and turned her over to the partisans.

I'm left to wonder: was the person who did this a persecuted Jew who was celebrating the coming Liberation, or was he a Nazi officer who took his revenge on a Jewish girl right before his final defeat?

Maybe on the night of the potlatch I'll be able to answer that. To me, it could be a lot of fun to be in the newspapers and on television as the captor of another fierce war criminal. Without a doubt, the most cleverly disguised one of all.

Silence DeWar.

B. 1918. But she's still hanging on to a few enchanting pieces of rubble. I can imagine more than one gentleman of advanced age, let's say a septuagenarian colonel, preferably an oilman, who still sighs for her.

"She is the daughter that Lady Brett would have had with that toreador who wanted to make her his wife": *Kiki dixit.* Yet, his description may not be sufficiently flattering, because, after all, I can't skip over one particularly revealing fact about her that can't be ignored: Kiki himself, despite being several years younger than her, must be included in the healthy legion of men who have fallen in love with her. ("My paramours," she says, exaggerating, and knowing it. She likes to make people believe that all of her lovers have shared some bed or other with her.)

Silence is a typical Southern Belle who grew up in the Dark Days of Prohibition. A childhood and adolescence surrounded

by a great deal of old-family pride and very little money. Her
father, a judge who liked his drink and enjoyed his violence;
her mother, a woman who prudently died when Silence was
only sixteen by setting herself on fire in the asylum where—and
there are people who say rightly—she had been committed by
her husband. Suddenly, a great deal of money and very little
old-family pride. In order to complete her education, a sister of
her father's, the wife of a multi-multimillionaire industrialist,
brought her up North to live. At seventeen, Silence was
already the favorite *maîtresse* of her uncle-by-marriage. Then
unexpected *Wanderlust* and the baby stays in Lausanne. Silence,
in Florence, learns to weave wall hangings, and in fact begins
to make such beautiful ones that they compare with the best of
the Quattrocento. In Madrid, in Segovia, everywhere in Spain,
she learns to drink that harsh vino *tinto*—and to this day, it's
still her preferred wine. Oh, I have to remember to have her
bring half a dozen bottles of her favorite brand so she'll enjoy
herself at the potlatch—she drinks it, with style and impeccable
precision, directly from the wineskin, like the muleteers with
their *botas* in the days of Gil Blas.

After she returned to Megalopolis, she was riding around
in the Village and crashed a car one night. Her loving uncle—
and in Silence's case, words more accurate than those have
never been uttered—suddenly died of a heart attack, perhaps
provoked by the many upsets she had caused him with her
incessant rule-breaking (she had even stooped, it is said, to the
level of joining the Communist Party). As always, Silence was
again lucky. She learned that her uncle was proposing to make a
new will and testament, in which he was going to cut out most
of her inheritance. But her uncle's death occurred in 1941, just
in time for the major part of his important fortune to come to
her.

Now, close to fifty years old and still full-bodied, she keeps
crashing cars and drinking with impeccable aim from her old

bota with the silver adornments, she keeps it with her; she keeps falling in love (always easy for her) and having affairs that, nevertheless, almost invariably leave her partners devastated; and she's still designing and manufacturing wall-hangings that are more beautiful all the time, so beautiful you would think they are treasured tapestries that were ordered by Lucrecia Borgia.

She was my first friend in Megalopolis, when I was just a youngster. And it's right that she is also my last friend here. I hope that at the end of the potlatch I'm still lucid enough to give her a kiss on the forehead and ask her, for the last time, to forgive me for never having been able to fall in love with her.

Isis Da Cunha.

Can you believe that this old girl, if you see her from behind, say leaving someplace with the still curvy Silence, is about the same age as she is? Would you also believe that this awful looking thing, her face obviously Negroid, and lacking all semblance of good health, is nothing less than Silence's old nanny? From back in the day on that ruined Southern plantation. Isis—my compatriot, my contemporary, is the girl Mama dreamed would be her daughter-in-law ("such an old, distinguished family, the Da Cunhas").

That splash of white in her bloodline has only served to give Isis the quick-to-age skin and face that are the principal curse of the white race. And she will never fully recover from the shock she got when she learned that I was categorically rejecting the request for her hand that Mama, by every means available to her, was trying to impose on me, using even the cruelest kind of extortion (for three weeks, she refused to let me sleep beside her holding her hand). Still, Isis has followed me, all these years, all over the world. She has pursued me with as much persistence as Javert hunting for Jean Valjean, but always trying to make herself likeable to me. She has studied the highly varied arts and sciences of my fleeting passions for this or that, puncturing her pride, humiliating her intelligence—though the latter was not so small, at one time, as it might be believed today by anyone who knows her now.

She has irritated me unspeakably on more than one occasion (most of all in the days of my first "enthusiasms"). But she has finally become a habit of mine, something inevitable, someone I always count on to be there. For example, at a potlatch.

Rebuffo, Victoria.

Age: twenty-three.

A twig. Or, a better way to describe her, the imp inside a twig. Or inside a bolt of lightning. If, as Kiki has suggested, Silence would be Lady Brett's daughter, then little Victoria— yes, "little," despite her height of 5 feet 9 inches—would be Silence's daughter.

"Queen of the Happening," that is what the most popular weeklies in Megalopolis and around the world have proclaimed her. Her very *life* has been a happening. And she's capable of so much enthusiasm for the idea of my potlatch that she—but she would certainly never use these words!—could offer up her life by throwing herself into the Great Holocaust.

Here is a typical episode in the life of little V.R. (and it's all perfectly true, for I was one of the witnesses). She is in her apartment, completely naked, as she always is at home, and she is wearing that sign she hangs around her neck whenever she's naked. On it, you can read her name. Some visitors arrive. V.R. apologizes for her slovenliness and, after serving them drinks, she asks them to excuse her for a moment to make herself look a little more presentable. Despite the looks they are soon giving her, she nonchalantly starts to get dressed: stockings, garters, brassiere. Then she puts on a red silk dress, opens the bathroom door, climbs into the shower, rubs water and soap all over herself, scrubbing with a large brush, and gets out of the shower. The eyes of her guests, who are following her every movement in astonishment, watch her proceed to undress, and, without even drying herself, come and sit among her guests and, with perfect aplomb, begin to discuss the idea of what the proposed homage to Hans Richter will be.

Do I have any right *not* to invite her since she herself is a constant, tentative potlatch?

Ernie.

He's the oldest young man of his generation. He's about twenty-eight and of course wasn't alive in the days of Verdun, but, hearing him talk about that battle, you'd believe he had lived every day of it, from start to finish—and clearly as a German soldier, because he's an out-of-his-mind *boche*, but one of those who showed up about fifty years too late and adore Ludendorff anyway.

Squat and dark. No one would recognize in Ernie, at first glance, the typical Teutonic warrior. But, in fact, by osmosis or something, deep inside him there is more than one really Teutonic element. For example, he has the unconscious cruelty characteristic of a champion of the Kulturkampf. So don't go to him with stories of sweet little nuns sent into exile or hung by the neck, or about old, humiliated humanists!

Then, right into one of the most characteristic episodes of Ernie's life, enters a Patriarch of Letters from my country, who met him here at my house, felt an instantaneous pang of love at first sight and, unable to transform it into something more concrete, instead transformed Ernie into the principal recipient of his long, literary-philosophical-uranian epistles. Below is how Ernie tells the story of that episode with the chilling detachment and steel that always characterize him. He speaks of himself in the third person in the narrative and I will reproduce it fully and faithfully here, for, without his knowledge, I taped his words:

"He received two a week. Only once was the norm broken. That was because a violent fever laid the old man low. So, if he had kept them, they would now fill up at least fourteen shoeboxes. How could anyone even attempt to try to make such a thing work, especially knowing, as the old man certainly knew, about his financial difficulties and continual shifting from one boardinghouse to another? I mean, such a plan was too much to comply with. Why, in his incessant 'emigrations,' he had already lost the few books he had left, as well as a portrait of von Tirpitz! And now, today, he can answer him with the same words his landlady said to him just this morning, when he went in to take her to task for the lack of butter at breakfast: 'You get what you pay for.' Yes, if he had such an intention from the beginning, it wouldn't have cost him anything, with all his money, to accommodate him permanently in some quiet spot, for example, an elegant part of Suburbia. How nice of him to just convert him into his living file cabinet! And, extending the image, never providing it with ample and comfortable drawers! And, especially, now that he can no longer claim to deserve even the duties of friendship, he thinks of how hard he made it for him to tear up or burn some of them, filling them all full of confidences like that, because it seemed to him they were like pieces of the old man's soul or, as the latter would have said, 'the beating of his heart'! But now he is starting to catch on to the idea that all this has been nothing but a joke. Those confidences were probably nothing but a farce, inventions he made up just to fill pages, because—why not?—the old man probably didn't feel like his friend at all and only saw him as a useful tool, like an instrument for letting off steam from a distance, or a kind of scaffolding he could take down when the building was finished.

"Truthfully, his last letter, the one that, with a mechanical movement of unsurpassed perfection, he had torn up only moments ago, that's the letter that made his earlier 'probablies' even more ridiculous. As for the other letters, he doesn't remember a word of them and, it's true, lately some of them he didn't even bother to open before he destroyed them. But a fragment of this last one will stay with him forever: 'I am making you the repository'—the old man wrote to him, in his characteristically overblown style—'of my deepest secrets, the purest and most subtle of my whole life, my essential, most intimate thoughts. To you, in the course of these last years, I've entrusted my vital nature, my virginal being as an artist, which in the end is all that matters. All those letters that you've put away are my true masterpiece! That's why, when I'm alone, I laugh at the critics who think they've found it in this, that, or another of my many books. Those poor wretches know nothing! You and I share the secret. And now it's time. I authorize you to publish all of my letters to you, so the world will know.'

"After all, only one paragraph of that huge collection of letters has stuck in his head. So, if the other man wants him to, tomorrow he will publish it. And he's getting ready to write him back right now and find out what he thinks about that."

Of course the Patriarch of our National Letters was unable to survive the intensity of the pain that Ernie's blunt note caused him.

Ernie despises anything that isn't rigorously Teutonic. But, after all is said and done, he is a great, natural hero of the *potlatch*, that entertainment of the primitive *Völker* so unworthy of the inheritors of Goethe, von Moltke, and Herr Adolf Hitler.

Nanette.

At nineteen years of age, she has already collected two divorces and two deaths ("in self-defense," as her lawyers have effectively alleged, without a doubt excellent lawyers, paid for by two successive husbands, both men of wealth). It is reasonable to suppose that, if she keeps going at this pace, in her old age, little Nanette will leave in her dust the hardest, most libertine of the working matrons of ancient Rome. Particularly if you take into account that life expectancy is much greater now than in the first centuries of this era, which without a doubt will soon be over.

In this sense, she constitutes a perfect example of my principal argument for organizing the potlatch, which is this: Megalopolitan civilization today is much more decadent than the civilized world was at the time Imperial Rome's death rattle was heard. It's even more decadent, as much from the point of view of its refinements as its cruelties. And perfecting this progress is still another fact: here, now, decadence has acquired a nightmare quality, one that, certainly in those distant times, could not have existed, for ours is an industrialized, technologized, and popularized decadence. The only things still left for us to complete are our five- and ten-year plans for corruption.

But now I'm starting to sound sociological and before I would ever let myself do that, I'd rather start shouting sermons from pulpits.

Nobodaddy interrupts his reading again. He would have preferred to spend a little time meditating on what he's just read, but time itself is pressing. He grabs the apparatus he has closest at hand instead and orders one of his subordinates to take charge, on his behalf, of finding out which Louise J. Bird, among all the Louise J. Birds whose background files are hanging over his head, would be the one invited to O Jango's highly exclusive reception.

"Right away, Chief."

"Yes, right away *would be good!* So when you identify her, have her file brought to me *immediately.*"

"Understood, Chief."

Relieved at having taken control of an enormous task, Nobodaddy again begins to rack his brains on (as he also takes great delight in) *Emaux et Camées.*

Tim.

Fifty-six years old.

As intelligent and refined as the best of them. But really stupid.

He wastes no opportunity to make a fool of himself. So, since his novels and stories can't be criticized for stylistic insufficiencies or childish arguments, people can instead criticize him for exhibitionist behavior, personal affectation, commotions he causes, and idiotic blunders he thinks up to commit in public every day. I believe that there's no scarcity of reporters who live to follow his footsteps.

He's an artist, the kind who sacrifices himself to his art. Oh! If I could only buy up the many different drafts of his works and throw *them* on the fire!

So, at the very least, I must invite him to it.

Ragazzino, Nino.

Forty-four years of age.

Thinking about him, I've written the following parable:

"The same thing always happened. Whenever he was joyful, whenever people seemed to be at their best with him and each thing seemed to be at its most brilliant, that's when he would have to pull back. He would be filled with terror, panicked at even the thought they might discover he wanted to sing. That meant his joy would always be so brief, that things could quickly slip under a cloud, and, instead of friends around him, there would be no one, only strict guards.

"They had convinced him that he didn't know how to sing and he ought never to sing. Were they satisfied? He knew he sang very, very badly. But deep within him, on days when he sang anyway, he felt an unadulterated, pure harmony penetrating his whole being. Was it really so important that he didn't know how to communicate it fully to others? Could that matter so much? Inside, his viscera and muscles and bones would be urging him to do it and, outside, the world itself would also be urging him to do it.

"His body ached from so much silence. His soul was in pain, even now, even while a little sunlight was breaking through and a little bit of sea was washing over him. And he could no longer resist. The sun and the sea demanded song. Every man and woman in the world was clamoring for song . . .

"'What a splendid voice!' a passerby said to himself and stopped to listen to the overwhelming sound coming from a window of that little cottage, evidently a bathroom window. 'That voice! So powerful yet so tender at the same time! What consummate mastery!'

"And it filled him with satisfaction."

Is it necessary to elaborate? Don't people say that a good listener needs to hear few words?

How does Nino manage to get those neckties he uses and boasts of owning at least five hundred of?

Estirol, Argentina.
Sixty-five.

She had a husband who died at just the right time and left her a son who—who can doubt it?—will also die at the right time and leave her as the only heir to the entire family's intellectual fame. A deceased spouse and a son who survives him: two more tentacles she can already work with. They are but two of the tentacles that will add to the ones Nature has already given this true human octopus, this "grand dame of letters"—a designation that has become permanently associated with her name in the women's publications offered by the publishing house she rules. This she-octopus presides over committees, teaches university seminars, inaugurates monuments, writes prologues that considerably lengthen her son's monographs, gives lectures on her dead husband's work, engages in intrigues at various ministries, deceives customs agents, travels constantly but is always present in Megalopolis, and undoubtedly keeps the most used of her tired tentacles in reserve for writing edifying stories in which there always appears a selfless and brilliant young female student of arts and letters who, of course, is a flashback to her own assiduously polished self-image.

And even with all this and everything else, there are still those, who, being more or less in their right minds, find her "interesting," even seductive, despite her robust figure, unexpressive face, and general resemblance to a cook in a third-rate boardinghouse.

I'm already fascinated by the edifying story she'll extract from the potlatch.

Dumb, Bella.

Forty.

Cultured, sexy. Cultured despite how copiously she perspires and sexy despite her notoriously equine features and the accentuated down that covers her vast upper lip.

The potlatch demands the presence of a human factor that shreds the patience of everybody in attendance, one that gives even the dullest sensibilities goose bumps and wounds even the most plausible vanities, one that can break down stubborn wills and annihilate the intelligence of the brilliant. Bella is certainly the woman for the job.

Idlestone, Agnes.

Age: twenty-one.

Pretty. Also really obtuse. Pretty much a lesbian. Made for the cover of *Harper's Bazaar* or *Vogue*. Celia has been pestering me to let her come along, and I'm finally giving in to her begging. On one condition: they put on a free exhibition. But, even more than seeing their exhibition per se, I want to be able to witness the face that L.J.B. will make.

On second thought, I don't think the girl is really all that young.

Emérito de la Galette, Rubén.
     Age: sixty-five.
     But he easily looks seventy-five and is in the category of those
who think they look thirty-five. His life is a cliché of old 1920s
films, and he really does resemble Valentino, except he dances
the tango with a lot more gestures. He also possesses a special
antenna that lets him know about great social events months in
advance. Maybe he even suggests them! Maybe even the potlatch
owes its existence to the fact that he suggested to me how
appropriate it would be to say goodbye to the Megalopolitans
by means of a gathering of extraordinary originality and bright
lights. Naturally, I had to invite him.

Uestis, Bijou.
     Approximately, fifty.
     A comedy writer. His play *Love of the Cob* achieved a
fabulous run of two performances. All his other pieces, despite
his tireless efforts, have remained unperformed, finding no
impresario willing to risk the sumptuous sets and multi-stellar
casts that he demands, against probabilities of success that are
more than dim.
     Nevertheless, Bijou doesn't lack a certain talent for getting
into scholarly anthologies and inspiring professors of dramatic
literature to impose the reading of his works on their students. I
accepted Dieunon's suggestion and invited him, because I want
to know what evidence the latter has at his disposal when he
describes him to me as a man of charming sociability. In reality
he strikes me as an opportunist of the worst kind.

Estercita.
     Age: Thirty-four.
     She is the greatest mistress of ceremonies of children's
specials on television in Megalopolis. Maybe her presence will
help promote disorder at the potlatch. I understand that some

of her shows often end in a real ruckus, with blood flowing from battered little noses, a profusion of bruises, and eyes galore looking like boiled fruit in a compote.

I can't neglect to invite her, especially because also coming are her two principal lovers, I mean Almeida and Moshe Hurenstein.

Toñita.
Age: Thirty-six.
A worker at a shoe factory. She was Fred Ovinario's fiancé for five years, during which time, sharing her room in a tenement house, the Benefactor saved even his exhaled breaths in order to keep buying stocks in Standard Guns. This nice Puerto Rican girl will add a proletarian touch much needed at the potlatch and maybe her presence will accelerate the unleashing of the class war they all tell me is inevitable!

What a wonder it will be to see the Benefactor and Toñita face-to-face again after so many years.

Leni Ragazzino.
See "Ragazzino, Nino."
She's twenty-eight.
Her mother made Nino believe that marrying Leni would enable him to receive a rich dowry (that without a doubt he avidly hoped for in order to enlarge his stock of showy ties). The marriage materialized, but the dowry did not.

Her father made Nino believe that marrying Leni would make him welcome in a family of purest Iberian heritage. Nino, shortly after the wedding, was able to confirm that the paternal grandfather of his eye-catching bride had come to Megalopolis as an illiterate in the hold of a cargo ship and got his start at the bottom rung of the ladder in a cleaning crew of the City of Megalopolis. Goodbye to the title of *marchese* Nino had dreamed of for his first-born son.

After causing him so many bitter disappointments, Leni now hates Nino. She hates anything in any way associated with him. I've seen her, pregnant, point to her stomach and refer to the tender embryo she was carrying inside it, in the following way: "Ay, this hijo de puta." After that I decided that Leni and her husband would never be left off the guest list of any of my agape-*partouzes*.

Elma.

Thirty-two.

She believes in witchcraft and she believes that she's a witch and she fears her own infernal powers. According to her version of things, her powers work themselves involuntarily and always against her good fortune.

She consults horoscopes and prepares potions using formulas from the best-accredited grimoires, and she protects her apartment on the thirteenth floor with a magic circle. She never allows it to be stepped into by any man, for like a modern Circe, she's fearful of turning men into dogs, cats . . . or a pig, or a woman, for example.

So, although many say she's crazy, I take her to be a real conjurer. The woman is young—and pretty, she doesn't fail to satisfy the high aesthetic merits of her Varsovian blood. In all Megalopolis, I dare say, it is she who has conquered the most men simply with her valiant aloofness, in which can be perceived only sincerity, there seeming to be an absolute absence of any artifice in her that could be used to make her more interesting or more coveted.

The potlatch will let her compare her magic to mine. She'll see that men turned into dogs, cats, pigs, or women, can actually come out the best.

Nadal, Macoco.

B. 1900.

He's a noticeable, low-key Charles II of England. What you could say about that king, you could also say about Macoco: he's unable to follow the Ten Commandments and so follows the Ten Thousand Commandments (of good manners) instead. How many millionaires today are capable of facing the certain knowledge that they'll die with their finances and reputation ruined and feel no terror? Macoco can. And, by the way, he shows no indication of stoicism because of it.

A country would be lucky to be ruled by a Macoco. How refined all of its customs would become.

Beside, I have to thank him for making that episode with the Hairy Spider Woman possible for me.

Ensor, Nick.

B. 1923.

He will come: what he will get out of it is to envy and criticize. I know this. But more fundamentally, he will get to drink, a lot and at someone else's expense. He is the epitome of "the intellectual properly speaking," in the words of Adonis. This says everything there is to say about him. Nick Ensor is a survivor of an already extinct fauna that picks up every new fad and adopts it as dogma, for he's possessed by his terror of being seen as old, because he's sure he's flotsam.

But I cannot deny that he is a master at envying. He safeguards his resentments like others keep family relics. His soul is filled with bell jars in which he keeps his hatreds always within sight; he dusts them every day. He'll surely put the potlatch in one.

Adonis Lest.

B. 1913.

Ingenious, lustful, and treacherous. The one work that accounts for his celebrity is absolutely genuine and consists of the finest interweaving of his genius and his lechery . . . and his treachery. He had a friend, a painter who was already famous when Adonis was not even thought of as a writer yet, and his friend suffered horrible mutilations in an automobile accident. Adonis, who had never taken an interest before, convinced his friend's wife to abandon her invalid husband and go away with him; he argued that it wasn't acceptable for a beautiful woman still so young to sacrifice the rest of her life for a man who could be her husband in name only. Annie let herself be persuaded and ran away with Adonis, and the invalid painter committed suicide. A week later, Adonis nonchalantly let Annie know that she could consider their relationship over and done with. He sold the half dozen oils and the temperas he had convinced the painter to give him in the course of their long friendship—the artist's work had increased enormously in value, of course, after his death. With the income from that sale, Adonis went to Europe by himself and enjoyed a long retreat; during that time he wrote the work that made him famous. "Every Other Minute!" as everyone knows, is about a painter who has a terrible accident, after which his wife runs away with his best friend, etcetera, etcetera.

How could I not invite such an intrepid champion who knew exactly how to save me from being horribly raped by the Hairy Spider?

Narko.

B. 1921.

He's a man who has had important mystical experiences. One day, while his doctor was removing wax from his ears, the indescribable physical pain that this was causing him was suddenly sublimated into "a great internal peace"—I repeat his own words—when he raised his eyes and saw that the crucifix on the wall of the doctor's office was smiling at him, encouraging him to resignedly endure this extremely hard test.

He will be able to see the potlatch as a descent into the rings of hell; I think it would be a good idea to have a Dante there on my last night in Megalopolis.

Trinidad Delpeje.
 B. 1923.

Ever since she was very young, she has been haunted by an obsessive dream: in some part of whatever city she's residing in at any given time and in every country she has lived in throughout the course of her life, there is a Negro who, at midnight, year after year, furtively leaves his hiding place and stealthily approaches her dwelling to rape her and then immediately strangle her. Trinidad has told me her nightmare so often that I believe it's time for her to experience another one. It will parallel hers: I am that Negro.

At the potlatch we will both be safe, for at least as long as the pleasant evening on which we're all gathered goes on neutralizing our two obsessions.

Nobodaddy finally raises his head from the volume, which he slams closed. His gaze, uncertainly for a moment, wanders among glasses and mugs of beer that cover his worktable. Ah, yes, eat something. He takes a bite of a stale ham sandwich and notices his dry throat.

"Right away! Yes, *now*, a bottle of ice-cold beer and two ham-and-lettuce sandwiches."

Nothing, think of what they call absolutely nothing until they bring the order. But first he wants to glance at the rap sheet of that woman with the name, the name alone, the exception, who stands out in *Émaux et Camées.*

"Oh, yes, chief, indeed, sir, yes, your assistant Mason dropped off the file with information on the Louise J. Bird who was invited that night. He left it on your desk, didn't want to disturb you, saw how very busy you were."

"Then thank you! That's all!" His tone is harsh. He silently chastises himself for the forcefulness with which he has demanded the documents. A red cover shrilly calls attention to itself now from the tops of several mugs of beer where it sits.

Calmer, he has decided that conditions are now right, he can leave his mind blank while he waits for his order. He sighs, relieved, and his eyelids close halfway. He almost has them completely closed when someone knocks on his door.

"Pardon me, chief, sir, I've brought you your . . . order." But the sight of the large bottle of ice-cold beer has revived his thirst and, rapidly, while the orderly is still holding the tray, he has taken the bottle, filled a glass, and emptied it in one swallow.

"Thank you. Now clear away all those glasses and plates and bring me another bottle and two more sandwiches, but make these tuna and onion."

"Certainly, chief, right away, sir."

Nobodaddy eats and drinks for ten minutes without interruption. As his hunger and thirst slake, his anxiety builds, until he again feels what he has felt for a good number of days now as he has searched for a solution to the very complex enigma that those charred human remains have presented him with.

He downs the rest of the beer in one of the new bottles and realizes that it is imperative for him to spend a moment in the small bathroom next to his office.

The mirror reveals a tired face under a significant growth of new beard and the large, dark circles that have formed around his eyes. He removes his jacket and loosens his tie, then plunges his head a couple of times into the basin he has filled with cool water from the faucet, and, not caring that his shirt is getting wet, he immediately splashes the back of his neck with more water because it is burning hot.

He returns to his desk in his shirtsleeves and sits down. The J. Bird packet is disappointing. A nutty lesbian multimillionaire, just like all the others. And did they try to make his disappointment even greater? Right on top of all the photos and clippings in the folder, someone put this terse memo: "It has been duly confirmed that on the night of the party under investigation Miss J. Bird was in treatment at the psychiatric clinic of Dr. Magnus Sapir. Dr. Sapir himself, in addition to his private secretary and the nurse in charge of Miss J. Bird's care, have all corroborated the woman's statement to this effect."

"I'll have to look somewhere else then," Nobodaddy says to himself. But he doesn't despair, because looking at things more closely, he sees that the case may now be seen as either simpler or more complicated. It all depends on how you want to look at it. The solution may still be hidden in the pages of *Émaux et Camées* itself.

If that's the way it is, it's essential for him to proceed to the job of deciphering and, at this moment, Nobodaddy can see only one possible way to focus his search: understand the guests' names. O Jango may have chosen his guests precisely for their names in order to employ them in the service of some hermetic meaning that would itself be the key to the deaths that occurred in the course of that strange party. So, for now, in order to convert the document into an intelligible form—if there is really anything in it to decode—only two possible courses of action occur to Nobodaddy. One is to make himself a list with the names of all the guests in alphabetical order. Why, after all, did the author of the new version of *Émaux et Camées* not follow alphabetic order? Number one, perhaps because it simply seemed too *democratic* to him. Nobodaddy has now already formed an opinion—*adverse, of course*—about the effeminate, South American, plutocratic aesthete and author. The second way to proceed is to add up the ages of all the individuals who figure in the gallery of character portraits accumulated under O Jango's vicious pen. For why did he bother so much about his guests' ages? Then Nobodaddy remembers something: in O Jango's text the exact age of everyone does not appear! In some cases the author has limited the age to an approximate calculation. About one guest, for example, he writes only "she must be about thirty"—and in another case he has omitted any reference at all to age. Therefore, no, it's better to discard immediately the possibility of finding a clue in the ages the author has provided.

Nobodaddy takes a sheet of paper and writes in a single column all the names that appear in the book, in the same order in which they appear in it:

Lys Vallée
Honey De Sucker
Olga Riesling
Mosca, "Fatso"
Ojal, Renato
Solar y Soler, Marie-Louise
Albamonte, Elodio
Pip
Ígor Pérez-Smith
Epinal, Silvina
Néstor de Talleyrand-Berrichon
Soledad Weisskopf
Elka Trakl
Sol Whitman
Tilbury, Marcia
Mariana Marx
Omar del Ramo
Roslyn Lupescu
Topaze McCulloch
Alenzar, Isabela
Jambon, Iris
Almeida, Jefferson
Minos, Kiki
Ayesha Flintless

Ixion, Friedrich Wilhelm
Selene Freund
Enos, Rodolfo
Tríada, Joaquín de
Incatasciatto, Mongho
Louise J. Bird
Van Boren, Laura
Ovinario, Fred
Uirakocha, Joachim von
Silver, Don
Ferroni, Amleto
Almirón
Ulises
Troika Soares
Celia de Minos
Hurenstein, Moshe
Orvieto, Camillo
Israel Goldstein
Silence de War
Isis Da Cunha
Rebuffo, Victoria
Ernie
Nanette
Tim
Ragazzino, Nino
Estirol, Argentina
Dumb, Bella
Idlestone, Agnes
Emérito de la Galette, Rubén
Uestis, Bijou
Estercita
Toñita
Leni Ragazzino
Elma

Nadal, Macoco
Ensor, Nick
Adonis Lest
Narko
Trinidad Delpeje

The list tells him nothing. The only conclusion it allows him to come to is this: foreign names predominate.

"Which is not at all unusual," the chief is forced to concede, when in reality he would have preferred to find a clue precisely in the exoticism of the majority of those names, especially taking into account the fact that the author of the list is himself a foreigner, with whose country, on top of everything, there exists no treaty of extradition, and bound for which, of course, the author left the very day after the party and will be impossible to bring here to be interrogated!

"For the third time in my career I'm now forced to admit defeat," the chief is already confessing to himself, his expression one of resignation. "Or, no, slow down, as my maternal grandfather always used to tell me: '*piano, piano, si va lontano.*'" Success is still a possibility, but he may have to slowly trudge the distance to get it.

Obviously, the merit, at least all of the merit for it would no longer go to him and his ingenuity alone, as it has with so many of the other enigmas that his intelligence has so effectively resolved. But, no, after all, it's not such a big deal to be forced to turn to the services of the automatic computer just installed in Records. So why consider himself beaten or compare this to asking for help from another investigator. He sighs, it may signal relief, and Nobodaddy makes a decision:

"Connect me to the head of Cybernetics-Records."

The head of Cybernetics in Records is a bald, thickly bespectacled, very short, little person (*i.e. he is a dwarf*) with a large beard. If he appeared in a comic book, he would make people laugh because he is the prototypical mad scientist. But it's he who laughs now, in silence, when he hears Nobodaddy's request. He's remembering the terse comment the chief as commissioner wrote when the new computer was installed: "Useless. Money wasted." The mad scientist inside the cyberneticist feels tempted to ask if the costly machine still seems useless and a waste of money to him, but he represses this desire. He knows that a victim of wrongs always pleases more when he suffers in silence.

"As soon as the materials you send me process, I'll call you with the results. No worries, sir," is all he answers.

Nobodaddy calls home now to reassure his wife about his extended absence. He then falls asleep thinking nostalgically of the cabbage and sausage that he missed out on at suppertime last night. It isn't easy to persuade his wife to make his favorite dish because of the smell it leaves in the kitchen and the whole house. Sometimes the neighbors have even complained.

"Chief! We have a first result, but the computer will keep working unless you order otherwise, sir."

The telephone buzzer has just pulled Nobodaddy out of a sweet culinary nap and he awakes alarmed and with a sense of guilt; as he always does, let it be said, when he falls asleep in his office.

"Well, *give* me the *information*," he rudely responds, because Nobodaddy is never ruder than when he feels at fault.

". . . It doesn't seem to make sense, chief."

"Kill the comments, I just want to know what it says! Well, then, what does it say? Is this something you do understand?"

The voice of the intelligent comic-book character suddenly grows grave.

"It says: '*Homo sapiens* has died and you all have to choose between God and nothing.'"

A long silence follows.

"And that's *it*?" Nobodaddy asks.

"For the moment, sir, everything. But the computer is still processing the material we received."

"OK, fine, that's fine. Talk to me if there's any new result. But, first, tell me something. Is there any possibility of an error in a result 'processed' by your infernal little machine?"

"Practically not the slightest, chief."

Homo sapiens has died and you all have to choose between God and nothing? Really? This is nonsense: these words are gibberish. This must be the result of some careless calculation, or maybe a failure in the transistors of that damnable quasi apparatus.

And Nobodaddy, whose body is still processing his lunch, again falls into a stupor.

What just now happened? Is he still asleep and dreaming? What is going on here! A powerful voice or some such thing has thundered through the intercom and stunned him like a bucketful of cold water dumped on his head!

The voice starts up again:

"Here in our village, there have been so many unusual events lately that people on the outside are starting to talk about us in the most disgraceful way. They exaggerate and distort the real facts so much that they are even unrecognizable to those of us who have lived them. But the facts themselves are so strange. Any little thing added on manages to make their details seem even crazier.

"But if I'm going to tell this honestly, I have to say that the truth is, we ourselves, those of us who are the witnesses, have been changed by the actual events. So much so, that I've barely been able to find, even among friends, two versions that more or less coincide in any aspect of them. So it would be very unjust of me to dare reproach the strangers, who, by the by, have never looked at us with much sympathy. For I observe their same things every day in the people I have known all my life, including my godfather (who I have always held up as model of wisdom), and, I don't know, maybe even in myself.

"Water tanks with water that appears to have been turned into fruit brandy, scandalous desertions by the most virtuous mothers, a vicious scarcity of food that could only be explained by an invasion of invisible gluttons—all these facts rile you, inhibit your talk, keep you from really listening. That is why I can't blame my wife anymore, if, when I finally get up the nerve to hint at an explanation, instead of paying me any attention, she repeats at the top of her voice, so all the neighbors and even non-neighbors can hear it all, that I am hallucinating, that I am a drunk and I am driving her crazy, and that that's probably all I really want anyway. I'm truly sick of hearing my wife rail against wine. But I'm even sicker of this—no, the truth is, I can't take any more of this huge confusion we're mired in everywhere! I only hope that someone will be able to really hear what I'm saying. That's why, since nowadays it has become practically impossible to come across a good listener, I've opted for writing down my version of something that happened and that I sincerely believe set off this whole series of calamities on us. And you can be sure that this narration is perfectly truthful, insofar as my faculties will let it be.

"I'm a man with only a little learning and I would have rather had my local pharmacist, like he usually does when I have to write a letter, check these lines over before I just submit them willy-nilly. I'm stopped short in his case, however, by the thought that the kind druggist is the biggest unbeliever in our village—he's always fighting with churchgoers—and, besides that, because on one occasion he had to come to my aid when I drank too much, so maybe he shares my wife's opinion of the truthfulness of this account. And it is the right thing for me to do, so I say right up front that I am—or, rather, I was—employed as a guard in the jail here. Since this is a small town of peaceful people, farmworkers and such, not many are the kind to wind up behind bars, and when this happens to happen, what is at the heart of it, usually, is just a pocketbook secretly emptied or a glass or two too many had by someone. That is exactly what I was thinking about when I applied for a job at the jail, for to honor the whole truth I've never been a big fan of very tiring duties. Although, and I ought to acknowledge it here, my laziness has now been sorely chastised.

"None of the other guards or even the Chief himself were ever noted for their work ethic; and this was the reason that it surprised me so much when, all of a sudden the Chief ordered us to get the cell ready, because he was about to leave in pursuit of a dangerous bandit who, naturally, he was hoping to catch. I remember that during that whole day we talked about nothing else, the other three guards and me. We were convinced that said dangerous bandit could be none other than the one who used to commit his depredations several leagues from town many years ago, so many that when I was a boy they already talked about him like somebody really old, though still active: like a volcano, you could say.

"Among ourselves everybody knew that that man was a highly dangerous criminal whose evil and daring accounted for the most abominable outrages that were committed all up and down the shore road. Business men with their throats cut, little boys sliced open with their insides falling out, big girls deeply insulted—all of that formed part of his atrocious rap sheet. It was even known *how* he pulled off so much evil so easily. Out there in the narrow ravine, where the long dry bed of an old stream (and where could those waters have gone? I've always wondered), right at the place where two enormous rocks have squeezed together and formed a, like a bridge, that is where the vile assassin would lay in wait, a sentinel of the road, and when prey happened to pass below his post, then with incredible rapidity he would fall on the unfortunate wayfarer and in an instant make short work of him. Or her. It was also known, because, over and over the cases of it would crop up, how on other occasions he'd fall back on tricks of a very different kind, so much so that it became possible to attribute to this monster a genuine capacity to divine the characteristics of his victims, and then, so calmly, as if he was just another peaceful traveler, he would come out to meet up with some, instead of waiting for them up in the streambed, and, in a minute or two of lively chatter, persuade them of the advantages that his abject lifestyle provided, so much so that he succeeded in sending them back amongst us, or to the neighboring towns, as his accomplices on some criminal mission.

"All this was known about that dark character, although never, if there was an opportunity, did we ever talk about it to strangers. We suspected—and not without reason, no—that they would throw our cowardice in our faces for the despicable flaw we would be betraying every time we might admit that, almost before our very eyes, that mortal threat was still going on. And the truth is we were afraid whenever we heard what people said about him, but we were also afraid of killing our greatest hope, which was to put an end to his ferociousness. For, if, by some error of calculation in our plans, when the moment arrived to undertake the punitive expedition, the bandit managed to escape our punishment, without a doubt, he would immediately go out and repeat his acts of bestiality, now with even more energy.

"That's why we got so nervous when our chief ordered us to prepare the cell, which, at the moment, was used for storage. And, although not one question that could have been taken as indiscreet came out of our mouths while the chief was present, as soon as he left, the four of us did not, as I said, stop talking about it all for a whole day, letting off all our nervous energy, although someone—I now don't remember who, it may have even been me—and maybe just to feel better through a statement that deep inside had to be considered the most flagrant of lies, maintained that the prisoner we were waiting for could <u>not</u> be the criminal we were all thinking about.

"Maybe he wasn't. But in the dim light of the corridor, at dusk, there we were when the warden and his procession came in. In among them, moving very slowly and almost strangling on all the ropes that were holding him, came an unknown stranger, and when the group got closer we managed to see the prisoner's face very clearly, and then our fear dissipated after our wait that had been made even longer by dark forebodings that had got so thick we could barely stand our mutual company or our own bodies.

"It was this really thin man, truthfully, nearly a skeleton, on whose head every other feature got lost because of his enormous whale of a forehead, which was as free of wrinkles as a bald head. His eyes were tiny and besides that were half-closed, and almost looked like they had been wolfed down by heavy, purplish bags, his eyelids, their rims so red, so big, they almost looked like lips. His real lips, though, were barely noticeable. You noticed his mouth only because of his teeth, a few kind of dancing in there. And his whole body was trembling inside the bindings. It was so bad, that I started to feel sorry for the prisoner, and through my mind flashed another poor guy who I remembered and was all cut up.

"It was myself who gave the key three good turns in that big lock and another guard lifted the heavy wood plank to free up the secure door. The warden, surrounded by his riflemen, was giving the orders and we complied without cracking a joke, it was a solemn moment, truly, one of those moments in which your feelings of duty and sorrow either combine or crash head-on with each other. And right away, irritation and probably disgust started growing in us, and then later, terror.

"Locking anybody up is something that hurts and especially when the captive looks like he's in weak condition surrounded by big tough men armed to the teeth, who you know are coldhearted killers. Keeping him there, week after week without knowing who he really was, never hearing him move around, him more like an exhausted mouse caught in a trap, it all gets to be too hard for someone who has sensitive feelings and even holds certain notions that justify the law breaker.

"Besides, us four guards could see that they were plotting a really wicked trial for that poor man. People were murmuring about it here and there, but nobody would dare demand the investigation be done by the rules. They didn't tell us who was being judged or why the stranger was on trial, but everybody in town had to contribute to his maintenance—not very costly, it's true—and the four of us had to mount guard outside his cell as if it was about protecting some bloody killer or criminal, like the one up at that bridge, and not some poor old scarecrow who, at the very most, might have been a trafficker of noxious herbs.

"Why, I even started to think that we could help him escape! I even talked about it with the other guards!

"And, meanwhile, the wretched man was stuck in the cell, in solitary, always more silent than even the grave, never touching the whole-grain bread we brought him every day or so, barely surviving on a swallow or two of water. That's how it was, and it made us think that the people in charge of the place had gone crazy and were horribly cruel and, one by one, they would start eliminating us because we would be in the way of their plot, because, having everything, they also wanted to flatter themselves by taking our poverty too: like the silver-plated knives and forks of one or the trained dog of another or some other's blond-haired daughter. Or <u>your</u> daughter, I said to one guy. Or maybe your <u>wife</u>, he answered me right back, but we felt so angry, we didn't have it in us to laugh at either thing. That's how the prisoner had become our very obsession. He took up all our time, night and day, and when we were sleeping he was in our dreams, as a red deer or a snake.

"Who was he? I believe I've insisted enough on the fact that we did not know; and for that very reason we would speculate endlessly about his name, his age, and his crime. As for a name, we opted to call him "Old Man," that's all, although nothing in his weak nature might justify that moniker, for we also didn't know his age, however much we might try to fool ourselves at least in that respect.

"And his crime? Did we ever get to know anything about his crime? Do I right now even know what they were accusing him of? Truth is, inside me now is a contending notion and I can glimpse a certain explanation, but on the day the chief came to alert us that the prisoner had been condemned to death by hanging, none of us knew what crime was imputed to the poor wretch.

"Anyway, we had to comply with the orders we got, and it was decided that the execution would take place the next day in the little patio behind the prison; the authorities seemed very anxious to eliminate every possibility that the prisoner, through some unforeseen maneuver, would escape. For that very reason, without a doubt, our chief took me and another guard in with him and only breathed a sigh of relief when he saw that his prisoner was still there, as quiet and shaky as on the first day.

"Then came the orders, given to us by the chief as always in a threatening tone, almost like relegating us to the condition of prisoners too. The chief commanded us to stay on watch the whole night, posted in pairs, two in front of the cell door and the other two at the end of the corridor, and he even demanded, in a tone of resolute threat, that we drink only water all night and, insofar as it was possible, not to even drink water.

"It was the saddest night of my life. While the carpenter out on the patio was lording it over his apprentices and building the gallows, even the rhythmic blows of the hammers were drowned out by his loud, brandy-soaked voice that would yell for this or that tool. And meanwhile I was mounting guard with Juan beside me in front of the cell.

"Finally, when I'd gotten myself convinced that the sun would never rise again and our watch would have to go on as long as the earth itself did, in my desperation I started talking to myself. Juan was nodding off, cowed alternately by sleep and our chief's threats, and the other two guys, as seen from where we found ourselves and in almost complete darkness, looked like two huge replicas of rivals standing there looking at each other, each one in fear of the other.

"Nobody heard me, if I actually spoke out loud. Only the prisoner could have heard me, supposing he wasn't asleep (for night—no matter how well our chief pretended not to notice—was made for sleeping and, besides, that wretch in the cell always seemed lethargic).

"I stopped talking when I heard the sound of footsteps approaching, and suddenly I felt a sense of duty: I gave Juan a big elbow in the belly to wake him up, and he writhed in pain a little, and I sharpened my hearing, trying to identify who it was who was coming. Then I noticed that the sun was already lighting up the corridor walls and, at the same time, I saw our chief, with his tireless henchmen, making his entrance into the corridor.

"I've written too much maybe and my hand, little accustomed to the task, is starting to hurt. My doubt is growing strong now too, and I think it would have been enough for me just to depose, without processing any other steps, the event I'm immediately going to refer to and to which I attribute so much importance in our lives. But, I've already written the earlier stuff down and it's better to leave it all as it is, and maybe it will be of use to someone who might get to read my explanation, by helping to dissipate certain objections about the accuracy of this account that his mind would have every right to raise. It tells an event that is too strange to be believed all at once, even if the one narrating it was a great magistrate or a rich landowner, when the one who is really telling it is hardly even—or to put it better, was—a small-town prison guard, on top of which are his previous bad habits in the area of intemperance.

"I've just left off where our chief is waiting there in the corridor a moment ago, although, in reality, he didn't slow down or stop a second after he entered the corridor, but came directly to where Juan and I were posted and ordered us to lift the plank and unlock the cell.

"That's what we did, as rapidly as we could in our pitiful state after such a night of guard duty, and the riflemen readied their weapons as if expecting that, as soon as the door opened, a wild beast was going to charge at us.

"Then, through the door, came no one. Nevertheless, and since the chief was rather corpulent, he made me and Juan and his fiercest looking sharpshooter go in first. And then confusion reigned.

"And I realized that we had fallen for a trick and not even the most subtle and perverse mind of our entire village could have come up with it. After that trick, I'll never be surprised at anything ever again in the future. Because what we witnessed, what we were sensing, all came together to mean the defeat of human reason itself. Because we went into the cell looking for a prisoner, and in there, side by side, elbow to elbow, were two.

"Two prisoners wearing the same irons, their scrawny legs lined up in exactly the same position, both equally silent; they were two beings who couldn't be called, for example, 'very similar' or 'twin brothers' because they were identical. And they were identical because they were exactly the same one. Yet they were two.

"I would need to come up with some really tortured language to describe exactly what we were seeing, words that surely the kind pharmacist, even as well-read as he is, could not tolerate. But, equally insufficient, it turns out, is just to say either 'they are' or 'he is.' Damage to our language is inevitable with such need to describe something as either 'he are' or 'they is.' Personally, due to a sensation whose cause I still can't manage to discern, the first of these two very bad ways to deform our language seems to me better able to transmit the experience of that horrifying moment. But, however that may be, I'm convinced that it will turn out to be very hard to give this account any credibility, because of which, seeing no other way out, I'll fall back on an expedient that will test my own self-love.

"I usually drink too much and this has earned me severe reprimands by my superiors and more than one punch on the jaw by my wife. I know very well, then, what constitutes the property of seeing double, a characteristic of the drunkard that is prone to much exaggeration and a lot of stupid jokes.

"Therefore, I've repeatedly suffered that experience and so have seen two lampposts instead of the only one that was there or two wives instead of just the one, both mine—what a nightmare! But this is something completely different. It was like having the sensation that I was the one had doubled, and now with two pairs of eyes was now looking at two prisoners . . . only because I was looking with both my pairs of eyes.

"Because it was as if, beside me, stuck to me, there had suddenly grown another individual identical to me and he himself was looking too; and, it's obvious, between the two of us we were seeing two prisoners. And both of them were sad. They were both laughing, though."

"This is all the computer has been able to extract from the material you sent us, chief," says the comic-book-mad-scientist character, much more softly. His voice is almost mellifluous.

"Thank you. But I can't use any of it. Therefore, please have them return all the texts and material I sent you originally. And thanks again."

Nobodaddy comments inside his head, "I like the straight-talking computer's tone much better than that sophisticated O Jango chatter," and he immediately thinks, "It's imperative that I continue my inquiry now. I will have to go in a new direction. I'll go back to the psychological angle." He picks up the list he made with all the guests' names.

He has memorized the characteristics that O Jango assigned to each one. And, after all, considering the poisoned pen aspect, only two of the characters really stand out. The camerawoman with the Germanic surname and the painter undoubtedly of Latin origin.

"Since they're completely free of O Jango's snide judgmentalism, aren't they the absolutely most suspicious of all?" he asks himself. "In the middle of so much corruption, who could *not* get infected?" he adds. "We know that, in the infected person, an illness tends to acquire its most virulent characteristics. Yes, of course! The so-called Elke Trakl and the subject known as Omar del Ramo could be a pair of killers perfectly shielded by their appearance of detached purity. But it's too late to question them tonight. I'd better go home and pick up the investigation tomorrow."

After six hours of very agitated sleep, a delicious aroma succeeds in waking Nobodaddy. His first reaction is to glance at the alarm clock on the nightstand. It says 8:50: "Confound it! Now I'll get to the office really late." And maybe he would have hurried to wash up and dress but the delicious smell coming from the kitchen is very tempting, for his wife left the kitchen door open when she went in to prepare his breakfast. It isn't so much the aroma of fresh bread toasting or the bacon in the frying pan that make him want to spend a little more time in bed. It's a strong fragrance of last night's cabbage, absolutely glorious, the cabbage he didn't get to eat. Martha has clearly kept a big portion of it for his lunch. This expectation comforts him and, feeling more secure, he decides not to get to the office before 10:30 and burrows back down into the sheets:

"Martha! Breakfast, my love!"

"It's coming, it's coming! Have a little patience, I have to make your toast again."

His wife comes into the bedroom with the morning paper and finishes her explanation about the late breakfast. It just so happens that the toast burned when she went into the basement to get some clothes out of the washer.

"But here is the paper. You can entertain yourself a little while I finish up breakfast.

"Which I'll have in bed."

"As Your Majesty commands." Having recently turned forty, Martha is still an attractive woman and there is something quite youthful in her demeanor right now. Nobodaddy watches her go out of the room, feels nostalgic, and proceeds to follow the wise instructions he has just received.

In Vietnam things are as bloody and confounding as ever. Deaths and more deaths. "German-American Camerawoman Disappears in Ambush":

"UPI, 18. – The distinguished television camerawoman, Elke Trakl, who just returned to the zone of operations after a brief vacation in Megalopolis to receive the annual distinction that TV-Megalopolis awards its prized graphic reporters, was part of a squad of U.S. Marines ambushed yesterday morning by Viet-Cong guerrillas. All members of the team are missing in action, including Miss Trakl.

"Miss Trakl, born in Dessau (E. Germany) on October 14, 1939, was a finalist in the competition to choose Mademoiselle Télévision Française in Paris five years ago, when she was in training with French TV. She began her career as a camerawoman . . ."

Why keep reading? Nobodaddy is irritated. He throws the newspaper to the floor. Why doesn't that damned breakfast get here! Now only one viable suspect remains.

At last Martha enters carrying a tray laden with succulent things, but he is now suddenly rushing to get dressed. He is not going to let the painter disappear on him.

He drinks his coffee in a single gulp, scalding his throat. He pecks his wife on the forehead without bothering to wipe his mouth—"such manners!" she chides him inwardly, an expression of disgust on her face because her forehead feels wet—and there he goes, already on his way to the office. "Omar del Ramo! I have to interrogate at the very least *this* one."

Nobodaddy will in fact not be able to interrogate the painter either. Omar del Ramo, just three days ago, suffered an extremely violent nervous crisis. This has required him to be placed in a psychiatric clinic. The only consolation Nobodaddy has is to sit here in Omar's studio, for more than an hour, listening to the endless, complicated story that he's told by a small, bearded man as modestly dressed as any office worker and who introduces himself as an intimate friend of the great painter. He has let it be known that he is someone who the artist's wife has put legally in charge of caring for her husband's material interests.

Nobodaddy makes no claims to be a connoisseur of fine art, but the canvases that he has before him seem sufficiently atrocious to justify the following meager observation that, without realizing what he's saying, he states in a voice quite audible to his interlocutor:

"I see why he went crazy."

And then the little man who looks so much like an office worker, as if swept along by some need to justify himself (but for several moments continues to seem suspicious to Nobodaddy), begins to tell him everything he knows about the celebrated artist's last few days of lucidity.

"Of course, in all honesty, not even I could agree with him when he started to make those things. And that was even though I was known as the most ardent defender of his painting. But who knows . . . Here are evidently things that go beyond, beyond intelligence or sensibility, or perhaps one's intelligence and sensibility all at once. Of course, I defended him when he was starting out, when Meyer Meyer used to dedicate barely a line of his critiques to him, and that was only to make fun of him. Because, from the beginning, what spoke to me in his work was that audacity in his way of using color, a kind of ferocity that could reconcile one to the idea of a modern art that was so genuine, that is to say, as modern and genuine as the art of the Middle Ages was modern and medieval. I was in awe. Nothing could stop him: he painted feverishly and, I dare say, even brilliantly. And the way he applied color! At times he piled on so many at once that it seemed color itself was going to collapse. But, no! Not only did it not collapse, it didn't even quiver. It was almost a miracle . . . And his brushstrokes! If he was sketching a foot, for example, apparently for no reason and against all rules, at odds with academics and the vanguard, some line in that foot would abruptly narrow then immediately thicken. I suppose you're following me, Commissioner? He achieved admirable effects. You could see the foot palpitate, *exist*, not as just a simple, drawn object.

"Just think of it. Then suddenly he started *those* abominations . . . I never imagined he would go in that direction. I had been able to see how well he was progressing, and he was already so close to achieving something enormous and splendid, so close to the quality of a new Cézanne, don't think I exaggerate. The first painter from here to have gotten so far! Because Omar, despite his name, is from here, born here. Then one morning he asked me to come see him at his studio; that day I realized that I'd been wrong. I even thought maybe the whole time I'd been completely wrong. But I also thought he could still find a good solution to all this, could find his way again, as they say. And I even thought that, sometimes, just when a man is at the edge of

fulfillment, he loses his vision, loses his balance for a moment . . .
But for only a moment!

"I can see him now, just the way he was that day. He was—
and it's important that you know this, Commissioner—he was
very *excited*. I didn't notice it right away, although I can clearly
see it now; I'd been constantly in his company and had grown
so used to his manner that any oddness in his behavior just
went by me unnoticed. And the truth is, he always seemed very
excited to me.

"But on the morning I'm telling you about, his level of
excitement perhaps reached its zenith, Commissioner, because
when he had barely started talking—he hadn't yet even shown
me those canvases you see there—he tried to lean against an
easel and almost went down with the heavy thing! Then he
started kicking it and he was insulting it as if he were dealing
with a human being! Something alive, anyway, not just some
broken sticks. After that, the tone of our conversation that day
became more and more violent; he had gotten used to talking to
me as if I were some scullery maid. I'm sure that in his heart he
loves me, despite everything. But that morning he was insolent,
and, I might say, cruder than ever. When he showed me those
images, truthfully, I felt a little afraid of him and couldn't hide
my reaction to them. Accustomed as he was to my endless
praise and total submission to his dictates—and now I can see
that it was *unfortunate* that he was so accustomed to it—he
became furious with me as soon as I made a few observations.
Of course, I had known for some time that he was egotistical,
but until then I'd let myself be soothed by the notion that, on
the other hand, a certain amount of vanity isn't all that bad
in an artist. It can even provide his nutrition—no, excuse me,
what I meant to say was "food." So I had never been irritated by
all that. It was only when he got so furious that day that I could
appreciate the real magnitude of his selfishness and I found it to
be, I can only say, monstrous, Commissioner.

"The same way those two 'pictures' there—well, one has to call them something—that had him so worked up that day were monstrous. But I won't attempt the impossible, by that I mean, I won't describe them. At the very least, it wouldn't be fair to them, and I've always thought certain critics were ridiculous to try to describe any image, I mean, insofar as the thing is its full measure—which is the measure of the painting itself. For a visual image isn't literature or geometry or even cookery. But believe me, Commissioner: if there were ever anything *indescribable*, without doubt those two repellant, repulsive canvases were that. They made you immediately want to run away from them.

"And, the truth is, in the end, I had no choice but to run away from this place. I mean, I escaped, from him, his studio, and his pictures. I thought Omar had gone crazy and was in the most serious emotional crisis possible. Let somebody else put up with him, I told myself. But ten minutes later I was struggling with my regret and that afternoon I went back. I wanted to get in touch with his wife, to warn her; they certainly loved each other very much, though they didn't often see each other, he was always somewhere with his fancy women. But she didn't pick up the phone. Maybe that, more than anything, is why I went back. From lunch on, till he went to sleep at dawn, Omar usually could not be found in the studio; always the fancy women. Generally speaking, he was invisible for the rest of the day, you understand, unless it occurred to him to go to the café or someplace, and that only happened now and then in the afternoon. Omar wasn't keen on the Espresso or the White Horse, unlike almost all of his colleagues, who thought they couldn't be real painters if they weren't at one of those places for hours and hours. But the thing is, this time was different: I had no doubt that a man in the state of mind Omar had been in, if he had an ounce of sanity left, would shut himself away voluntarily and be sitting in here quietly, in a corner. Otherwise, since he had been so enraged by my comments, those *images*, those damned 'pictures,' those so-called *paintings* would be creating so much agitation in him, that he would be out somewhere starting fistfights with anybody who crossed his path. And honestly, I was a little afraid of that when I started banging on the studio door. At that very instant, it occurred to me that, all in all, he might have gone out. I could see him at that very moment lying in a hospital with his head knocked in or maybe sitting in jail or maybe, a sad premonition, wearing a straightjacket somewhere.

"I don't know how many times I knocked, though I clearly remember that, when I stopped, my knuckles were red and sore. I'd been obstinately insisting that he open the door because I was struck by a sudden certainty that Omar was right there on the other side of the door. In my desolate hope, my impatience, you know how these things go, Commissioner, I was suddenly convinced that he'd locked himself in his studio. But it wasn't because I heard even the slightest sound from the other side. No, there really wasn't any indication of that. I felt his presence there in some more tenuous way, which was also vibrant, subtle. It seemed urgent, as if he were a small, caged animal in there, a little animal, such as a Black Widow, let's say.

"Then all of a sudden there he was standing right in front of me and I couldn't choke back a scream, of fear more than surprise, at his sudden, silent apparition; at the time it seemed uncanny. His face was extremely drawn, nothing left of the healthy petulance normally never absent in him, not even the time, many years ago, when he was still an unknown, a bachelor, and was in San Vicente Hospital and, don't think I'm exaggerating, Commissioner, his fever was so high that time that his elastic bonds radiated heat.

"He said nothing, just invited me in with a slight movement of his right hand, which I could see was heavily stained with bright colors, though he usually kept his hands scrubbed clean. That slight movement of his hand was accompanied by a smile

I'd never seen on his face before; it was, actually, unlike any I had ever seen on anybody. It was—I don't know if I'm explaining it well enough—it was hollow. It was a smile constructed without supports of any kind, as if it were free, present but independent of the muscles that could move it and of the soul that could give it life. Equally hollow—I mean empty—was this room! I had the feeling it had been dismantled, or, at least, that a lot of the furniture had been moved out to another part of the studio. But I couldn't place exactly which furniture was missing, although I am sure the 'infuriating' easel from that morning wasn't here anywhere. And I couldn't count everything, as I wanted to, Commissioner, because he immediately started talking and I had to concentrate all my attention on his voice. Rather, my focus got fuzzy, I got lost in his voice.

"And in his endless spew of words! Hot words! Cold words! Hot and cold at the same time in an excessive torrent of speech! If I tell you that he kept me more than two hours without giving me a single opportunity to say a word, I know you're not going to believe me, Commissioner, but that's exactly how it was. Only once did I try to get him to clarify a concept, though *every* concept he stated seemed to me to be terribly obscure. And when I did interrupt, I had to shut up immediately. Starting that morning, I'd begun to notice that a very disagreeable sensation, unprecedented, was insinuating itself into our relationship; a pure, icy fear I felt only at the moment when, very softly, it should be said, I tried to interrupt him and, believe me, I saw in his eyes the fangs of a rabid dog.

"Still, he didn't show his anger the same way he had in the morning. He now spoke in a very patient manner, at least in comparison with the state of outrage he had been in earlier. What he said was also very confusing—as I believe I've already told you—so it's a great challenge to make clear to you everything I heard him say that day. In short, so as not to get into other infuriating references we'd never see the end of, and also to reduce his labyrinthine exposition to what matters most directly to us, I'll try to repeat for you—just as he expressed them to me—those words of his that seemed at the time and still seem to me to express his thoughts most clearly, although, as artistic aims, I consider them silly things to say and as ridiculous as everything else I heard from him that afternoon.

"'What is really happening to you, what will not let you see what I'm trying to do now, if I haven't already done it,' he started telling me, 'is that you try to judge these paintings as if they were what all the other painters have done or are doing, when, to understand them, to tell the truth, you would need an entirely new perspective that you can't even suspect the existence of. A beast like Meyer Meyer is unable to understand Rauschenberg because he is incapable of conceiving that a painter has the right to reimagine, to remake whatever anybody else may have done, by applying his own critical-creative capabilities. And you're no less stupid than Meyer if you believe that these new pictures of mine can only be appreciated using canons that serve for the appreciation of a Titian or a Chagall or a Francis Bacon. That is to say, with canons that establish as the supreme norm either the eyes of the flesh or the eyes of the mind. In reality, a new norm, without precedents, is indispensable to the comprehension and attractiveness of what I now perceive and of the thing, it seems to me, that I'm beginning to do.

"'The established canons I've mentioned to you place emphasis on man, whether it's the man in the street or the one making art. But, for the paintings that I'm beginning to make, it's essential to put yourself, contradictorily, in the place of the other things, the things that are not men, and accept that *they* are capable of assuming the function of agency and can order themselves as they will, as what really happens.

"'I try—what the hell, I believe I'm doing it already, I'm painting a world devoid of men and women, as if that sixth day of the Creation or of the Australopithecus, whichever you prefer, had never happened. In other words, I'm trying—and I repeat, I think I'm already getting it—to be humble, that is, to be in the world around me, to let myself be led by the hand by an *it*, instead of arbitrarily disposing of it.

"'This morning I showed you some houses I'd painted in two successive stages of my new style, which will be, let me warn you, my only style from now on. I already know, yes, *know* that both of them seemed abominable to you (or, if not that, what would be even worse, seemed to just be stupid). Even so, I want to explain to you what principle they obey, why they are so different in appearance from the house you live in'—and, Commissioner, I remember this very well, Omar emphasized this idea in particular—'and from the building we're in right now and every house you've ever seen in your life. But really and truly, do you understand what I'm saying'—he insisted—'do you see why they are so different from all houses painted before *me*?

"'Because, when I first thought about the problem that I think I've now solved (and, let me just say, that's why I dared to show you the new paintings this morning), which, anyway, I'm very close to solving, I had only one question: what is nature like? And I included in *nature* everything man creates, plus one's neighbor and even oneself. So the thing I'm asking is what is nature like *outside* of my intelligence and my sensibility and my imagination, what is nature like *from inside itself*?

"'And then I felt a tingling, felt something that after a while was more like a heart beating. That's when I *saw* it! For example, I saw a house, but from far beyond our human sense of its construction with a specific end in mind. I was experiencing, let's say, the essence of nature's innermost structure and rhythm, its unique nature per se, nature's own infinitely unique nature. Showing my discovery through my brushes was immensely difficult. But I decided to take the first big step. It became for me a question of winning it all and I didn't care if, on the other hand, I lost it all in the attempt.

"'I wasn't satisfied with what I already knew and had considered my secure possession. I decided that the most effective way to conquer so many obstacles . . . was simply to add to them! And, then, once the problem of houses came up (because, of all the objects surrounding me, houses are the ones that attract me the most, though I don't know why), I risked doing a treatment of them that could express their uncountable difficulties, the ten thousand mini-details in them, the human beings that wear them out and ruin them, or only make them worse.

"'Right away I was sure I'd gotten to the heart of the matter. Before, my error consisted of the perfectly human, grotesquely human attempt to conceive of an "in-itself" or a "per se" of things, an isolation of each thing according to an analog that my own "I," out of all its experiences and deep in its solitary abyss, permitted me to devise. Suddenly, as I said, I had gotten past the deep problem, everything was solved except maybe a little technical problem here or there, something so insignificant when compared to the almost insurmountable obstacles I'd just overcome.

"'And thus the houses you've seen were born, houses in which there are babies in cradles, rows of books in libraries, rich ones and humble ones, strings of stored onions, a rusty iron pot or two, and I myself, as if I lived in one of those houses, as if I were really a part of them . . . That's how I've achieved these triumphs,' he said to me and ended his impassioned speech. He blushed and stopped talking.

"I'm sure Omar must have been embarrassed to call a 'triumph' something, as he could ascertain from the faces that I was involuntarily making in the course of his exposition, that I, on the other hand, considered a painful defeat. Silence, dense, asphyxiating, suddenly overpowered this whole room and us and I didn't know how to break the impasse. I didn't dare contradict him openly, but I also didn't want to support such a glaring error. I simply opted for saying nothing. I never again heard him speak, Commissioner.

"Little by little I got over the hard blow I had suffered, until it finally lessened and gradually released its claw from my throat. I'm talking, of course, I'm sure you understand me, of the moral blow, for in a couple of days there was no trace of the physical beating he gave me. But all the while my moral turmoil was following its course, I was drowning in it. Every time his name was mentioned in my presence—and this was beginning to happen with alarming frequency, often with gales of laughter—I contributed my bit of malice to the general gossip about him. I'll tell you truthfully, Commissioner: I was delighted when someone who had just come from Omar's studio would tell me everything he or she had been alarmed to see there. I loved having the opportunity to explain the pictures, although deep down, I confess, I knew I was lying, because it's impossible to explain what they were. But even if some night I'd be lying in bed reproaching myself, the following afternoon, at the Espresso or the White Horse, I'd do my part and add to the collective fun and games that his craziness had provoked, and I believe, at least to a certain extent, this all helped stimulate the public's curiosity, which was first aroused when his exhibition was announced. Just look at it, he put up a show so quickly, when he had always been so meticulous about his shows before, and it opened him up to the questions about his artistic medium that had been generated by my acerbic comments. So much so, in fact, that that night my comments drew murmurs of disapproval from the recent escapees (I mean those who had just gotten out of Omar's show), who a minute earlier were making the most disparaging remarks about his mental health and, if you like, even stronger condemnations of the poor guy's artistic ability than I had.

"And as soon as *The Herald* came out, a week ago today, the morning after his opening, I turned immediately to the visual arts column, which as you probably know is under the byline of Omar's *bête noire*, that Meyer Meyer I spoke to you about earlier. And I believe that for the first time in my life the pedestrian thinking and despicable style of that great champion of all the '-isms,' as long as they're old, were very satisfying to me. For all of us—and I say again, for Omar in particular—Meyer Meyer was like a massive tumor that was impossible to excise but hardly deadly (because the members of the public who gave him any credit would never affect our wallets: that was a given). Therefore his negative judgement could not have surprised Omar because he was doubtlessly expecting it. And that was exactly the problem: Meyer Meyer's attack, for Omar, became praise. But this time the vile hack had got it right, or that's the way I understood it, Commissioner, as soon as I was able to exercise some equanimity. And, oh my, events very quickly confirmed my analysis.

"Someone came into the bar and said he had just been talking with Omar, whom, of course, he'd had to come here to his studio to see clearly just to pump him for information. What bothered me the most is that that so-and-so, who, among other things, couldn't remember anything for two minutes, walked straight over to me as if I were still Omar's best friend.

"He stated, well, he told me that Omar was delighted with Meyer Meyer's revision, that he had said 'that miserable man couldn't have done me a bigger favor.' He was waiting for a favorable review from our friendly critic, or at least for a prudent one. It was a given that he wouldn't understand anything in the show, because Eisenberg, our friendly critic, why lie, I can't say he's very perceptive, Commissioner, but, yes indeed, he's always very careful. When Eisenberg doesn't understand something, take it to the bank, he'll fix it up with two or three words of German. Besides, Eisenberg admired Omar immensely, thought he was the most talented, if not the only real talent of us all.

"However, well, to me it appeared likely that Eisenberg would *not* actually praise Omar's new approach. I'd already seen a pair of representative pictures of that new 'manner' and I knew that, even if Eisenberg wasn't an intelligent critic, at least he was always very careful. I knew Eisenberg couldn't possibly give praise to eyesores like those, which only an imbecile or a very dumb snob, like Jango, could take seriously, whom you yourself were mentioning to me a little while ago, just one of those snobs whose mouths water when they hear talk of a new '-ism.'

"And I certainly got it right. *The New Nation* came out two days later—a good weekly in its coverage of the art scene— although I too, and I beg you to believe me, Commissioner, am against the advanced political views expounded by them—but good, as I was saying. *The New Nation* arts section came out with its Eisenberg articles, and I realized immediately that the blow struck by Eisenberg was going to be much harder than the idiot Meyer Meyer's. It was also much more detailed and this time Eisenberg didn't beat around the bush with big words in German. He understood perfectly, had perfectly grasped that Omar's new 'manner' was a mistake.

"And, yes, I felt sorry for poor Omar after I read the review. It was OK, you must understand, that we weren't friends anymore. For me—and I'm sure for him too—certain links remain intact or barely compromised no matter what. There's a certain kind of loyalty that words and even deeds can go against but that endures everything.

"And, besides, I knew, through more than one experience of my own, how sad it is to completely trust in something that then fails completely . . . Oh, the influence of critics' judgments in the life of painters! Sometimes they make you think, but, unless painters have an irresistible impulse and are able to become their own promoters and salesmen, it's the critics who can grant or deny them the right to thrive, to live in luxury, who can stave off suffering or condemn you to starvation. And it seemed to me that from now on the critics would condemn Omar to death. Though it was perfectly clear to me that nobody had done more than Omar himself to earn such a sentence. I compare his attitude to that of a brutal killer, since Omar himself was the one who had murdered his artistic ability. Yes, Commissioner, that's what I thought then.

"And the fact is, they found him here in the studio, sitting in a little, broken chair, the only piece left of all his furniture, yes—apart from the walls, the floor, the ceiling, and himself—it was the only thing here when they came in looking for him. It's important for you to know, Commissioner, that these chairs we sit in and this little table you see here—I brought them from Omar's apartment later, following his wife's instructions.

"'Pale as death,' that's how they said he looked and I imagined him exactly here, perfectly quiet, his eyes popping out of his head and his face like a great, purplish stain. 'He was freezing to death,' they told me.

"Of all his work, only a couple of things were left, the ones you were looking at just now. Of course, anybody who knows poor Omar's capacity for work, knows what he was able to produce in a single day, and would calculate that, at least, hundreds of objects should be here in the studio, and where are they? If not more, at least the thirty-something pieces from the recent show. Certainly none of them had been sold at the gallery. Their price—I want to clarify, so you don't think robbery is a possibility—their price, at the highest, any vendor would put at pennies, those things looked so awful.

"As for him, he would never speak again. They found him looking at that canvas, the one right there, which, by the way, I've acquired only today, Commissioner, after finally convincing your subordinates. Indeed, I got to see this horrendous painting almost at the very moment of its inception and I saw it again when the local officers came looking for me to give me the sad news.

"'When we came in,' a very excited sergeant, named Murphy, I believe, told me, 'we were with the doorwoman, she had asked for our help because she was very nervous about the long silence in the studio, it had been quiet for three days. And we saw him, sitting there, and he barely changed position after he noticed us. I still didn't know it was him, and I got irritated because he hardly paid us any mind, so I shook him. I admit I was pretty rough, being as he was a man. I asked if he was the painter and had to repeat the same question no less than five times before he responded, finally, with this thin voice that didn't seem to even come out of his own body, or anyone's even, but I heard him, though he was barely speaking. He said: *The door opened and he came in. If you want to see him, you'll find him in there*, and his eyes were glued to those doodles he had in front of him. I finally realized I was dealing with a madman. It was necessary to *drag* him out, and took two men to do it, but he didn't kick, like I've seen other crazies do before, and his body weighed no more than a sack full of stones. Out in the vestibule, the doorwoman, who could hear all this, suddenly appeared and she yelled, she was terrified, "oh, no! The poor thing! Just look at him!" And she fell to the floor and we had two unresponsive people to take care of.' Well, sir, Mr. Commissioner, all that was what that sergeant who came to find me said, yes, I'm sure his name was Murphy.

"Then Sergeant Murphy took me to see Omar, they were still holding him provisionally in a cell at the police station. And, maybe this was a good idea, maybe not, but out of pity for the poor guy, who was so fascinated by his own scribbles, the sergeant had ordered that they also bring into the cell where they had him that picture, which I told you a little while ago that they have now returned here.

"And so, seeing him with that painting in front of him, I shuddered. Seeing his body again was worse, believe me, Commissioner, than looking at a cadaver. You could tell that blood was still circulating through his veins, but it was impossible to ignore the obvious fact that all his blood and all his flesh and his entire nervous system no longer made any sense, that they were still functioning as well as they could—and this is especially valid in terms of his nervous system—but they were kept working only by pure inertia. Their only *true* authentic move would have been to abruptly stop. But, Commissioner, he was worse off than a cadaver, because cadavers don't make you feel sad—the one you're sad about is the one who has gone forever—and, in this case, there were two of him whom you had to feel pity for: the one who had gone, or rather, Omar del Ramo, the best painter of his generation, so prosperous, so happy and generous; and the one left behind in his body, the idiot he had turned into. In that cell's weak light was someone who used to be Omar, lying on a cot, with his legs drawn up tightly in his arms.

"Such a crazy thought flashed through my mind then, and, even in such dire circumstances, a smile crossed my lips. I thought he looked like a fetus in the womb of something I'd never known, something my presence, or my interference, rather, was violating in there. In front of him were his 'doodles,' as the sergeant called them, as you, Commissioner, will un-doubtedly have successfully realized to be true.

"So many disagreeable things had happened since I saw these images the first time that I started. I realized that my natural feelings of repulsion at their ugliness were now magnified by my having to witness a great evil. I realized that things like those don't get painted with impunity, that things like that are crimes against the world *and* against the one who makes them. Nevertheless, my curiosity was stronger than my repulsion and fear, and I moved closer to observe the painting again. For a second I had the feeling that poor Omar had become the way he was because all of us were too stupid and helpless to admit his greatness as an artist, that maybe a careful, truly impartial examination of his new style could prove Omar right and then he would heal and everything would begin anew, with me the first in line to go to him and humbly beg him to forgive me and to let me contribute to his vindication.

"But, no, I considered the situation that way only a moment or so, for soon, as I kept my eyes on that canvas, a prolonged shudder ran through my body and I tried to look away from the hideous thing. 'My home,' he had titled it, I remembered very well, in the catalog from his recent exhibition. Then I noticed that something was going wrong, something didn't fit. I focused my attention again, but still didn't realize right away what was wrong. I had started to feel uneasy because I saw vividly that, simultaneously with mine, his eyes were fixing on the canvas and radiating something that was reflected from it, a . . . like a black sun, I'd call it. I finally realized what was happening and I quickly ran out of the cell.

"Now, Commissioner, I want you to pay close attention to what I'm going to tell you. Do not think I'm bragging. What I'm going to tell you is a fact: I've always had a good memory and my visual memory has been classified as even amazing. But it's played great tricks on me, too, back when I would be painting and unconsciously start to imitate this or that maestro! Because of what I've said to you, I trust you will have confidence in what I'm going to tell you now.

"It is exactly the thing I've told you about, the second time when I saw the painting. My memory conserved very clearly the image I had seen, but my mind did not manage then and still can't manage to order it rationally or in any way explain it. However, within the layering that is there in the painting, a series of elements are discernible that can be recognized without too much difficulty. You can see the tiles of a roof, and, over there, a chimney, and further on there's a staircase. There is also a wooden door with a great bronze knocker. But, and here is the most extraordinary thing, when I saw the painting for the first time, I'm sure—indeed, I can almost swear it, Commissioner—that the door, the one I'm pointing to now, was closed. Nevertheless, when I saw it the second time, it was half-open, as it is now.

"At that moment, everything suddenly became clear in my mind, phrases I heard before fell into place and I understood that Omar was lost forever, that he would never return, would not be here with us ever again. 'As if I lived in that house, as if I really were part of it.' You remember, he told me that the first time, just after he had painted that house. And then there is the response that in some way came out of his body when Sergeant Murphy shook him: 'The door opened and he came in. If you want to see him, you'll find him in there.' And also this enigma of the disappearing furniture; and above all, all, all, his missing paintings.

"Yes, Commissioner, I'm sure that he is somewhere *in* there, as wise and as sensitive as ever, living peaceably, enjoying his paintings, maybe sometimes picking up his brushes and painting *us*, as he sees us, and, in that way, attracting us little by little to his kingdom, without our being able to do anything to prevent it. So, if you want to see him, that's where you will find him. There's a lot of irony in those words! How can anyone voluntarily be won over by such a destructive principle, and then again, how do we resist it, if it's beyond our powers?

"And this, Commissioner, is all I can tell you with respect to my friend, the great painter Omar del Ramo."

"Well, that was a lot of talk for nothing," Nobodaddy says to himself, "I've stupidly wasted my time again." Immediately the chief takes his leave of the little old man, who has turned out to be very dislikeable; he gives the impression that he loves to tell his friend's misfortune.

"This investigation will never end," the chief prophesies as he leaves the studio. Inexplicably, outside on the street, the fresh air makes him think of Martha and cabbage with sausages. He instructs his driver to drop him off at his house. All in all, he has reasons to feel happy. Though this is the third failure of his career.

But precisely its being his third comforts him in some way. Nobodaddy is getting used to failure; and that is good. Even Inspector Maigret, who is his favorite hero, has had his failures a few times. Not to mention other, more eminent investigators.

As for the cabbage, a night in the icebox has only improved it.

"This is exquisite," the chief proclaims, serving himself another helping, a little larger than the first.

Martha smiles at him and asks if he also wants another beer.

* * *

The leader of the Viet-Cong recon party approaches the body of a young female, a blond, lying there with a bullet in her brain. The Bolex-Paillard camera may contain very important information and, in addition, is a magnificent camera that wouldn't be bad for them to have around. He hands it to a subordinate and makes the observation that it's intact and that that's the condition in which it must arrive at general headquarters.

He proceeds to remove her boots, then lifts her left wrist and pulls off the identification bracelet: Elke Trakl.

The commander has read something about her in an edition of *Time* magazine he found the day before in an abandoned jeep, beside another cadaver, a major in the Marines. He's ready to order the body doused with gasoline. The invaders must not be allowed to follow our footsteps by identifying their dead. He takes it upon himself to make them all unrecognizable, however disagreeable the task proves to be.

But why not take advantage of her wealth? Her chronometer

has already passed from his hand to one of his pockets.

This poor girl, a victim of the system she served, is very beautiful. So blond, so white. If only there weren't a hole in her forehead. It's also a shame to let her excellent campaign clothes just be consumed by the fire.

"No time to lose. They will be on us any minute." Still he can't resist the temptation to strip her of her undergarments. They will be clean, as pretty as silk, fragrant even in this mud hole! He knows that with objects like these he can get everything he wants from girls in the capitol. What is this? Along with the brassiere, her breasts have come off. Rubber breasts. Nothing left but the chest of a boy, as flat as a board. "That's how the capitalist regime is, everything always false," he says to himself, the disgust on his face is apparent.

"And those rubber boobies will be very entertaining."

He moves to the lower part of her body. It isn't easy to remove her underpants, of a beautiful, thick, shiny fabric. He finally gets it done.

The exquisitely beautiful graphic reporter Elke Trakl's male genitals leave him stupefied. The enemy is near. He has to get out to the highway. First, quick, splash the bodies with gasoline. Toss the match.

Oh, if O Jango had only known!

THREE
A REPUBLIC OF COCAIGNE

December 14. "Today at last we leave (I shall get married today too). I don't know why, but, for the past few days, when I'm at my apartment, I suddenly have a feeling of something like apprehension; it borders on revulsion. I've told myself it could be because I keep constantly hoping that Celia will drop by for a visit (of course, she never has before). Or it could be that I get disgusted, sad almost, when I see all the empty shelves in my library. I sold all of my books to pay for my part of the trip. (The Neo-Anthropic Foundation agreed only to cover my passage. And, since I'm still no eminent scientist, B.A.D. didn't want to hear anything at all about allocating living expenses for me.) I'd already gotten rid of my best ones to finance the divorce.

"Strangely, it's galley proofs of Bloy's *Le Désespéré* that I miss. I bought the thing years ago, a real steal, about the Quai Voltaire. But for me to miss it is really strange, above all, because I never read any of his work, not counting, of course, a glance or two out of sheer curiosity at the author's hand-written corrections. (As if I would sit down and read a religious fanatic!)

There is also a possibility that, here in this place, Nick's death might be making me feel apprehensive, because the first thing I thought when I decided to make the trip was how I wanted to let him have the apartment. He liked it so much and it would undoubtedly have come in handy for his amorous flings behind Roslyn's back. (Oh my, if he only knew! While his remains were still at the *morgue,* that idiot woman moved into repulsive Fatso

Mosca's bed!) I'd already decided to offer the place to him as a pleasant surprise when I found out he was dead. I might have even come across as generous in the poor guy's eyes. But, that's the way things go . . .

"Then, thinking back from my wedding (which will take place today, immediately, *en route* to the airport we will leave from to start our search for the Baikas) to the day of Nick's death, everything seems to have conspired to upset me during what are my last days in Megalopolis until who-knows-when. As if I wouldn't have been nervous enough already! Naturally, after what I saw at O Jango's party.

"So don't even *think* of the possibility of a reconciliation with C. That night I saw very clearly, definitively, exactly what her problem is. And its solution is not and maybe never was within my powers to influence. Still, not seeing her again now and also not even hearing news of her since the night of the party make me feel uneasy. Could she just be embarrassed? If she is, that's her problem. *She* has always made me suffer plenty, whenever she could . . . But thinking about it this way doesn't help me feel any less concerned.

"Maybe I'm on the verge of a new breakdown: these last few days I've had the feeling that I'm being watched on the street. And that's not all. I'm *sure* someone has been following me. Well, if that's the way things are, I'm going to respond to their espionage with a noble gesture. I take it for granted that, as soon as I leave the apartment today, someone will invade it, since, without a doubt, this involves people who . . . I wonder can it be the police? Could this have anything to do with Nick's death? Well, somebody is investigating something. Precisely for that reason I'm going to leave my old notebook here and in it pleasures and heartaches that read something like 'a man's diary.' But it will be the diary of a man who, from now on, will be the assistant on an anthropological mission; who, in other words, will be 'a diary's man' (*vide* Unamuno).

"Because, in fact, chronicling the mission is, so far, the main task that Dr. Jambon has assigned to me. (I've *got* to get used to referring to her as 'my wife' and calling her 'honey' when I talk to her. *Quelle blague!*)

"I don't think these, my first entries in the anthropological expedition's chronicle, are at all beside the point. Behold white *Homo sapiens*. His are the principal traits conferred on him by the most advanced technological civilization of the second half of the twentieth century.

"With all my fears and tribulations, I will, I think, serve as a specific point of comparison to primitive men—who, I have no doubt, are very much happier and suffer from their raw nerves much less than I.

"*We are ready to plunge in among them.*

December 17. "Stuck until tomorrow. We are in São Paulo, where we've been since day before yesterday.

"We've finally received the Ministry's indispensable authorization to undertake our exploratory trip through the interior; and I hope their suspicions that we're in search of uranium have completely dissipated. (It is a different source of radioactivity, if you will, that we're after: archaic man's knowledge, in its *status nascens*.) It will now be tomorrow before we can get the military helicopter that we'll have at our disposal so we can travel deep into the jungle to an outpost nearest the area where the Baikas are generally supposed to have settled.

"In the last few days, alleging to the old nymphomaniac that the state of my nerves will not let me get on with our life together as usual, especially at night, I've been able to keep her away from me and use my nights alone to write these field notes. But, poor thing, she is disappointed. (Under no conditions should I let this notebook fall into her hands!)

"Right now I can see my doorknob turning. But in vain: I've locked and barred the door. Now she's calling to me, in a voice she considers soft, and I have no doubt it resounds through the entire hotel. (I think she thinks her voice sounds provocative.) I'll just let her think that I've fallen asleep with the light on; the state of my nerves justifies any extravagance. She eagerly awaits (laying plans for her ambush!) the day when my life among the primitives gets me back on track . . . And no one should ever doubt that she is infinitely cunning. Even in the way she uses her emotions: tonight, as we had dinner, she talked to me about Métraux's suicide in the Bois de Bologne, deep within it, I gathered. For it seems that, when surrounded by the great excesses of a refined civilization, he longed only to return to the jungle, to his Matacos and Tupinambás. The old know-it-all's eyes actually filled with tears at this detail.

"And, by the way, as she explained it to me, neither Métraux himself, nor any of the great ethnographic specialists working in this region had yet succeeded in studying the Baikas. Not even von der Steinen or Curt Nimuendajú.

"So could these Baikas be nothing more than a legend created by known primitive tribes among whom are the Waikas, whose name is noticeably similar to that of the tribe we're going to try to find?

December 18. "The things they say about the Baikas provide the specific reason for this expedition; but they also seem to make hypothetical deception all the more conceivable. On the other hand, reports of old tribal relations with them lend credence to their existence. And Doctor has been strict on this point, above all when I've tried to argue my skepticism based on the close similarity of the terms 'Baika' and 'Waika.'

"She points out to me that: (*1°*) The existence of the Baikas is, in fact, strongly *affirmed* by the Waikas, who, furthermore, even seem to feel a kind of reverential fear of them, claiming that, in the past, many Waika people who walked into Baika territory never returned. And (*2°*) the account of a Protestant missionary's travels here, published in Zurich seventy years ago, also tends to confirm these Indians' existence, notwithstanding the fact that his description of the Baikas is elusive rather than explicit, from an ethnological point of view.

"Indeed, 'my beloved wife' has been adamant whenever I've attempted to state my skepticism. She has shown me a whole lot of photos of Waika Indians. They're so culturally primitive that they still have no knowledge of *pottery*, and their physical appearance coincides broadly with their cultural backwardness.

"The Protestant missionary's and the indigenous versions of the enigmatic Baika people are, nonetheless, categorical regarding their physical aspects (*about which, on the other hand, not one major reference is found in the Jesuit records from the end of the eighteenth century*). I'm talking about a population whose "somatic traits"—I've picked up one of my know-it-all honey's favorite expressions!—seem to be practically identical to those of the white man. All the different versions coincide in the description of at least the majority of this aboriginal group as quite tall and blond with light-colored eyes. The Protestant missionary's account, which Doctor has seen—well, a Xerox copy of it from the archives of the Neo-Anthropic Foundation—states that only their slightly more coppery skin differentiates these singular natives from us. That's why some scientist, his name has slipped my mind, has brandished like a drop hammer a hypothesis that's not at all convincing to my humpbacked honey. He proposes that the Baikas are the descendants of Iberian conquistadors who got lost in the jungle after heading into the interior in search of El Dorado.

"The *profesora* (I think it's better for me to use her titles, the poor thing, it's not her fault, after all, that she's so ugly and has those erotic fits . . . and is my wife), well, so she also refuses to admit that the most unbelievable characteristic attributed to the Baikas certain aborigine fables may be purely legendary. It seems that, among the region's indigenous, there circulates a version of the Baikas in which they are not only not in the least astonished by the existence of certain two-headed monsters, they also worship them.

"In the doctor's view, a bizarre condition like that actually seems believable. She deduces that it might be caused by some genetic mutation and her driving interest in mounting this expedition has been to be able to corroborate such a hypothesis.

"Also, it is my belief that her enthusiasm for sharing these themes of her specialization with me helps her forget the failure of my most important conjugal duty (*quelle corvée*). Nonetheless, this morning at breakfast—during which, one after another, she kept casting glances at me charged respectively with reproach, ardor, and suspicion—she suddenly declared that she had lost her appetite. Oh, if her loss of appetite were only a different one!

"Word has just now come that right after lunch they will arrive to take us to the airport, where, thanks to the proverbial generosity of this country, the helicopter that will be at our disposal is now ready and waiting and the game is afoot! And, it's curious, but I'm starting to feel like a man of science. What's more, today, as I was standing beside her, I was photographed for what I've heard is the main newspaper here, *O Jornal Paulistano*. This is really happening! I'm becoming an explorer like the intrepid Fawcett, or maybe an ethnologist as famous as Lévi-Strauss. If only the people in the Village could hear about it! And maybe they *will*, through O Jango, if he has really come here as he claimed he would in Megalopolis.

"But can you count on a multimillionaire aesthete to even read the newspaper?

December 20. "Reality imitates fiction. Reality is stranger than fiction.

"Both propositions are true. But insufficient, when you come face-to-face with Baikas. She is disappointed but doesn't at all regret our loss of the expedition's technical equipment in the helicopter crash. The truth is, simply through some miracle, we ourselves survived (more scientifically, of course, she prefers to say, 'just by accident'). Doctor counts the pilot's death among the sacrifices imposed by the march of science. Well, we're alive and, what is much more important, we are with the Baikas!

December 21. "I find it difficult, with all these temptations around me, to get to my chronicle. Resuming the main points:

"We came in search of savages and found ourselves among more or less perfect French courtesans of the Ancien Régime. Yes! As incredible as it must seem, *French courtesans of the Ancien Régime.* I know, I know. When the scientific results of our expedition make it into print (if this actually happens someday), the scientific world, to say nothing of the general public (who are, without a doubt, even less credulous than the scientist-types), may believe that what we've published is a big hoax. A remnant of perfumed, enlightened France from the time of the last Louie, in the middle of the Brazilian jungle! It does seem too cockeyed to be believed.

"Nevertheless, our photos—at least we've managed to salvage one of the cameras and a lot of film—will corroborate it.

"That's the reason I've been hard at the shutter release all day, photographing the 'natives,' their buildings, scenes of typical life, etc., etc. Everything will be there in the graphic material required for ethnological enlightenment.

"And the Baikas collaborate with authentic enthusiasm.

December 22. "Who are these Baikas? Well, I'd better start at the beginning.

"Dr. Jambon, who, it may still be remembered, is my distinguished wife, and I managed with great difficulty to get out of the burning helicopter, with our clothes somewhat scorched and ourselves a little bruised. We were on the side of a mountain covered with thick vegetation and we were absolutely alone in the middle of a savage world. We had no weapon with which to defend ourselves from wild animals or belligerent natives (and the jungle is thick with both) and our only food consisted of the large canteen of whiskey I had slung over my shoulder. I silently cursed my scientific wife, most of all because she gave no sign whatsoever of feeling downcast. But I urged her, practically forced her to take a big swig of whiskey, with the excuse that she needed to regain her strength. In reality, counting on the fact that she's not very accustomed to drinking alcohol, I hoped a colossal dose of it would make her fall asleep. I needed a chance to think about what might be done to get us to safety (but mostly to get myself to safety). The old thing fell asleep after a while, that is to say, after a period of euphoria that she spent trying to teach me the hair-raising war cry of fierce Arakuan headhunters.

"While she snored off her inebriation, I took stock of our situation. And we had no possibility of rescue. Given the fact that it would have to be air patrols they would send to search for us as soon as they discovered the loss of the transport helicopter, it would be impossible for them to spot us on this wooded mountainside. We were, therefore, condemned to die exactly where we were; I wondered if perhaps it would have been better to die with the pilot.

"This sad reflection brought me completely down. I grabbed the canteen, still almost full despite my spouse's copious swallows, and started to drink like a crazy man. I was sprawled beside a wooden-faced old woman, and 'I want to drown my sorrows' I remember whining to myself very softly. A moment later, I was fast asleep.

"I woke up and thought I was dreaming. Just as in any adventure story, we were surrounded by a group of warriors. But all similarities with adventure stories ended there. They were observing us with great seriousness, it's true, and you could even say with less than friendly faces, but they were individuals of the white race, or looked it, although they were very suntanned, and they wore clothes typical of the eighteenth century. Short breeches and powdered wigs seem to be de rigueur in the uniforms of Baika warriors.

"So when I woke up, Doctor was already using her spotty French to address a person who seemed to be the chief (to judge from his sky-blue jacket and its decorative fastenings of embroidered gold, as well as the beautiful, jewel-covered hilt of his dress sword). This shocked me even more than our captors' physical appearance. (I immediately classified them as captors and only later learned to see them as our saviors.) I would have expected, rather, that Doctor would talk to them in one of those dialects that (unlike her French) she knows to perfection and that sound like a mix of owl screeches and barnyard grunts.

"The chief—yes, it was soon clear that the one with the beautiful ceremonial sword was the chief—answered her in impressively good French. His French gave me the impression of being slightly archaic, a little 'deformed' (without a doubt, a result of isolation); it was quite similar, in fact, to the French spoken by French Canadians from the rural zones furthest from big cities. However that may be, he was very easily understood.

"I see now that it's time for me to get ready for lunch, and I also want to rest, even for just a few minutes, before I go over to the dining room. Luckily, the great anthropologist is busy taking notes somewhere. I'll continue the story of our first encounter with the Baikas this afternoon.

"The chief is a very tall man, quite burly, who, except for the missing grand mustache, looks extraordinarily like O Jango. But his way of talking—virile, deliberate, and exact—is the furthest you could imagine from the incessant, banal chatter of the São Paulo magnate.

"The chief's name is Pierre de Pauw, and, as he explained to us, he is a direct descendant of an author of some notoriety who, in the eighteenth century, was known to be the bitterest enemy of Rousseau's theory of the *bon sauvage*. In his curious French, the chief has also explained how his group got their start deep in the Brazilian jungle.

"'In Paris, in 1795,' he said, 'a group of citizens formed, bringing together as principals aristocrats of both sexes who were hostile to the Old Regime. Among them were also priests who had renounced their clerical robes in order to embrace the rules of revolution.

"'With great trepidation after all the excesses that had been committed during the Revolution, these enlightened *citoyens* saw how the revolution itself would end; they even foresaw France's eventual return to the hated Bourbon regime. Fervent readers, well-versed in the most advanced political theories, the most audacious books—as was the norm among the *éclairés* in those extraordinary times—they conceived the project of crossing the ocean to found a new society that would not only remain faithful to the French Declaration of Rights, but would also perfect whatever had already been achieved in the matter of sociopolitical renewal. They would continue to adopt the governmental framework and collective structures that were described in the most frightening of all books published in France that year: a novel loaded with dark forebodings against Reason. It was *Aline et Valcour,* by *citoyen* Donatien Alphonse-François de Sade.

"'The citizens entered into negotiations with various ship captains they knew who were also worried about the immanent installation of a reactionary government in the country, and at last they persuaded one of them to lead their great adventure. Jean Janin out of Marseille had an excellent ship at his disposal, *la Redoubtable*, in which they embarked from Nantes, on the twentieth of October, 1795. They were a select group of thirty-two Sadian utopists, among whom were not only men and women, but also children.

"'The group's initial idea had been to establish themselves in the virgin forests of Canada. That land's original French inhabitants, victims of wicked oppression by the British government, would most certainly extend their hospitality to the new refugees from the Old World. They, in turn, could spread to the Canadian hosts their system of successful revolution following their utopian ways. But their *marseillés* captain, once his frigate was on the high seas, energetically opposed this part of the plan, declaring that he would sooner throw any of his passengers overboard than expose his crew to the firepower of the mighty British armada. The latter guarded the entire Atlantic coastline of their Canadian territory jealously, precisely in order to prevent any attempt, especially by the French, to disembark on it intending to proselytize or merely to loot.

"'Conversely, the captain talked to them about the marvels of Brazil, such a benign place, such a sweet climate, the flora so splendorous, the birds' plumage sumptuous. He extolled the general ease of life in that immense, barely populated, rarely governed country, and pointed to the fact that the government, Portuguese, watched one and only one section of the long coastline. He brought to their attention the enormous riches that awaited them in the heart of that true *pays de Cocagne*. The captain exaggerated a little, that is clear, but he feared a mutiny among his passengers, should they remain resolute on establishing themselves in Canada, as originally agreed in their secret negotiations in Paris. Without a doubt, the passengers also would have feared the formidable aim of British naval artillery and they let themselves be won over by the astute Marseilles mariner's suggestion. He, in reality, was interested more than anything in returning home with rich cargoes of tobacco and coffee, and maybe even diamonds, but this was discovered too late, in conversations overheard aboard the *Redoubtable* after the tongues of the crew loosened as she traveled full sail ahead in the waters of the south Atlantic.

"'Indeed, it was already too late once the passengers assented to Captain Janin's proposal. As it turned out, several of them would have no choice but to disembark when they were about three hundred kilometers from the village of Santos. A new change of plans had been insisted on at the very last minute by a handful of the utopists because they were terrified of the region's relentless, shocking heat, which grew more and more stifling as the ship approached the beaches of Brazil. It was now the beginning of December and the implacable Brazilian summer had only begun. Most of the French had resolved to return to Europe with the ship and disembark in Amsterdam.

"'The remaining twenty-seven people, including three children, initiated, without protection, their odyssey into the middle of an exuberant solitude. They carried complicated luggage on their backs—from armchairs to a full library of five thousand volumes, among which certainly would not be missing a full set of the *Encyclopédie*. They would stop walking several months later, having lost several members of their party. They founded a colony and baptized it La Nouvelle Tamoè, in homage to their prolific author's genius.'

December 23. "How can I resist the beckoning of delicious Ninon? She comes into the hut assigned to me and I get tired of so much writing.

"What a beautiful girl! But, to tell the truth, here there are no less than two hundred other such beauties, all completely naked . . . and available. There is no doubt about it: when the Baikas imitated the customs of the aborigines with whom they freely intermingled at the beginning—those primitive Waikas, whose name they took, corrupting it (that is so French!)—it was they who invented European nudism. And they did it long before German and Scandinavian 'naturists' came upon it. I mean, from here I can see two hundred Boucher models, beauties all, duly plump and shapely, their muscles invigorated by their rustic, outdoor life, their skin, exposed to the hot sun all day and golden. If he had seen them, the Marquis himself would have defined them this way: *faites à ravir.*

"So how can I resist? Above all please keep in mind that Dr. Jambon spends almost all day with the chief in his hut, the guy who every day looks more like O Jango, because, as it happens, he is now evidently proposing to grow himself a mustache.

"And I have absolutely no doubt that he finds Doctor fascinating. His curiosity is insatiable, he wants to know everything, absolutely everything relevant to the people he governs. But I also must acknowledge that their arrangement has, at least, liberated *me*.

"So: how can I resist Ninon's beckon? If I may already say she's 'mine,' should I not exercise what is my unquestionable right?

"Why, one could almost believe that Nouvelle Tamoè is heaven on earth.

December 24. "Doctor asked me to take down the following as she dictated it. She did this, it occurs to me, because she has caught on to my affair with Ninon, but I agreed to do it anyway. After all, I'm still her assistant, and this is still a scientific expedition. Here is what she dictated, now in a clean copy that I polished a little in the redaction.

"'Recently a well-known scholar from the United States wisely wrote that the meaning we attribute to any fragment of reality that we submit to analysis has its point of origin and its reference in a domain well outside of the analysis *per se*. I don't have the text at hand, of course, in order to verify the exact wording of the quotation now, but I'm sure that I have stated its meaning. Therefore, if we start from this intelligent observation and complete and perfect it, the following can be affirmed: at least in the matter of big discoveries, like Columbus's discovery of America or the discovery of the Baikas, we are only capable of discovering what has already been quasi-discovered; to put it another way, we only discover what is already processing, already opening a path into consciousness from within our unconscious mind.

"'Providence? A miracle? Is this the nature of our discovery of the Baikas? Well, even if the tribe's chief is telling me that, barely

eighty years ago, there lived among them for a while a German
Lutheran missionary who had gotten lost in the jungle, and that
missionary afterward was able to return to Europe—where his
monograph on Baika customs became, until now, the principal
source of scientific knowledge about this population—even so,
that Protestant missionary did not see in them what *we* see,
what we came here searching for in them, because we already had
glimpsed it within ourselves.

"'The Vikings didn't discover *America*, a new continent that
was not Europe or Asia or Africa, no—as unearthed documents
have corroborated—*they* were clearly only aware that they had
found someplace that was unlike their known world.

"'And the first peoples, primitive Mongol hunters, early
Polynesian fishers? They simply migrated, spontaneously. Given
the very spontaneity of their movements, they actually were
discovering everything, but, in reality, discovering nothing, for
the simple reason that they had not set out to make discoveries
using a process of *knowingly* coming across *new worlds*. They
were merely content to settle naturally within immense
territories that, until then, were as yet untouched by a human
presence; they paid no attention to the absolute novelty of their
relocation as an experience of *Homo sapiens*.'

January 5. "The bicephalous are not a legend after all. Doctor
brought me to see one (very badly embalmed, I might add); the
chief keeps it in his hut. The body could be that of an individual
who was about eighteen years old when he died.

"It was a matter of bicephalism and hermaphroditism at the
same time.

"The image of the monster I saw still nauseates me and I
shudder when I think of it.

"If one of them survives to the age of twenty, it is expelled
from the tribe. The Baikas, after enduring unspeakable hardships,
abandoned most of the basic principles of rationalism long ago,
and two-headed hermaphrodites are the tribe's scapegoats par

excellence. They're born to certain girls who are easily identified because the girl's eyes are of two different colors.

January 5 (that afternoon). "Ninon has one brown eye, the left one. Her other eye is light blue.

January 22. "Doctor has laid out (and very plausibly, I feel obliged to say) her scientific hypothesis to explain the shocking generation of bicephalous individuals in the middle of the Brazilian jungle. It seems that, around 1820, the Baikas, still quite devoted to their Sadist principles, gave aide to some members of an aboriginal Waika group who were wandering lost near Nouvelle Tamoè. Some of the Baikas soon even cohabited with them, and the savages, in gratitude, taught them how to use the bark of a certain species of palm as if it were tobacco. Its taxonomic designation escapes me at the moment (I'll have to ask Doctor for it again!), but that drug, which they call *wakana*, causes hallucinations that its addicts interpret as divine revelations.

"By the time the Baikas had learned of the existence of this drug and mastered its preparation, they were already disillusioned with their initial utopian plans. Perhaps they refrained from reversing their journey and returning to civilization then only because of dangers they perceived lurking here in the jungle's depths. Those dangers, without a doubt, had magnified in their imaginations with the passage of much time since 1795, the year the founding group actually had to come face-to-face with their own ups and downs. So the new Baikas had nothing to lose by putting into their pipes the mixture the generous savages were offering them, and after they tried it, they took it up as a definitive part of their culture.

"And, now to the point, Doctor maintains that this drug is probably responsible for producing chromosomal changes that determine the appearance from time to time of 'special female individuals.' (This is the pompous phrase she likes to use for it, trying to sound professorial when she refers to these beautiful

women, each distinguished by her un-matching eye colors.
But in reality she just seems to be speaking with the cold voice
of a spurned woman.) Those enchanting 'female individuals'
presently number seventeen among the Baikas, according to
Doctor's calculation. Their sad, inevitable, biological destiny is
to give birth to bicephalous hermaphrodites.

February 1. "There is no longer any doubt: Ninon is
pregnant. The poor thing has known since childhood the nature
of her sentence. As soon as she has given birth to the monster,
she will be thrown into a nearby stream and the piranhas that
infest the region's rivers will devour her.

"Doctor insists that I acknowledge that Ninon should have
been more careful. She should have either renounced certain
pleasures or at least asked me to use the *capote anglaise*, as they
still call it here; they know how to produce them with great
refinements from the bladders of peccaries.

"In truth, I must recognize that there is a lot of sense in
what my wife is saying. Am I becoming infected with her
coldheartedness?

"No, there is a certain level of impartiality required for the
work of anthropology, i.e., the observation of strange customs.
All cultural values *are* relative. And this notion can lead the way
to a new planetary civilization.

"But is mankind becoming more plasticized, more adaptable
all the time? And is this the same as 'becoming more human'?

July 7. "It's been weeks since I've seen Ninon. I haven't talked
with her since the summer. Doctor now plans to postpone the
return trip until after the monster's birth. According to her, it
should be an easy trip, and would be even for a person traveling
alone (as long as he or she is sufficiently provisioned).

September 9. "Doctor has explained to me that, when it's
time for one of the two-headed children to be born, while
the woman giving birth is struggling with her labor pains, her
husband or lover is surrounded by the principal men of the tribe,

who pretend to assist him. He, meanwhile, mimics the mother's complaints and actions. This is the *couvade*, a ritual commonly practiced by diverse archaic groups across all latitudes, as my beloved wife has told me. (I wonder why I didn't limit myself to the enjoyment of her company and her charms.)

"Even though I'm a foreigner, it is clear that I'm expected to follow the custom.

September 10. "It's almost time for the birth and the strange ceremony whose principal enactor I must become.

"The chief, brandishing his great walking stick with very evident phallic symbolism, has come to visit me in my hut. He is richly decked out in his short breeches and sky-blue and gold jacket, clothes he must have found as he rooted around in the huge old chests of Nouvelle Tamoé's founders (but how could they have stayed so well preserved for so many years, especially in conditions imposed by the ambient humidity and the large number of damaging insects around here? Those clothes look almost brand-new!).

"I now know that the protagonist of the *couvade,* starting a few days before the ceremony, is made ready for it; the men make him smoke the diabolical drug that they call *wakana.*

(*that afternoon*). "I will now report my first experience as a *wakana* smoker.

"The chief stands in front of me, seriously preening. I inhale smoke from the pipe they hand me and standing in front of me is O Jango! There is no doubt whatsoever that it is he and I want to cry out for help. I realize immediately that this is nothing but magic and I am the magus.

"Besides, it's not the first time this has happened to me, I mean, the part about being the magus. I suck on the pipe again and, yes, I can remember it very clearly. I was on the crossing from Cherbourg many, many years ago on the *Queen Mary.* Lois Jefferson, a gorgeous singer I never saw again, and I are elbow to elbow at the railing and she starts talking about magic.

I say I'm a magician and tell her to ask me for a prodigy so I can demonstrate my magic powers for her. And Lois asks me to make her see a whale. I make a few swipes with my hands, like I saw the charlatans do at fairs when I was a child back in my native country, and I stop looking out over the railing, distracted by my mimicry. Then Lois shrieks: 'Look, a whale, over there!'

"I did everything I could to see it. And it wasn't just that I was distracted, I had also come out without my glasses, so that my Egyptian eyes, my Egyptian-cat eyes, would look more attractive to her.

"Did Lois really see a whale? Or is it some kind of subtle trick she played on me in return? I suddenly feel uneasy. It goes without saying that my nervousness explains what happened a little while later, the fiasco in Lois's cabin, a fiasco as Stendhal would have understood it. But Lois was indignant. She sat up unexpectedly and screamed: 'Are you a man or what?' And I fall asleep in her bed. And, after that second pull on the *wakana* pipe, I also fall asleep. I don't remember anything else until I woke up a little while ago.

September 12. "I hear drums. It's the signal that Ninon's labor has started.

"Inside of a minute, the chief and his henchmen will be here, surrounding this big bed in which I sit writing. Finally I'm done with all this superficial note-taking!"

A silent crowd surrounds Kiki, their faces grave. The chief hands him the already smoking clay pipe. There is a flash of blinding white light.

O Jango laughs raucously and smooths the ends of his enormous mustache. Everyone is laughing. Kiki can't resist their contagious joy. It's a contagion, a disease. It's the plague.

Kiki is locked in with plague victims! What kind of monster would keep him locked up in here with them? Let me see him, who is it! He is required to show himself and someone better put us together face-to-face, even if it's by force!

Kiki feels somebody inside his head, poking around in his brain, lacerating neuron after neuron. A stranger. He senses that the intruder enjoys pulling his synapses apart, one after the other. His brain is now as big as the world. It *is* the world. Someone keeps scraping his neurons with something very, very hard, pricking one, then another, then another. His perverse, unknown torturer, Kiki realizes, knows everything about him, is already his absolute master. Poor Kiki! Poor, poor, tiny Kiki!

Kiki has to scream. He howls, he is howling. What monster holds him in this prison? Who is his kidnapper, his torturer? What Kiki has locked him in here? Why does this diabolical Kiki keep uprooting his poor brain like that? Who is it, this Kiki they keep talking so much about?

He wails, simpers, yells, kicks! He makes multiple attempts to escape. *All is in vain, Kiki.* He has been taken over by another Kiki and Kiki can't stop screaming, he cries out, he whimpers, whines, whines louder. He searches and searches, and searches. looking for a way out of the belly of his whale.

Oh, Jonah, you *are the whale!*

Kiki is watching TV, sprawled comfortably in the large living room of his suburban *chalet*. He deservedly enjoys his Sunday rest after mowing the lawn of his little garden for an hour. It must be exactly one hour. This helps him stay trim better than any sport. And mowing has the other extraordinary advantage over sports of letting him avoid leaving his house, like he used to have to do when he drove his car more than half an hour to play golf at the country club.

Although he's been married four and a half years, his adored wife is still as indispensable a companion for him as she was during their first days together. "Still on the honeymoon?" their friends ask them with affectionate irony.

Nevertheless, Kiki knows that one of his principal duties is to stay trim, not only for reasons having to do with his health, but also in order to favorably impress his clients. Although his accounts at the publicity firm he works for are going great guns, there's no point in putting any of them in jeopardy. The client must always perceive him as fresh and agile, solid and sensible as he always seems to be: this is the rule he set for himself at the very beginning and at no time should he ever deviate from it. And because he has always been faithful to it, he can now feel very satisfied, perfectly serene in his downtime.

Kiki sucks delightedly on his fine Cherrywood pipe and immediately exhales a great mouthful of smoke to make a comment to his beloved wife, his ideal companion:

"Interesting, isn't it? These programs about primitive tribes, I mean. Such a strange custom, wouldn't you agree, the one at the end? The, ah, what did they call it, a *co . . . cu . . .* ?"

"A *couvade*. Anthropologists currently use the French expression," his beloved Large-Headed Woman explains to him.

Across the screen flit familiar scenes from the central park and Kiki stops talking. Another educational program is starting. Yes, another educational program. They are all so educational. This one is about the life of squirrels, those agile, graceful little animals, so fond, the little scalawags and gluttons, of nuts. A little boy about six years old carrying a shiny toy sailboat runs, leaving his nanny far behind.

"A little picaro, the boy is a scamp," Kiki murmurs and is going to say something else, but an imposing look silences him. The boy is trying to give a little squirrel a nut.

"Bad, bad squirrel! Why is he biting the little boy? Bad! Bad!"

A repugnant close-up of the severed finger appears over the narrator's voice: "Yes, our fun little friends, so adorably quick, can become quite dangerous when they go into heat."

This expression seems to have gotten the child's attention and he stops pouting. He no longer seems very concerned about the other boy's mutilated finger.

"Mama. Mommy. What did he say, the man on TV? What do squirrels do?"

The Hunchbacked Anthropologist gives her little Kiki a harsh look. Without answering him, she gets up and turns off the television set. Kiki immediately starts bawling, as he does every time he figures out he has done something stupid.

Manhattan (EE.UU.) – Córdoba (Argentina).

ENRIQUE LUIS REVOL was a well-known Argentinian writer, critic, and translator. He was also a professor of English and French literature affiliated primarily with the National University of Cordoba, where he had taken a baccalaureate in Philosophy (1946) and a doctorate in English and French (1958). He authored five books of poetry, two story collections, and a novel. He also translated a wide array of fiction and philosophy, including works by Herman Melville, Czeslaw Milosz, Lewis Mumford, and George Steiner.

PRISCILLA HUNTER, PhD Spanish and Emerita Professor, is a poet, literary translator, and literary translation workshop designer. Her publications include poems, translations, book reviews, and literary, film, and translation criticism. She holds a Certificate of Applied Literary Translation (University of Illinois/Dalkey Archive Press). *Abrupt Mutations* is her first book-length publication.

MICHAL AJVAZ, *The Golden Age.*
The Other City.
PIERRE ALBERT-BIROT, *Grabinoulor.*
YUZ ALESHKOVSKY, *Kangaroo.*
SVETLANA ALEXIEVICH, *Voices from Chernobyl.*
FELIPE ALFAU, *Chromos.*
Locos.
JOAO ALMINO, *Enigmas of Spring.*
IVAN ÂNGELO, *The Celebration.*
The Tower of Glass.
ANTÓNIO LOBO ANTUNES, *Knowledge of Hell.*
The Splendor of Portugal.
ALAIN ARIAS-MISSON, *Theatre of Incest.*
JOHN ASHBERY & JAMES SCHUYLER, *A Nest of Ninnies.*
GABRIELA AVIGUR-ROTEM, *Heatwave and Crazy Birds.*
DJUNA BARNES, *Ladies Almanack.*
Ryder.
JOHN BARTH, *Letters.*
Sabbatical.
Collected Stories.
DONALD BARTHELME, *The King.*
Paradise.
SVETISLAV BASARA, *Chinese Letter.*
Fata Morgana.
In Search of the Grail.
MIQUEL BAUÇÀ, *The Siege in the Room.*
RENÉ BELLETTO, *Dying.*
MAREK BIENCZYK, *Transparency.*
ANDREI BITOV, *Pushkin House.*
ANDREJ BLATNIK, *You Do Understand.*
Law of Desire.
LOUIS PAUL BOON, *Chapel Road.*
My Little War.
Summer in Termuren.
ROGER BOYLAN, *Killoyle.*
IGNÁCIO DE LOYOLA BRANDÃO, *Anonymous Celebrity.*
Zero.
BRIGID BROPHY, *In Transit.*
The Prancing Novelist.

GABRIELLE BURTON, *Heartbreak Hotel.*
MICHEL BUTOR, *Degrees.*
Mobile.
G. CABRERA INFANTE, *Infante's Inferno.*
Three Trapped Tigers.
JULIETA CAMPOS, *The Fear of Losing Eurydice.*
ANNE CARSON, *Eros the Bittersweet.*
ORLY CASTEL-BLOOM, *Dolly City.*
LOUIS-FERDINAND CÉLINE, *North.*
Conversations with Professor Y.
London Bridge.
HUGO CHARTERIS, *The Tide Is Right.*
ERIC CHEVILLARD, *Demolishing Nisard.*
The Author and Me.
MARC CHOLODENKO, *Mordechai Schamz.*
EMILY HOLMES COLEMAN, *The Shutter of Snow.*
ERIC CHEVILLARD, *The Author and Me.*
LUIS CHITARRONI, *The No Variations.*
CH'OE YUN, *Mannequin.*
ROBERT COOVER, *A Night at the Movies.*
STANLEY CRAWFORD, *Log of the S.S.*
The Mrs Unguentine.
Some Instructions to My Wife.
RALPH CUSACK, *Cadenza.*
NICHOLAS DELBANCO, *Sherbrookes.*
The Count of Concord.
NIGEL DENNIS, *Cards of Identity.*
PETER DIMOCK, *A Short Rhetoric for Leaving the Family.*
ARIEL DORFMAN, *Konfidenz.*
COLEMAN DOWELL, *Island People.*
Too Much Flesh and Jabez.
RIKKI DUCORNET, *Phosphor in Dreamland.*
The Complete Butcher's Tales.
RIKKI DUCORNET (cont.), *The Jade Cabinet.*
The Fountains of Neptune.
WILLIAM EASTLAKE, *Castle Keep.*
Lyric of the Circle Heart.
JEAN ECHENOZ, *Chopin's Move.*

STANLEY ELKIN, *A Bad Man.*
The Dick Gibson Show.
The Franchiser.

FRANÇOIS EMMANUEL, *Invitation to a Voyage.*

SALVADOR ESPRIU, *Ariadne in the Grotesque Labyrinth.*

LESLIE A. FIEDLER, *Love and Death in the American Novel.*

JUAN FILLOY, *Op Oloop.*

GUSTAVE FLAUBERT, *Bouvard and Pécuchet.*

JON FOSSE, *Aliss at the Fire.*
Melancholy.
Trilogy.

FORD MADOX FORD, *The March of Literature.*

MAX FRISCH, *I'm Not Stiller.*
Man in the Holocene.

CARLOS FUENTES, *Christopher Unborn.*
Distant Relations.
Terra Nostra.
Where the Air Is Clear.
Nietzsche on His Balcony.

WILLIAM GADDIS, JR., *The Recognitions.*
JR.

JANICE GALLOWAY, *Foreign Parts.*
The Trick Is to Keep Breathing.

WILLIAM H. GASS, *Life Sentences.*
The Tunnel.
The World Within the Word.
Willie Masters' Lonesome Wife.

GÉRARD GAVARRY, *Hoppla! 1 2 3.*

ETIENNE GILSON, *The Arts of the Beautiful.*
Forms and Substances in the Arts.

C. S. GISCOMBE, *Giscome Road.*
Here.

DOUGLAS GLOVER, *Bad News of the Heart.*

WITOLD GOMBROWICZ, *A Kind of Testament.*

PAULO EMÍLIO SALES GOMES, *P's Three Women.*

GEORGI GOSPODINOV, *Natural Novel.*

JUAN GOYTISOLO, *Juan the Landless.*
Makbara.
Marks of Identity.

JACK GREEN, *Fire the Bastards!*

JIŘÍ GRUŠA, *The Questionnaire.*

MELA HARTWIG, *Am I a Redundant Human Being?*

JOHN HAWKES, *The Passion Artist.*
Whistlejacket.

ELIZABETH HEIGHWAY, ED., *Contemporary Georgian Fiction.*

AIDAN HIGGINS, *Balcony of Europe.*
Blind Man's Bluff.
Bornholm Night-Ferry.
Langrishe, Go Down.
Scenes from a Receding Past.

ALDOUS HUXLEY, *Antic Hay.*
Point Counter Point.
Those Barren Leaves.
Time Must Have a Stop.

JANG JUNG-IL, *When Adam Opens His Eyes*

DRAGO JANČAR, *The Tree with No Name.*
I Saw Her That Night.
Galley Slave.

MIKHEIL JAVAKHISHVILI, *Kvachi.*

GERT JONKE, *The Distant Sound.*
Homage to Czerny.
The System of Vienna.

JACQUES JOUET, *Mountain R.*
Savage.
Upstaged.

JUNG YOUNG-MOON, *A Contrived World.*

MIEKO KANAI, *The Word Book.*

YORAM KANIUK, *Life on Sandpaper.*

ZURAB KARUMIDZE, *Dagny.*

PABLO KATCHADJIAN, *What to Do.*

JOHN KELLY, *From Out of the City.*

HUGH KENNER, *Flaubert, Joyce and Beckett: The Stoic Comedians.*
Joyce's Voices.

DANILO KIŠ, *The Attic.*
The Lute and the Scars.
Psalm 44.
A Tomb for Boris Davidovich.

ANITA KONKKA, *A Fool's Paradise.*

GEORGE KONRÁD, *The City Builder.*

TADEUSZ KONWICKI, *A Minor Apocalypse.*

The Polish Complex.

ELAINE KRAF, *The Princess of 72nd Street.*

JIM KRUSOE, *Iceland.*

AYSE KULIN, *Farewell: A Mansion in Occupied Istanbul.*

EMILIO LASCANO TEGUI, *On Elegance While Sleeping.*

ERIC LAURRENT, *Do Not Touch.*

VIOLETTE LEDUC, *La Bâtarde.*

LEE KI-HO, *At Least We Can Apologize.*

EDOUARD LEVÉ, *Autoportrait.*

Suicide.

MARIO LEVI, *Istanbul Was a Fairy Tale.*

DEBORAH LEVY, *Billy and Girl.*

JOSÉ LEZAMA LIMA, *Paradiso.*

OSMAN LINS, *Avalovara.*

The Queen of the Prisons of Greece.

ALF MACLOCHLAINN, *Out of Focus.*

Past Habitual.

RON LOEWINSOHN, *Magnetic Field(s).*

YURI LOTMAN, *Non-Memoirs.*

D. KEITH MANO, *Take Five.*

MINA LOY, *Stories and Essays of Mina Loy.*

MICHELINE AHARONIAN MARCOM, *The Mirror in the Well.*

BEN MARCUS, *The Age of Wire and String.*

WALLACE MARKFIELD, *Teitlebaum's Window.*

To an Early Grave.

DAVID MARKSON, *Reader's Block.*

Wittgenstein's Mistress.

CAROLE MASO, *AVA.*

HISAKI MATSUURA, *Triangle.*

LADISLAV MATEJKA & KRYSTYNA POMORSKA, EDS., *Readings in Russian Poetics: Formalist & Structuralist Views.*

HARRY MATHEWS, *Cigarettes.*

The Conversions.

The Human Country.

The Journalist.

My Life in CIA.

Singular Pleasures.

The Sinking of the Odradek.

Stadium.

Tlooth.

JOSEPH MCELROY, *Night Soul and Other Stories.*

ABDELWAHAB MEDDEB, *Talismano.*

GERHARD MEIER, *Isle of the Dead.*

HERMAN MELVILLE, *The Confidence-Man.*

AMANDA MICHALOPOULOU, *I'd Like.*

STEVEN MILLHAUSER, *The Barnum Museum.*

In the Penny Arcade.

RALPH J. MILLS, JR., *Essays on Poetry.*

CHRISTINE MONTALBETTI, *The Origin of Man.*

Western.

NICHOLAS MOSLEY, *Accident.*

Assassins.

Catastrophe Practice.

Hopeful Monsters.

Imago Bird.

Natalie Natalia.

Serpent.

WARREN MOTTE, *Fiction Now: The French Novel in the 21st Century.*

Oulipo: A Primer of Potential Literature.

GERALD MURNANE, *Barley Patch.*

Inland.

YVES NAVARRE, *Our Share of Time.*

Sweet Tooth.

DOROTHY NELSON, *In Night's City.*

Tar and Feathers.

WILFRIDO D. NOLLEDO, *But for the Lovers.*

BORIS A. NOVAK, *The Master of Insomnia.*

FLANN O'BRIEN, *At Swim-Two-Birds.*

The Best of Myles.

The Dalkey Archive.

The Hard Life.

The Poor Mouth.

The Third Policeman.

CLAUDE OLLIER, *The Mise-en-Scène.*

Wert and the Life Without End.

PATRIK OUŘEDNÍK, *Europeana.*
The Opportune Moment, 1855.
BORIS PAHOR, *Necropolis.*
FERNANDO DEL PASO, *News from the Empire.*
Palinuro of Mexico.
ROBERT PINGET, *The Inquisitory.*
Mahu or The Material.
Trio.
MANUEL PUIG, *Betrayed by Rita Hayworth.*
The Buenos Aires Affair.
Heartbreak Tango.
RAYMOND QUENEAU, *The Last Days.*
Odile.
Pierrot Mon Ami.
Saint Glinglin.
ANN QUIN, *Berg.*
Passages.
Three.
Tripticks.
ISHMAEL REED, *The Free-Lance Pallbearers.*
The Last Days of Louisiana Red.
Ishmael Reed: The Plays.
Juice!
The Terrible Threes.
The Terrible Twos.
Yellow Back Radio Broke-Down.
RAINER MARIA RILKE,
The Notebooks of Malte Laurids Brigge.
JULIÁN RÍOS, *The House of Ulysses.*
Larva: A Midsummer Night's Babel.
Poundemonium.
ALAIN ROBBE-GRILLET, *Project for a Revolution in New York.*
A Sentimental Novel.
AUGUSTO ROA BASTOS, *I the Supreme.*
DANIËL ROBBERECHTS, *Arriving in Avignon.*
JEAN ROLIN, *The Explosion of the Radiator Hose.*
OLIVIER ROLIN, *Hotel Crystal.*
ALIX CLEO ROUBAUD, *Alix's Journal.*
JACQUES ROUBAUD, *The Form of a City Changes Faster, Alas, Than the Human Heart.*

The Great Fire of London.
Hortense in Exile.
Hortense Is Abducted.
Mathematics: The Plurality of Worlds of Lewis.
Some Thing Black.
RAYMOND ROUSSEL, *Impressions of Africa.*
VEDRANA RUDAN, *Night.*
GERMAN SADULAEV, *The Maya Pill.*
TOMAŽ ŠALAMUN, *Soy Realidad.*
LYDIE SALVAYRE, *The Company of Ghosts.*
LUIS RAFAEL SÁNCHEZ, *Macho Camacho's Beat.*
SEVERO SARDUY, *Cobra & Maitreya.*
NATHALIE SARRAUTE, *Do You Hear Them?*
Martereau.
The Planetarium.
STIG SÆTERBAKKEN, *Siamese.*
Self-Control.
Through the Night.
ARNO SCHMIDT, *Collected Novellas.*
Collected Stories.
Nobodaddy's Children.
Two Novels.
ASAF SCHURR, *Motti.*
GAIL SCOTT, *My Paris.*
JUNE AKERS SEESE,
Is This What Other Women Feel Too?
BERNARD SHARE, *Inish.*
Transit.
VIKTOR SHKLOVSKY, *Bowstring.*
Literature and Cinematography.
Theory of Prose.
Third Factory.
Zoo, or Letters Not about Love.
PIERRE SINIAC, *The Collaborators.*
KJERSTI A. SKOMSVOLD,
The Faster I Walk, the Smaller I Am.
JOSEF ŠKVORECKÝ, *The Engineer of Human Souls.*
GILBERT SORRENTINO, *Aberration of Starlight.*
Blue Pastoral.
Crystal Vision.

Imaginative Qualities of Actual Things.
Mulligan Stew.
Red the Fiend.
Steelwork.
Under the Shadow.
ANDRZEJ STASIUK, *Dukla.*
Fado.
GERTRUDE STEIN, *The Making of Americans.*
A Novel of Thank You.
PIOTR SZEWC, *Annihilation.*
GONÇALO M. TAVARES, *A Man: Klaus Klump.*
Jerusalem.
Learning to Pray in the Age of Technique.
LUCIAN DAN TEODOROVICI, *Our Circus Presents...*
NIKANOR TERATOLOGEN, *Assisted Living.*
STEFAN THEMERSON, *Hobson's Island.*
The Mystery of the Sardine.
Tom Harris.
JOHN TOOMEY, *Sleepwalker.*
Huddleston Road.
Slipping.
DUMITRU TSEPENEAG, *Hotel Europa.*
The Necessary Marriage.
Pigeon Post.
Vain Art of the Fugue.
La Belle Roumaine.
Waiting: Stories.
ESTHER TUSQUETS, *Stranded.*
DUBRAVKA UGRESIC, *Lend Me Your Character.*
Thank You for Not Reading.
TOR ULVEN, *Replacement.*
MATI UNT, *Brecht at Night.*
Diary of a Blood Donor.
Things in the Night.
ÁLVARO URIBE & OLIVIA SEARS, EDS., *Best of Contemporary Mexican Fiction.*
ELOY URROZ, *Friction.*
The Obstacles.
LUISA VALENZUELA, *Dark Desires and the Others.*
He Who Searches.

PAUL VERHAEGHEN, *Omega Minor.*
BORIS VIAN, *Heartsnatcher.*
TOOMAS VINT, *An Unending Landscape.*
ORNELA VORPSI, *The Country Where No One Ever Dies.*
AUSTRYN WAINHOUSE, *Hedyphagetica.*
MARKUS WERNER, *Cold Shoulder.*
Zundel's Exit.
CURTIS WHITE, *The Idea of Home.*
Memories of My Father Watching TV.
Requiem.
DIANE WILLIAMS,
Excitability: Selected Stories.
DOUGLAS WOOLF, *Wall to Wall.*
Ya! & John-Juan.
JAY WRIGHT, *Polynomials and Pollen.*
The Presentable Art of Reading Absence.
PHILIP WYLIE, *Generation of Vipers.*
MARGUERITE YOUNG, *Angel in the Forest.*
Miss MacIntosh, My Darling.
REYOUNG, *Unbabbling.*
ZORAN ŽIVKOVIĆ, *Hidden Camera.*
LOUIS ZUKOFSKY, *Collected Fiction.*
VITOMIL ZUPAN, *Minuet for Guitar.*
SCOTT ZWIREN, *God Head.*

AND MORE...